BLUE, RED, AND DEAD

~Deadlock at the Electoral College; A "too close to call" presidential election thriller~

A Novel

BY

TIMOTHY BURTON ANDERSON

Table of Contents

PROLOGUE

No matter how hard he tried to wipe the blood off his hands, it was never gone. So, he stabbed his hands into a vat of acid and then pulled them out. Nothing but blunt stubs remained. He stared at the gore, and the shock blocked his senses, leaving only dizziness and numbness. However, the hands were back...red, blood-covered bone-white knuckles and bluish fingers in spasm, in oscillation, out of control, extruding forth from the fat palms of his hands at the ends of his wrists. The re-emergence, the regrowth! It forced him to scream, even shriek —loudly, or so he hoped. Then, accepting that it was only hollow echoing within his body, never heard by anyone or anything, made it more terrifying. He screamed louder! Visions of needles—the caustic odor of lethal liquids maliciously filtrating into his veins. Suddenly, his eyes shot open. He stared frantically into a void of seemingly endless blackness, straining his optic nerves to the limit to sense even the faintest glimmer of light.

It must have been midnight, he thought. Less-than-quality vision at 59 years of age caused the red digits on the alarm clock to merge into a blur, only further magnifying the memorial image of the bloody hands from his nightmare. At least it was light, and the light was good. He fumbled for the lamp, switched it on, and looked at the clock all at the exact moment. It took a few more seconds for him to remember where he was. Every night was a new place, leading to early morning struggles with the question, "Where am I?" Then, usually, about twenty seconds into the perennial confrontation, he would put his existence back together in terms of place, time, and even, on rare occasions, identity. More frequently than not, the battle would be joined with the irreconcilable question: "Why?"

Robert Cannon kicked back the covers, got out of bed, and planted his feet on the clammy cold floor to make his way to the bathroom. In a sleepy trance, he stood still, giving his bladder plenty of time to empty to the slow, rhythmically simple cadence of dribbling in the toilet. He appreciated the duration of the event as it allowed time for his cold sweat to begin to warm while he culled through his memory of the haunting, recurring dream of the bloody hands. It would not go away nor diminish in intensity. He knew that.

Robert Cannon's hands had ended lives. In his earlier years, his activities had been played out as tasks performed for the good of the country. Creative thinking had often lent a hand in allowing him to suppress reality. His victims had seemed so fictional and distant — even non-human. Over the past several months, however, it all began flooding back—relentlessly revisiting him in a way that twisted his stomach and frayed his nerves. Like a recurring cancer or a stubborn seasonal virus, it returned, more powerful and invasive than ever. It was all about a time that he knew would come, but he had hoped that somehow a bullet, a knife, or something as mortally permanent but less painful would stop him before he arrived at this point in his life. He had been seemingly willing to go to hell for his deeds. Now, he was discovering that going through actual hell was quite another thing.

1

"Bentley, you've got to come over and see this," Charlotte Reid ordered. "I don't think Georgia is in now either."

Bentley Wilcox, the Chief Strategist to the Charlotte Reid Presidential Campaign, broke away from conversations on two separate cell phones. "Char, you're right; nobody is going to believe this. It just can't be! It just can't!"

The network anchor's voice boomed from the speakers on the large screen monitor, announcing the long-awaited results of the electoral vote:

"IN AN ALMOST UNTHINKABLE AND CERTAINLY UNPRECEDENTED RESULT, THE ELECTORAL COLLEGE HAS MET AND VOTED. NEITHER CANDIDATE HAS GAINED THE 270-VOTE MAJORITY NEEDED TO WIN. NO ELECTORS FROM THE STATE OF GEORGIA HAVE OR ARE GOING TO PARTICIPATE! THE RESULT OF THE ELECTORAL COLLEGE IS 267 IN FAVOR OF THE VICE PRESIDENT AND 255 FOR GOVERNOR HOUSTON. I PRESUME THIS MEANS THE MATTER WILL BE TURNED OVER TO THE UNITED STATES CONGRESS AND, MOST CERTAINLY, THE COURTS TO RESOLVE."

Bentley had been close to Vice President Charlotte Reid since their early days at Harvard Law. He was the only person in the vice president's circle who could use the name "Char" and survive the steaming glare. "We've got to do something about this, and we've got to do it right away!"

"I thought you already did!" the Vice President barked as she stormed out of the banquet room, visibly irritated by the report, and ascended the stairs to the personal quarters of the huge mansion.

Bentley sat quietly, staring out through the tall windows. From his Bainbridge Island vantage point, he gazed across Puget Sound at the City of Seattle, where the setting sun transformed thousands of skyscraper windows into glowing plates of gold. Positioning his one-time soulmate forever for the most incredible run of her life had been a formidable process. The effort had paid off. After serving in Congress for only two terms, she had been invited right onto the presidential ticket.

It had been the hallmark event of a long-term political strategy hatched years earlier—when Bentley's vision ranged much farther than Charlotte's. Bentley had recognized the potential early and had paved the way to come by tying down every valuable political contact possible throughout the country before Charlotte had even finished her first congressional term. With incessant energy, he had Char Reid, in effect, running for president before she had even hung any pictures on the wall of her cramped attic-level Cannon Building office. Four years later, just one week after she accepted the nomination for Vice President of the United States—and without waiting to see if she and presidential candidate Senator Ronald Minton would even win—Bentley shut down his polling and consulting firm in Houston, Texas, and moved, lock, stock, and barrel, to Washington, D.C. From that moment on, there were no more casual talks of simply getting her elected; the stakes had become undeniably real. The discussions were all serious in his mind-deadly serious and expensive.

Bentley's vision was focused on his certainty that Charlotte Reid could be the first female President of the United States. However, Reid had her detractors. Often portrayed by Republicans and opponents within the party as the woman who had gained prominence by sleeping her way up the corporate and political ladder, she carried baggage. After graduation from Harvard Law School, the young fashion model-quality lawyer had taken her sassy blonde hair and classy figure to an in-house position with one of the largest software companies in the world, headquartered in Seattle. After less than five years on the job, she had already been promoted to personal legal counsel to Bill, the famed founder and CEO of the company.

Three years later, Bill divorced his wife of twelve years. It took just ninety days after that for Bill and Charlotte to fly to Bali for an extravagant private wedding, which dominated the tabloids across the English-speaking world for months.

ASHES OF TREACHERY

It had been the juiciest scandal in the software industry. Soon, even Bill was feeling the heat from the boardroom. Charlotte's position as chief counsel was viewed as a prime case of nepotism that could not be tolerated by senior officers and stockholders of the company. So, she stepped down and began to look around. After taking more vacation than she was used to, she dedicated an entire summer to writing what she believed could be an industry bestseller—a *Software Law Guidebook for Dummies.* It went nowhere. Even being married to Bill wasn't enough to curry favor with the New York publishing world.

Discouraged by publishers' rejections, she found herself even more depressed just hanging around Bill's Puget Sound waterfront mansion, trying to be the woman of the house. She took a serious stab at redecorating, threw elaborate dinner parties, and supervised the full-time team of housekeepers, groundskeepers, and chefs brought in from choice parts of the world. She even put on a stellar performance from time to time as stepmother to Bill's teenage children when they would dutifully appear for their semi-monthly visitations. But after several months of floating from one undefined role to another, she found herself emotionally spent and unable to function without the powerful brew of French Roast from Seattle's Best Coffee—and a tinge of vodka.

It was at this time she turned to her old friend, schoolmate, and one-time lover from Harvard, Bentley Wilcox. It was Bentley who, while operating a reasonably successful public relations and political consulting firm in Houston, popped the question, "Why don't you go into politics?"

As soon as he asked the question, it seemed to make all the sense in the world. After all, Bentley had been pressing her to do it ever since the Harvard days, but she had never taken him seriously. Looking back, she realized she'd simply been too close to the forest to see the trees. She truly needed someone else's perspective to help her step back and take a good look at her life from a reasonable distance. No one had been better at this than Bentley Wilcox, whom, she had often thought during her early days at Harvard, would not have been just a good advisor but an excellent husband as well. For her, it was the best marriage that never happened as it eventually answered the politician's biggest question, "How are we going to finance this campaign?" Even before the question could be fully asked, the answer was already in place. It had taken only one night out for dinner with husband Bill, and $200 million was in the till the next day just to prime the political pump.

With Bill making strategic celebrity appearances throughout the campaign and providing first-class use of everything from mailers, signs, brochures, and billboards to television ads and the most massive online campaign the world had ever seen, the Seattle area voting public had no problem being convinced they needed Charlotte Reid to represent them in Congress.

Substantial sums of money flowed into the pockets of Bentley Wilcox and his team of expert consultants. Hiring the best and brightest from across the country came easily, as the campaign quickly became the most expensive congressional election in U.S. history. In comparison,

Reid's opponent, though well-financed by typical standards, barely registered as a blip on the election expenditure radar. From the very first day, the money showed up in the campaign account, Bentley was profoundly appreciative of the fact that he had never married Charlotte Reid. The ending of soulmate forever had been a good thing.

For her part, Charlotte was more than just a powerfully financed politician. She was also a formidable candidate in her own right. The fact that her striking appearance and fashion plate clothing worked as constant fodder for pundits, critics, and cartoonists alike was not lost on her advisors. Her "spin doctors" hammered an image into the minds of the public that was not easy to forget. Tasteful sexual innuendo was built into the promotion of her persona, creating a sort of Hollywood flair that sported a very broad appeal, especially to men. It was every publicist's dream—the consummate union of sex, brains, and money.

SEEDS OF CORRUPTION

The brains had been easy to establish. In her days at Harvard, Charlotte had not been known as a socialite. The late-night rendezvous with Bentley Wilcox always took place after the doors to the law library had been locked at closing time. She studied incessantly and, as a result, achieved the position of Note Editor of the Harvard Law Review. She logged long hours during the week and even on Saturdays and Sundays. When others were playing, traveling, and otherwise avoiding coursework, she was riveted to her studies and was, by far, the most attractive library jock that the prestigious school had ever seen. By graduation day, she emerged from her life as a sort of law library urchin to that of a very marketable talent. She graduated third in her class. The interviews went well with major law firms and businesses across the country. It made perfect sense to accept the position with the massive software company in Seattle, which not only offered her a salary competitive with anything on Wall Street but also came with a stunning, brand-new pearl white Jaguar convertible—the car of her dreams, at least up until that point in her life.

It had been a long journey from Charlotte's rather simple life in Champagne, Illinois. There, she had been encouraged by her parents to matriculate to the University of Illinois and pursue a degree in elementary education. She had not been fully excited nor in disagreement with the plan. The life of a schoolteacher had sounded like the thing to do, that is, until she found herself pulling exceptionally high grades, scoring well on SATs, and being offered scholarships to several major schools around the country. It was in her second year at Wellesley that she realized law school might be a possibility. It was in her third year, after scoring in the 95th percentile on the LSAT that she knew even before she applied that she was on her way to Harvard.

As a congresswoman, Charlotte proved to be an astute tactician. She was adept at cozying up to senior members and committee chairs in both the House and Senate while at the same time applying her best womanly assets to garner attention in the largely male-oriented halls of Congress, picking off privileges early that others had taken a political lifetime to get, which made her that much more formidable and dangerous. She was the darling of the Washington social scene. As the wife of one of the richest men in the world, Charlotte had her choice of subcommittee assignments normally reserved for only the most senior members. Before the end of her first term, some considered her as influential as one, if not both, of the long-term Senators from her state.

The relationship with Bill tended to improve with their separate residences on opposite coasts. The bi-coastal presence also projected a greater sense of power. They each had a Gulfstream G660ER corporate jet at their disposal. The toughest part of the Thursday evening commute from D.C. to Seattle was the one-hour-plus drive through traffic from the Capitol out to Dulles. Charlotte used the time on the plane to unwind and return the calls that had piled up over the week. By the time she landed in Seattle, she was fully prepared to humor Bill and navigate the local political scene with a carefully calculated agenda designed to propel her forward. Exactly where she was headed remained a bit uncertain, but one thing was clear: it was exhilarating and fun. Everyone wanted a piece of Charlotte Reid, pieces she would offer at a considerable price. By the end of her first year in the House, she had become the most photographed woman in America. Charlotte's innate sense of style, combined with the incredible power center that she created for herself, was a force to be reckoned with. Among those paying the price was Ronald Minton, the Democratic nominee for President. Public opinion polls had shown Charlotte Reid leading the race for the Democratic nomination ahead of all five of the candidates already announced. Yet, Bentley had run even more precise polls that supported his conclusion that despite all the notoriety, it was not yet time to run. It would be better to wait, and be invited. True to his plan, it was only a matter of time before Senator Minton came to her to pop the big political question.

On an afternoon in April, he called Charlotte from his campaign headquarters in Atlanta and invited her to serve as his running mate. The call was far from a surprise; Bentley Wilcox had already effectively orchestrated the approach with senior staffers for Minton. Charlotte's affirmative response enabled Senator Minton to surge to the top of the polls. Over the next three weeks, all other Democratic Party contenders graciously withdrew from the race. Throughout the summer campaign, the Republicans found themselves left in the Democrats' dust. By the time of the November election, Ronald Minton was poised for a significant victory. Seventy-two percent of the country voted for Minton/Reid, marking an astounding triumph—a virtual walkover.

The broad coalition, ranging from conservative retired folks to NASCAR junkies who supported Reid to the old-guard Democratic Party anchored behind Minton, was far too strong for the Republicans to overpower. But the ultimate winner was Char Reid. Charlotte had her sights set on the Oval Office, and she intended to do whatever it might take to get there.

One Sunday morning, fourteen months after the inauguration, the country was stunned by the news of a massive heart attack that had struck the popular first-term President, Minton. Only the exceptional training of the White House paramedics, along with the heroic efforts of the President's personal physician, allowed the prominent farmer from Georgia to survive beyond that day. However, after spending two weeks at George Washington University Hospital and another six weeks recuperating at Camp David, the pressing question on the political street was whether he would ever be able to resume his duties at the White House. It was evident that the 62-year-old President was only partially the man he had been before the illness struck. He had been in excellent health—a marathon runner. He had grown tobacco but never smoked it, nor had he had any history of heart disease whatsoever. But as the chief cardiologist at Bethesda Naval Hospital blandly explained, "Heart attacks are frequent in men of the President's age, and even those who show no symptoms and maintain a healthy lifestyle are still vulnerable."

During the two months of the President's absence, Vice President Reid carefully steered the ship of state with the ease and sophistication of a seasoned sailor. Making every effort to visit the ailing President but avoiding raising issues that might affect his recovery, she was the perfect symbol of a Vice President in charge but still dutifully bound to the recovering President.

It was also during this time that Bentley Wilcox brought a fashion consultant from New York's Bergdorf Goodman to the White House to further refine Charlotte's image. The efforts of the two caused the long-stemmed, plus-sized Vice President to become even more endearing to the American public. Camera shutters were clicking and video rolling, recording the Vice President making appearances at every possible high-visibility event. Each time her notorious husband Bill would show up, it would elevate into even more of a major media event. By the time President Minton returned to the White House, the spotlight had significantly shifted, and quiet conversations about his early retirement were more than just pensive rumors.

It was Memorial Day, the third year into his term, that President Minton, having seemed to regain much of his strength but now suffering from cognitive issues as well, appeared at a nationally televised broadcast from the Oval Office and grimly announced that he would not run for a second term. The country seemed to register this announcement with calm acceptance. In his absence, his presidency had lost steam. The public had grown tired of the nightly medical reports. He concluded his speech by announcing his support for Charlotte Reid as his successor and declared that he would support her vigorously for the Democratic nomination for President in the next election. The metamorphosis of Charlotte Reid had been nothing short of incredible.

THE DAWN OF RECKONING

Now, despite having poured more than $400 million dollars into her campaign to match an equal amount from party faithful across the land, the Vice President was deadlocked with the brash young ex-governor from Oklahoma, David Houston, and the Republicans' answer to Charlotte Reid. The debates—ten in total, reminiscent of the Lincoln-Douglas struggle during the 1860 election—had been nothing short of pure, unadulterated, and audacious verbal combat. No issue was deemed too extreme to bring to the table. For the most part, the discussions revolved around the standard Republican versus Democrat rhetoric of previous years. However, one significant issue that captivated much of America's attention was the Houston proposal to overhaul the government's intelligence system. His approach was straightforward yet highly controversial. In a time of war, he reasoned, all intelligence operations should be under the military's control. Simply put, if elected as President, he would fire the director of the CIA, put a general in charge, and run the whole Agency out of the Pentagon. Reid fought him tooth and nail on the issue, with the country largely split right down the middle.

On the first Tuesday in November, Houston bested Reid by just over

100,000 votes. But, for her part, she had "won" the all-important electoral vote, or so she thought. The official tally was 267 to 255 in Reid's favor, and 15 votes not even cast. The state of Georgia had been too tight—so tight, even in the weeks that followed, the situation there had become extremely confusing. By December 18th, the day the Electoral College voted, Georgia had become so infested by swarms of lawyers, lawsuits, and restraining orders that the state was simply unable to certify electors, resulting in one inconsistent recount after another. No one really knew with reasonable certainty how the state had voted. This left Reid with less than the 270 votes needed to win. The question of the Presidency was up in the air.

Convincing the courts and the U.S. Congress would now be a very different journey. It had long been presumed—at least in modern times—that in the event of an Electoral College deadlock, all states would be involved. By the fifth week of the process, the situation had become as chaotic as the discovery of thirteen missing voting machines and ballot boxes submerged at the bottom of a remote shallow eddy in the Chattahoochee River, nestled in the forested Georgia outback near Lake Lanier. It was the ultimate dilemma, the political horror story of horror stories – an election for President of the United States of America, simply and absolutely - too close to call.

2

"You've gotta admit, she gets your attention," David Houston remarked as he leaned over to his Campaign Manager, Sam Rusk. They were watching Vice President Reid on the bar large - screen on the penthouse level of Oklahoma City's Petroleum Club.

"Yeah, she looks good, but what a ruthless bitch," Rusk responded.

"You are so right about that, my friend... and you could call her a lot of things. But, ruthless...well, she certainly is that!" Houston paused. "But her back-stabbin' days are over. Congress will put me in. "There's no way she's ever going to turn this one around. Our forefathers didn't allow for screw-ups in the Constitution," Houston began to pontificate, as he often did on the campaign trail, taking a strong pull from his glass of swirling, amber-colored scotch—straight up, with no ice. Aged scotch was his preferred 'thinking' drink. "They weren't planning for shysters like her to come along."

Houston contemplated his surroundings—the old mahogany bar shrouded in wafts of cigar smoke floating through the air. Thickly textured rugs on hardwood floors shouted masculine power. Houston's staff had transformed most of the penthouse's interior into their temporary campaign command post.

Rusk replied, "At least half the country can see through her, and to be honest, that's more than I thought we'd achieve. I'll concede that she's a force to be reckoned with, but soon enough, she'll be on the outside looking in."

The two continued to pitch theories back and forth as other members of David Houston's inner circle worked feverishly on the phones, checking their sources in each state capital. Another group of campaign workers was in the lounge nearby, carefully watching each of the major networks and C-SPAN on a bank of ten screens arrayed precisely for monitoring every sound bite to make certain the Electoral College findings were confirmed.

Thus far, there appeared to be no hitches. Reid was not getting the 270 votes needed. It left Houston as the popular vote winner and neither candidate a winner in the Electoral College. The State of Georgia had stayed home from the vote, leaving the Electoral College inconclusive and, from the Republican point of view, of no consequence to the selection of the president. To them, the question of when a concession declaration might come from Vice President Charlotte Reid was the most pressing issue of the evening.

"You're gonna have to face the reporters pretty quick, you know, David, or should I say Mr. President! She's got to know that Congress will put you in." Rusk said with a wry smile. "So, let's talk about what you're going to say." But Sam quickly retreated from his optimistic stance. "You know, the lawyers are still saying that there are some out there who think it's not over. She's still got—"

"I know, I know," Houston interjected, waving him off with his left hand like a trial judge cutting off debate, while finishing a sip of scotch from the glass in his right. "Don't get hung up on legal technicalities, Sam."

"There are those who argue that, because of the Georgia situation and how close the election was, you should meet with her and reach some sort of agreement that reflects the will of the people," Sam continued. "You know, some kind of power-sharing scenario. You've got to be prepared to at least address that question."

"True," Houston said. "But I think the public is sick of her. With her billionaire sugar daddy trying to buy this election for his bitchy manipulative wife, she'd be a liability even if l liked her, which I definitely don't!"

Rusk watched Houston closely. He enjoyed listening to the confident Oklahoman talk tough and boast at the same time. It usually happened when they were at a bar, solving the problems of the world, and well into a bottle of scotch. He was slightly put off at Houston's evasion of his questions.

Houston continued, "She needs to go back to Seattle and focus on a long, shallow life with her nerd husband and his money. If we gave her any part of the leadership of this country, she would do the same thing to me that she did to Ronny Minton. He was a good man. I always liked him, even if he is a Democrat. But we've exposed her for what she is. If we could show how she set him up...and I swear to God, if I could prove somehow that she caused that heart attack, I would—because I think she did! She's dangerous...she's got an insatiable appetite for power," Houston concluded, tilting the snifter to get the last drop of his beloved Glendive.

The discussion was interrupted briefly by press reports about the possibility of an announcement from the Reid camp. Houston found himself trying hard to avoid any chance of engaging in a responsible discussion with anybody. He had enjoyed a few too many shots of scotch and now was paying for it. He knew that most of his past politically incorrect behavior involved 'letting the gorilla out of the cage' at inopportune times. He had no intention of being caught looking anything but presidential during the last leg of his long march to the

White House. So, it was time to slow down and quit drinking for the night.

LAYERS OF DECEPTION

The journey had begun long before politics was a part of Houston's vocabulary. He had been the Oklahoma Sooners' quarterback for two of their three national championship seasons. In his senior year, he was awarded the Heisman Trophy, but then did the unbelievable. He declined a lucrative NFL contract in favor of a Rhodes scholarship to Oxford. The sports world was shocked, as were most alumni and friends. His father, however, was not surprised. The family fortune needed to be managed wisely, and David had long aspired to take over his father's legacy. As the third generation to head the family's oil field servicing conglomerate, an NFL early first-round pick contract was mere chicken feed. David would make more money in one year in the oil business than he would in ten seasons in the NFL. He also had no illusion about what a 6-foot 7-inch 340-pound defensive tackle with half of his IQ could do to his 6-foot 2-inch 195-pound frame. He had managed to keep his body healthy through a brilliant college career while watching so many of his friends do long stints in the orthopedic ward. He hated general anesthesia. A long night with hard liquor was as close as he ever wanted to get to that. He didn't need the money, nor did he welcome the inevitable injuries that modified the gait of so many of his football friends. Therefore, he headed off to England—ending up with a Ph.D. in economics.

True to form, on the day of David's graduation, his father handed him the keys to the front door of Houston Industries. It took only a few short years for David to establish himself as the man to be consulted if any major project required a servicing crew, drill rig, or supply shop anywhere across the mid- western United States and certain locations across North Africa to the Arabian Peninsula and even Siberia.

David's personal life followed a predictable course. He married his college sweetheart. They had two sons in the first three years of marriage, making the Houstons the epitome of the perfect Southern family. Involvement in church and their dedication to various charitable causes helped nurture the legacy of high-quality Christian living established by David's grandfather.

At about the same time Charlotte Reid was suffering the boredom of trying to run Bill's estate after failing as an author, David Houston was growing weary of the oil business. One thing he had not done was get involved with politics. So, with the current Governor leaving office after two terms, David decided to throw his hat in the ring. As expected, the campaign was a landslide victory. He was sworn in as Governor of Oklahoma two years before Charlotte Reid was elected to her freshman term in Congress.

Houston's youth had not hampered his ability to become revered as an astute and capable Governor. He immediately gained credibility by putting on his economist's hat—focusing on the severe economic pain wreaked on the state by fluctuating energy prices resulting in unbelievable prices at the pump. David was no stranger to the subject. Even before his favorite art was hung on the walls of his new office, he was headed to the Middle East as Governor of an American oil state to negotiate production terms with sheiks, sultans, dictators, and pirates.

Initially, the trip was low profile. He carefully avoided publicity and fanfare, afraid the initiative might fail, and was also cautious to avoid creating an opportunity for terrorists. The adventure evolved into a resounding success. By the time his tour wrapped up breaking bread with the dictator in Caracas, Venezuela, the Governor of Oklahoma, despite criticisms about a state official violating the law by conducting foreign policy, returned to America as a national hero of sorts. The commitment to increased production, which would result in an eventual lowering of prices at the gas pump, was an accomplishment only he could have put together. After all, a large portion of the equipment used by the oil recovery and production system in the countries he visited had the

Houston Industries name extruded in the metal next to the serial numbers. Begrudgingly, the White House, the U.S. Trade Representative, and eventually Congress acknowledged him for the assistance.

David had been secretly working on something that would astonish the country even more than his oil diplomacy. As the filing deadline approached for his second term, the media was "caught looking" when Governor Houston appeared at a press conference and announced his decision to step down, endorsing his Lieutenant Governor to succeed him as the next Governor of Oklahoma.

That announcement, as unprecedented as it was, paled in comparison to the second part of the news conference. The Governor revealed that he and a group of business partners had been engaged in secret negotiations to purchase the Dallas Cowboys football team. The deal, which had been in the works for months, was completed discreetly, right under the nose of the news media.

FRACTURED PACTS

As amazing as this was to political junkies and sports fans alike, they hadn't seen anything yet. The Dallas Cowboys purchase was only the beginning of one of the most spectacular events in the history of professional sports. On a warm summer, morning in Irving, Texas, at the Dallas Cowboys' rookie camp, there was a new face. This face was none other than Number 10, former Heisman Trophy Winner and recent Governor of Oklahoma, David Houston. With his ownership interest in the team placed appropriately in a blind trust under the control of his partners, David Houston made it clear to the coach that he was just another one of the guys and he wanted no special treatment. He gave his word that he would do his best on the field or on the bench. He also vowed that he would not entertain any media interviews until the end of the first season. The sporting and political world came to understand very quickly that this was no publicity stunt, but a bonafide effort by an overage rookie to do the impossible.

But the impossible had never been beyond the reach of David Houston. As a high school quarterback, he had experienced defeat only once, and that was in his sophomore year. At the University of Oklahoma, the team enjoyed a record of 38 and 2. The last B to show up on his report card pre-dated his driver's license. The Heisman Trophy he had won had been the largest balloting landslide in the history of the award. As soon as veteran sportscasters discovered the identity of the new rookie in camp, there were already many acclimating themselves to the long-shot possibilities of Dallas in the Super Bowl behind the strength of the left-handed Sooner.

Governor Houston also outlined other reasons for not seeking re-election. As early as March, he had anticipated a Minton/Reid ticket on the Democratic side, which would undoubtedly lead to a lopsided national victory for the Democrats in November. At one point, he had considered pursuing an open Senate seat but ultimately decided against it, not wanting to engage in a contentious battle—especially with the looming possibility that the Senate could tilt in favor of a Democratic chain reaction.

He preferred the prospect of a few years in the NFL to that of a junior Senator in a minority party in Washington. He also knew that he was substantially at the tail end of his life from an athletic standpoint and that running, throwing and working out daily would only preserve him for so long. This was his last big chance—and he took it.

Early in his first season at Dallas, the team dropped its first three games. David had been playing sparingly as a backup in the first two games and didn't play at all in the third. His appearances had been respectable, but not of a caliber to overly impress the seasoned Dallas offensive coordinator and his staff. By the fourth game, he was relegated to third string and found himself standing on the sidelines holding a clipboard. He suffered under the reality that the game he was now playing was very far removed from the experience he had during his years at Norman.

By mid-season, the starting quarterback had suffered a serious elbow injury, and the team was barely hanging on to play-off hopes with a 5 and 5 record. Suddenly, on a Friday night before a Sunday game, David received a call at his home in Oklahoma City, where he had returned after practice on Thursday. The coach explained that the second-string quarterback who had taken over for the injured starter had been knifed in a brawl outside a Dallas nightclub. They would be hustling to scrape together some backups, but Houston would be starting on Sunday. He was told to report to the team offices in Dallas immediately to be ready for the teams' pre-game shakedown on Saturday afternoon. Within an hour, David had loaded up his Corvette Sting Ray and was headed south on I-35.

Sunday's game turned out to be nothing short of incredible. Houston proceeded to pick apart the Philadelphia Eagles' pass defense in an almost flawless performance. By day's end, Dallas had won the hard-fought battle by a score of 32 to 17. Houston had completed 22 of 35 passes for 285 yards. He threw for three touchdowns and ran for one more with no interceptions. The sports world had something new to talk about; the ultimate poster boy for success in business, politics, and sports.

By December, Dallas had nailed down the Division Championship, and David Houston's quarterback rating was the fourth highest in the NFL. The lead story of every cable and network sports show was about the new quarterback in Dallas who was living the fantasy of walking into an athletic arena many years after college and making a difference. This time, the difference was beyond anyone's imagination. Dallas' season came to a heartbreaking end in the second round of the playoffs as the Cowboys fell to a last-second field goal in overtime, orchestrated by a sensational comeback led by Tom Brady and the New England Patriots. The dramatic conclusion was as astounding to the sports world as David's oil diplomacy had been to the political realm less than three years earlier.

David then spent the off-season helping to run the family business as well as supervising shrewd trades to improve the Dallas defense. He acquired one additional wide receiver needed to complete the suite of offensive weapons for a serious next season run at the Super Bowl. His plan had been to find the most skilled and experienced wide receiver in the business who, like him, had one more year to give it everything he had. At the May press conference, the golden hands of the finest receiver in history came to Dallas by way of Philadelphia. Houston considered himself in the same position he had been in when he ran for Governor of Oklahoma—the race to the Super Bowl was his to lose.

During the course of the next season, the second-year quarterback rewrote the record books, passing for over 270 yards in each of his first seven games, without an interception. By the end of the regular season, the team had suffered only one stumble, and that occurred in a non-crucial late season game when David had to sit out with the flu. The team then went on to survive the playoffs. Finally, the entire sports world was riveted on that important day in January when the Dallas Cowboys faced the Steelers at the Super Bowl. Houston was unstoppable, but so was the youthful, high-speed, high-energy quarterback/running back leader of the Pittsburgh Steelers. By the time the game ended, Dallas had come up short, losing by a score of 37 to 34 in what many a sportscaster declared to be one of the most exciting Super Bowls in the history of the game. For David Houston, he had proven his point to himself and the world. He returned to Oklahoma City and his family to contemplate the prospect of yet another year of football, or so he thought.

THE TWO MOST BEAUTIFUL PEOPLE IN THE WORLD

The story, as Houston remembers it, was somewhat different from the way Sam Rusk might have told it. But there were enough similarities in the two accounts that most would assume it did spawn from a common origin. It went as follows: David Houston arrived at his Nichols Hills home with a crowd of post-Super Bowl well-wishers assembled behind police barricades on the opposite side of the street. Still having the energy to visit with fans, he walked over and began shaking hands and signing autographs, taking care, as was his political nature, to treat everyone courteously. As he reached out to the last person in the group, a man established eye contact with Houston and introduced himself.

"Hi, I'm Sam Rusk, and I'm *not* here for your autograph."

Houston was quick to retort, "Well, that's actually perfect because I think my pen's out of ink."

"Well, let me put it a different way, Governor Houston," the man replied. "I still need your signature, but it will be on a piece of paper that is going to change your life."

"I've heard that before," Houston said sarcastically. "So, are you selling athletic shoes, sports attire, or men's cologne?"

"Governor Houston, my name is Sam Rusk, and I am Chairman of the Candidate Selection Subcommittee for the RNC. I need your signature on a document that will save this country, nothing less, and nothing more."

Within a few short minutes, the two men were in David Houston's den as Rusk soberly outlined the Republican Party's worst nightmare— an Evita Perone-style takeover of the country, which was becoming apparent as President Minton's illness was catapulting the popularity of Vice President Charlotte Reid to new heights. He disclosed the secret polling that had been conducted in anticipation of an election, which would occur two years hence. It showed no elected Republican leader in the country having any significant numbers in a contest against Charlotte Reid. The committee decided to look elsewhere and stake its future on the one man who had dominated the sports world to even a greater degree than Charlotte Reid was dominating politics. Strategists anticipated a crossover from Reid's support if they started early and if Houston's high-stakes exploits as Oklahoma's governor some three years earlier could be brought back into center stage in the minds of the voting public.

Within days, David Houston left football and never looked back. The ensuing campaign devolved into a war of words, dragging politics to new lows. To counterbalance their youthful exuberance and brashness, both candidates chose running mates from the senior ranks of the U.S. Senate. This decision was made well before the convention, following the same strategy that Minton had originally used when selecting Reid. The Democrats chose the venerable Senator Thomas Rosenblat from New Jersey on the assumption that he could pull in the strong Jewish and senior vote to add to Reid's liberal power among Generation Y.

Houston called on a prominent Senator and former Republican Governor from the otherwise liberal State of Massachusetts, Talmadge Smith, who, like Houston, had established himself as a powerful industrialist-financier before running for the Governor's seat. It was presumed that Smith would help the ticket appeal to the largely homogenous religious vote, along with the more liberal and centrist Republicans in the eastern part of the country. This would supplement Houston's appeal to sports fans and middle-of-the-roaders from both parties and maybe he could steal back part of the NASCAR vote, not to mention the female voters, as well.

The debut of his "Dashing with Dave" workout DVD coincided with the first month of the campaign. As the fickle winds of fate would have it, the intense, high-energy video turned out to be wildly popular with women as his sculpted body and ability to effectively take the viewer through an intense 60-minute workout quickly trumped Charlotte Reid's gender appeal. By the sixth week of the campaign, among female voters most likely to vote, the Harris Poll showed Houston leading Reid 2 to 1.

The greatest equalizer, however, was, by far, the first shot fired by

David Houston across the Charlotte Reid bow when, in his announcement for his candidacy, he took a shiny copper Lincoln penny from his pocket, held it up, and declared, "Not one penny more!" He went on to define his motto. He declared that he would not invest more than a single penny of his own money into his campaign, despite the wealth of his family, which, it must be said, was considerably less than that of Charlotte Reid—even under the most conservative interpretation of her share from the prenuptial agreement with Bill. Nevertheless, it was still a substantial amount. He vowed to rely on small donations from individuals across the board and throughout the country to fund his campaign. He then mounted an attack against the $250 million that Reid had already invested in her campaign before even "penny one" had come from an outside contributor.

So, it stood on that December night, as the Electoral College returns showed Reid's hollow 9-vote victory with a 267 to 255 vote. The two firebrand candidates, icons of what could be labeled the two most beautiful people in the world, had all but torn each other's tracheas out while betwixt in political combat. Both had plans, and both had strategies. As every effort came to a standstill in a sort of strategic back-and-forth, the courts and Congress would be tasked with untangling the mess. Each candidate was becoming more desperate as the race to become the most powerful person on earth was dramatically distant in both concept and reality from any sort of resolution.

3

A light snow fell from the sky with a periodic flake shattering into a thousand crystalline shards across Robert Cannon's nose as he walked briskly from his townhouse in Georgetown to the busy corner at M and 32nd Street. Dirty gray clouds skimmed the vast sky above him. He looked up at the ornate Jeffersonian architecture and the golden dome of the three-story Riggs Farmers and Mechanics Bank on the corner. It was the kind of building that had lost its prominence over time, yet its majesty still lingered. Robert pondered how such an unrefined name could exist on a bank in such a cosmopolitan area. He couldn't imagine many farmers or mechanics doing business at a bank on Georgetown's bustling main drag. The trendy shops, restaurants, and upscale art galleries simply didn't seem compatible with crops, pickup trucks, or country western music.

As the crosswalk sign illuminated "walk," Robert joined the surge of human traffic that stepped off the curb, making its way across the street to the west. Despite the cold, he felt warm inside. Robert had made it through another night—a night of terror, fear, and hopelessness. The thought that at least he was still alive and he hadn't killed anyone was enough to comfort him. His struggle with the darkness, to hold together long enough to even see and feel a ray of morning sun, was over. With the light of day, he had hope. Warmth of the day made him feel courageous. But, as darkness returned at day's end, so did his fears and memories that, once more, would drive him to hide—to mourn the fact that he had ever lived.

Making his way south along M Street to 30th, he turned right and continued halfway down the block, crossing the street to enter the courtyard entrance of the Georgetown Suites Hotel. Skipping the hotel itself, he ventured into an office complex on the west side of the cobblestone courtyard. As he pushed through the heavy-gauge double glass doors, he greeted the crisply uniformed African American security guard seated behind the reception desk, who was enjoying a steaming cup of coffee. Robert then ascended the circular staircase to the second floor. Entering the heavy polished glass doors into the stately mahogany-paneled Fischer, Cramer & Morrell law firm, Robert was relieved to be present and accounted for.

FLICKER OF CURIOSITY

Robert had worked as an investigator for the firm since his retirement from the CIA seven years earlier. Although much of his work was done for other law firms and businesses throughout the D.C. area, the billings were run through the Fischer firm. It was a solid arrangement for him and the firm, supplementing his agency pension.

Normally, he would pass through the reception area, turning left to navigate the circular hall leading to his office—a sanctuary he cherished. His patio on the south side offered a picturesque view of the historic locks of the Chesapeake and Ohio Canal. However, this time, his routine was interrupted by an enthusiastic "Hi!" that rang out from the reception desk, as if a long-lost relative had just arrived. He turned to see a different face—a vibrant newcomer, not the usual receptionist, who rarely spoke even when addressed.

"Hello," he responded, "Aren't you..."

"The new receptionist...Kim moved on." She laughed softly. "Oh, I don't mean she died, she just got another job."

The woman's face was tinted slightly red as she rolled her eyes, acknowledging her own silly remark. Only lonely people talk to me, Robert remarked to himself. Then she tilted her head sideways to cause a strand of hair to fall over her left eye, only to be met in the next second by a jet of air from her slightly extruded lower lip sending the bangs back into place. It caught Robert's attention. He found himself pleased by the energetic yet soothing voice coming from a woman who looked, at first glance, very attractive. He could feel her large, bright eyes focusing on him as her shoulder-length blonde hair bounced in tandem with her soft pink cheeks angling upward to complete a warm smile. Her eyes sparkled and sent out a clear message that she was going to have fun with any discussion ensuing between them.

"I'm pleased to meet you...I'm glad you're here." He wondered why he had said that.

"Well, I'm glad I'm here too. My name is Cindy Wilstead."

Robert took a few steps across the glazed hardwood floor in the direction of the reception desk, nodded, and spoke, "I'm Robert Cannon. I work here as..."

"The investigator," Cindy interrupted, "I know who you are!"

For a moment, her statement shot a chill down his spine. No one knows who I am, he thought to himself. Why would she say that unless she really did? His paranoia was always just a lame thought away.

"So, you do, do you? Well then, who am I?" He popped a rare smile, suspicious that she might know more than she should.

"The lawyers here say that you are the mystery man. They say you do their investigations and that I should expect you here at about a quarter after eight in the morning. And guess what?"

"What?"

"You are exactly three minutes late!" She smiled, sensing that her humor was appreciated.

Robert checked his watch then looked back at her, wondering why the flirtation was directed at him. "You are right. I came in exactly three minutes late, and maybe four, if my watch is not synchronized with yours." He smiled again.

"Oh no, it's not my watch. It's the clock." She pointed to a cherry wood antique clock on the entry wall. "So don't forget it...I just thought it would be good for us to get off on the right foot. We need to make sure you are always punctual."

As she spoke, he noted her poised and attentive posture behind the high counter of the receptionist station—an air of calm confidence. Her professional demeanor and the elegance of her attire intrigued him, and he found himself wanting to know more about the person behind the friendly voice.

Cindy was about to speak again but was distracted by a telephone call. "Just a moment, let me get this. "Fischer, Cramer & Morrell," she rattled off the firm's name, even making a law firm sound like a fun place to call. As Robert approached, he noted as she turned to answer the phone, her shoulders moved almost with the same rotation of her head, as if working from the same axis. Then, in the next moment, as he approached the counter, a flicker of curiosity urged him to glance down at her legs. He noticed they were drawn to one side, held together by a belt-like device. Almost simultaneously, his gaze traveled upward, revealing the rubber handle grips atop a wheelchair, followed by the unmistakable presence of an electrical motor—this was anything but a simple chair.

"So, you like my wheels?" She had transferred the call to the firm's managing partner, Landon Cramer. He quickly broke his stare. She was cheerful. "So, what's a little muscular dystrophy between friends? I got the wheels when my legs gave out and, frankly, my wheels are really not so bad!"

She smiled and Robert found himself looking directly over the counter into her eyes. They were green with robin-egg specks decorating the iris, adding luminescence to her gaze.

"In fact, I can get this baby up to 15 miles an hour and keep it that way for five miles. I bet an old fart like you couldn't do that...not even in your prime!" She tossed a mischievous grin across the room as if she were challenging him to a race. The hair flopped down again, this time to stay.

He didn't mind being called an old fart as he deftly tried to unravel the mystery behind why this attractive woman would flirt with a 59-year-old like him. In a rush to recover from the awkwardness, he realized that the hired help at the firm—hell, in any office—had never spoken to him like this. "Well, that's okay; I guess it really does go fast," he stammered, his embarrassment palpable. He knew he sounded foolish, floundering for the right words as he navigated this unexpected encounter.

He paused again, but this time she held up as well, and just looked at him and smiled as if she already knew his next move. "Well, I guess I better get to work." He started to walk in the direction of his office, trying to avoid the gaze that begged for more words. As he reached the door leading out of the lobby and into the office hallway, he found himself wishing that he could say something more, maybe clever.

Then he heard her voice call, "Bob." He turned around to look at her once more, giving her his full attention.

"What?" He answered almost dutifully.

"You need a haircut!" She was accusatory and direct.

Robert reached up to run his hand through his hair as if responding to an order from the boss. "Well...I guess I do," he admitted, as he felt the hair hanging slightly over his ears.

"I'll expect it to be done some time this week, got it?" Cindy demanded with a chuckle.

"You bet Cindy… I've got it." He then turned and walked down the hall to his office, noting it had been a lifetime since anyone had called him 'Bob'.

"I know what you're thinking!" Robert heard the friendly voice of Landon Cramer, who followed him into his office and gently closed the door. "She comes on a bit strong for a receptionist."

"Or any employee at the law firm." Robert responded, while at the same time privately pleased with the woman's way. He sat down at his desk cluttered with unopened mail.

"Last week while you were out, Kim just called us one morning and said she had a new job and needed to start immediately. Didn't even clean out her desk, saying it was a government thing, so I didn't ask many questions."

"I thought Kim was quite content here. It's been what, about four years?" Robert asked.

"At least, but it was apparently too good a deal to pass up. We were kinda stuck and she mentioned her friend Cindy." Robert knew he could piece together the rest of the story without asking any more questions. Landon Cramer had a heart as big as his broad smile—a bit of a 70s throwback at first glance. Cramer never missed an opportunity to lend a hand. Surely as soon as he discovered the applicant for the job was in a wheelchair that iced it in her favor. Cramer had long established his own personal affirmative action rules in life—those with disadvantages were drawn in under his umbrella and given every chance to succeed. The new receptionist, no matter her qualifications, would inevitably be another individual influenced by the benevolent hand of Landon Cramer.

"So, did you vet her, or did you just put her in the position without any consideration?" Robert inquired. "She had a reference from the

Pentagon, I believe," his boss replied. Robert understood the implication. His boss likely had a staffer make a quick call to another staffer, and negative references were rarely the outcome of such informal inquiries.

"But she'll be good, Robert. Just give her some time. She'll figure out what it takes. Doesn't she possess the greatest smile?" Landon grinned again, causing his horn-rimmed glasses to rise slightly upward as his freckled cheeks widened.

"Linda and I had her over for dinner last week. She's been through a lot."

Robert, again, marveled at the Cramers, who would find time to invite a new receptionist to their home for dinner even before her first week on the job was over. She was probably a project for them, much like he felt he had been. Cramer never gave up—always positive, always probing—to uncover something good in every situation.

Everyone is good to Landon Cramer, Robert thought to himself. He often wondered how a person like Cramer could traffic so well year - in and year - out in Washington circles with no caution for bad people. It was as if Cramer had succeeded with the attitude of ignoring the evil to make it run. No matter how slight the good might be in anybody, he would pull it out of them and put it up in lights.

"So, how was the vacation?" Cramer asked.

"Great." Robert had been working his other job—one that he could not share with Cramer. "Got some storage lockers cleaned out...been waiting for a long time to get it done." The story was partially true.

"Two weeks to do that?"

"Well, I did some other stuff too."

Cramer was not one to pry and could see he might be striking a sensitive chord with his long-time investigator. But he was still unwilling to back off from a personal discussion. "We really enjoyed having you over for Thanksgiving. Linda and the kids...well, they just think you are the man!"

Robert was hoping that a Christmas invitation was not about to be made. The Thanksgiving dinner at the Cramer home in McLean had been wonderful, but also very hard. It had been the result of his first affirmative response to a hundred invitations by Cramer and the other lawyers. The food was wonderful. The sensation of love in the Cramer home had overwhelmed him. It caused him to feel, for one afternoon, like he had had a glimpse of heaven. But he was pained at the end of the day to leave, and for all intents and purposes, return to hell. As wonderful as it was, he was leery about suffering through the transition again.

"I enjoyed it, Landon. You've got a great family."

"So, how about Christmas? Are you doing anything?" Cramer asked. "We'd love to have you for Christmas Eve dinner at our place. We've got a couple of young guys from our church who are away from home during the holidays coming over too." They're away from home for the holidays. They're pretty interesting guys...you know...sort of like you!"

CHAINS OF REGRET

Robert pondered how Landon Cramer would feel if he really knew what he did for a living. But the same thought was framed by Robert's suspicion that Landon Cramer could spend Christmas Eve on death row and still walk away with an extremely positive experience and a new set of friends.

"Thanks Landon. I'll check my schedule. I do have some stuff to do over the holidays." Robert was lying. "Let me get back to you, if that's okay."

"Sehr gut!" Landon shot back in German, a language that he had mastered as a young missionary in Berlin twenty years earlier. Cramer stood up, headed for the door, then stopped, closing on one last thought before leaving the room. "Now, don't worry about that receptionist. If she gets rough on our clients, I'll talk to her. She'll come around. I know she will."

He headed to the hall. Robert could hear the fading whistle of the theme song to *Bridge Over the River Kwai*. Cramer was incredible, he thought to himself. Truly incredible. Throughout the morning, Robert struggled to focus on the piles of documents on his desk. His task was to review tens of thousands of adverse event reports issued by the Food Safety Committee of the FDA. The goal was to assess the legitimacy of the FDA's push to ban certain exotic Asian herbs used in dietary supplements. As he turned the pages, he found the process interspersed with thoughts of Cindy. For a moment, her sexuality swept through his mind, arousing him enough to slow his work. In the next moment, a visceral pain at the thought of a once-magnificent woman, her muscles and limbs severely affected struck him, just struggling to navigate life. The image tormented him, yet he couldn't shake it. As the morning wore on, Robert could hear Cindy's gentle voice echoing down the hall, interacting with lawyers and their clients as they moved through the lobby. He felt a pang of envy, even jealousy, stirring within him.

She was so kind—her words coated with infectious goodwill. Her version of a smile in a law firm was a rarity, too familiar, too quaint— too genuine. Why I can't be like that, even a little bit, he thought to himself.

By late morning, Robert had placed calls to dozens of trauma centers and emergency rooms across the United States as he tried to track down the sources of reports of severe illnesses and in some cases, death, attributed to patients who had been taking herb-laced products. He uncovered a pattern that could greatly benefit the law firm's clients. In typical bureaucratic fashion, instead of reporting the actual number of individuals who had fallen ill, the FDA was merely reporting the number of calls regarding potential adverse events. This meant that adverse events were being reported based upon the count of calls received by the FDA, rather than the total of actual incidents. Apparently, no one had even bothered to tackle the question of how many people were reporting the same incident more than once.

The outcome, in some cases, as many as ten adverse events were merely different people in the same emergency room reporting the same event to bureaucrats calling at different times over a two-year period. The evidence was mounting that the government's case against the target herb was significantly flawed. By noon, Robert had already discovered that as many as eighteen reports of deaths by the FDA were, in reality, only two. This would support the contention of the dietary supplement companies that their products, after millions of dosages, were much less hazardous than diet sodas with caffeine.

"Bob," the rich timbre of Cindy's voice pulled him from his thoughts. She sat casually at his office door. "I was serious about that haircut. I have connections at the salon over at the Four Seasons Hotel." Then, adopting the sultry tone of a 1940s Mae West, she added, "You just go over there and tell them Cindy sent you."

Robert couldn't help but wonder how this woman he had met just a few hours ago could make his heart race with a simple intercom call. "I might take you up on that, but I already have a barber," he said, attempting to deflect her suggestion.

"That's exactly the problem, Bob," she countered. "You go to a barbershop and get the $23 special. What you really need is a professional stylist to update your look. We're talking style here! I think a guy like you can handle spending more than twenty-three bucks—and live to tell the tale."

There was a brief silence. Robert expected Cindy to fill the void, but she didn't. "Well, I'll see what I can do, but right now, I've got to keep this work moving along," he spoke slowly, feeling his way.

"I understand all that. I'm here to make sure you keep going.

Anything you need, just give me a buzz." Cindy wheeled on down the hall, put her chair in gear and darted into another office, burning rubber in the process.

"Thank you, Cindy. I appreciate it. I really do." Robert meant what he said, even though he knew she did not hear him.

For Robert Cannon, unlike most of the rest of the world, Mondays were usually good days. The weekends, more often than not, dragged into invariable loneliness—loneliness that he spent a large part of his life attempting to keep at arm's length from everyone and everything. The weekend was sometimes survivable, at least on Friday evening. By Sunday, he had normally exhausted all his habitual diversions, and the weekend could not be over fast enough.

ECHOES OF KINSHIP

One healthy habit Robert had acquired over the years was a love of running. His favored route was to start in Georgetown and run up the C&O Canal trail paralleling the Potomac River all the way to the chain bridge at Glen Echo. His turn-around point was a water fountain in a small regional park on the Potomac. He had followed a routine at least three dozen times over the course of the year. That corresponded with the number of weekends business had not taken him away from D.C.

Monday was a day of rest. At noon, Robert would regularly go to *J. Paul's* on Georgetown's main drag, a busy sports bar frequented by locals and tourists alike. He usually ordered nachos, more out of habit than a genuine preference for the dish. His regular visits over the years had earned him a small table—sometimes for two, but usually just for one— tucked away at the back with no wait. It gave him the comfort of blending into the crowd without feeling completely alone.

Robert returned from lunch at 1:35 p.m., feeling a bit more energized than usual. However, his brief burst of enthusiasm was quickly overshadowed by a swirl of conflicting thoughts.

On one hand, he wanted to see the woman who had stirred him in such a clever way earlier in the day. On the other, he wanted to avoid the recurring and overwhelming sadness that he felt deep inside for her. It was a distraction.

As Robert came through the door, he saw one of the mail couriers covering the front desk in Cindy's absence. Cindy was probably at lunch, he thought to himself, and he realized he was glad to avoid her. Suddenly, it was easier to get back into his work. Robert figured that if he could wrap up his current project by 7:00 p.m., he'd reward himself with a late spaghetti dinner and catch Monday Night Football at one of his usual spots, just a block from his townhouse on Dumbarton Street. For him, this was about as good as life could get.

"Mr. Cannon," a few minutes later he heard Cindy's voice on the intercom, sounding professional and without the touch—the familiarity. She must have returned from lunch. "You have a call on line two, and the gentleman will not give his name."

Such calls were not uncommon in a law office, but the message did cause a slight gastric alarm as Robert pushed line two on the twelve-line phone. "Robert Canon here."

There was a momentary silence and then a person with a mechanical sounding voice spoke, "This is a message for the 'Lever.' May I receive a clearance?"

A sharp pain shot through the pit of Robert's stomach. With Pavlovian reflex, he responded, "The weather is clear in Spitzbergen." Instantly, he felt a pang of shame for having uttered the words. He turned away from his desk and his work, stood up and stared out the window into the quaint old-world street. There were so many things to see along the C&O Canal below his window. The mechanical voice continued, "Tomorrow—1400 hours—the boathouse. So how is the weather in Spitzbergen?"

Like a pilot communicating with an air traffic controller, his words were monotone yet unmistakable: "The weather is clear in Spitzbergen." With that, the voice disappeared. Robert set the phone down and turned to the window, now watching as the early 19th-century lock filled with water on the old C&O Canal. He stood there in silence for minutes, then half an hour, and finally, for the better part of an hour, before he almost trance-like settled into his desk chair. He realized he would need to concoct an excuse for his failure to complete the FDA report on time for the Fischer, Cramer & Morrell lawyers.

The distress was settling in at a level that would forbid him from reading, writing, or in any other manner comfortably navigating through the day. The order was very much a command, and he intended to respond obediently, as he did on so many occasions.

4

Atlanta was burning. Not literally, but figuratively as the legions of lawyers that had converged on the city were wreaking carnage not seen since General Sherman's arrival in 1864 on his march to the sea. Holiday goodwill had taken a back seat to fractious election warfare. It had spread well beyond the city. Nearly every county courthouse became the battleground for election fraud litigation. It was evident that both sides had adopted a Ulysses S. Grant-style strategy: attack on all fronts.

In predominantly Republican voting counties, Democrats were filing lawsuits. Conversely, in the Democratic-controlled counties, Republicans were doing the same. Each party aimed to prevent the other from gaining control of the recount audit and hand-ballot counting process. Both sides were convinced that, if given the chance, they could manually disprove what machines had reliably established over many years of civility in the electoral process. In one county in northern Georgia, armed Republican locals, wielding rifles and shotguns, stood guard against several busloads of paid out-of-state protesters who threatened to storm the courthouse and seize the voting machines and ballot boxes. So much for Christmas cheer; in some places, ballot boxes were missing. In some cases, machines had been confiscated for claimed forensic examination and testing, though neither supposed experts nor judges could even explain what that testing entailed.

The Georgia chaos continued to fuel the national anxiety over the unfinished election. It had been assumed that the election would be resolved once the Electoral College had spoken. Republicans nationwide emphatically called for the winner of the popular vote to be declared president, disregarding the provisions of the Constitution. The popular consensus was that Congress would likely support the Houston/Smith ticket, provided there were no defections. In the Senate, the Republicans held a razor thin majority of 51 to 49. In the house, there were still seven more Republicans than Democrats, despite substantial gains made in races across the country. The division of Republican vs. Democrat delegations, on a state-for-state basis, had drawn to a virtual tie with most experts, and even Democrat pundits begrudgingly projecting a slight Republican advantage if the Presidency actually came to a vote.

FRAGILE PRECEDENT

Within a week after the November vote, Democratic power brokers had already anticipated the direction of the election. With over two hundred and ten million votes cast, the race remained a dead heat. It was so close that several states found themselves in a gray zone, with Georgia being the most contentious. A civil war of sorts had erupted at the local level, where the party in control of the county election process dictated the terms. Charlotte Reid's surrogates, along with her public relations team and a battalion of New England lawyers, were relentlessly launching attacks against the officials in outlying counties. Except for the Atlanta metro area, a surge in the rural counties seemed to be successfully projecting the Houston cause. Democrats claimed voter irregularities at many rural sites. Statewide, the lead changed sides daily depending upon which wire services claimed to have the latest word.

By the third week, however, public opinion polls were starting to steer largely in favor of the Democrats.

As the National Democratic Chairman argued on the Sunday morning *Meet The Press* and any other friendly show he could muster; "IT

WOULD BE ONE THING TO ACCEPT DEFEAT IF THE ELECTORAL COLLEGE VOTE ALLOCATION TO VARIOUS STATES HAD BEEN CLEARLY ESTABLISHED. BUT IT IS QUITE ANOTHER WHEN COUNTING THE VOTES OF 537 ELECTORS IS EVEN MORE CONFUSING THAN DETERMINING THE OUTCOME OF 123,000,000 PLUS POPULAR VOTERS."

The Democrats sought to reassess the voter results, address the issues in Georgia, and reconvene the Electoral College for a second vote—all before the January 20th inauguration. If necessary, they were prepared to request a restraining order from the U.S. Supreme Court to delay the inauguration, fully aware that this was a fragile argument lacking legal precedent. Nevertheless, they believed that if they could reach the Supreme Court, they still had a chance to prevail. This route was clearly preferable to the one-state, one-vote process mandated by the Constitution for a decision in the House of Representatives.

* * *

THE UNYIELDING EDGE

Robert Cannon rolled over in bed and glared at the red digital alarm clock. The clock displayed 4:31, reminding him that two hours and twenty-nine minutes remained until sunrise. He had spent most of the night awake, alternating between watching late-night talk show comedians and flipping to CNN and the Weather Channel. To make things worse, the Weather Channel has switched to running documentaries about famous hurricanes from ten years ago. Mentally numb, he realized he had seen the same stories more than a dozen times. He assumed there was nothing new in the world and nothing to distract him from his heart of darkness.

Periodically, Robert would turn off the television, bury his head in his pillow and try to let sleep take over. In the early stages of rapid eye movement, the nightmare of the bloody hands pitched him out of his sleep and into a state of conscious fear. He turned the TV back on and started the process all over again. But then, he would run into an old movie-ancient enough to surmise that every character on the screen was now face - up in a dark coffin somewhere reduced to a morbid skeletal blob, or even worse, ashes in ajar. Old movies felt haunted by the presence of dead people—a disturbing thought. His mind was like a dangerous intersection, where his thoughts collided. Even if sleep were possible, he knew he wouldn't find it; the night drained his energy in ways that few could ever understand.

Robert found himself wondering how anyone could ever reach this place in a lifetime, as his mind cast visions of two beautiful babies now grown with children of their own, desiring no contact with their father or grandfather. Other visions projected images of village chieftains and community leaders being blown away by his Navy SEAL team, under the guise of clandestine pacification operations in remote parts of the world populated by America's enemies. The past was often more real than the present. He remembered the day, after ten years with the CIA, he accepted a job beyond that of a mere CIA pipeliner and became an operator, which was tantamount to that of a professional assassin.

Although Robert had never personally pulled the trigger or placed anyone in the crosshairs of the many weapons he was trained to use, the label "assassin" still felt apt. As an expert in accidents, illnesses, and explosives, he had caused the deaths of many and shattered the lives of even more. Along the way, he conditioned himself to ignore reality, convincing himself it was just another job. For a time, this denial was effective; the pay was good, and he had a growing family to support.

Robert's career was nothing short of legendary at the Agency to the few who had a "need to know." Among his more prominent jobs was that of causing a socialist dictator from Chile a perilous death from cancer. Another early assignment to help a North Korean turncoat return home had failed badly. A Soviet pilot in a Sukhoi-15 fighter had shot down Korean Airliner Flight 007 in September of 1983 over the Krill Islands of the eastern Soviet Union killing hundreds including his turncoat and even a U.S. Congressman.

Recently, Robert took down a member of the President's own cabinet in a fiery crash on a mountain in Yugoslavia. He had even caused a Japanese Prime Minister to suffer a non-fatal heart attack, changing the government and the future of Japan.

Robert's work was in some cases the standard in intelligence circles across the world. He operated under the code name, "Lever," a name he had used for decades. Lever's identity was a national security secret, known only to a very few of the top CIA echelons and usually they were changing as often a computer access password. Some in the service took great pride in knowing the Lever which and that included many who knew neither him nor his whereabouts by any other name. His work was always meticulous, thorough and often accomplished leaving no trace of the true cause of death. Outwitting medical examiners resonated his work. It was his forte.

For his part, Robert Cannon considered his tasks to have been reasonably simple. Eliminating the Marxist Chilean president in the early '80s had been as simple as switching a vial of medication at the National Hospital in Santiago with one containing an AIDS-contaminated solution. All it took was a careful study of the President's medical charts and one bribe. By the time the truth of the illness was discovered, officials were either too embarrassed or too confused to disclose the real nature of the death. Officials announced it as cancer, but Robert and the CIA knew otherwise.

It struck Robert as strange that the Agency relied so heavily on him. Perhaps no one else at the CIA had ever fully embraced the level of depravity required for such tasks. But he knew better. But he wondered if his singular services gave the CIA the insulation needed to lay the blame on one man, should the work of foreign assassination of certain U.S. and foreign leaders offshore become known. The story that the

Agency might tell would likely be one of denial and blame. He was reasonably certain that he would not be around to hear it told.

FRAGMENTS OF REDEMPTION

The Korean airliner shoot-down had facilitated the most basic approach to east/west relations in the late 80's. A reasonable bribe could get any result in Russia. In that case, it took just two payments: one to the head of the Soviet Naval Forces stationed in Vladivostok, and another to the commander of the Air Defense Radar site on the Krill Islands, off the coast of eastern Russia, due north of Japan. The plan was to force the airliner to land at the remote military base at Krill with a slight adjustment to the inertial guidance system in the Boeing 747 cockpit during a refueling stop in Anchorage, Alaska, Korean Air flight 007 would accidentally fly over Soviet airspace.

The Air Defense commander had in place a long-standing order to shoot down any foreign aircraft violating the airspace. The plan hadn't been for the plane to be shot down, but rather forced down. The passenger list featured a Korean intellectual accompanied by a U.S. Congressman. In a convoluted deal orchestrated in the shadows of the intelligence community, the CIA had agreed to hand over the Korean to North Korean dictator Kim Jong-un in exchange for a significant rollback of his country's nascent nuclear and missile programs. The North Koreans claimed that the man had revealed the identities of the assassination team responsible for a mass killing of South Korean government leaders in Burma, and Kim was eager to capture him. It was a calculated exchange: a political objective traded for the life of a traitor. The CIA hated traitors no matter which side they were on—that is, if the traitor had lost his value to the CIA.

As life goes when dealing with the Russians, the word passed on to the Air Defense Commander from the Naval Commander, in a situation where one or both were either drunk or not listening, had been "shoot down" rather than "force down." This mistaken word, not uncommon among the disoriented Soviets, resulted in the deaths of 269 passengers. When dealing with Russians, uncertainty is always a given, and one must tread carefully with requests, Robert mused.

The assignment involving the Commerce Secretary had been straightforward. Robert drafted specifications at the CIA for modifying a cell phone so that each time it charged, it would automatically activate and stay in 'transmission' mode, regardless of whether it was manually turned off. The modified phone was handed to the Secretary of Commerce as his plane departed from Ramstein Air Base in Germany. For the Secretary, it functioned perfectly well as a regular cellular device.

What he didn't know was that it remained engaged and continued to emit a high frequency signal as the aircraft worked its way through the stormy conditions of the Balkan winter. The subtle but powerful emission threw off the navigation system. Although the pilots had successfully corrected their position visually on two dangerous landings, they met with disaster on an instrument approach to Dubrovnik Airport in Bosnia. They crashed into a mountain, killing everyone on board, including the Commerce Secretary, who was rumored to be a drug addict, money launderer, and, most notably, a Democrat campaign fundraiser whose ran a rather successful albeit illegitimate solicitation of Vietnamese contributors in Hanoi was at risk of being exposed.

One of Robert Cannon's more celebrated assignments had been one in which he had not been involved at all, namely, the death of Princess Diana. As experts gathered across the world to determine just what had happened, they grilled Robert in an attempt to detect any involvement by him. A roll-over in a Paris tunnel sounded like a "Lever" take-out. Once the CIA convinced British MI5 that Robert had been sidelined on this one, the British hired him to investigate the scenario to determine whether it had actually been an accident. It was his final opinion that, in fact, there had been no professional hit involved, but rather the life of the Princess had been snuffed out in a tragic event where the assassins were speed, alcohol and a perceived sense of invincibility.

Robert trained himself never to ask why. His well-used motto was, "To know is to know you don't know!" Over so many years, he found it easier not even to wonder. There had been times that he had rationalized his situation as a soldier merely doing his duty for his country and being no guiltier than he who kills in war. Other times, he took an even more distant view as the meat eater who has not a clue where the slaughterhouse is or what really happens there. Still, more and more frequently, the tortured distress of his existence was blotting out any sense of purpose or duty. He was in pain most of the time.

Robert could never forget where his sense of real guilt began. After seventeen years of marriage, he felt he was struggling through a relationship that had become less fulfilling over time. The many months he spent on the road each year, coupled with special assignments that called him away at a moment's notice, had strained his marriage at nearly every turn.

The couple's sex life had largely died, and they had distanced themselves from one another in almost all of their interests. Despite years of temptation, he had always fended off invitations from other women. Then one day he met Gina while jogging in Rock Creek Park. An intern for a California congressman, the sexually experienced graduate student drafted Robert into the major leagues of eroticism. It was all too incredible—that is, for every part of him except his conscience, from time to time.

ECLIPSE OF REALITY

On a Sunday afternoon, less than a month after the shoot-down of the Korean airliner, Robert kissed his wife goodbye at their cottage on the South Jersey shore. She boarded a commuter flight from Cape May Airport, heading back to Dulles and their family home in nearby Vienna, Virginia. The cottage, located not far from the Cape May lighthouse, was intended to be the perfect getaway for family and friends, providing a respite from the frenetic pace of Washington. As he watched her board the plane, a sudden wave of nostalgia washed over him, momentarily eclipsing his current distress with memories of happier times. Gina saw him and leaned back, waved and mouthed the words "I love you" followed by a blown, passionate kiss. He remembered blowing a less than enthusiastic kiss back. He had other thoughts on his mind.

The plane hadn't even taken off before Robert had returned to his car, picked up his cell phone, and made the call to Gina, waiting in an Atlantic City hotel. The plan was for her to drive down the Garden State Parkway and join him at the cottage once the coast was clear. She arrived within two hours. However, thirty minutes later, the incessant ringing of Robert's cell phone interrupted their frequent moments of intimacy. Robert froze as a Federal Aviation Administration inspector informed him that his wife's plane had crashed on approach to Dulles, and no one had survived.

As Robert slowly began to thaw, extreme self-deprecation took over. The pain, the turmoil, the guilt, combined with buried memories dripping off the walls of his dark world, culminated into one massive nauseating condition of self-loathing. He sent Gina on her way, never to see her again. His soul continued to die over the next several months. The anguish was fierce, in his mind a punishment for all he had done— a punishment that would be with him forever.

In the nightmare of the moment, Robert found himself frantically sifting through the reports of the commuter flight crash, trying to determine the likelihood of a "quid pro quo" hit connected to the Korea Flight 007 disaster. His search proved inconclusive; nothing seemed to fit together. The only factor that stood out was the coincidental timing, which, in his tormented state, led him to the harrowing conclusion that he had, in essence, pulled the trigger on his own wife.

The pressure of the ever-deepening around-the-clock depression had caused Robert to run. In his desperation, he sensed an inescapable need to distance himself from anything that related to family or responsibility. He never made it to the funeral. He never saw his two children again. The last thing they needed in their fragile lives was a connection to their mother's killer. Robert decided to flee. For months, his whereabouts were unknown to everyone—except the Agency.

If there were lessons to be learned from this personal tragedy, he would have been a very poor student. The business of arranging death was one enterprise from which he could not step away for long. He was soon back on the job, creating an illness for the aging Communist President of the former East Germany..

Shortly thereafter, Robert parted ways from the CIA and freed himself from daily reporting responsibilities at the Langley, Virginia campus. Instead, he sought private employment and found success as an investigator for various law firms. However, he soon realized that there were still strings attached. The CIA continued to turn to the "Lever" for resolving serious foreign concerns.

Within the framework of a certain evolution in his life, Robert never really stopped accepting cases akin to death missions, just that he did fewer of them. The pay was exceptionally good. Each hit was worth $250,000 tax free US dollars, which, adding to his standard CIA pension, made for a very comfortable retirement. How the CIA arranged for the IRS never to flag him for an audit remained a mystery to him—along with the question why, after all these years, they were still corning back to him for more work.

Robert had been at the Fischer, Cramer & Morrell law firm for more than seven years. The job positioned him well to stay in the intelligence loop, giving him the perfect excuse to ask questions and make inquiries that might otherwise cause suspicion. The fact that he was using some of Washington's finest lawyers as his cover to carry out some of the world's worst mass murders caused him some pause, but only for a moment. He appreciated the cover, especially since he no longer had a desk at the CIA. In Washington, using friends and trusted people was more the norm than the exception. A skilled CIA operative was well-versed in that process.

After a long shower, alternating between hot and cold, Robert attempted to clear out the effects of a sleepless night. He had his normal breakfast of oatmeal with skim milk and toast, then headed back to the office, knowing that due to lack of sleep, no matter how simple the work, it would be a long and difficult day.

5

"Hi Bob! So, what's your take on this election? Are you a Reid man? Or a Houston kind of guy?" Cindy's words stopped him in mid-stride halfway across the lobby, competing with his overwhelming fatigue for his attention. She persisted, "Come on, everyone's an expert. Tell me what you think."

"I don't think what I say matters much...Congress will have to work it out. I think that's where it's going to end," he spoke almost with a slur.

Robert's condition did not go unnoticed. "You are reminiscent of something the cat dragged in, Mr. Cannon," she spoke with some delight. "I can tell that you are ready for a wonderful day." She was sarcastic.

If she only realized the kind of a day it was really going to be, Robert thought. He did not want to visit, but then it was attention of a kind he had not seen for a very long time, and part of him liked it. He could not ignore her sense of timing that had a way of giving added meaning to what she had to say. Though tired and eager to retreat to the privacy of his office, Robert felt compelled to pause. "I can't spend too much time on politics today. After all, I'm not even running for office this year." He managed a weary smile as he walked down the hall, hanging his winter coat on the hook behind the door. But if he was seeking an escape, he found it elusive. In less than five minutes Cindy was wheeling herself into his office, carrying a pot of hot coffee on her lap, and demanding to know one of Robert's most intimate secrets whether he liked it black or cream. He was truly appreciative. He knew that without the offer, he would have procrastinated until the coffee's effects would have been far too little, too late. "You surely know exactly what I need."

"Oh, it's just my job. So, don't come out of here until you get your work done!" Cindy shot a command in his direction. With a mischievous grin, she added, "Or until the coffee makes you need to use the little boy's room." Cindy disappeared behind the door, allowing it to close softly behind her.

Robert sat in silence and stared for a moment, sensing the puzzling effect that she was having on him. Then, he returned to focusing on the herb case, knowing that at the very least it would be a struggle, and at the very most it would be impossible to concentrate as he anticipated the meeting at the boathouse.

By mid-afternoon, Robert was catching a second wind. Two of the firm's partners, Landon Cramer and Stanley Fischer, had summoned him for an impromptu meeting to review his preliminary findings on the FDA's Adverse Event Reports. Although he wasn't entirely prepared, Robert felt confident enough to navigate the information and ensure the two lawyers felt they were getting their money's worth from his efforts.

FISSURES OF TRUST

Robert had always been touched by the fact that the tough business style of the Fischer, Cramer & Morrell lawyers never seemed to supersede their friendliness. He considered them consummate gentlemen and far more accommodating than anyone he had ever worked with. He had long since concluded that these men had much more going for them than just their enviable professional careers. They were family men, and despite not sharing that aspect of their lives, their high regard for him remained undiminished. Beyond the regard, he had little in common with them. He often found it difficult to tolerate normal family-oriented conversations, especially those centered on holiday plans and family gatherings. There was always a warm, positive story about children. He had no stories to tell.

Robert found it easy to acclimate to the Georgetown holiday lifestyle where the merchants and restaurant owners seemed to trade only superficially in the holiday season, enough to make money but nothing more. It was an international thing to do. Many in the area did not even celebrate Christmas. It was beneficial for people like Robert because he didn't want to feel the spirit or sense the joy. He simply wasn't equipped to handle sentimental matters, having long insulated himself from any unrestrained expressions of positive emotion. If he had initiated a Merry Christmas or Happy Hanukkah wish in twenty years, or, if he had uttered a response to someone else's wish, he hadn't meant either.

There was one distinct seasonal expression that Robert could hardly ignore. Starting with the first Christmas after his arrival at the firm, he had received three packages on his doorstep. The first year it occurred, he received bags full of homemade holiday cookies and fudge. The real emotional pull came when Robert's stoic demeanor was softened by the handmade Christmas cards from the children. Over the years, he had transitioned from being the distant but cordial investigator for the firm to the holiday "special project" for the families of the lawyers at Fischer, Cramer & Morrell.

More than once, Robert had planned to acknowledge the gifts. But fear that such recognition might open the door to further gift giving obligations had steered him away from such a response. He was devoutly inclined to avoid closeness—finding it easier to disappear on the holiday than to be a part of it. Why should Christmas be any different? A half-hearted nod at the end of Christmas Eve would typically represent his maximum effort. However, Thanksgiving dinner at the Cramer home would now make it much harder to maintain such emotional distance.

By 3:30 p.m., the meeting had finished. Robert slipped out of the office as fast as he could, walking through the lobby without even acknowledging Cindy.

* * *

Within minutes, Robert was at his row house on Dumbarton Street, just two blocks east of the Georgetown main drag. It was a narrow three-story residential building. He had a storage shed in Reston, not far from Dulles. It was there that he stored items, especially deadly items used in his job. He wasted no time in getting himself decked out in his cold weather jogging gear. He finished the process by lacing up a pair of New Balance running shoes that had been worn or less than a month. His heavy pronation necessitated a change of shoes roughly every four hundred miles. This meant every month and a half he was spending upwards of $150 on a pair of shoes. Robert had long accepted that it was impractical to spend serious money on a pair of dress shoes when he could easily buy a perfectly good pair of running shoes instead.

Before shutting the front door of his townhome, he retrieved a tape dispenser from a drawer. He tore off a piece of tape about an inch long, then used scissors to cut it down the center, creating two thin strips. After that, he surveyed his exit route, glancing out the window before squinting through the peephole in the door.

He then proceeded outside and closed the door nonchalantly. While glancing off in another direction to distract the attention of possible observers, he reached behind him and stuck the tape between the door casing and the door at about the height of his thigh. It was a sleight-of-hand maneuver he had done thousands of times over the past years. He then looked in all directions, walked down to the street and braced himself for about a minute against a light pole for a runner's stretch.

SPITSBERGEN

Robert ran along Dumbarton northward to the corner of Wisconsin Avenue, going slow to avoid cars and people. He turned left and went past Riggs Bank, across M Street NW, Georgetown's Main Street and then one block further west in the direction of the Potomac River until he reached the Chesapeake & Ohio Canal. Turning right, where the rear wall of the Georgetown Park Hotel overlooks the canal, he made his way north along the towpath, which is used to pull tourists in replica 18th-century barges during the summertime. The path had long since become a favorite for joggers and bikers. Now, off the street, he could run faster and more relaxed.

The mid-afternoon sky was already beginning to fade as the dreariness of December normally required. The towpath left the Georgetown business district entirely and followed north along the river-paralleling canal for about three miles to the Chain Bridge turnaround. After the first half-mile, Robert's heightened metabolism began to help with the day's fatigue. He kicked up his speed to his 7.25 minute per mile pace and knew, based on his many years of running that he would need to maintain the pace for the rest of the run in order to reach the boathouse on time.

During the decades of his thirties and forties, Robert had run seventeen marathons, or as he would put it during a rare conversation about himself, sixteen too many. The pace steadied and he began to feel comfortable. There was no strain—just gliding motion. The thought of a massive heart attack while running crossed his mind from time to time. His family history validated his concern, as his father died of a heart attack at age 53 while Robert was out of the country on an extended assignment. The sudden death of his father had served as a strong wake-up call, motivating him to work out on a regular basis.

Sometimes, Robert envisioned a small gathering at a graveside memorial service, knowing he would never attract enough mourners to justify a church funeral. He imagined many would settle for the trite aphorism, "At least he died doing what he liked best." It was hard for him to gauge how much running truly meant to him. In many ways, it had simply been a way to pass the time and keep himself occupied against the backdrop of a life that was difficult to understand and even harder to feel. He imagined the lawyers from the firm showing up with their spouses and maybe a few of their children, standing around saying a few good things, thinking they knew him when in fact they really didn't have a clue. Most of what they didn't know, he did not want them to know anyway. It would be better to pass from life under the cover of trite sayings than to allow anyone to remember him in the horror of his reality.

Another realistic death scenario Robert had imagined for years involved someone from his past catching up with him. The CIA had normally been quite adept at keeping the names of its most effective operatives under lock and key. With the fall of the Soviet Union and the demise of the KGB, however, the CIA, with no deadly institutional adversary for more than a decade, had become relaxed, and less stringent in its security procedures. With the rise of Putin, the CIA had still been seemingly slow to pull itself back together. He often worried that someday, someone other than the Agency would discover his role in events that had resulted in the deaths of so many and exact their own remedy. If he ever had to face the consequences of his actions while he was still alive, he hoped the punishment would come swiftly and decisively.

The turnaround was situated about one hundred yards shy of Chain Bridge, which crosses the Potomac just below the section where the rapids make the river unnavigable. As he ran, he scrutinized each biker and jogger on the path, attempting to make eye contact—something he rarely did. After completing the turnaround, he headed south along the riverbank, making his way back toward Georgetown.

It was now after 4:00 p.m. and most of the cyclists on the path were heading north away from the city. Some were exiting the trail and making their way across the bridge to the off-campus student housing just north of Georgetown University. Others continued under Chain Bridge toward the bedroom communities northeast of D.C. As he ran, Robert considered the purpose of his journey. This was not a run for fun or a workout. Rather, a required approach pattern had to be successfully executed if he were to receive any instructions at the boathouse. This caused him to be more aware, more cautious of others on the trail.

Many of the bikers were couriers who had finished their afternoon shifts delivering important documents that were too sensitive or bulky to be emailed or faxed around the nation's capital. Each wore a similar uniform consisting of a heavy black windbreaker with prominently placed bright yellow, fluorescent stripes to alert drivers. A leather carrying pack was strapped over the cyclist's back. A key piece of equipment was the cell phone attached to the courier's waist with a black wire running up into an earpiece underneath the helmet. This time of year, goggles were necessary, making the face close to impossible to see. With steam pouring from his mouth and quickly dispersing into the air around him, the sleek, compact figure of the biker, fully equipped, resembled more of a "Robo Cop" than a high-tech letter carrier. In Washington, D.C., letters remained highly significant, allowing them to stay off the tech grid and out of the cloud.

Robert knew that there were a few in the group who were neither students nor couriers nor ordinary cyclists. Rather, they were young officers, kids from Langley with scanning equipment in their backpacks. These agents would ride right next to him as he ran ... first, to observe and make certain that it was, in fact, Robert Cannon—the famous "Lever," approaching for the meeting. Second, the roentgen x-ray scanner device in their backpacks would determine whether he was carrying a weapon or recording device, both of which were prohibited at the boathouse encounters. The instructions had always been clear. He would run the entire six miles at a steady pace, wearing only his running attire—no wallet, not even a watch. Once he reached the boathouse, he would commit all instructions to memory, taking no notes and seeing very little.

In the past five years, Robert had made the run to the boathouse at least a dozen times. He found himself annoyed by the menacing look of the cyclists as they rode in his direction, crouched forward over the handlebars, peering at him with predatory eyes through the yellow-tinted goggles. His attempts at eye contact were a waste. Over time, he improved his ability to distinguish one biker from another.

The only bike Robert had ever ridden on the job was a stationary Life Cycle, in the gym at the CIA's Langley, Virginia complex. The new officers were different. They seemed to carry themselves with a Hollywood-like swagger, in accountant's attire, turning the overt image of dullness into a subtle but certain threat. They were quietly confident, suited soldiers, with a much higher potency than the couriers who were just grown-up kids on bikes. These officers were no longer kids; most had been trained to kill, which disqualified them from being considered "kids" in Robert's mind. If any of them had been trained for "Lever" missions, Robert figured they must not be doing a very good job—he was still receiving most of the big calls.

On Robert's fifth mile, the bike trail worked its way through the forested area where it parallels most closely to the river. The traffic on the other side of the C&O Canal to his left had become a frenzied rush of headlights and car noise as it funneled out of Washington, D.C. along M Street in Georgetown and on to Chain Bridge Road. The sky was dark and grimy, filled with the noise of low-flying aircraft crawling through the murky air on their final approach to Reagan National, tracing the route of the river southward until touchdown. He slowed his pace, glancing down the path beneath the aging concrete viaduct that served as the northern approach to the Whitehurst Freeway, leading to the Key Bridge, which crosses the Potomac just north of Georgetown. As he continued forward, feeling surprisingly strong despite his lack of sleep, he carefully scanned the row of buildings along the riverbank beneath the viaduct, where the bike path abruptly ended and a wide, industrial road began. It was the perfect setting for this kind of meeting.

The viaduct acted as an outdoor roof, sheltering the green-shingled boathouse to the right along the river and the two-story, almost nondescript barracks-like structures on either side of the road for several hundred yards. This setup created what the CIA agents referred to as a "control zone." Snipers could strategically conceal themselves in the superstructure of the viaduct, well positioned to handle any situation that would need to be resolved through the focused violence of a high-powered rifle. Of equal importance, from there they could make certain that no unauthorized person was watching who might be coming or going to the dimly lit, obscure boathouse, which extended off into the leafless trees where a dozen canoes were stacked on wooden racks near the shoreline.

Robert walked the last hundred yards, carefully surveying the eerie scene. The sole source of light in the sky was the orange-red glow of the city reflecting against a solid sheet of clouds. The long stretch of roadway under the viaduct was illuminated by the gloomy greenish industrial streetlights one on every third support column. Looking south down the road, he spotted an officer crouched in the shadow of the iron armature of the overpass, about two hundred yards ahead. It wasn't Robert's skill that led to this revelation; the officer was deliberately positioning himself to be seen while concealing himself from others. This was a signal for Robert to walk toward the boathouse just off the right side of the road. He could enter through the pale green door, marked with "NO TRESPASSING" spray-painted across its center in a mildly artistic urban graffiti style.

Once inside, Robert stood in a strangely familiar place. It was no larger than two telephone booths back-to-back. There was a door to his left and another to his right. Against a narrow wall adjacent to the door on his left was an old black rotary telephone. The same phone, he thought, that had been around when push buttons were still a novelty.

He quickly picked it up and dialed a 5 followed by a 1. Again, numbers he had used at this same spot for so many years. There are some things you will never forget. In the next ten seconds he heard some muffled crackling noises, which he presumed to be the sound of some sort of MRI-type scanning device from somewhere inside the wall, conducting an electronic identification process. Then all stopped. The light went out, and he was in coffin-like darkness. In the silence, he could hear his heart still beating fast from the run.

Suddenly, the door in front of Robert unlatched, revealing the awareness of another void that he knew from prior experience to be a larger room. As he had done countless times before, he walked through the door to listen to the voices of people he would hear but never see.

"Please give us a voice print," were the first words resonating through the darkened room.

Robert spelled his name out three times. Then, the blackness was broken by a thin ray of dusty light emitting from a three-inch projector through a hole in the wall. The beam projected onto the expanse of what he estimated to be a seven-to-eight-foot screen on the wall to his left. It was old-time technology, completely devoid of anything digital—totally off the grid. Robert recalled that it was the same as his first experience at the boathouse some twenty-five years earlier. Some things, particularly bad things, never change, he thought to himself. The room was damp and cold. There was, however, enough light for him to know that there was no one else in the room and that the source of sound was from an old low-tech, drive-in movie-like speaker mounted somewhere on the upper part of the black wall directly in front of him.

"My reporting name is "Lever. I am fifty-nine years of age. I have just finished a six-mile run," Robert spoke in normal, steady tones— starting the discussion using the same operating procedures as he had on so many prior meetings.

"Thank you." The voice, which Robert estimated belonged to an agent in his mid-thirties—definitely younger than the projection system—continued, "Your objective is a ninety-nine-year-old male from Biloxi, Mississippi, named Maxmillian Ormond."

The name instantly triggered a reaction within him. "You mean United States Congressman Maxmillian Ormond?" Robert replied, not overly surprised. He had taken out U.S. government officials before.

"That is correct." The voice from the speaker adroitly continued, "He suffers from a variety of aging-related illnesses. He had a pacemaker inserted originally in his eighty-first year. This was recently replaced with an upgraded model during his ninety-fourth. Incidentally, it is not microwave reactive. He also takes 120 milligrams of Inderal to regulate his blood pressure. Despite his age, he seems to be quite healthy, but his advanced age is a factor that should be to your advantage."

The video presentation lasted about five minutes. It was notably different from previous sessions at the boathouse, where the facts and circumstances had been so complex that Robert often needed to request several playbacks to remember everything. The facts about the aging Congressman Ormond were simple—the sort of plan Robert could put together in his sleep, and likewise carry out in the Congressman's sleep, as well. "So, when is the Congressman going to be out of the country?" Robert asked matter-of-factly.

The otherwise monotone voice paused before continuing over the speaker, "Uh...he won't be. The window of opportunity ends December 31st. Therefore, the work must be done in-country." "What do you mean?" Robert asked, alarmed. "I've never done hits in-country! You know that! That's not in the protocol!"

UNDER SHADOWS

The younger voice was ready for his objection. "We don't have a choice this time. The orders are clear: get it done. The most likely location is the Congressman's residence."

Robert stood quietly, thinking. He had terminated prominent officials of the government before. However, it had always been outside the borders of the United States. That was arguably within the unwritten leeway afforded to covert operations of the CIA. The fact that the agency had sometimes focused on American citizens seemed to have been of no consequence. Robert spent little time wondering if the orders came from the highest levels of the government. He always assumed such was the case. This time, he was bothered. The request was odd, and a gut instinct told him to refuse.

"I don't know about this," Robert stated. "It sounds like you've got your wires crossed on this one."

The youthful voice came back briskly, "As you know, we are acting within all appropriate authority. You know that—and that has always been the case."

"I'll ask for confirmation." Robert responded abruptly.

"That's quite all right. You know you have that right as well. Just don't hesitate if you want confirmation. Get it quickly." The young voice seized control once again.

The confirmation process was established after Robert retired from the CIA. When he was asked to undertake a mission through the usual procedures at the boathouse, he was assigned a MOTS contact, which stood for "Man on The Street." It allowed back-door contact with an Agency Deputy Director who would meet Robert at a pre-arranged spot on the street, usually, somewhere in the downtown DC area. There, Robert would rehearse a summarized version of the facts to the official. The meeting would be extremely short, and he could not ask questions. At least he would know that he had the nod from a real breathing member of upper management at the Agency. Robert planned to take full advantage of the MOTS contact this time.

"Lever, do you accept the assignment?" The voice demanded an answer. Robert had never turned down an assignment, but he still could not come to grips with the concept of an in-country hit.

"I need a moment to think, if that's all right?"

The response to the question was outright and quick, "If you have any hesitancy, just say so. If you are not up to this, that's fine. We will deal with that and, of course, you will not hear from us any further. You will be expected to adhere to every aspect of the National Security Act and the Agency's internal regulations. "You know you have no due process in this matter. Violate it, and you're out!" The voice was emotionless and stern, reminiscent of a police officer reciting a Miranda warning during an arrest. Robert couldn't help but wonder if the boathouse had been established solely for him from the beginning.

There was absolutely no doubt in Robert's mind about the gravity of the threat. The big question in his mind was that if he refused, would he really be left alone for the rest of his life? What would life be like without the Agency? Would he ever leave the boathouse alive? For a moment, he tried to view things from the Agency's perspective. He doubted the CIA could trust anyone with as much knowledge as he had—especially as he aged and might eventually start talking. Keeping an umbilical cord to the CIA provided him with some measure of protection. Once more, he rationalized that this would be an easy hit. A heart attack in the night would polish off Congressman Ormond probably only a few months or short years before his natural death anyway. He paused again, but for only a moment.

"Let's do it, gentlemen," Robert responded.

"Lever, as you know, you will be required to carry this out with urgency. If you become implicated in any way, you will receive no support from the Agency." The voice sounded slightly relieved as it continued with its formal dissertation. "Remember, you must comply fully with all the terms of the National Security Act of the United States. Should any police agency, authority, or division of the United States Government compromise you, you will be subject to termination." The funds will be handled as usual, at the customary compensation. Do you have questions?"

It bothered Robert that the youthful voice seemed to be reading the information from the script as if the words had never been spoken before.

"Yeah, I know all that," Robert interrupted.

"And will you seek MOTS confirmation?" The voice was harsh.

"I'll think about it," Robert responded, yet with every intention of doing so.

Robert left the building, turned left and ran to the north on the bike path next to the river. Consistent with the routine, he ran only half a mile to the first point and then worked his way up a set of crumbling concrete stairs, returning to the jogging trail on the towpath to one of the bridges over the C&O Canal. From there, he went east across the Georgetown main street and finally on to Dumbarton Street where, in the murky shadows of night, his nightmares would return.

6

The wet Vancouver Street reflected a thousand fractal images. It was late at night, but the town was still busy with restaurant patrons carefully making their way along the sidewalks. Many were bloated, struggling with what they could take to relieve the result of their overindulgence of choice. For some, this would become after-hours indigestion or, even worse, tomorrow's hangover.

The temperature was cool but manageable, with a faint, intermittent breeze. On the north side of West Georgia Street, in front of the Vancouver Art Gallery and one block northwest of the landmark Vancouver Hotel, a white Pontiac Grand Prix was parked in the emergency lane with its engine running. The driver watched carefully, ready to move the car if requested by a policeman. The passenger, wearing a broad-brimmed cowboy hat, waited quietly to participate in a meeting that every newspaper in the world would like to have as a scoop.

A woman disguised beneath an oversized raincoat and carrying a black umbrella walked southward down Hornby Street, a narrower road which intersected West Georgia at the Gallery's southeast corner. The two men in dark suits following her at about twenty steps suggested that she was more than just another restaurant patron.

The man with the hat got out and pulled the hood of his ski jacket over his head to shield himself from the drizzle. It was not the only reason for the hood. Republican Presidential Candidate David Houston didn't want to be recognized. He walked in the direction of the woman.

In the next minute, the two people who would be President of the United States were nervously standing underneath the umbrella. "You wanted a meeting, so here it is!" Houston broke the ice as he tilted his head down to look eye-to-eye into the face of the woman he loathed.

"I don't need any bullshit, David," the Vice President said, her tone tough and direct. "When I wanted to meet before, it was to keep everyone from going nuts over this election mess. But it's a little late for that now."

Houston leaned back, crossing his arms. "So, what do you have in mind? My people are adamant that I meet with you." He never entered a negotiation without a clear idea of what he expected to gain. For him, questions felt more like statements that deserved periods or exclamation marks rather than question marks. This clandestine meeting left him feeling off balance, a level of discomfort he wasn't used to.

CHAINS OF RESENTMENT

Both began walking slowly side-by-side to break the tension. They appeared as merely another couple walking along the street in the night, each well concealed in a heavy overcoat and hat.

"You know a meeting called by either of us would not have made any sense except maybe as a publicity stunt which, quite frankly, I have been trying to avoid," Reid said.

"Yeah, sure you have." Houston watched her break into a confident smile in reaction to his sarcasm. He was definitely in the very small camp of men *not* attracted to Charlotte Reid under any circumstance.

"Governor," the use of the term was designed to avoid the distress of actually having to say his name, "I find it hard to believe that the deadlock is even real. I feel very comfortable with my twelve-vote lead in the Electoral College. You know I won that. And looking at Georgia, it is simply too close to call. It's pretty impossible to conclude who won that state. There's just been too much junk around the ballot boxes...and with your folks throwing those ballot boxes in the Chattahoochee River.

Houston interrupted. "I've heard you've got every lawyer on the east coast saying they're gonna prove that, and that I should just quit. However, there's no proof...and you know it. With Georgia out, my lawyers say you haven't won anything. I've got the U.S. Congress waiting in the wings. "Just read the Constitution—especially the Twentieth Amendment. There's no reason for me to quit. And if you're not quitting, then what's the point of this meeting?" Houston said impatiently.

The Vice President was quick to respond. "Even without Georgia, I'm confident the Supreme Court will rule in my favor. I believe they'll override Congress. I'm counting on Ramona McCall's support."

"Don't be so sure about Justice McCall."

Charlotte fired back, "Even more than you being a Republican, McCall hates pompous, middle-aged male dictators, and along with your many attributes, you happen to be one of those too. But to be honest with you, I think this whole thing is getting so out of hand that Congress is getting damn tired of both of us... and that's even before either one of us litigates our way into the White House." She paused. "That's why I thought I should talk to you, and technically outside of the United States where such a discussion might not constitute a crime." Reid struggled not to say the word, but then she painfully spoke his name. "David, whoever ends up being President is going to be about as lame as a duck can get. Starting out a lame duck is not where either you or I want to be."

Houston could sense that she was attempting to engage in a rare moment of honest conversation. "I won't disagree with that," he replied, not even bothering to acknowledge her by name. Reid pressed on, her voice steady despite the weight of the situation. "What I'm about to suggest may sound really stupid, but I've thought it through, and I think it's the only way to be fair. I'm willing to give myself a 50/50 chance of becoming President. That's what I've got right now, and maybe even better. I think your chances are worse than mine, for a variety of reasons."

She met his gaze, her eyes revealing a mixture of determination and vulnerability, challenging him to consider her proposition seriously.

So, I suggest we do this: We arrange to have a ceremonial coin flip during half-time at the American Conference NFL playoff game on January 7th." She paused to let the idea sink in. "Midfield...50-yard line...whoever wins becomes President!" She quickly added with a conciliatory tone, "And whoever loses will likely be remembered as one of the most respected Americans to ever live!"

Houston stepped out from under the umbrella, holding it over Charlotte's head, looking back at the two Secret Service men keeping a discreet but able distance. "Have you been drinking, Madam Vice President?" David smiled, as his Oklahoma accent drawled out in a slightly indignant manner. "That's not the way it's done. We happen to have a constitution, you know."

Charlotte responded rapidly. She was ready. "Sure, we do. You should've picked up on the fact by now that we are in a constitutional deadlock. There's no certainty how the courts are going to rule or that this'll ever make it to Congress. Like I said earlier, I have a better chance than you."

"I see what you're trying to do," Houston retorted. "You're worried you are going to come up short with the courts, so you want to make a deal! Sounds like you're running scared and that's uncharacteristic of you, Mrs. Vice President."

She despised being referred to as 'Mrs.' It connoted, at a minimum, dependency on husband Bill that she claimed did not exist, and, at a maximum, a belittled reference to being the wife of a Vice President.

Reid didn't let her irritation distract her from the task at hand. She continued to reason with Houston. "Governor, at first this idea seemed ludicrous. But the more I consider where our country stands, it's clear that one of us needs to get the administration moving." It doesn't make any sense to be sitting around litigating. You may think you have Congress as a Republican, but remember, you haven't served there. You may think they like you. But they don't. They just tolerate you because you are the only stiff they could come up with to take me on. You know that! So, if they had a chance to put one of their own in and take control of the White House while you and I keep fighting in court, don't you agree, they might just jump at it. "There are rumors out there... you've heard 'em... I've heard 'em. And make no mistake, Governor," she said, positioning herself in front of him to block his path, her finger jabbing the air to emphasize her point, "if I don't make it, I know I have a good chance at keeping you out too. There are a lot more players in this game than you know! You're smart enough to realize that you're not the only game in town."

Houston felt the heat of her words, a mix of urgency and warning. She was laying her cards on the table, and he could see the resolve in her eyes. The stakes were higher than either of them had anticipated, and he couldn't shake the feeling that the political landscape was shifting beneath their feet.

The Vice President continued, "Don't assume it's just one of us. If the Supreme Court allows the litigation to go on and throws this into the House, there's a fair chance that neither of us will be President. Although that's not my preferred scenario, it's very possible to produce that outcome...with one exception. She paused for emphasis. "If you agree to the coin flip, it creates a solution so simple that even an idiot voter can understand it! That gives us both a better chance than we have now.

Either way, one of us will be back in four years. So, what do you think?" She continued to look at him, trying to use the alluring expression that made most men think lustful thoughts. She could see it had no effect on the Governor.

Houston knew the Vice President was shrewd and definitely a player. His intelligence people had picked up rumors of Chinese government money in her campaign. It was nothing he could prove, but only a real gamer would take the chance. His first impulse was to wonder what else she had up her sleeves. She had been a brilliant tactician in the debates. She had almost never spoken an ill-placed word or phrase requiring clarification or retraction. He had long concluded that the woman didn't take a breath without an agenda. Yet, deep down inside, he had to admit, at least to himself, that the concept of a 50-yard line solution was very clever. It even made some sense. He quickly began to consider what four years really meant to him. Maybe it meant getting back into football, or just running the company for eighteen months and then starting a presidential campaign again.

As he weighed the options, David decided to call her bluff. He still had no reason to trust Charlotte Reid. "Why wait so long? That's another two weeks. If we've got an administration to put together, let's do it now! You do yours! I do mine! Then, whoever wins will be ready to go." He leaned in slightly, probing her defenses, watching for any sign of hesitation or uncertainty.

Reid held his gaze, her expression unreadable. She was calculating her next move, and he could sense that she was weighing the implications of his challenge. "You really think it's that easy?" she shot back, crossing her arms defiantly. "There's more at play here than just us, Governor. This isn't a game of checkers."

He couldn't help but smirk at her response. "Life is just a game of strategy, Charlotte. The question is, who has the better pieces?"

"I've thought of that. But no one of significance is going to accept an appointment with the election still up in the air," Charlotte replied. "Nobody wants to really be your friend unless you've won. So, getting back to the deal...to make it work, the loser has to acknowledge the winner as the real winner. All lawsuits must be dropped. This gives the new President at least a fighting chance to be able to govern. And if we do this at the playoff game, the ratings will go through the roof."

"Another important part of this is to raise some serious money." She continued. "We could go to the networks, the NFL and the sponsors. With your athletic pedigree, it makes ultimate sense. If we move fast, they'll quadruple their advertising revenue. We'll require that half of the proceeds be contributed to...say...the top three cancer research institutes in the country, or other worthy charities. It would be the most watched event in history. "We'd want to strike while the iron is hot," Charlotte replied, her tone steady and persuasive. "We could announce it within the next week, ideally before the debates start heating up. It would give us a joint platform to showcase a united front, presenting ourselves as leaders willing to put aside partisan differences for a greater good. It would generate immediate media attention and public support."

David nodded, intrigued despite himself. The idea had merit; a collaborative effort to combat diseases that affected millions could resonate well with voters, especially if presented as a bipartisan initiative. "And what's the angle? What do we tell the press about our partnership? That we suddenly decided to play nice?"

Charlotte smiled, sensing his skepticism. "Not quite. We emphasize the urgency of the issue. We're two candidates who recognize that politics shouldn't get in the way of progress. We're both committed to helping our constituents and their families. We can frame it as a call to action, a commitment to finding solutions rather than just pointing fingers."

Houston considered her words, weighing the potential fallout against the benefits. "It might just work, but I need assurances that this won't backfire. If we're in this together, we both need to come out clean on the other side. No hidden agendas."

Charlotte met his gaze, her eyes sharp and focused. "I agree. Transparency is key. We set clear terms, and we both hold each other accountable. If we're going to do this, we need to trust one another."

David leaned back in his chair, pondering the stakes. The prospect of collaborating with Reid felt risky, but the potential rewards were hard to ignore. "Alright, let's start drafting a proposal. If we're going to go public, we need to be prepared."

"Agreed," she said, her voice tinged with enthusiasm. "Let's show them what real leadership looks like." Charlotte continued, "I think we should both appear at a Christmas Eve press conference to talk about peace on earth, good will to men and all of that. Then, we'll bury the political hatchet. It'll give the NFL and the network time to get everything in place...and advertising sold." She smiled, knowing David was still looking at her suspiciously.

"Do I get some time to think about this, Madam Vice President, or must I agree to your scheme right now?" he asked.

"Well, Christmas is only five days away. But take a day...two at the most. And don't forget, Governor, the risk is as big for me as it is for you. At the end of the day, the whole election mess will turn into a win - win for the country rather than an argument about who's the winner and who's the loser."

Charlotte nodded; her expression serious. "I understand the risks. But think about what's at stake—not just for us, but for the country. We have a chance to rewrite the narrative and emerge stronger, but it requires boldness. If we can harness the public's desire for change and unify our efforts, we can create something powerful."

"What's the timeline?" David asked, trying to gauge how quickly he needed to act. "We can't just sit on this. We need a plan and precise execution." "We have a window. The longer we wait, the more we risk losing momentum," Charlotte replied. "We should aim to announce it within the next few weeks. The holiday season is a time when people are more receptive to messages of hope and unity." David considered her words. "And if Rusk doesn't back me? He's been vocal about his doubts." "Then you convince him otherwise. This is about framing the narrative to benefit all of us," Charlotte said, her gaze unwavering. "You have to remind him he's part of this too. If we succeed, he stands to gain."

David sighed, running a hand through his hair. "Alright. I'll reach out to Rusk. But I need assurance you'll move quickly once we have his support. We can't afford missteps."

"Trust me, I'll be ready," Charlotte said confidently. "I'll have our team drafting a communication strategy while you speak with him. We'll ensure everything is seamless."

"Good," David said, feeling determination surge within him. "But if we're doing this, we do it right. No leaks, no half-measures. The moment anyone senses weakness, we lose everything."

Charlotte extended her hand. "Agreed. This is our chance to make history. Let's not waste it."

David did not like being threatened but he knew America, in general, was sick of the whole ordeal. He had seen the polls. The country was largely fed up with the election and tired of Houston and Reid. It sounded like time to make a deal.

"O.K., Madam Vice. I'll return the call or at least have Rusk call Bentley Wilcox. It would have been better if we had met like this more often."

Charlotte caught the jab. "Don't push your luck, Governor. The debates were as close as I ever wanted to get to you. Tough political times call for creative measures, and I believe this one will work. If you truly love your country, you'll take the risk." She turned and began to walk back up Hornby Street in the direction of the two Secret Service men. To David Houston, the Vice-President looked like an attack dog returning to its handlers.

Houston walked back to his car, cautiously looking in all directions to make sure that the meeting had remained secret. He and Sam Rusk then headed down I-5 to return to Seattle. Sam would handle the Border Patrol who seemed focused on prohibiting guns, drugs and terrorists. Two businessmen from Seattle were not worthy of any such excitement. Chances were remote that the media would discover David Houston's five-hour absence from the downtown Alexis Hotel, at least until the Border Patrol turned its logs in days later. Occasionally, it was even necessary to give the Secret Service the slip.

Before Charlotte got into her car, Bentley Wilcox emerged from his strategic position near the steps leading to the main entrance of the art gallery. "So what'd he say?"

"Well, he's being cautious with a capital 'C'! He doesn't have the balls to deal with this. I have to say—I really do hate the guy. He just makes me sick."

Bentley paused. "Char, I think you're jumping too soon. We can take care of this other ways. You need to be more patient."

Patience was not one of her virtues. "Bentley, I've heard your little plans...but nothing's happening...I've got no choice."

"Talking to him now doesn't help!" He shot back. "I've got something in the works."

"Bentley, you always say that. I've listened to you and the lawyers' ad nauseum. Fifty-fifty sounds good. I'm a risk taker...you know that!"

"But there are other things that can be done. It's not over." Wilcox was frustrated with Charlotte Reid's apparent dismissal of his advice.

A lengthy silence hung between them as they drove toward the airport. Finally, Charlotte broke the quiet. "You know, there aren't many people in the world I'd kill if I could!"

She spoke resolutely, her gaze fixed on Bentley. "But he's one of them." The silence returned. Bentley remained silent, feeling the weight of her words. There was a dark side to her that both excited and frightened him—often simultaneously.

Bentley couldn't help but entertain a fleeting thought before quickly dismissing it. The thought was that Houston was simply too close to kill. He began his dismissal with, "But then again," and ended it with, "maybe not."

7

Robert walked slowly toward the corner of Wisconsin and M Street only a few minutes before 8:00 a.m. The nighttime had been a struggle. He once again wrestled in futility with the phantoms of the past and the demons of the dark—a struggle that only caused greater fear of the future. He would surely need confirmation this time. An in-country hit was hard to conceive.

Even so, confirmation was always welcome. It allowed his conscience to view himself as a soldier for his country, carrying out covert operations. The identities of the victims, while intriguing, were not his concern or responsibility. The government had designated those targeted as enemies who needed to be addressed, just as if he were a special operator in Somalia or dropping into Bosnia, Afghanistan, or Iraq. The possibility of civilian casualties fell within the parameters he had been trained to accept by the CIA as collateral damage. He followed orders like a wingman in flight formation, adhering to his lead regardless of the situation.

Robert assured himself that if collateral damage had been unacceptable to the U.S. Government, he would not still be receiving assignments. Now, even in retirement, assignments kept coming. Maybe it was good to be needed, even if the needy were hidden faces and clandestine words. At least, it was someone.

Robert remembered his intensive training during his CIA initiation at the agency's secret facility, the Harvey Point Defense Testing Center on Albemarle Sound in North Carolina. With the Vietnam War having concluded just a decade and a half prior, it served as an ideal case study for the new recruits, providing invaluable lessons and insights into the complexities of covert operations. He had learned in classroom study that the business in 1968 as Operation Phoenix rolled out in the rural hamlets of Viet Nam. The SEAL teams who were the historical subject of the study would connect with the covert operations people who, even then, were about as non-military and evil as evil could get.

The SEAL team would storm ashore from its rapid assault boats at one of the hundreds of waterways of the Mekong Delta. They would then round up the inhabitants of the targeted village in what was designated as the "Red Zone" in the Viet Cong-rich parts of the coastal rice lands. The plan was to make the area safe enough to turn the village over to the control of the CIA. By nightfall, the SEAL team typically stepped back to let the CIA officers engage with the locals. The following morning, the surviving village elders would be gathered and transported in larger boats to reeducation camps, all under the pretense of the joint U.S./South Vietnamese Rural Pacification Program.

VEIL OF UNCERTAINTY

At that time, the terminations of the Viet Cong operatives all took place under the direct control of the CIA with the presumptive permission of the South Vietnamese government and the tacit knowledge of the U.S. military commanders in the field. This force protection allowed the covert forces to safely do their thing. At some point, it was explained by the instructors that the SEAL teams ended up in a village, helping the CIA do its vicious barbaric deeds.

In Roberts' SEAL team experiences, he had joined – in on an

incursion against FARC rebels in Columbia. At least he thought it would only be once. Then it happened again, and again. No longer was he on the outside ignoring reality, but on the inside creating it. It was a precedent he could not avoid if he was going to stay in the business. He tried to rationalize it, convincing himself that he understood the lengths some Americans would go to punish the enemies of freedom. As he walked away from the SEALS, he swore he would never engage in such actions again. Quite early in his career, even before the career with the CIA was one of them. Yet very soon after mustering out of the Navy, he was already pipelining for the Agency, and it was not long after that that he had his seat at Harvey Point. From such humble beginnings, he had grown to become world-renowned expert in some of the most awful things that Americans under the color of government authority can do to other human beings.

Finally, with the advent of retirement, Robert thought it was over. Months after his retirement, however, he had been called upon, not by the CIA, but by the US Army to arrange, of all things, the termination of Colombian drug lord Alberto Montero. This time, not in Columbia where he had operated years earlier as a Navy SEAL, but in Spain where Montero was taking a rare vacation.

The Army had been working for years with the DEA and Columbian security forces to eradicate the Montero family's cocaine processing and refining operation deep in the South American jungle. It was only by a stroke of good luck when the planets lined up for a group of analysts at Langley that they determined, with confirmation on the ground, that Montero would take a break from his life's work and spend a few nights with some teenage girls in a hotel in Spain.

During this operation, Robert collaborated with Basque separatists to plant a car bomb outside a downtown hotel in Madrid. Spanish authorities found it peculiar that the bomb was timed to detonate at 4:00 a.m., raising suspicions about the motive behind such an unusual timing. For the Basques, collateral damage was a major objective, a treacherous statement with political consequences. In the early morning hours, only three luxury rooms on the Villa side of Madrid's Hotel De Leon were destroyed when the entire wall collapsed, sending the unfortunate occupants onto the street. The blast killed everyone inside, including Montero, the then Kingpin of the Cali Drug Cartel, and two teenage girls who were not his daughters. Additionally, four bodyguards in the other two rooms died. Robert regarded this as one of his finest hits, given that all the casualties were linked to the Montero crime family. It was hard to argue that anyone who was killed was overly innocent, that is as long as it can be rationalized that the young girls by nature of their lurid participation were de facto members of the family as well.

There were times when everything went awry, such as his early experience with Korean Airlines Flight No.007. In that case, the huge loss of life was unacceptable to those involved, even Robert. Still, there existed in his mind a certain degree of avoidance in taking full responsibility, given the fact that his mission had been to cause the aircraft to navigate into Soviet airspace. The shoot-down had been a terrible quirk of very bad luck and incredible coincidence. Despite his work's horrifying outcome, Robert never considered himself violating the law in the United States.

This time, the situation had crossed the comfort line. Each step, from start to finish, would be directed at causing death within the country. There was no question he'd be breaking the law, and yet the CIA had no problem going forward. Robert couldn't fit this into any of his rationalized scenarios. He habitually flipped through cable TV channels at night, trying to distract himself from painful thoughts and the torment of the past. He moved from one news station to another, watching round-the-clock coverage of the battle for the White House. The stories were so repetitive that even history-in-the-making could be relegated to boredom within hours. There simply did not seem to be enough happening to feed the voracious appetite of the television audience craving new news, day in and day out, and Robert was the worst of them all. By midnight, everything was on a rerun, with yesterday's news being unabashedly shown again and again.

Following his normal nocturnal pattern, Robert found himself at some point shortly after midnight, thrashing around in bed, rejecting the reruns, desperately trying to find something live and wishing he had a more sophisticated system that allowed him to connect up with the part of the world on the other side of the planet that was not sleeping, not dead, not still even if in languages he could not understand. The sleepless night-time boredom that imprisoned him would at times drive him to overeat, to read, to go for walks in the D.C. nights, always armed with his 9mm. Shooting a street punk would undoubtedly end his career, so Robert viewed early morning walks as a last resort—necessary yet risky. He often wondered if it was worth the gamble, but it was a means to keep the ghosts at bay and avoid confronting the harsh realities of life, death, and his troubled past.

Finally, Robert began rapidly switching stations and relegating himself to the drone of a documentary on some innocuous subject that would allow him to avoid anything that forced him to think. It was not time to allow his heart to be touched by anyone or anything. Then, the supreme thought, moving from a passive to an active contemplation of suicide by reaching into the bed stand drawer. Each time he would pull out his 9mm automatic pistol with the resolve to end it all, the internal debate would begin all over again.

There would be no end to the rush of thoughts, visions, intensely encapsulated by loneliness that rendering him defenseless against the walls of darkness closing in on him from every direction, inching him to come closer to pulling the trigger. At some point, usually about 3 a.m., Robert's self-imposed isolation would surrender to the wish for someone to talk to—all the while knowing there was not a soul on earth, he could call who would not merely hang up on him, enraged at being disturbed from sleep. He could try to call his children, but what would he say? "This is your father. I abandoned you when your mother died." The one exception that kept passing through Robert's mind was Landon

Cramer. Occasionally, he imagined breaking the silence and telling Landon everything, so at least someone would know—someone who cared. But he knew the visit wouldn't come without a price. Even in Washington, where clandestine side jobs are common, staying at the law firm where his past—and sometimes future—were known to the managing partner might not be feasible or practical.

DARKNESS TO LIGHT

Still, in the confusion of the long night, Robert reasoned that he needed a friend far more than a colleague. He needed someone who knew and cared for him more than someone who was proud or confident in him. Cramer would never abandon a friend. To get there, Robert figured he had to follow up on the Thanksgiving visit and try to be a friend—something he hadn't been for as long as he could remember.

Robert wrestled regularly with the question of whether the handgun next to him was his greatest friend or worst enemy. Finally, he would fall asleep, worn out from the night's events and the heavy burden, overlaying his existence. When the sudden morning would come, he would be resurrected by the light, fresh air, the freedom to walk, the chance to eat and to run. He preferred the basic premise of existence to the blackness of a worm-ridden coffin that, in any event, was soon to come. With no sleep, his daytime jubilation was tempered by the fact that for all intents and purposes, he was dead to the world unless he could sleep in his office for a while soon after his arrival at work.

Once he was fully awake and the sun was shining, Robert occasionally found himself in a better mood. This was one of those moments. Despite the holiday blues layering onto his usual state, he felt oddly balanced and stable. Stable enough to be thankful; thankful that he'd never been seriously injured in his chosen occupation, that he could still run ten miles at a respectable pace and that, despite the hours of darkness and futility that controlled part of each day, he still had many hours of light in the day to help fend off the ghosts of the past. "Hi!" The voice startled him slightly, then a warm sensation radiated through his body. He wondered how a person could infuse so much meaning into a simple two-letter, one-syllable word.

He looked at Cindy, sitting behind the receptionist's desk. "So... how are you?" He found it odd that she genuinely seemed to want to know.

"Oh, fine. How about you, Bob?"

Robert liked being called Bob. It sounded friendly and made him feel as if he could somehow act friendly. He'd been called that name before—in another life—long before he had ever killed anyone. "You know, just another day, another dollar, or something like that," he paused.

"So, are you busy getting ready for the holidays? You seem like the kind of person who'd be all done by now, right?" Cindy looked at Bob, her eyes telegraphing an intense need for an answer.

* * *

Robert had seldom acknowledged Christmas, much less gotten "ready" for anything. Maybe a box of candy for the office and that was it. He also did not want to avoid the discussion with Cindy. "I guess it's now or never," he looked at his watch, "About five days away."

"You mean you're a last-minute shopper, Bob?"

The words created a sensation that the woman could somehow read Robert's thoughts and elicited an icy fear that she might discover more about him than he would ever want anyone to know. Feeling a twinge of jealousy, he pondered whether she treated everyone in the office with the same warmth she showed him. "I don't have many people to buy for," he said. "When you get old like me, you pretty much have everything, so it's tough for those who have it all to give anything meaningful to anyone else." He felt a sense of pride in his humor. "Does that make any sense?" he inquired.

"Not really, because when you have everything, you should have plenty to give away! Then, maybe you don't have everything after all... and, you know what? "You aren't that old. Heck, you can't be a day over... I'd say 49!" Cindy proffered as Bob removed his overcoat. Even small talk seemed to flow effortlessly from her.

Robert turned around, slightly embarrassed, and started walking toward his office. He couldn't think of anything to say. "You sure know how to make a guy feel good!" Without hesitation, Cindy looked across the lobby and replied, "Yes, I do!" With that, she answered a ringing phone, leaving him to ponder what lay beneath her words.

Robert walked into his office and sat down, feeling a sense of something he hadn't noticed in years. It wasn't just her engaging sense of humor; it was the way she looked at him that lingered in his thoughts. The effect was strange and powerful, rekindling a redeeming characteristic he couldn't recall feeling before as he searched through his memories for a similar moment.

Then the phone rang and over the next few minutes, Robert lapsed into a state of work. Work, along with Cindy's words, helped him to avoid the deep galling impressions of who he was and what he had done.

* * *

DIVIDING SILENCE

On the other side of the country, the whine of the generators on the mobile news trucks laden with satellite uplink dishes was contributing to the noise in the parking lot outside the Alexis Hotel. The coincidence of both presidential candidates being in the Seattle area at the same time sparked rumors of an impending meeting. It provided the news gatherers with a sense of purpose as they churned out speculations against the picturesque Seattle skyline. The Space Needle offered a refreshing change from the usual settings of the U.S. Supreme Court or the Georgia State Capitol building. For the most part, however, the country was tired of it all—same circus, different town.

The young male network correspondent was dressed in jeans and hiking boots, which the cameraman did not show. As a "talking head," he was appropriately attired with a heavily starched white shirt, a blue silk tie and plenty of makeup to camouflage his facial symptoms of fatigue. He stood under a black umbrella and practiced several times before he began the morning broadcast. His words would be heard on the morning show in New York, hours before anyone in Seattle heard it. Viewers in the Eastern Time Zone were getting ready for work, having breakfast and pursuing daily morning routines. The news correspondent began:

"RUMORS ABOUND IN SEATTLE THAT VICE PRESIDENT REID AND GOVERNOR HOUSTON ARE PLANNING TO MEET. THE COINCIDENCE OF BOTH OF THEM BEING IN THIS TOWN AT THE SAME TIME IS NOT SOMETHING THAT CAN BE OVERLOOKED. AFTER ALL, DURING THE HOLIDAYS WE CAN UNDERSTAND WHY THE VICE PRESIDENT WOULD BE AT THE RESTORATION POINT ESTATE, BUT MOST OBSERVERS DO NOT BELIEVE THAT GOVERNOR HOUSTON FLEW INTO WASHINGTON TO CONFER WITH THE GOVERNOR IN OLYMPIA ABOUT A POSSIBLE CABINET POST. WE HAVE NEVER SEEN GOVERNOR BROCK ON ANYBODY'S RADAR SCREEN FOR A CABINET POSITION GIVEN HIS SIGNIFICANTLY LIBERAL STAND ON ISSUES THAT ARE DEAR TO THE HEART OF THE CONSERVATIVE HOUSTON CAMPAIGN, IT WOULD SEEM AN ODD FIT FOR AN ADMINISTRATION POSITION. WHAT WE DO KNOW IS THAT HOUSTON IS STAYING IN SEATTLE'S ALEXIS HOTEL AND THAT HIS WIFE AND CHILDREN MADE THE TRIP ALSO. WE'RE NOT AWARE THAT HE HAS ANY OTHER RELATIVES OR SIGNIFICANT POLITICAL ACQUAINTANCES IN THE SEATTLE AREA AND WE DON'T THINK THERE IS ANYONE IN THIS PART OF THE COUNTRY

WHO HAS MUCH TO DO WITH THE EVENTS OF THE SUPREME COURT. WE HAVE SEEN CERTAIN MEMBERS OF THE REPUBLICAN SIDE OF WASHINGTON'S CONGRESSIONAL DELEGATION GO IN AND OUT OF THE HOTEL, BUT NOBODY IS REALLY SAYING MUCH, WHICH LEAVES US ONLY TO SPECULATE ABOUT JUST WHAT IS GOING ON"

The New York anchor weighed into the discussion, *"VERY INTERESTING. TO GET AN IDEA OF WHAT MIGHT BE HAPPENING ON THE OTHER SIDE OF TACOMA BAY, LET'S GO TO KAREN SHELTON TO SEE WHAT'S UP WITH CHARLOTTE REID."*

Then, the scene shifted to a split screen with the New York news anchor listening while his colleague in Seattle addressing the matter in the shivering cold of the December morning. *"I'M STANDING HERE IN FRONT OF THE RESTORATION POINT ESTATE OF CHARLOTTE REID AND HER HUSBAND. WE'VE BEEN HERE SINCE ABOUT 2:00 a.m.—WHEN WE WERE GIVEN AN EXCLUSIVE NEWS TIP THAT THERE MIGHT BE A MEETING UNDERWAY BETWEEN THE TWO CAMPS. WE DID REPORT A HELICOPTER LEAVING THE COMPOUND LAST NIGHT AT ABOUT 8:00 P.M IT FLEW TO THE WEST. WE THEN SAW THE SAME HELICOPTER LAND HERE JUST AFTER WE ARRIVED, COMING FROM THE NORTH. WE REALLY HAD NO VANTAGE POINT FROM WHICH TO SEE WHAT WAS TAKING PLACE ON THE GROUNDS OF THE SPRAWLING 125-ACRE ESTATE. WE DON'T KNOW WHO WAS ON THE HELICOPTER. THERE DOES SEEM TO BE A CERTAIN FERVOR THAT SUGGESTS SOMETHING MORE THAN JUST BUSINESS AS USUAL IS UNDERWAY. OBVIOUSLY, WE WILL APPROACH THE VICE PRESIDENT'S PRESS PEOPLE TO SEE WHAT IS GOING ON. AT THIS POINT, AS FAR AS WE KNOW, THEY ARE ALL ASLEEP. SO, REPORTING FROM JUST ACROSS THE BAY*

FROM SEATTLE AT RESTORATION POINT, BACK TO YOU IN NEW YORK.

* * *

Three hours later, David Houston was watching early CNN reports from the east coast while sitting in the lounge of the hotel's Presidential Suite along with the ever-present Sam Rusk. "Those folks are quick. You've got to hand it to em'. "But it doesn't sound like they've gotten wind of anything in Vancouver."

"I didn't think they would," Rusk replied. "Unless they were tipped off by the Reid people. I genuinely thought they were up to something and would try to use this to set you up."

"I haven't ruled that out yet. I'm just not sure what to make of it. This flipping a coin stuff—it's hard to tell if it's legit or not," Houston said.

Rusk shook his head. "I know—I'm not sure either, but I have already talked to the lawyers this morning. I'm ready to give you your legal briefing. The bottom line is you can't get a 50/50 chance out of them. They're telling me that they've counted noses and analyzed the judges right down to the bone. They think with Justice Hatch having recused himself, we can't get better than a 4 to 4. In addition, they think that Ramona McCall is one female justice who has absolutely no use for you. She carries both the other independents with her. In effect, she turns them into Democrats and there's not much we can do to change that. It might never make it to the House. The Court could just certify a gang of Reid—leaning electors from Georgia, even if they split, it'll only take three to get her over the top."

"So much for justice and abiding by the law," Houston retorted.

"Well, I don't think our people are telling us they're not following the law. The problem is, there isn't much law on this issue and that leaves it open to interpretation and that's risky. Should it be a majority of the electors or of all of the states? The Georgia situation has been the difference. Look where it's gotten us. Just one helluva lawsuit and an old lady on the Supreme Court that hates guys like you and will probably stop at nothing to get a woman into the White House."

"What a way to run a country!" The Governor was derisive. He walked to the window and looked out across the Bay, trying to forget which lights to the west originated from the estate of the Vice President, forgetting that it really belonged to Bill. The telephone in a nearby room rang and Houston walked in that direction.

"We've got to escalate this," Rusk said quietly, ensuring his words wouldn't reach the room where Governor Houston had just picked up the phone. "I'm not letting him go with this frickin' coin flip!"

A young assistant with a cherub face replied with a calculated, professional coldness. "Are you certain you want to do it now?"

"Yes. Reid's got something up her sleeve that's good for her and bad for us. We need to act. We have to make that call."

"OK, I'll get the STU-III phone— the one that's encrypted. We can't take any chances." The aide added, "When you call the Pentagon, I don't want it going through any hotel switchboard!"

"Let's do it," Rusk ordered again nervously. The assistant slipped quietly out the door, down a flight of stairs next to the elevator and into the communications room to retrieve the secure phone.

8

By noon, Robert had placed a call to the CIA offices at Langley to set up the MOTS confirmation. He had been told to be in Washington Circle no later than 3:30 p.m.

"Bob, it's the second day of me asking you to get a haircut." The voice crackled over his telephone intercom. Cindy's voice broke the monotony of work. He wondered if she knew how long it had been since anyone had paid attention to him on anything non-work related.

"You sure about this?" he asked. "I actually got one about six months ago and there's not much up there anyway."

"Yes, I think a new style would do you good. And I have some herbs that might help with that 'hole' on top of your mop," Cindy teased. "I could even massage it in for you—or better yet, maybe crack a few raw eggs on it!"

"Oh, no. I knew it! You're an Amway salesman."

"No way! These herbs are from a store over at Five Points. I go over there on Saturday and get a handful of good stuff, then go for a jog, do my shopping, carry all the stuff home and, by Saturday night, it's all back to my wheelchair!"

Robert was amazed at how she could joke about herself so casually.

On one hand, it was funny, but he could sense she was also trying to dodge her own emotions, perhaps running from a painful past just like he was. "Well, I'd like to take you up on that and see it for myself one of these days," he replied.

"If you are a real good guy and get your haircut, I will set that up!" The voice came back in a way that made getting his hair cut sound better all the time.

After a brief pause and wondering if she was still on the speaker, he said, "How about I visit your choice of salons and let them have their way with me?"

"Well, well, well!!! I like your compliance. Would that be like today, next week, next month or next year?"

"Today," he replied without pause.

"Good. I will set you up with Omar at 5 p.m. today. So," her voice was quick, "Don't be late!"

CONFIRMATION

He calculated the appointment momentarily, wondering if he could do the MOTS confirmation and get back in time for the haircut. He figured it would work if there were no delays or surprises. "I have a small task out of the office at 3:30, but it won't take long. After that, I'll head to your salon, so you won't have to be embarrassed about my appearance any longer!" Robert feigned a need for sympathy.

"Oh, I'm not embarrassed for you," Cindy teased. "I'm just worried about our clients. I want them to have the best experience possible when visiting the prestigious law firm of Fischer, Cramer & Morrell."

"I appreciate your sincere concern for our employer," Robert responded in like banter.

Then, Cindy was interrupted by a telephone call and quickly gone.

Ten seconds later, she was back. "I've got a message for you. You are to call Mr. Cedric Martin tomorrow at exactly twelve noon."

The levity of the moment suddenly surrendered to sober reality. "Great Cindy, thanks," Robert was quick and cold. In reality, it wasn't a great message. Tension gripped his chest as memories of Cedric Martin—a voice from the past—came flooding back. It had been contact from the Army, and specifically from Cedric Martin, that had led to the hit at Hotel De Leon in Madrid. He remembered Martin all too well....A towering black Army Colonel with a perfectly cut physique. He remembered being convinced that if he did not take out the Columbian drug lord, Martin would do the job bare-handed himself. He had not seen the man since the Spanish operation and had hoped never to lay eyes on him again. Few people could give Robert the creeps, but Martin was one of them. For a moment he wondered what this might have to do with the CIA. Again, he knew that the CIA was always a closed-mouth operation and that it avoided cross-fertilization with DOD on such matters. It made him curious, but there was nothing he could do until tomorrow.

Robert took a cab to Washington Circle and was dropped on the west side of the Ellipse where 'K' Street meets the circle. He arrived five minutes early. The afternoon traffic outbound on Pennsylvania Avenue was already heavy, flowing around the west half of the circle with most vehicles heading toward the Potomac bridges. A biting chill had set in, and the brief sunlight that had ignited the morning was giving way to a complex storm front slowly moving southeast from the Ohio River Valley over the Alleghenies into the Washington area. Robert noticed pedestrians hurrying along, hands buried in the pockets of their heavy overcoats, hunched slightly forward as if it would stifle the cold. No one looked left or right. People were grouping together like thirsty cattle at the street crossings. It was an impersonal place—ideal for a MOTS encounter.

Paranoia started to get the best of him. Robert imagined an Agency sniper perched somewhere in a window or atop a building with his head in the cross hairs. The order to kill would not be unlike those that Robert himself had followed. It made sense to him that the Agency, at some point, might not want him around. With nothing left to offer, yet much to tell, he was a liability. Showcased in the center of the park was George Washington's statue—weathered with a green patina. Robert kept his eyes on the windows and rooftops as much as possible. He knew that if the Agency wanted to take him out, there would be nothing he could do. It would merely be a question of when and where. Murders in Washington, D.C. were run of the mill, often competing on a per capita basis across the board with battlegrounds of other sorts, like Baghdad or Kabul.

DESCENT INTO PERIL

The drug trade in the north-central part of town, even near the White House, was thriving. It wouldn't take much effort to fabricate a story— his body found with a bag of cocaine conveniently tucked into his pocket. It would make him just another numbered corpse predestined for a comprehensive drug autopsy at the D.C. morgue. He reasoned to himself that if he were assigned to set up someone like himself, that's exactly how he would do the job. Maybe it would be a relief for it to all come to an end. With that thought, the fear started to fade, and he began rationalizing that as long as he kept accepting assignments, no sniper would take the shot. Perhaps work was his best form of protection.

Momentarily, he saw Jerry Rothman, Deputy Director of the CIA, walking across the Square toward him. Jerry was not alone. A younger man, well-built and clearly a line officer, followed not more than two paces behind. Robert took note that the stern-looking backup resembled a younger white version of Cedric Martin.

The two men approached, and faced Robert directly, with Rothman solemnly stepping forward. Consistent with the MOTS procedure, neither spoke. The person charged with talking under this scenario was only Robert. He looked around at the people in motion, making sure that no one had stopped or put themselves within listening range. He concluded that the din of the afternoon traffic was enough to block out the sound of any discussion from those passing nearby, and he could see no one loitering nearby.

Robert began, "I've been assigned to do a 'Code 10' on Maxmillian Ormond, the Senior United States Congressman from Mississippi, latest by December 31ˢt. I'm concerned with the fact that the procedure is to take place inside the country." He looked into the eyes of Rothman, one of the few members of senior management of the Agency whom he knew personally that had not retired. Rothman's eyes were clear but unreadable as he stared back at Robert and momentarily made a barely discernible up and down nod. The younger agent was stiff—maybe even indifferent. MOTS meetings were old - school.

Then, after a pause of not more than twenty seconds, Rothman and his cohort turned on their heels almost in unison like a pair of ceremonial palace guards, and walked away in a southwesterly direction as a slight puff of steam from hot breath floated up above them, telling Robert that one of them said something to the other. He wished he could hear what they were saying and kept watching as they hurried across to the other side of the circle, heading toward the crosswalk. Crossing the street, they then disappeared around the corner where the George Washington University Hospital Emergency Room entrance is located.

Robert began his ten-minute walk back in the direction of Georgetown. The MOTS had been done completely consistent with Agency procedure, yet he found himself searching his recollection for any expression of concern on Rothman's face. He failed to pinpoint anything to be alarmed about, nothing overt, and nothing subliminal. Still, much like the day, there was darkness falling. In the next instance, an ambulance came screaming down New Hampshire Avenue towards the Circle, another casualty of the drug wars heating up in the frigid, damp cold of mid-afternoon in northeast Washington.

As he walked away, he could not distill his sense of uncertainty about what had just transpired. While it was hard to decipher the expression on his longtime associate Jerry Rothman's face, there was something in the eyes of the younger agent that instilled a sense of caution. Beyond his typical paranoid instincts, an unsettling chill crept in that he couldn't ignore. It led him to wonder even more about the coincidence of tomorrow's appointment with Cedric Martin.

* * *

"You look like a million bucks!" Cindy said as Robert came in with his newly styled hair.

"Golly gee, Miss Cindy...I'm not sure there's enough here to cause too much of a difference." Robert's lighthearted impersonation helped him deflect the slight embarrassment from the attention he was getting as he ran his hand through his hair. "Well, Bob, you know what they say... it's not how much there is, it's how you use it!" Cindy teased. "So, what makes you think I should know that?" Robert asked. Cindy suddenly went on the defensive, lacking a quick response. "Because you're such a distinguished-looking man." With an exaggerated look of perplexity, she added, "My guess is you've got women stashed all over the country, just waiting for your next business trip. Am I right?"

Women had pegged Robert over the years as being the strong, silent type. It usually occurred on those rare occasions when loneliness would send him to a bar to try his hand at attracting female companionship. Routinely, he blew off such come-ons as nonsense. They were rarely successful.

Yet somehow, the same kind of nonsense from Cindy's mouth seemed real, honest, and just plain fun. It triggered a desire to just be silly in a way that Robert could not remember. There were no women across the country or anywhere, for that matter. When he lost his wife, he lost the love of his life, despite the hard road they had traveled together in their marriage. Even with the passing of so many years, he was still immersed in the guilt of rationalizing that because his wife had lost interest in intimacy, somehow, she would eventually have understood his seeking closeness with another woman. After all, it would have taken the burden off her, and if he could somehow have continued to cause her to feel loved, it would all have worked out. Worked out? No, just a cold awful death.

When the plane crashed, much of what Robert considered to be the consummate definition of "home" and "love" died with her. There was no way to repair the damage or recover from a stupid mid-life crisis mistake. He could not do it among the living, and certainly not among the dead. So, the times they had spent laughing, playing and being friends were gone forever. It was a sensation he thought he would never experience again. At times, he missed her so deeply that the hollow ache of longing became unbearable. It lingered with him, always.

Now, this strange woman was stirring ancient emotions—a sort of resurrection that felt so safe and good. Her almost foolish but tactically – placed words and taunts sparked sensations somewhere deep within which made him want to hear more and more. It was all very odd to him, but undeniably real.

When Robert didn't react to her teasing, Cindy responded, "Well, anyway, let me be the first of all your women to give you something. I bought it especially for you. You know, Bob, it's almost Christmas, and you're probably going to need what's in this box about six months from now." She placed a beautifully wrapped box tied with gold and red ribbons on the reception counter. "Go ahead, it's just for you. You can open it whenever the spirit moves you."

Robert was a bit embarrassed that he had no gift for her. The thought had never crossed his mind. Now, he was genuinely excited with the thought that he now had someone to buy for—a sort of holiday mission. It was something he could do. This was beyond any thoughts he had had in years. He usually loathed the holidays from Thanksgiving to New Year's, and the overwhelming feelings of failure and loneliness that seemed amplified through the season.

Gifts to the children had never happened. It was beyond the contact that his guilt could allow. Occasionally, he would send money, but the holiday season had lost its charm since Veronica's death. Robert picked up the box and made an exaggerated show of examining it from the outside, then looked again into the eyes of the enchanting woman in the wheelchair across the counter. He felt a pang of guilt for appreciating her presence so much. He concluded that he did not deserve the attention that he was getting. After all, he was the "Lever."

"Cindy," it was the first time he had spoken her name with feeling. Again, he said, "Cindy," as he walked away. At that moment, she looked up and said "What, Bob?" However, he said nothing else and disappeared into his office.

At the end of the workday, Robert waited until after Cindy had closed down the lobby and made her way to the parking terrace on the lower level, before he left the building. He bypassed dinner for a run up the Canal towpath. It was a murky night, with the sounds of the city echoing off the low clouds, the noise of rush hour louder than usual. He switched to the bike path about thirty yards down the hillside, closer to the Potomac River, for his return trip. Three miles later, he ran under the viaduct and past the boathouse, where no light emanated from the scant windows of the building. There were no cars parked in the "U.S. Government Parking Only" spots in front of the adjacent buildings. Everything felt vacant and lifeless, as if nothing had ever occurred there. Few would ever know that just days earlier, it had been the site of a death sentence for a U.S. Congressman. He made his way back, ate a light dinner and went to bed early. He found he could not keep his eyes open past the evening news. Sleep came peacefully for a change. The run helped.

At about 3:00 a.m. Robert awoke to use the bathroom. For a time after, he could not sleep and worked his way through the standard TV station switching. He found himself staring at the ceiling, struggling against the darkness as his memories closed in on him from all sides, as if he were inside an airtight coffin built especially for him. He closed his eyes, hoping morning would come and free him from the madness of the night.

Finally, Robert began to slip into a state of half-sleeplessness, the point where the darkest side of his mind exerted its greatest control. He stared at the weapon on the bedside table, awaiting the vision of bloody hands. It was time, and he knew it. At least once before sunrise, on a night that had rewarded him with sleep earlier, he would need to be punished.

Strangely, it did not come. Instead, Robert felt a trembling deep within, near his heart. It wasn't the familiar ache he had grown accustomed to, but something warmer, tied to a fleeting image of the woman behind the counter at the office. The thought lingered, stirring a sense of longing he hadn't felt in years. The darkness became a companion, as he imagined what it would be like to feel her warmth, to draw close, and to be with her in a way he had long forgotten. In stark contrast to the past, the darkness offered a moment of comfort as he found himself recalling her presence with unexpected intensity. His thoughts lingered on her elegance and the gentle allure of her expressions, wondering how she might respond to his affection. It had been years since he had felt such complete focus—a singular fascination that deepened as memories returned, moment by moment, conversation by conversation.

As the minutes turned into an hour, Robert found himself replaying every word she had shared, returning to their first meeting. He recalled her welcoming smile and the graceful confidence she exuded. Yet, it had come as a surprise when he noticed her wheelchair, a reminder of the strength she must carry, adding depth to his admiration.

MANGLED MORTALITY

The picture loomed vividly in Robert's mind, and he suddenly began to weep. Within minutes, he was crying like a baby, clutching his pillow and writhing on his bed, sobbing uncontrollably. The stoic strength of a man whose work had altered the destinies of nations was now reduced to emotional rubble as he struggled to catch his breath, overwhelmed by what he perceived as pity for the hopeless circumstances of a woman he hardly knew.

Robert stood up and turned on the light. He needed to figure out what was going on. For a moment, the Smith & Wesson again took the center stage of his mind. Was it time to do it? Time to finish it all? There was nowhere that he wanted to be any longer. He reached for the gun and walked to the mirror. Clicking off the safety, he raised the gun to his head and looked directly into the mirror, seeing who he might be for the last moment of his life, wondering if his eyes would focus as the explosion turned everything to permanent darkness.

Suddenly, just as Robert was about to squeeze the trigger, a thought seeped into his mind like a mystical cloud covering an otherwise desolate swamp. An inner dialogue began. I'm feeling sorry for myself, which is why I want to kill myself. I have plenty of reasons to feel this way, but now I'm sad because I don't have her. It's not pity for her; it's pity for me because she is crippled and broken, and I can't have her. Why am I so sad? Because I want her. She is the person I wish I could have in my life. So what if she's handicapped? So what?

In a trance-like state, a force almost beyond Robert's control caused him to slowly draw the gun down from his head and look at it as if it were no longer a solution, but as a foreign object that he had forgotten how to use. He nervously clicked the safety back in place, looked around the room and then began turning on lights.

Moments later, he sat down at his computer, logged onto Amazon, and began searching. He had a holiday mission: to find the perfect gift for Cindy. This task consumed much of the early morning, which felt less early as he realized he was trying to select a present for a woman he hardly knew.

By sunup, Robert had eaten two candy bars, something he had not done for years. He was always conscious of being in shape. There were so many things that he thought she might like. He wanted to know her better to find the perfect gift. By the end of the long roller coaster night, Robert appreciated those few things about life and living that delivered redemption. It even occurred to him momentarily that he could almost be thankful for Christmas as well.

9

It's difficult for the layman to genuinely understand how hard the lawyers were working at fighting the battle over the Presidency. Lawyers, billing at rates of $780 an hour, work tirelessly to navigate the complexities of law and governance. This reality underscores how, instead of relying on military might, democracy often depends on legal expertise and negotiation. In this sense, the relentless efforts of lawyers can be viewed as a modern-day substitute for the tanks that might otherwise be seen in the streets, reflecting the ongoing struggle for justice and power within a framework that values the rule of law. Sleeping only periodically and creeping across the mine-laden intellectual battlefields of the American judicial system, the glamour of a lawyer's life is a mere figment of the Netflix series scriptwriter's mind. The reality is hard beds, lousy food, long hours away from home, weird people on your side and the others, and the client's expectation that you will find a way to make the facts support the cause. Yet, you can't change the facts. You can't create votes where there is none and when someone tries to do so, you are bound by oath to report it.

The RNC wanted it their way and the DNC, theirs. The lawyers were stuck in the middle with clients who think that the fees being paid are a bribe for power, while the lawyer receiving the fee was armed with his exit speech regarding the limits to which he could go and still be ethical or keep his license. It was a strange dance which was playing out, in a close election where there were always those few who would let the ballot box be thrown in the river and think nothing of it. There were lawyers and there were criminals. Both kinds were in plentiful supply across the state of Georgia in the December of the Reid-Houston contest.

At least they were not shooting at each other, and their briefcases were full of iPads, papers, and not explosives. So, the relentless struggle to support their respective clients who would be President would continue. It was surely a bargain for the American people—given the fact that an M1A1 Abrams tank, together with fuel, armament and crews, costs more than $3000 an hour to operate. Then, when the battle is over, the tank lacks the ability to convert to non-government work, as is the case for most lawyers.

In addition to the lawyers, a battery of investigators had been herded into the fray to investigate the background of every elector of the Electoral College. Like a jury study, the assignment was to determine exactly who would be for and who would be against either candidate, as well as who might be most subject to manipulation from either side.

The Georgia State House had quickly become a battlefield all its own where emotions and issues were as vigorously argued as those in 1860, in the debate over secession from the Union. The result had been a deadlock. No electors could be agreed upon, and thus on the December 18 vote, Georgia, hoping that its absence would create a problem, stayed home. It did create a problem—a very big one.

The Courts were working feverishly to deal with the crisis and to construct a decision prior to the commencement of the congressional term in January. The timing was assumed by many to be favoring Vice President Reid—so long as her narrow coalition could hold at the Supreme Court. If the Supreme Court fails to make a decision before Congress convenes to certify the process for the Georgia electors, this could significantly affect the Electoral College meeting. Given the narrow Republican majority in the House and Houston's slight edge in the popular vote, he would likely emerge as the probable victor. The timing and decisions surrounding the certification of electors could ultimately determine the outcome, highlighting how procedural delays and judicial indecision can influence electoral results in a tightly contested political landscape.

* * *

PISCES V. SCORPIO

The lack of sleep from the night before failed to deter Robert's gait as he briskly strolled through the office doors, looked, almost timidly, in Cindy's direction, and hoped to be the target of a simple greeting.

"Hi!" The uptake was on the second part of the single syllable word. It wasn't a mere "Hi," it was a "Hi!!" ...one customized for him.

Robert wasn't ready to say anything; nothing clever had been planned. "So, what do you think of this election now?" Robert asked, thinking it sounded dumb even as he said it. He hated small talk, and it was something they had already covered on a prior occasion.

"Well, I've got it all figured out, you know." Cindy smiled as she spoke matter-of-factly. He assumed she would have something to say. "You see, the Vice President is a Pisces. Governor Houston is a Scorpio. When you put these two together, they are a very good match. If they would get together about two weeks from now, they'd create the baby of babies! It would be a Virgo or maybe a Libra. Either way, you get the ultimate leader—a disciplined, high-achieving, perfectionist, very smart, and someone who likes to please everyone!"

"So, what do you think of that?" Cindy asked proudly.

Robert paused for a minute. Watching her talk was sheer entertainment. He had hoped she wouldn't stop. "Cindy, I think it makes all the sense in the world," feigning with a slight smirk that he had been totally convinced.

"Well, of course you do, Bob," she responded, "Because I know my astrology and you know that I know what I'm talking about." She was talking with her eyes, as much as with her voice, and he could not help but notice the rest of her that he had dreamed of only hours before.

"I see," Robert thought for a moment, "So you know that I know that you know what you are talking about!" The flirtation continued.

Cindy paused and looked up. "Uh...I think you're right, Bob, and I'm glad you see things my way." To him, her cheeks and eyes brightened everything behind the reception desk. Robert began to take off his coat as he headed for his office. "So, what do you have planned for today?" he asked.

"Oh...you have some calls. I put them into your computer. Remember, I am here to help you...I don't want you to worry about anything. You concentrate on that pile of work on your desk, and I'll take care of the admin' stuff. O.K., Bob?"

Cindy looked up at him with a reassuring nod of the head. He found his heart melting. She's so incredible, he thought to himself as he walked to his office. Then he thought, what is going on with me? I do not understand this.

Even before making the first call, Robert noticed a slight change to his cluttered desktop. A beautiful card sat conspicuously on top of a stack of files, clearly demanding attention. It wasn't in an envelope and bore no resemblance to a basic Hallmark card. Instead, it was homemade—a serene image of ice skaters on a pond, reminiscent of a Currier and Ives motif, featuring skaters, a pond, and a tree, all accentuated with silver embossing powder against a deep blue background. Robert knew what was next as he opened the card. CHRISTMAS—CRAMER STYLE. PLEASE JOIN US.

SMOKE AND MIRRORS

The almost knee-jerk reaction had been as always—I've got to get out of this—how will I do it? As Robert looked at the card, the simple peacefulness of the scene, another thought began to evolve in competition with all the negative constraints, excuses and diversions. Robert imagined an after-dinner walk, if the weather allowed, or maybe just a closed-door session with Landon Cramer next to a warm fireplace in his study. This would be the moment when he would finally confront Landon Cramer and reveal everything. Landon would be taken aback, especially by the deceit of using the investigation job as a cover. Yet, if there was anyone capable of understanding and forgiveness, it was Landon Cramer. It would be a chance to come clean. It might mean the job—Landon probably had his limits as well. Robert, however, was confident that Landon was the one person he knew who would tell no one, but could still, perhaps, give him good advice on how to deal with his life.

Recognizing the importance of having a true friend to help fend off the ghosts of the night, Robert reasoned that it was worth a try. What better time than Christmas at the Cramer home? It was just an idea, a tentative plan, but perhaps a good one. With that thought in mind, he turned to his work; he had much to do.

The meeting with Cedric Martin was planned for the old Steam Plant by the C&O Canal on 30th Street which, coincidentally, was only one block south of the office. It would take him less than five minutes to get there. Constructed from an industrial-grade gray block, the square building rose about ten stories tall and had no windows. Supporting two tall smokestacks, the steam plant was a World War II relic designed to supply power to the rapidly growing northwest Washington, D.C., area. Its original purpose had long since given way to modern energy sources in Pennsylvania and other locations along the eastern seaboard, leaving the structure quiet and unused. The only signs of life were the guard stations at the two entrances, where armed security personnel in uniforms bearing the insignias of the civilian protection agency for the Department of Defense stood watch around the clock. Rumors were rampant about how the underground tunnels connected the plant to every important Washington site, including the FBI J. Edgar Hoover building, the Capitol and even the White House. They remained nothing more than local buzz. No reporter had ever been given access to confirm or deny the stories, nor had the government ever published any reports or maps of the building. The Steam Plant loomed like a mystery, a ghostly structure amidst the bustling activity on the northwest side of town. As Robert arrived at the guard gate, light snow began to fall. He provided his name, and moments later, the deep roar of steel against steel echoed as the enormous door—large enough for a dump truck to pass through—lifted. The guard gestured for him to enter.

Like the visit at the boathouse, Robert found himself standing inside a room with the entry door behind him slamming hard against the concrete. Again, the room was entirely dark, absolute blackness for what seemed like a very long minute. Suddenly, to the right side of where he stood, a bright white ray flowed into the room as a door opened. Standing directly in the doorway and silhouetted with the brilliant light behind him was the unmistakably recognizable figure of Colonel Cedric Martin, United States Army. A sort of magnificent entry—absent the music and artificial smoke. "Well, Robert Cannon. Come on in!" The Colonel's voice boomed, officious but friendly with the resonance of a James Earl Jones.

Robert was unprepared for the seeming fanfare—a sharp contrast from the meeting at the boathouse where he saw no one. He walked forward and met Martin in the doorway. The broad-shouldered colonel in a dark civilian suit had a prominent bald head that gleamed and wide black cheeks. He offered a strong handshake, matching Robert's equally firm grip. In his late forties, the colonel had already dedicated nearly thirty years to service in the Army. More than once, frenzied Redskins football fans had mistaken him for a member of the team.

Blue, Red, and Dead

The rumor in intelligence circles was that Martin had long since been awarded the rank of Major General, but due to his special position in covert operations at DOD, he could not be identified beyond the rank of Colonel. "It's good to see you, Cedric," Robert responded.

"Well, I'm not sure how good it really is," Martin said, his tone stern and distant. This wasn't the time for admiration. "Every time you and I team up, someone ends up dead!" Robert knew Martin was alluding to the Madrid Hotel incident but doubted Cedric Martin ever truly cared about anyone's death.

His gaze shifted to three other figures—two men and a woman— dressed in the green, non-insignia fatigues of the Department of Defense Special Security Service, commonly known as Black Ops. Much had changed since his days of chasing the fighters of FARC in Colombia. Although he didn't know them well, he recognized what they were at a glance. Each stood quietly on the opposite side of what appeared to be a heavy vehicle repair bay, a spacious room with a high ceiling filled with equipment, including a functional crane and intact hydraulic lifts.

"So, what do you have for me, Cedric?" Robert asked.

Colonel Martin gestured for Robert to take a seat in the folding chairs positioned in the corner of the room, beneath harsh industrial lights that bathed the scene in an unsettling yellow hue. As they sat down, the Colonel loosened his tie, crossed his legs, and leaned back, clasping his hands over his knee in a relaxed, yet deliberate posture. "I have an assignment from the Department, Cannon. It is a little different from what we have done before, so you need to listen very carefully."

Robert showed no response but was anxious to hear what Martin was up to.

"They tell me you're still the top 'passive exit man' in the business," the Colonel began. Robert always hated the term "exit man," and the "passive" reference was equally offensive. It was old guard, reminiscent of Ian Fleming. What it really meant was that no one was pulling a trigger, firing a rocket, or facing their victim as he helped them "exit" this life. His work typically involved chemicals, biological agents, and, on rare occasions, explosives—hardly passive.

"I thought you'd have some younger operatives in the business by now, so I'm a bit surprised to be called upon again. So, what's up?" Robert urged Martin to get to the point.

"Well, I'm not going to sit here and stroke you, so let me get on with the mission. We have a job that needs to be done quickly—there can be no hitches. None!" The Colonel was cautious, but Robert sensed a slight nervousness. This had to be significant.

"I realize that the jobs you've done for the Department have always been outside the country. Well, this one isn't," the Colonel continued.

Robert could feel cold sweat start to form under his arms and on his forehead. This was sounding too much like what he had already heard. Further, the discomfort in Martin's voice was showing through. And Martin was a pro. It put Robert on alert.

"The Department wants you to take out Ramona McCall," the Colonel spoke as if he had blurted out a phrase he had not wanted to say.

Robert's mind scrolled its memory for only a few brief seconds, realizing McCall was a Supreme Court Justice. The Colonel continued, "She's eighty- one years old, second oldest on the Court. She's lived a good life and has given plenty of strong service to her Country. There are reasons she has got to go now. This can't wait for the retirement party."

Robert could hardly believe what he was hearing. For the second time in two days, he was being asked to assassinate a high U.S. official within the boundaries of the United States. But he was also nervous about what he observed. He noted the perspiration beading on Martin's shiny black head. It sent a signal that he was trained to read. Martin was struggling with this one and Robert knew anything that made such an old pro squirm was far more than just another hit.

CONFUSION REIGNS

It was one thing to arrange a termination outside of the country, but quite another to be running around Washington, D.C. killing people. It felt cheap, almost like associating him with the D.C. Sniper. He decided to test the limits of what he could say. "I'm a little concerned about this, Cedric." This is very different from what I have done before. Don't I get any confirmation at all?"

"You know as well as I do that you are to follow through on these orders. You may be retired, but you're still a soldier and you always will be." The Colonel paused for a moment and then continued. "Frankly, I don't know what it means if you decide not to take the assignment. In fact, I'm not here to ask. I'm just here to tell you what it is and that it's got to be done no later than New Year's Eve."

New Year's Eve was etched deep in Robert's memory. The CIA had given him the same deadline on Congressman Ormond. "I don't mean to pry, Colonel, but has anyone ever suggested that maybe you could tell me why we're doing this?"

Martin rolled his eyes slightly and shook his head. He leaned forward, pointing at Robert. "You know as well as I do that we don't ask why. I do what I'm told, and you do what you're told, and that's the way it's going to be... for the rest of your life!"

Robert could feel the intensity of the Colonel's words as if the finger was being shoved hard into his chest as the Colonel spoke. Robert looked at the three young, trained killers standing on the other side of the room, clearly listening to the conversation. He reached the conclusion, based on years of experience, that a refusal on his part could be tantamount to signing his own death warrant. He wondered if the three were aiming to become like Martin—or worse, like him. The realization struck: self-preservation meant accepting the job, or he might not make it out of the building alive.

"Justice McCall lives in Potomac, Maryland. Her address is 2465 Stuart Court. That's just off Route 7. Her phone number is (301) 555-7481. The rest of the stuff, you know where to get it. It's all on Fed Web." Robert nodded. He had used the site many times for many reasons. The Colonel continued, "It's got to be natural. So, you need to mix your potion. She's had a lot of heart problems...been under the knife twice and is on 120 mg of Inderal and 20mg of Accupril twice a day for hypertension."

The coincidence of the moment was making Robert very uneasy. Was it a coincidence? Robert knew that Washington had a huge number of moving parts but more often than not, when they moved together, one of the city's major powers usually carefully orchestrated it. However, such was not always the case. There had been many exceptions. He also knew that any express violation of the National Security Act could create an open season on him, so it was not his place to open his own investigation. His options were few, and Cedric Martin was definitely not someone he could confide in about his doubts. "Alright, I'll get it done," Robert replied with the icy detachment of a man resigned to his fate. "Yeah, I'll handle it, and it'll be quick."

Within the next minute, Robert was back on the street, walking away from the Steam Plant which, if the truth were known, had been used to hatch the plots that led to the deaths of many over the years. For a moment, he recalled the look in the eyes of the three young soldiers as he accepted the job. Had it been relief or had it been disappointment?

10

"Bob, you left without even letting me know where you were going. You ought to be ashamed of yourself!" Cindy spoke as Robert came through the front door of the office into the lobby.

If she only knew, Robert thought to himself. "Well excuse me, Ma'am. I'll try to keep you posted." He spoke quickly as he walked directly across the lobby toward the hall to the offices without stopping at her receptionist desk to visit. He wanted to avoid Cindy. It was time to retreat to the office, to sit, think, and worry. Silently, he walked up the hall, the weight of uncertainty pressing on him. Kill two high government officials as the uncertain administration was being assembled, and in the middle of a deadlocked election. It raised a specter of possibilities. Could it be all linked together? Yet at the same time, Robert's years of experience reminded him not to spend too much time on the question of why. It was his responsibility to get the job done in dealing with enemies of the United States, both foreign and domestic, or so he rationalized in his more noble moments. This time, the enemies were two supposedly well-respected American citizens. At least they would go easily, Robert thought to himself. They were nearby, old and not very well protected.

As he sat at his desk, Robert found himself back in the dark world normally reserved for the night. Against the backdrop of his previous night's epiphany, killing anyone was not only distasteful, but it seemed impossible. He knew that, just as before, he would do it again. The epiphany would inevitably clash with reality. This time, though, he needed to think it through—carefully weighing the personal costs and benefits of his peculiar life, always questioning why he felt compelled to take these actions in the first place. When the analysis had run its course, he would return to his guilt-ridden internal dialogue of how he had ever gotten himself into this situation in the first place.

The answer to the first question was relatively simple. Robert had killed so many times before that his handlers at the CIA and DOD likely assumed anyone so depraved and consistent in his deadly undertakings could always be relied upon to get the job done. Only the most depraved individuals would do what I do, he thought. People like me are born, have mothers and fathers, and learn to walk. At what point did I learn to kill? I'm a psychopath... maybe I like it... and again, maybe I hate it... but I hate myself. What would Landon Cramer say? How might he react to the Christmas confession? Would it make any difference? Or should I continue to live with it all in silence?

As Robert sat watching the intensifying winter storm turn the mid-afternoon into darkness, he felt the terrible pain pushing upward from his stomach toward his ribs. It was a deep, sharp gut-wrenching visceral grinding that prohibited him from thinking about anything else.

Suddenly there was a knock at the door. Before Robert could answer, the door opened and Cindy wheeled her way into the office, smiling and looking directly at him, making him feel that she could see right through him. "Well, Mr. Grimm, are you working on another fairy tale or something?" she teased. He wanted to respond, but the effort felt heavy. She could tell Robert twas wrestling with something deeper, something from the emotional side of life.

"What you need, Robert, is something that I've got!" He still sat silently, but Cindy persisted. "Don't you want to ask what I've got?" she said almost like a mother talking to a child out of a bad mood.

Robert turned away from his steady gaze out the window. "So, what have you got, Cindy?" he asked, his tone more out of obligation than genuine interest, his words lacking enthusiasm.

"Bob, I've got a home-cooked meal for you, featuring my world-famous spaghetti complimented by some great Australian Merlot...and from the looks of you, you could use both." She spoke convincingly, at the same time looking for any sign of a positive response.

Robert shifted around on his swivel chair, "This isn't the time, Cindy...you don't want to ask for my company now." He spoke softly.

"Well, I'm not going to pull the 'you don't want to go out with the crippled lady nonsense!'" Cindy said, her tone sharpening slightly. "But I will take offense at the fact that you may be turning down the finest spaghetti and wine combination you've ever had in your life. I'll either take offense or at least feel sorry for you if you pass it up." "No, it's not that at all..."

Cindy interrupted, "Well, I hope you're not onto some anti-fraternization bent in the law firm, because you're just staff like I am, and we can cross-fraternize all we want."

Robert was slightly stirred but still not released from his depressive trance.

Cindy could see that helping him out of his funk was going to be a Herculean task. She made one more attempt. "You don't know anything about me, but I live alone apart from one very sensuous cat named Angel. I know you're going to find this hard to believe, and maybe even repulsive, but Angel creeps up on my bed sometimes at night and sucks on my earlobe while I'm sleeping. That's the kind of action that goes on in my house...not that it overly pleases me, but Angel purrs while she does this...can you imagine that feeling? Make me want to...you know." Robert simply stared at the woman, struggling to grasp the full meaning behind her words as she continued speaking. "So now you know the most intimate details of my life. Either way, it's a wonderful life and I don't know that I get grumpy, like you, except maybe when these damn wheels need some oil. That does bug me, but I get over it!" She looked at him intently and delivered a parting shot. "I hope you can get over whatever is eating you." She reversed the wheels, spun the chair around in athletic style and rolled out of the room, letting the door quietly close behind her.

Robert sat staring at the door, as if it didn't exist. His mind raced, trying to make sense of what he had just experienced while also grappling with the pressing concerns weighing heavily on him. Uncertainty clouded his thoughts—unsure of what to say or how to act. He knew that he did, in fact, feel uncomfortable for a variety of reasons. He had to admit to himself, with a certain degree of personal disgust, that the wheelchair was one of them.

CROSSROADS

For the next hour, Robert tried to press through the completion of several necessary telephone calls. He had a daunting list of returned email on his computer, only a portion of which he could make before losing his ability to concentrate and wandering out the door after 5:30 p.m., hoping he would see Cindy, but knowing she had already left for the day. Robert walked the ten minutes to his townhouse, quickly changed clothes and headed back out for a run. In his pocket, consistent with routine, were a couple of twenty- dollar bills. He always believed it was wise to be prepared for the possibility of not finishing a run; at the very least, he could hail a cab to get himself home. Forty dollars would more than cover the fare to get him across town if necessary.

A mild snowfall whitened the path as Robert ran northeast through Rock Creek Park, providing a surreal effect. Running had become an almost automatic action for him. As he drifted in and out of deep thought, he grappled with how to manage the assignments he had received from the CIA and the Department of Defense. Approaching the zoo, about two miles up the path from Georgetown, his legs felt like lead, making it harder to maintain his pace. He remembered running six miles just two days earlier on the route to the boathouse and several more the following day, so he couldn't comprehend why moving forward felt so laborious now. It felt as though pressure was closing in on him from all directions. What was it? Was it the realization that he was in a high crime area? It was dark. He recalled that the supposed Shaundra Levy murder site was in the woods off the path only forty or so feet from where he was now slowly jogging. It was not as if he was gripped by fear of street punks. He knew that he could quickly become very dangerous. No thug or gangbanger in D.C. had killed as many as he had, he thought. He was the most vicious animal in this forest. Robert wrestled with the roots of his paranoia. It wasn't the darkness that troubled him; he had navigated that before. He worked in the dark. It was one of his tools. His mind started settling on the distant past. It slowed him from a run to a walk.

His mind moved him out of the woods for a moment, to a time which had once been like yesterday, but was now like forever ago. He was driving off in the dark to the town where he and the beautiful young woman in the car with him were to be married in the morning. He had known Veronica for less than three months. Quickly, however, he had sensed how happy she seemed to be around him. He had always doubted that anything he might say or do would have such an effect. Certainly, in the FARC wars no one had experienced any joy in his presence. Then, driving away in the night, she had been gleeful, singing the fifties song "Going to the Chapel and We're Gonna Get Married," repeatedly. Soon there were. It had all been so phenomenal. He was sure it would last forever.

As the presence of the dark pathway began to invade his thoughts and painfully contaminate the past, Robert tried hard to hang on for just a few moments to the feelings that had so fully possessed at the time. Like an early morning struggle to keep the best parts of a dream clear in his mind, he recalled how he wanted to tell her that he loved her. He had said it often—and yearned to shout it out in the woods as if she were right there.

Dead people don't listen; they just haunt you in the present, making your heart heavy with the past. They nudge you toward where they are. Robert's memories abruptly shifted to the image of a decaying, wound-riddled corpse in the black abyss of twenty years in a coffin. That was where the body lay—once warm, once believing in him. He fought against the darkness to regain his focus. He envisioned a white dress, a beautiful smile, the mouth he loved to kiss. I killed it all! Darkness had triumphed, leading him down a path to a hollowed-out soul.

He was back now plotting against himself in the awful present; the killer of my wife, out to kill again, and again. If I refuse, they kill me: There is no hope!

Robert started considering his options and settled on one, which he thought he had overcome. The 9mm was again the solution. If I kill myself, they can't kill me. Then I won't be killing anyone else. The Congressman and the Justice were certainly doomed to die, no matter what he did, he thought. If he didn't get to them first, someone else would. Before he put himself away, perhaps he could at least warn them—they might still have a chance.

Turning around on the path, Robert began to make his way slowly back in the direction of Georgetown. Soreness was setting in on both hips. The need to walk was rapidly becoming irrelevant. Dead people don't walk. It had been such a momentous day, yet so anti-climactic. He had been so high and was now so low. It was time to drop back by the law office, send a warning letter, then go home, and end it all. It made sense in a way that it never had before. Reality had only made his wild imagination less bearable. Since the loss of his wife, he had regularly teetered on the edge of suicide. Only fear of death had allowed short spurts of relief to his senses and faculties and kept him alive. Now, it was time to die. It was too late, even to talk to Landon Cramer.

It took almost half an hour to walk the two miles back to Georgetown. During the hike, Robert composed a warning letter to his intended victims. He made his way back to the law office, checked in with the night guard and started searching around the office for something with which to scribble a note. He reasoned that it was important to compose a note that must not be attributed to him. His death would pose enough of a problem. He wanted to steer clear of any implications involving the law firm in a potential assassination scandal.

He remembered how kind each of the partners had been to him over the years. Mitigating the damage from his actions would serve as a cheap atonement for all his misdeeds, but at least it would mark the beginning of something that could never truly be finished. Even a person on his way to hell can maybe stop at some point to do something good along the way. Robert found himself rummaging through Cindy's reception desk to find paper and selected two sheets of plain bond paper underneath what appeared to be a carbon copy of a check that apparently was signed earlier that day by Landon Cramer. He took the two pages and was reaching for a pen when his eyes focused on the face of what struck him as so new, so different. In a small 3x5 portrait sat the woman with a large gray cat in her lap, looking at him in a pose that caused him to sit back and simply stare. She posed so beautifully and there was no sign of a wheelchair or her MD.

All he could see was a magnificent presence, which his senses told him was hope. Until that moment, hope had only been something he could feel—and only on rare occasions. As he gazed into her eyes and traced the contours of her noble face, he not only felt hope but saw it in its most brilliant form. The haunting memories of the death walk from Rock Creek Park began to fade from his mind. Maybe death, though imminent, could be postponed a little longer. In the next few moments, Robert found himself scanning the desk again, searching for an address. Once he located what he needed, he folded the two sheets of paper, tucked them into the pocket of his running jacket, set the alarm, and dashed out the door, catching a cab heading south on M Street.

Within twenty-five minutes, Robert was standing on the steps of a small but stately red brick 50's era single story rambler on a tree-lined street just off Glebe Road in Arlington. As the door opened, the face from the picture seemed to materialize, merging with the portrait in a moment of surreal clarity. "I think I need the wine and spaghetti you offered. Is there any left?"

11

This has gotta be absolute bullshit, if you will excuse my French, Senator." acknowledging his deference for the former governor, current senator from Massachusetts, and current Republican Vice - Presidential nominee, Talmage Smith Sam's bluntness hung in the air, a stark contrast to the polished decorum typically expected in such high-stakes political discussions. Talmadge Smith, a man known for his unflappable demeanor and carefully curated image, raised an eyebrow, his lips forming a thin line.

"Now, Sam," Talmadge began, his voice steady yet tinged with a hint of incredulity. "You know how this works. We can't afford to lose sight of the bigger picture here."

"Since when were elections determined by the flip of a coin in the middle of a football field? I mean, where's that in the Constitution?" Rusk continued to vent as he informed Senator Smith of the offer from the Vice President.

"It's an intriguing proposition," the Senator responded as he spoke with David Houston's right-hand man in the den of the Senator's Vienna, Virginia home. "It gives each side an equal chance. It is risk taking and brinkmanship at its finest, as far as I can tell."

"So, it doesn't bother you?" Rusk asked.

"No. The logic of it does make sense…and it helps preserve face even for the one that loses. I do find that intriguing."

Rusk was slightly irritated. "That's easy for you to say, Senator. You have your job in the Senate to fall back on. But for David—Governor Houston—if he loses, that's it."

"No, you're wrong there, Sam," Smith quickly replied. "You might lose if your man doesn't become president. David Houston is a young man with a bright future. One misstep by Charlotte Reid during her presidency, and she'll be a one-term player." The fact of the matter is that you're upset because you are not getting everything you want right now. That's the way life is young man." Smith was known to be soft spoken, but very direct and circumspect with his words. He was not one to be pushed around by the likes of a political party operative like Sam Rusk, who Smith had always considered a "hack," at best.

"I don't think you're being fair with us on this Senator," Rusk was irritated, "It's the Presidency of the United States we're talking about, and you talk about it like selecting which team gets to receive. Just think of everything we've put into this, all the money, time, effort, sweat…" He was about to say the word blood but chose not to. The Senator cut in during Rusk's pause, aware of the direction Rusk was taking with his tirade. "You have to understand, Sam—the other side has done the same thing. Both sides have invested enough money in this deal to lose their objectivity."

"I bet Governor Houston would love to hear that!" Rusk shot back, his tone dripping with sarcasm.

"If you think you're gonna go tattle on me, it's too late." Smith was prepared to tee off on such a puny lightweight comment. "Governor Houston knows exactly how I feel about this election, and he also knows that I don't cater to lightweights like you!

"I'm not here to impress you!" Rusk retorted. "I'm just here to let you know what the other side has brought to us so that if this thing leaks out, the next big story won't be that you were caught unaware." Rusk was starting to retreat, overwhelmed by the powerful Senator. It was time to sound diplomatic rather than vitriolic.

"I really appreciate that." Smith said sarcastically, "Well, what about my input. Do you want my opinion or does that matter?" "Of course it matters, Senator," Rusk replied, his voice losing some of its earlier intensity.

Smith pressed on. "I think you should let me talk to Tom Rosenblat and see how deep this proposal goes. It could just be political posturing... you know, for the next sound bite."

"That's exactly what I think it is."

"We need to find out," Smith continued. "If it's genuine, it could also be an excellent way to bring closure to this issue. The American public is tired of it, you know. Flipping a coin is something people can relate to. It could resonate well. If you turn it down, you might still win the election but lose the support of the people."

ABYSS OF LOYALTY

"Yeah, I know," Rusk interjected, inferring that he could care less about the will of the people but also knowing that Char Reid and the Democratic strategists were not born yesterday.

"I agree; it could also be a delay strategy or some kind of ploy. If you're going to consider this, you need to have it put in writing as an agreement between the two camps, and congressional leadership should sign on as well." Because, you know," the Senator reminded him, "they're the ones that are going to ultimately make this decision."

"I'm not so sure of that, Senator. I'm worried that the Supreme Court will resolve this issue before we can even get to the coin flip. Our legal experts tell us that the Court may certify the Georgia electors and set up a new electoral vote. If that happens, there won't be a chance to flip the coin—even if that's what the public wants."

"Yes, I'm aware of that," the Senator acknowledged. "In the end, I think they'll stick with the Constitution and send it to the House."

Rusk attempted to regain control of the discussion. "And that's precisely my point. I don't think we're ready to hand the Presidency over to the flip of a coin. This election needs to go to Congress. We know we can win there. You and your Senate buddies will secure it for us!"

"Well, you seem quite confident about all this," the Senator replied, slightly offended by the implication of cronyism. "I know you have plenty of political contributors who don't want to lose their investment. Those individuals understand that when they contribute, it may or may not pay off. They're big boys—and girls. If you have people applying pressure on Governor Houston that's more than he can handle, let me know, and I'll take care of it!" the Senator said, jabbing his finger directly at Sam Rusk.

Rusk could sense the Senator's resolve and was not disposed to carry the matter further. He had delivered the message and had gained the Senator's input, which he intended to convey to the Governor. Causing his image to slip further with the powerful Senator was a bad direction to go, and he knew it. He chose not to press his point further.

"So, why didn't you just call me instead of coming all the way out here to Virginia?" the Senator asked. "I thought you'd stay in Oklahoma for the Christmas holidays."

"This situation is too fast and too furious. We watched the Electoral College fight flow into the Supreme Court, and we are concerned the court will convene a special hearing and act during the holidays. So, I've had to stay right on top of it. I've got meetings here..." His voice trailed off, not finishing the sentence.

The Senator did not completely believe what Rusk had to say. To him it was odd that Rusk would still be in D.C. Even in the middle of the crisis, it seemed that everybody was away from the District, with the exception of the major law firms that were spending their holidays on non-stop election skirmishing and preparation for the post-holiday fight. For his part, Senator Smith was going to fly back to Boston and spend Christmas with two of his seven children and eight grandchildren. As important as the election dispute was, Talmadge Smith refused to let it interfere with his Christmas.

* * *

THE PUZZLE

Never had spaghetti and wine tasted so delightful. Fortunately for Robert, he hadn't arrived too late to enjoy the meal. Cindy could hardly contain her joy at his appearance at her door. Within half an hour, she had pulled the dinner together and set it on the table. Robert was impressed that she had planned a spaghetti dinner with or without him. The meal turned out to be exquisite, and Robert savored every bite.

Once he had finished two helpings, he joined Cindy as she put dishes in the dishwasher. From there he moved to the sofa as the carbohydrates worked in his system. He settled in to watch television, letting the gray cat, Angel, rest its head on his leg and purr contentedly.

Robert did not try to fend off the feelings of contentment that seemed to be so naturally present. It was all such a sharp contrast to the almost terminal events of the previous hours in the cavernous darkness of Rock Creek Park. Death had seemed so imminent; now it was so remote.

For her part, Cindy seemed comfortable. She busied herself with a cross- stitch project next to the sofa that would have caused any third person viewing them to assume that they had been together as a couple for years. It felt like all the typical first date questions had already been answered, making small talk unnecessary. As the news played in the background, they hardly spoke. Cindy hoped she was interpreting

Robert's relaxed demeanor, along with the cat and the television, as signs that he had enjoyed the meal. With the effects of the thick pasta kicking in, Robert nodded off.

As CNN droned on with its persistent around-the-clock reporting of the Presidential standoff, Robert was suddenly aroused from his slightly hibernated state as a certain face on the newscast caught his attention. He could see the Vice President's entourage leaving a Christmas party at the Kennedy Center. In the crowd, Robert thought he could see a man whose name he didn't know, but nevertheless recognized from a recent meeting. It was...as he resurrected his thought processes from their state of relaxation, the CIA officer that had accompanied Deputy Director Jerry Rothman at the previous day's MOTS confirmation in Washington Circle.

Suddenly, Robert was wide awake. He looked closer, puzzled by why a CIA officer would be so close to the Vice President. From what he could gather from the report, it became clear that the young officer was serving as the lead inner-ring security person. Having often studied the protection arrangements for world leaders, Robert understood this meant the officer was one of the agents closest to the person being protected, essentially approving and, in some cases, selecting the Vice President's every move. It was strange; it made no sense that a CIA officer, of all people, would take on the role of a Secret Service agent.

Cindy noticed Robert's startled reaction to the TV report. "So, what's going on there? What is it?"

"This is so weird Cindy...really weird!" Robert moved across the room and knelt in front of the screen. "Look at this guy." He pointed his finger, trying to keep track of one individual while the scene continued to move with the news report. "This fellow does not work for the Secret Service, Cindy. He's CIA!"

"So, what makes you think that?" She seemed confused.

Robert paused for a moment, recognizing that he had overplayed his enthusiasm. Blowing his cover would undoubtedly end everything swiftly. Why he should know these things was meant to remain a mystery. Yet, he couldn't hide his astonishment from Cindy. "I know him!" he exclaimed, then impatiently awaited the end of the report and the switch to coverage of the latest developments on the Houston side.

After a commercial, the news correspondent moved to another Washington, D.C. holiday celebration. This time, it was the Republican candidate, Governor David Houston, leaving a holiday party at the Mayflower Hotel. The commentator was artful in pointing out that each of the candidates seemed to be spending an inordinate amount of time in and out of the nation's capital as if, through association, they were laying claim to the seat of power. The Governor had just arrived from meetings in Washington State to attend a Christmas benefit concert and a fundraiser at the Mayflower Hotel. Within moments, Robert grew more troubled as he spotted another familiar face, this one closely associated with David Houston. Again, among the Secret Service detail, he thought he recognized the young female who had been in the group of three Army Special Operations soldiers in the steam building in Georgetown only six hours earlier. This time, she was elegantly dressed in a tailored business suit. He was certain it was the same person. As the camera panned the crowd, he thought he spotted another young male soldier. Before he could be certain, the report ended.

"So, I knew someone in the Secret Service years ago," Cindy began to reminisce, nonchalant and apparently oblivious to Robert's alarmed state.

Robert interrupted, "It's not that Cindy. It doesn't make sense. Why would a CIA agent be protecting the Vice President?" He continued to think aloud. "And why are people in the Department of Defense mixed in with the Secret Service detail protecting Governor Houston?"

"You mean you can really tell that just from watching the news?" Cindy asked, somewhat incredulously. The report had passed quickly, causing Robert to wonder if he was too tired to entirely trust his initial perceptions of the television report. It had been a long day, and he was exhausted. The media has a way of presenting things so you can never be sure what you are seeing, he thought. Maybe everyone was looking familiar at this point. "If I could... just see it again. I guess I can watch CNN at home tonight until they re-run this segment." "Oh, I don't know if you need to do that," Cindy said. "I've been recording this stuff. You know, this is historic... a huge constitutional crisis."

Robert interrupted, "What have you been recording it? What have you got?"

"Well, since I don't get home from work until after the evening news, I record the news every night. I'm one of those people that actually know how to program the recording device side of the world. Do you?" She smiled.

"Not really," Robert said wryly. "But let's see what you've got...that could really help me...maybe."

Cindy spun her wheelchair around and headed for a bookcase not far from the television. The news started to play.

"Well, why is it such a big deal? I mean, the people with the candidates...I assume they've got Secret Service crawling around everywhere," Cindy said.

Robert was only half listening to Cindy as he focused intently on the recorded scenes of the evening news reports from the previous week. She had been diligently recording the first ten minutes of the CBS evening news every night since the legal battles kicked off in mid-November. As he fast-forwarded through the segments, his heart raced when he reached the December 1st report. The segment, titled "Battle for the White House," prominently featured Jerry Rothman's associate from the MOTS confirmation meeting, bringing a rush of adrenaline as Robert anticipated what revelations might follow. Robert carefully made sure that it was him and then reran the report back to the 30th of November. The footage displayed an event featuring the Vice President and her husband, Bill, as she gathered with her campaign advisors. The security detail was present, as expected, but Robert couldn't spot Rothman's cohort anywhere in the scene.

BROKEN BONDS

Fast forwarding to December 1st and then to the segment of the 2nd, Robert was amazed at what he saw. Not only was Rothman's associate in the picture, but as he switched back and forth between the 30th of November and the 1st and 2nd of December, he noticed that all the faces after December 1st were different—a new security detail appearing to be led by yet another CIA officer. Then he wondered, could it have been a Secret Service agent who was accompanying the Assistant CIA Director to the MOTS meeting? If so, why?

Robert then switched to a careful focus on the Houston campaign news coverage. "I can't believe this Cindy...I simply cannot believe what I am seeing, but I am seeing it!"

She wheeled closer to the TV.

"Now, look at this," Robert pointed, running the picture backwards and forwards from November 30th to December 1st. "In the Houston entourage, look at these security people. Now, this is a guy and a woman who are assigned to a special Army Unit." He looked at her for a moment, seeing that she was slightly perplexed. "Don't ask me how I know this; just take my word for it. When I rewind this to the day before, look at all these people. Do you see any of them in the news report on December 1st? It is a completely different group."

"Well, maybe they just had a shift change or something," Cindy responded naively.

"That could be true. When I go over to the reports on Vice President Reid, I see somebody who I know is probably not with the Secret Service...it's really weird! I'm not sure what to make of it, but it's weird!"

Robert thought to himself as he processed the information, his suspicions starting to align. However, he hesitated to reveal too much to Cindy, aware that any slip could lead to unintended consequences. With a determined focus, he hit play on the news segment again, hoping to catch any details that might clarify the unsettling situation further. Running through each of the evening news reports from early to mid-December, the bodyguards appeared to be the same group of people.

Robert shifted his focus back to the earlier coverage, freezing the frame on a group of agents from late November. He meticulously scanned each moment, and then fast-forwarded into December, pausing again at different points. Each freeze frame captured a new angle of the evening news reports, highlighting the candidates with their respective entourages, as he sought any overlooked detail. There were always a few new faces, but clearly, certain faces remained constant throughout the reports. The CIA and the U.S. Army Special Services Unit, respectively. The Secret Service was either in the background or not even present.

Suddenly, while running through a December 17 report, a cold chill shot down his spine as he saw another face within the middle ring of security around former Governor Houston. There, unmistakably, under a heavy coat and black hat, were the dark face and blazing malevolent eyes of Cedric Martin. Robert quickly froze the frame so he could see several other bodyguards. Looking closely at the picture for several minutes, he concluded that all three of the soldiers from the Steam Plant meeting were working the close-in security for David Houston. "This is too incredible...I mean there is something very sinister going on."

By now, Robert had Cindy's full attention. She was pleased to see him so engaged with the television in her home, particularly with the news reports she had recorded "So, are you working on something involving this? I mean...are the lawyers at the firm working some angle with respect to presidential security?"

"No, it's not that." Robert felt a rush of anxiety at the thought of revealing too much and quickly dialed back his tone. He didn't want to raise any suspicions, especially not during what was meant to be a pleasant first date. This sudden discovery felt like a precarious thread that could unravel everything, and he needed to keep the conversation light. "Just...something caught my eye, that's all. I'm a bit of a news junkie, I guess." He forced a smile, hoping to steer the focus away from the brewing tension in his mind.

"Robert, do you mind if I ask you a question?"

Robert backed away from the screen , looked at her and said, "Sure, ask away."

"Are you some kind of spook?" Cindy asked very directly using a term that, broadly interpreted inside the Beltway vernacular, meant spy.

"So, why do you ask that, Cindy?" Robert asked calmly.

"Well, what is it with all this on TV...the candidates for President?"

Robert glanced away from the television, his gaze shifting to the sofa where Cindy sat. He sighed, deciding to change the topic. "I'm getting too wrapped up in this election," he admitted. "It's frustrating, like it is for everyone. It feels like we just can't settle on a President."

Cindy was not easily put off. "No, Robert. There's something going on and it's really about those two presidential candidates. Are you just not able to tell me? Are you doing some kind of undercover work?"

"Well, I guess I forgot to tell you." He began to smile, "My name is really Clark Kent, and I am Superman!" Robert smiled, trying to break the tension of the moment.

Cindy appeared put off by Robert's avoidance but chose not to press the point. She allowed him room to change the subject—that he tactfully did. Over the next hour, the discussion moved away from the election and in the direction of their lives. For the first time, Robert began learning much more about the beautiful woman in the wheelchair. She shared her story with a calmness that belied the turmoil it had caused. "I grew up in Charlottesville, Virginia," she began, a hint of nostalgia in her voice. "Life was as normal as one could imagine—family dinners, school events, all the usual stuff. That is, until one winter morning during my sophomore year at UVA."

Cindy paused, her expression shifting as she recalled the day. "I remember waking up and feeling this strange numbness in my left thigh. It was like I had lost all sensation, and it didn't make any sense. I thought it would go away, but as the morning wore on, it only got worse. I couldn't even yell loud enough from my bedroom for my parents to hear me in the living room."

Then, the numbness in her legs set in over the next few months. After days in and out of the University Medical Center in Charlottesville and then trips back and forth to Johns Hopkins in Baltimore, the numbness came and went. She hoped and prayed that it would only be temporary. By age 25, she could no longer use crutches or a walker. Muscular Dystrophy had taken control of her life and she'd been in a wheelchair ever since.

The illness felt like the final blow in a series of personal disasters. As Cindy recounted, she had spent her teenage years caring for her mother, who suffered from Alzheimer's, while her father struggled to cope with his wife's decline. Although her father provided money for the treatments, as well as for Cindy's schooling, his emotional state had kept him distant from his daughter. As Cindy's condition worsened, so did the overall family situation. Eventually, her father suffered a nervous breakdown. Within ten years of the first M.D. symptoms, her mother was dead, and her father estranged. Cindy was on her own.

Cindy explained how a stroke of fate transformed her life, forcing her into self-sufficiency she hadn't fully embraced before. Always a swimming and water sports fanatic, she intensified her workouts to combat her condition. "The result was incredible upper body strength," she explained, "but it didn't stop the challenges."

She moved to Washington, D.C., initially landing a job as a legal secretary. But her continuing debilitation soon relegated her to answering telephones and assisting in office management. "No one wanted me as a legal secretary," she admitted, frustration evident.

"I could type more than a hundred words per minute," she reflected. "Now, it's down to less than eighty and getting slower. Even with conditioning, I couldn't stop the gradual loss of dexterity in my hands."

Robert sensed the bitterness in her voice and nodded, encouraging her to continue. "It's not easy, is it?" he asked softly.

Cindy spoke of how her chances at children, a family and a normal life had also long since been lost. It had been what she wanted the most. She had watched many stricken with M.D. suffer destruction at an early age, and was thankful that her version of the disease, especially with a new regimen of drug therapy, had a slow progression. A born optimist, she explained her appreciation for the reality that she had fared much better than most. She learned early in the process that the only way to survive was a positive attitude. To that end, she had created within the walls of her small home in Arlington, a world of imagination filled with happiness. She looked forward to sleeping. Her dreams were full of happiness when she walked, danced and ran.

Robert followed her story carefully, forgetting, for the moment, the strange events of the television news. He envied those who had the comfort of good dreams. Her story, filled with hardship, tugged at his heart in a way he wasn't used to. Normally, he avoided sadness, but this time, he felt an inexplicable urge to listen, to share in her pain, and be part of it.

Although he shared ideas and feelings with Cindy that evening, Robert also avoided disclosing too much. He avoided the details of Veronica's death. There was no way he could explain his disappearance to New England following the death of his wife. He doubted that Cindy, or anyone for that matter, could truly grasp the weight of his decision to leave his children behind. Maybe one day he'd tell her the truth, or maybe he'd spin a lie instead—something that would fit seamlessly with the deceitful thread woven through his life. She was such an attentive listener, and he had no one else who offered that kind of understanding. If he were to tell her everything, then at least someone would know and maybe someone would even care.

By the time he got into the cab, it was after midnight. Even with his unwillingness to trade the truth about his life for hers, as first dates go, he felt it had gone well. For once, he was thinking about something good in the future.

12

The litigation over the Presidency had taken on an odd form of combat. The lawyers who had erstwhile been spending their time trying to find lost votes were now putting their efforts toward the art of suing. The State Courts in Georgia were inundated with issues ranging from vote counting to voter fraud and voter qualification lawsuits. It seemed that every county official involved in the voting process had a restraining order slapped on him by one party or the other, and in some cases, both. The practice of law had become, at least for a season, a booming business across the state, as nearly every local firm found ways to add higher-than-normal fees on top of the hourly charges of out-of-state lawyers admitted to practice in the state for specific cases, pro hac vice.

The Federal courts were busy too. By early December, a whole package of cases had been filed before the Federal Court in Atlanta. Then, by mid- month, following one mini-trial and then an ultimate consolidation of issues, the 11th Circuit Court of Appeals had certified the matter to the U.S. Supreme Court. In its wisdom, the Court took a preliminary look at the boat load of issues and determined it would accept certiorari and at the same time consolidate all appellate issues into one mega-hearing. The Court, in taking stock of the entire situation, was still in no rush to get the work done. Hoping that some sensible wind might blow into the sails of the politicians, it announced that it would put off the resolution pending an extraordinary session before the full court, to be held beginning the second Monday in January.

The Court's temporary withdrawal from the fray a week before Christmas sparked widespread speculation. Pundits reported that the Democratic leadership appeared most fearful of the outcome if the House and Senate resolved the issue themselves. Those familiar with the Court believed that President Minton's two appointments, with the aging Ramona McCall's support, could sway the decision in favor of Vice President Reid before Congress could convene. Rumors of a possible emergency session during the holidays were fueled by the unusual fact that all nine judges were remaining in town.

The Republicans viewed it differently. They had their own set of fears. On more than one occasion, it was reported that Governor Houston, in private, had proclaimed his disdain for the Supreme Court, calling them "a group of geriatric untouchables." It had not been a politically smart thing to do, especially with the media not just chewing, but ravenously feasting on each candidate's misstatements. Even with the Republicans, the narrow margin of the majority in Congress and the apportioned one-state one-vote as required by the Twelfth Amendment was clearly a problem. Although the House could elect the President, the 51-49 standoff in the Senate could possibly produce Thomas Rosenblat as the Vice President. After all, Rosenblat was far senior to Talmadge Smith—and beloved on both sides of the aisle. The Court's temporary withdrawal from the fray a week before Christmas sparked widespread speculation. Pundits reported that the Democratic leadership appeared most fearful of the outcome if the House and Senate resolved the issue themselves. Those familiar with the Court believed that President Minton's two appointments, with the aging Ramona McCall's support, could sway the decision in favor of Vice President Reid before Congress could convene. Rumors of a possible emergency session during the holidays were fueled by the unusual fact that all nine judges were remaining in town.

Republican legal strategy with the Supreme Court had been to load the Court with as many issues as possible on appeal in order to cause delay and confusion.

"AND THE HARDEST WORKING LAWYERS WILL BE THOSE JUDGES WHO SIT ON THE U.S. SUPREME COURT. CONSIDERABLY OLDER, AT LEAST IN MOST CASES, AND HOPEFULLY WISER, THAN THE DOZENS OF LAWYERS WHO ARE POUNDING AWAY OVER THE CHRISTMAS HOLIDAYS TO BRIEF THE ARGUMENTS TO BE SUBMITTED BEFORE THE COURT, JUSTICE RAMONA MCCALL WILL BE EIGHTY-THREE YEARS OLD ON NEW YEARS DAY. MCCALL IS VIEWED AS THE GRAND DAME OF THE COURT, HAVING WEATHERED MANY JUDICIAL FIRESTORMS DURING HER ALMOST TWENTY-FIVE YEARS ON THE BENCH. WITHOUT QUESTION, NONE ARE SO HOT AS THE CASE OF REID VS. HOUSTON.

THERE ARE REPORTS THAT HER EYESIGHT IS FAILING AND IT'S KNOWN THAT SHE HAS SUFFERED VARIOUS COMPLICATIONS RELATED TO DIABETES. IT IS ALSO KNOWN THAT THE MALADY HAS BEEN UNDER CONTROL AND SHE HAS BEEN VERY EFFECTIVE AMID RUMORS THAT SHE WOULD BE RETIRING FROM THE COURT THIS YEAR. IT LOOKS LIKE HER RETIREMENT MAY NOT BE SOON ENOUGH. THE REPUBLICANS HOPED THAT SHE WOULD REMAIN ON THE COURT LONG ENOUGH TO SURVIVE THE APPOINTMENT POWER OF PRESIDENT MINTON. MANY OBSERVERS SUGGEST SHE WILL SIDE WITH THE LIBERALS ON THIS ONE—AND THAT'S NOT LIKELY TO BODE WELL FOR DAVID HOUSTON!"

There she was, the person Robert had been ordered to kill before New Year's Day. His instincts kicked in as he focused on the video, instantly assessing her weaknesses—a natural reaction given his past. He was momentarily struck by the gentle kindness in the old woman's face, a face marred by irreversible frailty. His analytical mind quickly shifted to the question: how could someone so small and seemingly weak possess such power? He reasoned that her frailty would make it easier. To end her life would require a minor accident or a low dose of a natural solution. He knew that accidents were investigated more thoroughly than deaths by natural causes, especially concerning prominent individuals, regardless of their age. The natural death scenario seemed the best route to take.

A TEST OF WILL

As the report continued, Robert had little doubt that he was being drawn into the national crisis. The nation's overseers did not want to be implicated, and that made sense. Their desire to do the worst of things secretly is what had kept him in business over the years. He reasoned, the country needed soldiers, soldiers to quietly do in foreign lands what it might otherwise take a major military operation, even a war to do publicly. It had often been in America's best interest to vanquish an enemy without taking credit for the deed. Overt military ventures were too risky—especially if there was a chance the opponent might not surrender quickly. The American military excelled at many things, but dying wasn't one of them. When faced with a foe willing to die or fight for a cause, it was always better to eliminate their leaders through assassination.

In every assignment, Robert felt assured that the national security interest had been justified at the highest levels. He had never focused on the analysis; it was beyond his pay grade. However, this time, with two clearly stated missions to kill, he found himself questioning where the critical national security interest lay. Killing spies and traitors—clear enemies of the United States—was terrible, but still within his range of toleration. He reasoned that he never expected it to be acceptable to most.

But again, it made even more sense in the case of certain in the case of major drug traffickers and treacherous dictators. He had always avoided the reasons. That was left up to the analysts and CIA Directors and Presidents. But this time, he had to ask, what did Congressman Ormond, the most senior member of the House of Representatives, have to do with it? Why Justice McCall?

With his mind focusing heavily on the question, he continued to watch the experts on the news spend the airtime presaging all the angles of complication, and then trying to interpret the variety of outcomes as to how the courts and Congress might handle the presidential deadlock. It was a confusing situation; the real outcome of choosing the President might rest on factors far beyond anyone going to the voting booth.

To confirm his suspicion, Robert switched on his computer to conduct some research. Until now, he had blocked out most of the technical noise surrounding the election system at the center of the crisis. He needed to understand it quickly. He began browsing through scholarly and less scholarly articles about the election standoff. Within an hour, what had seemed complicated was coming into focus.

The closeness of the election was only part of the problem. A much greater issue emerged as he read article after article about the legal battle over Georgia's inability to certify electors to vote with the Electoral College.

The argument of the Democrats was that the Electoral College vote should be allowed to stand even though all the states did not participate. Their claimed precedent was a reach back to the second term election of Abraham Lincoln, citing the fact that eleven confederate sates did not participate, yet the country had no problem electing Lincoln over George McClellan.

The Republicans were seeing it much differently. Having selected one of Harvard's most prominent historians and a constitutional lawyer, they argued first that the Twelfth Amendment that set up the Electoral

College contemplated all states participating. Second, they claimed that the Civil War election analogy did not apply because the election of 1864 was not even close. Lincoln received 212 votes, and McClellan only 21. So, there was hardly anything to fight over. Even more compelling was the argument that Georgia, unlike the southern states during the Civil War, was not a state in secession, and its citizens should not be disenfranchised by a court system freezing its ability to select electors. Restraining orders, quick to be issued but slow to be resolved, were now in place. By December 18, the courts were only beginning to sift through the dozens of orders entered by state and federal courts regarding every aspect of the election.

Favoring the judicial logjam, the Democrats responded with the argument that the time to vote had come and gone, and that it only made sense that the majority winner of the electoral vote, Charlotte Reid, should be declared the winner. If the Court was unwilling to apply this straightforward approach, certifying electors in Georgia and holding a second electoral vote would be the next best option. Surely the Democrats could secure at least three electors to win. With the Supreme Court scheduled to hear arguments on the ultimate issue in early January, Robert realized that the Houston camp was likely anxious that Ramona McCall could end the whole matter long before it reached the House of Representatives.

Why Congressman Ormond? Robert continued to dig. Ormond was from Mississippi, a Republican state with staunchly Democrat roots. He had originally been a Democrat but switched parties during the Reagan years. Robert pulled up an article that traced the balance of power between the two parties in the House and Senate. It pointed out that for the first time in the history of the country, the house was so evenly split that it might be impossible for the House to pick a President despite the language of the Twelfth Amendment. Simply put, if each state had a vote, it could result in a 25/25 tie. Since the District of Columbia did not have a vote in the House, as it did in the Electoral College, the deadlock would persist. The article noted that if this occurred and there was no resolution by Inauguration Day on January 20, the Constitution allowed the Senate to elect one of its own—either Thomas Rosenblat or Talmadge Smith—as Vice President. This individual could then preside over the country as commander-in-chief in the absence of a President, effectively leaving both Reid and Houston out of the running altogether.

SPLIT DOWN THE MIDDLE

Robert then looked carefully at the political equation in the State of Mississippi. The state was split right down the middle—two congressmen and two senators from each party. It was still not clear how it would help the Democrats if Ormond was gone. He was tired, but working through the night, putting all nightmares on hold. That's how he liked it, so when he finally laid his head on the pillow, he would not be thinking and would be unconscious within thirty seconds.

Robert left the computer and went to bed. He switched out the light, hoping to think about Cindy, but just could not get Ormond out of his mind. Why Ormond? He looked at the ceiling, then focused on the small Christmas tree in the corner, and then turned on his side and tried to sleep.

Suddenly, Robert's heart began to race. He switched on the light, returned to the computer, and went back to the Mississippi site. It took less than a minute to find the answer to what happens if a sitting Congressman or Senator dies in office: the Governor appoints someone to fill out the term of the deceased politician. In the state of Mississippi, the Governor had even appointed himself to fill the Senate seat on several occasions. Would a Governor appoint himself to a mere congressional seat?

He then scrolled through more information on the state's official site. There it was, the Governor of the state was a Democrat. Searching even closer he found that the Governor was no average Democrat. He had served as chairperson of the Reid for President Committee since its inception some three years earlier. The Governor of Mississippi was a Charlotte Reid insider. If anyone could deliver a state from the Republican column to the Democrats, it was him. All he needed was for Maxmillian Ormond to be dead. Now, it all made sense. With Republican Ormond out, the House vote would swing 26 to 24 in favor of Reid.

As he returned to the ritual of turning out the light and trying to sleep, Robert became increasingly aware that choosing the most powerful person on earth might ultimately be up to him.

Could it really be the Department of Defense standing behind Houston and the CIA backing Reid? Had the country truly come down to something so cut and dried—a sort of dictatorship of the agencies?

It caused him to wonder how often in the past the military or the CIA may have stepped in to make the rules of the election game. Now, in a close election, it wasn't just the clash of ideas that put the democracy at risk, but very possibly a quiet, deadly war between two departments of government.

Robert finally quit the political speculation in favor of his own deeper worries. Time and time again, the darkness of the night closed around him as if his victims were collectively wrapping him up in thick black sheets. As evil as he had rationalized them to be, he knew he was much worse.

Robert would run through the list of his life's events time and time again. Uncertain how he had reached this point in his miserable life, he would ask himself every probing question about the past. He had not sufficiently worn himself out on his effort to dissect the election. Now he would pay the price. Surely it was time, Robert reasoned, to bring someone else in—someone who might understand. He began staging a Christmas Day talk with Landon Cramer in his mind. It would be hard and painful—hardly a subject of good cheer for Landon—but it was necessary. If there was ever a chance for change, survival, or even some form of forgiveness that might lead to reconnecting with his children, it would need to begin with Landon Cramer.

Robert's mind slipped into a darker focus. He envisioned Veronica lying next to him in bed, reading her magazines. A warm memory surfaced: he had always kept her well-stocked with home and family-oriented magazines, their pages turning softly as he drifted off to sleep. For a long time, that had been enough for him; it was sometimes even a substitute for sexual intimacy. He missed her terribly.

Deep, throbbing mental pain accompanied him for another hour of wakefulness, and the memories of his murderous missions on behalf of the government became vividly clear again. Each time, a new nightmare would stage its premier in his mind—an event he hoped to avoid by shutting his eyes, but then the re-run of the bloody hands would emerge, more strong and powerful than before.

Yet, amidst it all, something was starting to stir within, powerful enough to sometimes dull the sensations of torment and despair. Cindy! The name dislodged a thought, that somewhere, deep in the stone-cold emptiness of life, a hope or a dream might remain alive. While fighting for his last breath of air, a last extra second of life, Robert found himself thinking that maybe Cindy could give him both.

13

Arriving at work on time was typically a chore for each of the three name partners at the law firm of Fischer, Cramer & Morrell. It was the Christmas season, and these were family men. Their legal practice had always been a means to an end: to care for a diverse array of corporate and business clients for many years. Honest and straightforward, each of the three had served the community well. A finer firm would have been hard to find in Washington, D.C., or anywhere else.

Above all, their greatest accomplishment lay in the sanguine image of family and community they projected, which made each man mean so much to so many. Their influence extended beyond their families and the northern Virginia suburbs; they were also active in a variety of national and charitable cultural endeavors.

Landon Cramer had served for many years as a member of the National Council for the Boy Scouts. With the organizational skills of a field marshal, he had specialized in bringing back to life failing scouting programs across the country. His personal style was warm and friendly with an incredible aptitude to never forget a name, face or a positive experience as well. As a result, everyone he interacted with considered Landon to be a close friend. This trait greatly aided in fundraising efforts. Many recognized his potential and encouraged him to pursue a career in politics, but Landon viewed politics as corrupt and self-serving. His focus was on uplifting those around him, showing little concern for his own welfare. It was a trait with a well-formed result. Thousands of boys, especially underprivileged Boy Scouts, made the trip every summer into the Shenandoah Valley or into the forests of northern Maryland because of Landon. He was a paragon of power with a very humble touch.

Stanley Fischer, along with his children, organized a crusade against hunger at their church. The program gained traction throughout the D.C. area and was successfully replicated by community food banks in Baltimore and Philadelphia. Each Christmas became extra special because of Stanley Fischer's initiative. Although the program intensified during the holiday season, it operated year-round.

It all began on Christmas Eve when the Fischer children were young. To teach them the true meaning of the holidays, Stan and his wife arranged for the family to volunteer at a Salvation Army soup kitchen in a rundown part of northeast D.C. The experience went well, and when their oldest son turned fourteen and needed a community service project to qualify for the Eagle Scout award, he created his own plan to help the needy.

Working out of the back of the family van, he and his fellow scouts canvassed the inner-city freeway underpass and bridge areas for street people to deliver to them warm chicken soup and hot chocolate. It soon evolved into blankets and thereafter to a database of scouts and other teenage boys and girls ready to help in places where the need was the greatest.

Stanley and his family were members of the Mormon Church. By the time his son left for his church mission in Italy, the two of them had formed an organization that was far more than the mere scouting project of its original intent. The program had been studied and replicated in downtown areas of several major cities, exemplifying how the lawyers at the firm and their extraordinary families had positively impacted many lives.

Kevin Morrell, the youngest member of the firm, was a lawyer of a different sort. His daytime job in a lobbying practice for businesses in the western United States often took a backseat to his night job as a violinist with the Washington Philharmonic Orchestra. He was the only member of the orchestra to effectively have another full-time job. It was not uncommon for him to leave the law firm by noon, perform a matinee with the Philharmonic, and return to the office by 7:00 p.m. to work what he called "The Night Shift."

REMNANTS OF THE PAST

His talent had not fallen far from the tree as each of his three daughters had become so proficient at the cello, violin and harp that they were already, despite their tender ages, veritable shoe-ins for Julliard.

For the three lawyers, the work in the law practice, like any other, was long and hard, requiring early mornings and late evenings. The commitment to so many other aspects of life had established a local quality in the law firm, which did not go unnoticed by many clients and business associates. The law firm of Fischer, Cramer & Morrell, though small by Washington standards, made a significant contribution to the community. During the Christmas holidays, each child sought ways to share their best wishes with the staff, including the quiet, peculiar man who worked in their father's firm.

Their efforts had not been entirely unsuccessful. Robert had overcome his aversion to sentiment enough to stack the presents, cards and mementos in a corner of his reading room, allowing the items to form the triangle of a Christmas tree. Seven years' worth of Christmas gifts, less the perishables he had eaten or thrown away, gave a certain joy to his living room, whether he liked it or not. The fact that he had kept the cards and gifts around for most of the year was largely lost on him. No one visited his Georgetown townhouse, so it was not an issue to leave them out beyond their time. However, another reason remained. Often at night, he would look at the cards, the crayon pictures from the youngest children. In moments of indefinable melancholy, they brought him closer to a part of his life, long lost, yet still, at times, so near. He found himself wishing that he had even one such thing from his own children. How often his daughter or son had climbed on his lap and shown him a paper from pre-school or just a watercolor project having been done at the kitchen table with mom. Even one such paper, old, torn, wrinkled or faded, would be fine.

* * *

Blurry eyed and awakened to the sound of tires crunching new fallen snow on an old street, Robert focused first on his Christmas corner. For a moment, as so often in the past, he had to think for a few seconds, clear his head and determine exactly where he was. But as he remembered he was at home in his own bed, his vision cleared. Most prominent was a card from one of the Cramer children. Then, he noticed something he hadn't seen before—a card from several Christmases earlier with the name "Bob" on the front. Nobody had called him "Bob" since his early years, except for Cindy, who gave the name a pleasant ring. Now—he could see the word "Bob" written in red crayon across the top of a Christmas card from "Rachael."

"Age 5" was proudly scribbled in another color of crayon across the bottom of the card. That must be Kevin Morrell's daughter, one of the violinists, he thought to himself as he tried to remember how old she might be now—probably eight and no longer thinking of me as "Bob." The pleasantness of the card pelted his heart with needed warmth.

Robert looked at his watch: December 23rd, the day before Christmas Eve. As he got out of bed, a sensation stirred within him—a blend of what he wished to call the Christmas spirit and a tender remembrance of his previous evening spent talking to and gazing at Cindy. He lay there for a moment, trying to recapture those feelings, as if he had just awakened from a dream he was reluctant to forget. The warmth of their conversation lingered in his mind, filling him with a bittersweet nostalgia that seemed to intertwine with the holiday season.

A few minutes later, as Robert fixed his usual breakfast of oatmeal and yogurt, he realized that despite the late night, he had slept deeper and better than he could remember. Most of all, he could not dislodge the pleasant feeling. It was new, profound and real. The more he thought about it, the more it caused him to formulate a plan—something he couldn't believe he was going to do. When he left for work, if he still had the courage, he would try putting his plan to work.

Over the next few minutes, rather than following his usual routine of turning on the TV to track world events, Robert concentrated on his own world. It felt strange to find himself humming an old Dean Martin Christmas song as he climbed into the shower. By the time he stepped out of his townhouse, he had resolved to take a different route to work.

EMBERS OF RESOLVE

Despite the snow and cold, which would typically make the day feel miserable, Robert headed toward the shops along M Street. The festive atmosphere, close to Christmas, prompted a few stores to open early. Within minutes, he was the second customer of the day at Barnes & Noble, specifically drawn to the New Age section, where he browsed for books on angels.

After considerable browsing, an endcap filled with a variety of gift items caught Robert's eye. Among them was a candle adorned with a small metal angel affixed to its side. A sense of purpose washed over him as he made the purchase, envisioning the special recipient in mind. But he wasn't finished just yet; he felt compelled to seek out something more.

As he wandered through the aisles, he pondered the significance of angels and the comfort they might bring to someone feeling lost. He continued searching, feeling a sense of determination to find the perfect gift that would resonate with hope and light.

He spent the next hour wandering through the toy store in the

Georgetown Mall buying toys—hoping he could amass enough playthings for all the younger children of the staff and lawyers at the Fischer, Cramer & Morrell law firm.

Wandering down M street from store to store, hauling three large bags, Robert was momentarily a different man. The snow was still being flung wildly around the street and against the cold buildings by a stiff twenty mile per hour wind blowing both debris and pedestrians alike. It was the kind of breeze that knifed lungs and made bare skin numb. It was the sort of day that would have normally imprisoned his spirit and condemned him to a stolid state of depression. There was at best, an antagonized sun, intermittently elbowing clouds aside to allow a brief appearance. Unexpectedly, another spirit had intervened, the spirit of the season. It had a grip on him like never in his memory.

As Robert walked from the shopping area toward the law firm, his gait was decidedly joyful, a smile lighting up his face. No one would have suspected that he was the mysterious operative known as "Lever," a legend within the intelligence services' lore across the globe. Today, he could easily have passed for a blissful and carefree grandfather on a final shopping spree before his grandchildren arrived from over the river and through the woods. Suddenly, life felt different.

"Hi!" came his favorite word as he entered the law firm. Cindy looked more beautiful to him than ever.

"Merry Christmas!" Robert stumbled over the words, as if they were fresh out of a foreign language dictionary. He noticed her gaze shift to the shopping bags he was carrying. "I've got a few things for people here," he declared, trying to sound casual.

Cindy wheeled around the receptionist counter, her eyes wide with surprise and delight as he set the bags down on a chair in the waiting area. "My goodness, what have you done, Bob?" she exclaimed, her smile infectious.

Robert couldn't help but chuckle at her enthusiasm. "Just spreading a little holiday cheer," he replied, feeling a warmth spread through him. Each gift represented not just a physical item, but a piece of his heart he was sharing with those around him. Cindy leaned closer to one of the bags, peering in with curiosity. "I hope you didn't go overboard. You know how we like to keep things simple around here," she teased, her eyes sparkling.

"Simple is overrated," he countered playfully. "Besides, this year feels different. I wanted to do something special."

She straightened up, regarding him with a mix of admiration and concern. "Well, whatever it is, it's nice to see you in such good spirits. You seem… lighter somehow."

Robert felt a flutter of warmth at her words, realizing just how much he needed this connection. "Thanks, Cindy. It's the season, I guess. Or maybe it's just the company."

Cindy laughed softly, and for a moment, Robert allowed himself to savor the moment—a fleeting glimpse of joy amidst the weight of his secret life. He could almost believe that everything was normal, even if just for today.

"Well, you know, 'tis the season." Robert started to pull a doll out of a bag. "These are for the kids; you know the children of the lawyers. They always remember me."

"You too, huh? That's right, you saw all the presents they gave me at the house. Well, we need to wrap this, don't we?" Cindy asked.

Strangely, the concept of wrapping gifts had not even occurred to Robert. As soon as she suggested, it was automatically a good idea. "I didn't bring any wrapping paper," he responded.

"Let's throw it in your office and…," Cindy thought for a moment, "We can send the runner out to get wrapping paper as soon as he gets here. I'm sure he'll do it for this. This is going to be fun!"

"Yeah, I think so." Robert responded. This was different...very different, he thought.

"Well Bob, let's put all this in your office and out of sight. You don't want any of the lawyers knowing what you're up to—that is, until it's all wrapped."

Robert agreed and, picking up two of the bags with Cindy carrying a third on her lap, they together went from the lobby down the hall and into Robert's office, where the sacks were stashed in the corner until the wrapping paper arrived.

* * *

BALI NIGHTS

It was mid-morning, and the Washington Post headlines had already been in the blogposts and newsstands for six hours. **"REID DENIES CHINA CONNECTION,"** were the words spread across the front of the newspaper in 40-point type. The story was tough and to the point. It linked several U.S./Asian import companies on the West Coast, whose subsidiaries and thousands of employees heavily contributed to the Reid campaign, to a Southeast Asian opium trafficker. To make matters worse, it centered on a Bali trip shortly after the Minton election victory, where Charlotte Reid had gone to great lengths to entertain a group of Chinese billionaires. Her less-than-vice-presidential decorum was now exposed in a spread of photographs featuring Charlotte in a hot tub with what appeared to be a group of naked capitalists from the communist state.

Reid was not imbued with the holiday spirit as she slammed the newspaper down on the desk in the study of Bill's mansion. She pointed her finger at Bentley Wilcox, and declared in no uncertain terms, "I thought you had this buried! They are acting like we are still in the middle of a campaign. You're trouble, Bentley! Just like you were back in college, and you are one now too! Nothing's changed!"

Bentley Wilcox' retaliation was quick. "I don't know where you were in November. If I recall, the election didn't get over on that day." His voice was stiff and irritable. "If you hadn't thought it was cute to fill the party war chest with Chinese dollars three years ago, you wouldn't be in this fix today! Wasn't Bill's money enough? I told you not to do it, and you did anyway. Then…" his anger intensified, "You didn't just take their money; you even met with them—not just casually. Hell, you did everything short of sunbathing in the buff for the paparazzi while entertaining them at Bill's place in Bali. What did you expect? I'm just amazed it didn't come out before the election!"

"It was not like that, and you know it Bentley! You said we had all the pictures." Charlotte's words bounced off the bookshelf covered walls of the soundproof room. "It was just good diplomacy."

Bentley interrupted. "Diplomacy my ass! You were suckin' up to foreign money because you hate every dollar that Bill puts behind you! No one can match him, and so the party has been dropping the ball on the fundraising. So, you think that if you can get your own big dollars without Bill, it'll salve your female ego…Well, it did just that. Your last quarterly report gave the RNC everything to howl about. I wonder how many votes that forty million really cost you."

His voice was stiff and irritable. "If you hadn't thought it was cute to fill the party war chest with Chinese dollars three years ago, you wouldn't be in this fix today! Wasn't Bill's money enough? I told you not to do it, and you did anyway. Then…" his anger intensified, "You didn't just take their money; you even met with them—not just casually. Hell, you did everything short of sunbathing in the buff for the paparazzi while entertaining them at Bill's place in Bali. What did you expect? I'm just amazed it didn't come out before the election!"

There was a pause as Charlotte reached for a drink. Then she asked with more reverence for her long-time partner, "Bentley, I've thought a lot about it. I still think I've got to go with the flip. This Chinese thing doesn't help me, not with Ramona McCall or the House. The way it's going this still might get to the Congress."

"Well," Bentley pulled her to him, "Trust me...just one more time. McCall will get it for us, and if she doesn't, and it goes to a vote in the House, we'll be ready to break that deadlock...you know we will. You can drag the coin flip idea around, but you'd be crazy to really do it." He smiled. She ignored his advice and asked nervously, "You think that old guy really is gonna be gone by then?"

"Oh yeah, the CIA has him in the bag. They've got the top man in the business on him." To her, Bentley was morbid and gross, but also clever. Charlotte couldn't help but love that sort of man. Since the beginning of the Minton administration, she had been the go-between on intelligence matters. President Minton wanted nothing to do with them. With Bentley working closely with the Agency as well, there was a level of security that allowed her to feel assured she would win in the end. At the same time, she doubted whether the CIA was as aligned with her as Bentley made it sound. Vice President Reid had never thought the whole campaign funding process through. But the frolic on the beach in Bali had certainly attracted the Chinese. They loved her, and she knew it. What she knew even better was that she had her hand on the floodgate of soft money dollars surreptitiously pouring into PAC coffers from companies around the world, which spoke much louder than votes.

"You don't seriously think that even the CIA can track this thing back to you and me?" Charlotte asked.

"Maybe," Bentley responded.

"But it all seems too easy. There's got to be a hitch."

"Just self-interest, my dear. The CIA is protecting you because of the intelligence that they have on the military. It'll show that merging the intelligence services, especially the military with the CIA, was a bad idea. That's the CIA's big deal. The Agency could really care less if you don't protect Taiwan. They've got themselves to protect politically. That was dumb to take the Chinese money, but everybody knows it bought something.

"Having one old fart finished off who has already seen his day is a mere walk in the park for those people. So, I wouldn't get all lathered up and plus, if it's any consolation to you, it ends with me. I mean, I go down for you...I arranged the money...even though you know I didn't...I go to prison and the works. That's just the way it would have to be if anything ever came unglued here. I guess that's the way it was back at Harvard. Why should it be any different now?" Bentley smiled. Charlotte leaned across the table, grabbed him by the lapels of his suit, pulled him up, and kissed him powerfully on the mouth, kissing hard for at least ten seconds to make her point. When she pulled back, his face was covered with lipstick.

"I'd get that mouth fixed, at least before you walk out of here. It looks like it has blood all over it." Charlotte walked to the door and paused, looking back at Bentley, who seemed to bask in the warmth of her apparent confidence like a teenager after a sexual conquest. She was bothered by what she saw and decided to pop his bubble. "If Houston accepts the flip, I'm going to do it. So, if you've got something to do, you'd better do it quickly!" She left the room, leaving Bentley alone in her office.

14

It was around 2:00 p.m. when the runner returned from a mail run, having made a detour to the store to purchase several rolls of holiday wrapping paper. Robert had not taken lunch because of his late arrival at work. Cindy reciprocated by skipping eating in favor of teaching Robert how to wrap presents quickly, while making them look nice as well. Before the hour ended, they were shuffling through the last bag, staring at the twenty some presents that Robert had picked up in his whirlwind shopping spree between 9:00 a.m. and 11:00 a.m.

"What's this?" Cindy asked, holding up the Angel Candle she had found at the bottom of the sack. "Who does this go to?"

Robert was nervous. "That's for you." He worked up a half smile but was unwilling to make eye contact.

"Oh, look this is an Angel, isn't it Bob?" she asked, as her fingers delicately touched the soft metal charm.

"Yeah, I think that's what it is."

"So, are you my Guardian Angel?" Cindy asked, tilting her head to increase the moment's intensity, as if she wanted an immediate answer.

In his heart, Robert wanted to say there was nothing more he would rather be. Instead, he tempered his deeper thoughts and replied, "Well, I guess I could be...sometimes." Their eyes met for only a second before he looked away, while she continued to gaze at him.

"Well, sometimes is good." Cindy broke the seriousness with a laugh. "I'll take sometimes because...sometimes that's all there is in life...sometimes...hmm." Her profound philosophy lightened the tone, allowing Robert to escape the weight of intense feelings.

"I think you're right, I really do," he replied.

"So, once we get all of this done, what are we gonna do?" she asked.

Robert floundered for a moment. "Do you think you could get a hold of the keys to their cars?" he asked. "The lawyers park over in the parking terrace at the Georgetown Suites Hotel, don't they?" he asked.

"Yep, I'm sure they do."

"The parking lot attendant keeps the keys."

A Cottage by the Sea

Cindy found herself juggling the tasks of answering phone calls and assisting Robert with finalizing the tags on the packages. Then, she put her charm and persuasiveness to work over the phone, causing the parking staff at the hotel to join in the Christmas cause, with one last sorting of the presents for Robert, along with helping him understand the description of the cars. They piled the gifts on Cindy's lap, and Robert pushed her chair to the elevator. Minutes later, they reached street level, crossing the circular courtyard to the parking terrace below the Georgetown Suites Hotel. In the dark caverns of the third level down, they identified the cars and loaded the gifts into each.

The whole event had taken longer than Robert had anticipated—the better part of the afternoon. For once, it truly felt like Christmas to him; no one was keeping track. It felt like an invitation to share happiness as they giggled, joked, and had fun.

As they returned, walking in the door to the lobby, with Cindy preparing to take the fall for the rest of the staff for missing calls, Robert had one more question to ask. It was one he had thought about, wanted to ask, but was fearful. Still, he tried it. "Are you planning on going down to Charlottesville for Christmas Eve?"

Cindy nodded playfully. "Yeah. That is...unless you got something better in mind?"

Is she serious or just playing with me? Robert thought. He decided to take a chance and find out. "I've got this place over on the south Jersey coast, just down from the lighthouse at Cape May." He started to perspire, feeling tongue-tied and struggling to get the words out. "What I mean is, it's a cottage on the ocean..."

Cindy interrupted, "Of course I would like to spend Christmas with you. Do you think I'm nuts?" She was suddenly exuberant-looking at him with a piercing examination.

"Nuts? What do you mean nuts?" He was perplexed, wondering if he had offended her or if perhaps, his premonition of where he was with her was way off base.

"I'd be nuts not to go, Bob. I'd be really nuts."

Robert was surprised and even thrilled by his accomplishment. He was right where he wanted to be with her. It caused a strange, cold excitement, melting of the heart. Rather than allow the moment to carry into anything awkward, Robert retreated to his office and tried to get back to such work that could be done in the few hours remaining in the day.

By evening, the euphoria began to fade. The excitement surrounding Cindy had temporarily made him forget about the Christmas invitation from Landon Cramer. It would be such an opportune moment, he reasoned. Cramer was pleasant at work, and always very busy. There would be no opportunity here, especially with the end of year rush on legal work. If there ever was the right moment, it would be at Landon's home. "Was it another opportunity lost in favor of time with a woman?" he thought to himself. "Seems like I've done this before." Robert walked out of the office and down the hall to the reception area with the intention of attempting to withdraw the offer of the Cape May trip, but Cindy was already finished for the day and had left the office.

* * *

"Where in the hell did they get a hold of him?" David Houston yelled as he paced the floor in his home in Oklahoma City. He was gesticulating wildly while talking on the phone to Talmadge Smith in Boston.

"What do you mean by 'him,' do you know this guy?" The deep measured voice of the Senator boomed across the telephone. "You've denied ever since they first raised the issue that you had anything to do with that knife incident. I have always believed you on that, Governor," Smith continued.

"Now Talmadge, don't you think that if this guy had any credibility at all, they would have had him on every talk show in October? It seems like they had everybody else, so why not him?"

SOME TYPE OF GAME

The Governor rolled out his Oklahoma drawl, furious. "I don't know about that," Smith responded, "but it just came out in what looks like a copyrighted story in the *Boston Globe*."

Let me read you this: *"Walker Williams, a one-time quarterback for the University of Texas, says that while working as a bouncer at a nightclub known as the North Dallas Sweethearts, he was given $8,000, to pick a fight with Rashad Watson, the then quarterback of the Dallas Cowboys. He said no one ever told him why he was to pick the fight, but he was told to do whatever was necessary to put Watson out of commission so he would at least be finished with football for the season.*

Williams claims that he then approached Watson a few times during the evening while he was at the bar with his girlfriend. After he bought Watson several drinks, Watson left the bar with his girlfriend and Williams engaged him in a discussion in which he, Williams, told Watson that he had been spending time with Watson's girlfriend. Watson jumped back out of a limo and grabbed Williams. Williams defended himself by plunging a knife into Watson's thigh. According to Williams, the only reason he picked the fight was to get the remaining $4,000 of the $8,000 that was promised. He claims that a man, who said he was a private investigator and had given him the first $4,000 in cash, was waiting in a car two blocks from the bar to pay him the remaining $4,000 as promised. It was his understanding that the man was a private investigator. That is, until he saw pictures of Jerry Starkweather, the newly appointed Press Secretary for former Oklahoma Governor and Republican Presidential Candidate David Houston. Starkweather has been contacted for comment, but at press time has refused to comment.

Bentley Wilcox, Chief Strategist for Vice President Reid, speaking for the Reid campaign, commented, "This is an unfortunate disclosure for Governor Houston. However, we are not surprised as we have always maintained through the course of the campaign and even now, as the election is being determined, that there are many reasons why the Governor should not be President, and this is one of them."

"So, this is what's circling the country on Christmas Eve, Governor Houston?" Smith's voice grew increasingly irritated. He was not one to use expletives. "What I want to know is what's really happening. Is there any truth to this?"

"There is none!" Houston shouted into the phone. "None!"

Senator Smith paused, trying to gather his angered thoughts. "Let me tell you this, David, there had better not be! Because I have listened to all the trash through the campaign and figured, it would be over now. "Here we are at Christmas, and it just keeps on coming! I've served in the Senate for seven years, and it seems like I've always been able to avoid these kinds of problems. They have never been on my radar screen. Yet, since I accepted this appointment as your running mate, I keep hearing my name getting tagged more and more with things that neither my wife, my children, nor my grandchildren would appreciate or could even relate to!"

"Well, blame that on the DNC," Houston interrupted.

"No, you don't get it!" Smith had cornered the presidential candidate and was not going to let up. "You think this is just some type of game...a game without any rules...a game where whoever can hit the hardest somehow will end up scoring the most points. It's not! It's messing up this country worse than anything that I have ever seen or heard of. The fact that the Democrats would even raise this sort of allegation against you is bad enough. The mere thought that it might be true absolutely turns my stomach and makes me believe you're no different from Charlotte Reid!

"What the hell makes you think you can talk to me like that? You want off this ticket?" Houston yelled into the phone, as Sam Rusk walked into the den, wondering what the commotion was all about.

"That may not be such a bad idea. I've got to make this decision anyway within the next short while because the Governor of Massachusetts is wondering whom she should appoint to my seat. At this point, I'm not sure that I want to lose it."

"Well, you think long and hard about this Senator." Houston was trying to sound tough and in command.

Smith uncharacteristically interrupted and shot back. "There's nothing for me to do that requires long and hard thinking where the Vice Presidency is concerned! You know as well as I do that if I decide to opt out of this coalition, you're finished...absolutely finished. The House may very well choose not to vote for you. Even if it does, there's a good chance the Senate will vote for Rosenblat as vice president, which would be fine with me. I wouldn't be surprised if the courts turned you out before you ever get to the Congress. At this point, most of your credibility comes just from being seen with me... and you know it! The decision is mine, not yours! If you think it's yours, you just take your best shot, stand back, and watch your world melt like ice cream in a microwave! My reason for hanging in there for you is not out of any respect or loyalty. It's because I think there is still some good that can be done for this country! And my worries about the future of Taiwan if Reid gets in. But whether it will come about because of you being President is, in my mind, a major question!"

Smith's words were so loud, that Sam Rusk, sitting in an overstuffed office chair several feet away from Governor Houston, could hear every word. "Whew...wee!" Rusk waved his hand in the air as if trying to cool down burning fingers. "He's really fired up tonight, isn't he?"

Houston was watching Sam and trying to respond to Smith at the same time. He could see that he was effectively pinned down by the Senator's highly effective verbal gunfire. "Well, I think this conversation needs to end! It's not leading anywhere but to..."

"To a lot of shame, disappointment, and dishonor if things don't straighten up!" Smith interrupted, "Both in your camp and in Reid's!"

Houston presumed that Smith and Rosenblat had been talking to each other on the side. He knew they were both cut from the same stone—decent, good and well-respected men. At times, he wished he could be like them but had his doubts about his ability to rehabilitate himself from the demeaning reckless combat of the political campaign. Even being presidential for the next four to eight years might not erase the memories of this campaign. "I'll see what I can do, Senator," he said in a mildly dutiful response that sounded like a surrender. "I'll talk to you tomorrow."

"Merry Christmas in spite of it all!" Smith offered these last words in conciliation before hanging up.

Houston threw his phone onto the nearest couch and walked to the window, looking pensively out into the hazy late afternoon Oklahoma sky. It was just beginning to get dark, and he had family things to do. He had been ignoring his children in favor of politics for months and thought maybe Christmas Eve would be a chance to make up for lost time.

He did not want to discuss his being taken behind the barn and horseshedded by Senator Smith with Rusk—or anyone. Just outside the window of his den, walking along the patio, was Cedric Martin from the U.S. Army's Executive Protection Unit. More than once, Houston had wondered who made the decision to bring in the Army and replace the Secret Service.

. He knew the Secret Service was out there somewhere, but no longer noticeable among the inner ring of protection. It was time to move to another subject. "So, when was it, Sam, that the Army started protecting me? Wasn't it around the first of the month?" he asked.

"I remember exactly when it was," Rusk responded with certainty, "It was when you gave that Veteran's Day speech just about ten days after the election."

"I thought it was later, about the first of December or so." he remarked. "That's when Colonel Martin and his troops showed up. It seems like things changed by the end of that day that you declared that you would cancel the Executive Order on the permanent job status of the CIA Director...and threw in the stuff about putting the Pentagon in charge of all intelligence. We just didn't tell you they were there."

Houston continued looking out the window wondering why they hadn't told him. He then moved to a different thought. He turned to Rusk and said, "Call Bentley Wilcox and tell him I'll accept the deal. I know we didn't close it by Christmas, but New Year's will do." At the game on the 7th, we'll flip the coin."

Rusk was mildly stunned. "Are you sure you want to do this David? I mean be the 50/50 President?"

"Yeah, I'm sure I want to do it."

Rusk continued to protest. "You can win. You've got a lot of things going for you."

Houston interrupted, "Like what? Like Starkweather, paying that punk to knife Rashad Watson? Like I'll do okay in the House if we can get past Justice McCall? She's not going to do us any good. McCall could blow us out. I know a Republican President appointed her. But she is no Republican and is no friend of mine!"

"And that's why you've got to be careful." Rusk cautioned in agreement.

"I do need to remember a few things." Houston had been admittedly humbled by the exchange with the Senator, "Remember what Talmadge Smith just said. There are many screw-ups around here. Moreover, maybe he's right. Maybe I'm one of them. Maybe it wouldn't hurt to get historic and turn this whole election thing into some big fundraiser for charity and have everybody walk away feeling good when it's over...Is that impossible? Am I just dreaming?"

"Yeah, Governor, you are just dreaming." Rusk was hardened, "There's too much money, too much influence, and too much power behind this whole thing. You can't just turn it into some glorified United Way drive. Your chances are much better than 50%. Plus," he paused.

"Plus, what?"

"Uh," Rusk paused as if he was going to say something important, but then went another direction, "You're gonna win this one, David!" He sounded trite, like an Evangelist. "I know it deep within that this one has your name on it. Just take my word for it. You can't get weak now! You can't show any weakness! Most of all, you can't let the other side know that you are weakening. They're watching you close... Everybody's watching you. At the end of the day, Congress and the courts are just people too." I would advise, Governor, that you pass on this deal."

"No, I'm not so sure I am going to pass," Houston continued, mildly struggling with what he perceived as mixed signals from Rusk. "I think it's better odds than your optimism. When I trust guys like you, I end up in a tie! Well, screw that."

"Governor, let me warn you!" Rusk's words were penetrating, "This whole thing is a ploy. You know what kind of cheap shot artist Charlotte Reid is. She already put President Minton out to pasture. She just took a page out of Flossie Harding's book of tricks and found a way to poison a President. It happened to Warren G. Harding back in the '20s, and it has happened again. Do you really think she is going to now flip for it with you? Do you think that it's anyone other than Bentley Wilcox that uncovered that Williams story? She just wants to get under your skin... she wants you to commit! However, she'll never go through with it!

Houston was silent. He was looking out the window again and after a long pause, he turned around, shook his head and said, "I don't know, I guess I'll sleep on it."

With that concession, Rusk quickly exited the room. He was irritated by the whole event. It seemed like there was always a big problem whenever Talmadge Smith showed up to infect politics with the fever of conscience.

15

About 920 nautical miles northeast of Oklahoma City, the winter storms from earlier in the week had blown out to sea and the weather had taken an unseasonably warm turn. The couple pulled up in a rented van to the seaside cottage, hidden amidst the dark, largely leafless coastal overgrowth. Robert Cannon and Cindy Wilstead had arrived at the seldom-used Cannon family summer home, located about a mile north of the Cape May lighthouse on the south Jersey shore where the Delaware River wide opens and flows into the Atlantic. It had been a comfortable drive. After crossing the bridge at Wilmington, Delaware, Cindy had reached over and nestled her hand into Robert's, holding it firmly until they reached the town of Cape May an hour and a half later when he needed to drive with both hands. Cape May was a quiet town on Christmas Eve. It was a good place for families to retreat for the calm of the special season.

For Robert, however, the home had enjoyed very little activity for many years. There had been no Cannon family event at the home since the day his wife left to board the airplane for her last and fatal flight. After a few meager attempts at putting it in a rental pool, he had simply winterized it each year and let it sit. For almost eleven years, a caretaker and handyman in Cape May had looked after the home and kept it in the best possible condition.

The handicapped van from Avis Rentals was very convenient. It allowed Cindy to bring her regular wheelchair, which she preferred inside the home, and a motorized wheelchair for moving across paved surfaces outdoors at a reasonable speed. She needed both during this trip.

LIFE ON EMPTY

After pulling into the driveway and entering the house to ensure the caretaker had turned on the heat earlier as requested, Robert returned to the van. As he walked around to the passenger side, Cindy shifted to the edge of her seat, threw her arms around Robert's neck, and pulled herself into his embrace. Her move was consistent with the aggressive style that Robert appreciated. The full form of her body curled up against him as he carried her into the house and gently sat her down on the sofa. The absence of leg strength made her cling to him very tightly. He liked that. She thanked him and then he returned to empty the van of its supplies and get things set up for a winter's night in Cape May.

Once situated in her wheelchair, Cindy began exploring the ground floor of the old beach house. She moved from one empty dresser to another, examining the early-American furniture and the faded black-and-white photographs hanging on the worn dark burgundy wallpaper and redwood beams. "So, who are all of these people?" she asked, taking in the musty atmosphere that felt like a museum barely surviving the deterioration of the coastal climate.

"A lot of them are people I don't know, but I guess if you want to see my wife, Veronica, that's her." He pointed to an oval picture in a frame on a wall with a beautiful dark-eyed woman in a crisp, white lace, almost Victorian- style dress with a high pearl-lined neck, puffy sleeves and white dressy boots. The face that peered out in an almost haunting eternal gaze was neither a smile nor a frown—a sort of modern Mona Lisa. On either side of her were two small children, a boy and a girl, both under five years of age, in a neutral pose.

"And when was this taken?"

"Oh, that was over thirty years ago. That's when the kids were young, and life was really pretty simple." Robert spoke, trying not to allow his voice to reveal that he was forcing an answer.

Cindy could see that it was not time to talk about sensitive things, so she wheeled to the kitchen in search of a corkscrew for the wine bottle.

Robert made his way briskly up the stairs and returned in less than a minute with some blankets, hoping they would be enough to cover the rollaway bed in the living room. The main sleeping quarters were upstairs, but he assumed that Cindy would prefer sleeping downstairs where she could be close to her wheelchair.

Over the next hour, the mood improved as they joined forces to create the perfect meal. With all the groceries in place and both of them hard at work, the outcome was still Italian—lasagna and wine. As they cooked dinner, there seemed to be little discussion, as each sensed the other's unspoken requests. It felt natural. As they finally began to eat, conversation flowed between them. With Robert's past still too sensitive to discuss, they shifted the topic to the lawyers—Fischer, Cramer, and Morrell. It was the one thing they had in common.

Robert had known the three lawyers for many years and spoke with admiration of his past with them. In response Cindy asked question after question. She seemed amazed by the incredible detail with which Robert described each person. As he continued, she could see that he was opening up. Robert described them as the finest men that he had ever known, spending considerable time relating stories about the kindness extended to him by the children. He explained how he especially looked forward to the visits by the children, which turned the stodgy law office into a lively place.

"What about the children?" Cindy wanted to get back to the subject Robert might now, on a full stomach, be willing to talk about.

"Which children?" Robert asked.

"I mean your children in that picture. They are adorable, Bob. They really are. Why aren't they in your life now?"

INEVITABILITY

Robert had so often tried to dodge this question. He knew that it would be futile to avoid Cindy's attempts to try and figure him out. He knew she wanted to get to know the real Robert Cannon, just as he yearned to understand the true Cindy Wilstead. This time, however, the truth would sting. He began, "When I got word of the plane crash, I didn't go home." He looked down as he spoke. "I simply got in my car and headed north. I was so emotionally ripped apart; I ran out of gas and found myself wandering along the New Jersey Turnpike to get some help... to get gas for my car. "I remember thinking that maybe it would bring me to my senses, and I could go back to Vienna and somehow take care of things. After all, I had two kids, and they didn't have a mother. But the depression, the pain, and the guilt were so overwhelming. I couldn't... I couldn't look into their eyes, or worse, have them look at me. It was killing me. It would have ended my ability to care for them in any way." He paused, his voice heavy. "At least I've provided for them financially."

"You mean you really have not seen them since way back then?" Cindy asked cautiously.

"That's kind of the way it is. My children are grown and have children of their own in high school. Other than sending money to a trust in Chicago, I have had no contact. I have not seen, nor spoken to, either my son or my daughter since three days before that plane went down."

"What about the funeral and those things?" Cindy asked.

"I didn't go," Robert blurted out, expressing something he had no other way to convey. Darkness pressed down on his words, heavy and suffocating. "After eating practically nothing for over ten days, I found myself in Montpelier, Vermont, sitting in a park, getting bothered by a cop who had accused me twice of being a vagrant. After I convinced him that my car was mine, he arrested me for public intoxication. "I really wasn't intoxicated, though I had been drinking a little. I was so out of it, emotionally, I barely knew who I was. They couldn't figure it out, so they put me in a sanitarium, and that's where I stayed for another month."

"What about your job? What happened to that?" Cindy asked gently, probing for the answers she needed without causing more pain.

"I was still working for the Agency." The memories were hard. "The Agency tracked me down. They knew where I was most of the time. "They awarded me a month of bereavement leave and actually considered it a positive thing that I was in a sanitarium. I think that's exactly what they wanted."

"What do you mean by that?" Cindy asked.

Robert was silent. He knew there were things he could never tell her, or that he had to at least try to withhold from her as long as he could. He continued cautiously, "By the time 1 came back, they thought I was in pretty good shape. They reassigned me to my job, and I just kept on working."

"Back to the kids, so...so, what about the kids?" Cindy asked.

"That's all there was about them. They were picked up by my wife's family and through a lawyer acquaintance at the Agency, I arranged to have a trust set up which has funded a good part of their lives ever since."

"So, what are they doing now?" Cindy followed up.

"I don't know exactly. All I know is that they are alive, that they both got through college, and that they are both married. My daughter lives near Chicago. I've gotten that from my sister who intentionally avoids talking very much about it. I think she knew a lot about me, at least enough to know that I was wacko enough that my ability to care for anyone, even myself at that time, was entirely questionable. "At least I've sent money… that's the most I could do. They were a part of her…" Robert pointed to Veronica's picture, his voice beginning to break. "They reminded me of her so much." I was…"

"Let's change the subject," Cindy interrupted in her normally assertive manner. "This is too serious for Christmas Eve. I think what you need is something positive, like having your palm read or maybe getting your fortune told. I've got cards in my purse." She spoke with positive energy, trying to move the discussion away from his past. "The future is a lot better than the past. Let's talk about those things."

Cindy laughed, her eyes sparkling with mischief. "No, of course not! But I had you going for a second, didn't I?" She pulled her blouse back up and winked. "I'm full of surprises, Robert. You'll just have to keep guessing." Robert chuckled, relieved by the sudden shift in tone. "Well, I wouldn't put anything past you at this point."

"You'd be surprised what I can do," Cindy teased, still smiling but with a hint of mystery in her eyes.

"Well, of course there is, you silly man." Cindy was starting to tease. "According to the Americans for Disabilities Act, every stripper's stage must have wheelchair access and that's so people like me who are attractive enough to express ourselves in the same way as those G-string babes. They got legs. We got beauty!"

Robert was starting to laugh, he played along. "So, what does a guy have to do to get you to strip?"

"Oh, that's easy. All he's got to do is take his pants off and he'd be totally amazed at what happens to me!" Cindy shot a nasty smile in Robert's direction.

Robert pretended to struggle with his belt buckle, sparking a playful laugh. Cindy surprised him by moving from her wheelchair onto the sofa, wrapping herself in his arms as they shared a lighthearted moment. As he held her, their laughter softened, and she looked up at him with a gentle smile. Their eyes met, and in an unspoken moment, they leaned in, sharing a warm, tender kiss. They drew closer, her arm resting around his neck as they nestled comfortably together, enjoying the quiet warmth and closeness they had found.

Robert found his mind racing in odd directions. The tension between them was palpable, and Robert could feel his desire intensifying. Yet, as strong as his instincts were, a part of him hesitated, unsure of how to navigate this unfamiliar territory. But being with Cindy, the natural connection between them, made it feel right. The fact that her legs didn't move didn't seem to matter anymore—it was irrelevant in the face of the energy they shared.

Cindy, sensing Robert's uncertainty, took control, her confidence shining through. She embraced him tighter, her actions clear and direct, showing him that she was ready, that she wanted this. In that moment, her strength, both emotional and physical, overcame any doubt he had. Robert, captivated by her assertiveness and the depth of her desire, found himself giving in fully, drawn into an intimacy that felt both inevitable and overwhelming.

At some point during the evening, he found her certain parts more alive than he could have ever imagined, and they made love until total exhaustion gave way to the serene quiet of the night.

* * *

Air Force Two had taken Vice President Reid and Bentley Wilcox three time zones to the west, to celebrate Christmas Eve and Christmas day in Washington State. The Vice President had stepped off the ballroom floor and into one of the side studies in her palatial home, clad in a stunning ecru satin evening gown. Charlotte had been dancing with

Bill until a somewhat inebriated woman from Seattle's upper crust had cut in with a giggle, relieving Charlotte of her partner. Bill didn't know how to dance, and it always bothered Charlotte that the richest man in the world had never taken the time to buy a few dance lessons. After relieving herself literally in the private quarters restroom, she returned to the side room to discuss the latest developments with her lover, Bentley Wilcox. "So, how's that Starkweather and the night club knifing gig playing?" she asked, clearly hoping for a positive report.

"Well, it's out there and gaining traction," Wilcox responded. "It didn't make a lot of sense to release it at Christmas time, but the press couldn't hold back. If they hadn't let it go at the Boston Globe, somebody else would have gotten it. But you know, half the world's watching the Pope celebrate mass on television right now, and nobody really cares much about David Houston." His voice was cynical and indifferent.

"So, what do we do to keep it in the forefront...you know, keep people focused?" Charlotte asked.

"It certainly impeaches the guy. It shows how corrupt he really is. That's got to get a lot of attention, even during Christmas. Whether they admit it or not, those Justices are gonna take it into consideration." Bentley explained.

"Yeah, and the House too?" Charlotte responded with a hopeful question.

"Maybe a little less so. I mean, they all have their histories. I still think we've got a big problem. You know, the Minton problem."

"You think that's still out there?"

"Well, the Republicans are certainly gonna run parallels of this knifing incident to you socially climbing past President Minton." But then again, aside from the cartoonists and the right-wing talk show hosts, nobody seriously believes you had anything to do with the President's heart attacks. The knifing, on the other hand, is a different story."

She looked at Bentley, walked in his direction, then backed up slightly and stopped, making sure she had his attention. "So, what do you think, Bentley?" she asked in an evil tone, but also demanding of an answer. "Do you think I had anything to do with those heart attacks?"

Bentley took the challenge head-on, his eyes locked on hers as he ran his hands through the strands of her blonde hair before checking the door. His touch became rough, grabbing her forcefully by the waist where her dress clung to her lower body, pulling her hard against him. "I know you're a killer," he growled, his gaze unflinching, "but life's too short not to be one when you need to be."

They held each other in silence, the tension palpable, neither one speaking for nearly a minute. Charlotte then stepped back, straightening herself and regaining her composure. "Now, what about the deal—are we going to have one?" she asked, her tone turning strictly business again.

"We intercepted a conversation between Talmadge Smith and Thomas Rosenblat. By the way, neither thinks very highly of you just in case you wondered," Bentley interjected but noticed that the comment didn't seem to bother her. "The CIA guys are very good eavesdroppers. The Secret Service protection around Vice Presidential candidates is pitiful. Anyway, both VPs think the flip is a great deal."

She changed the subject slightly. "So, what else did our loyal VP's talk about?" she asked.

"Pretty much the same old stuff. Smith is trying to get a commitment from Rosenblat that if you win, he will try to discourage you from giving the Chinese the green light."

She acted mildly offended. "I'm not giving the Chinese the green light. I'm just taking all our forces out of the Formosa Strait. The Chinese can do the rest."

"Smith is in this to protect the Taiwanese. In fact, if he had assurances that you would keep the fleet there, I think he might bag Houston. He thinks Houston is a total loser."

The Vice President paused for a moment. "I'm not willing to give him that assurance ... the Chinese at least need to get what they paid for...that is, unless he'd quit Houston. If he'd quit, I'd reconsider."

Wilcox's response was calm, almost dismissive. "I don't think that'll be necessary. Trying to double-cross your contributors from Bali is something we'd have to strategize carefully before making any moves. But don't worry—the China deal has to hold."

The Vice President's face tightened as she brought up her next concern. "What about Ormond? He's not dead yet. I'm going to have to go through with the flip," she said, her tone sharp, fully aware that Bentley despised the coin flip idea.

Bentley's jaw clenched, but he stayed quiet, loathing the thought of the unpredictability that the flip could bring.

"Don't you worry about that either! I'll work it out."

Charlotte was hopeful, but doubtful, as she walked back across the room, aggressively kissed Wilcox on the mouth and then backed away. "It's that bloody face again, Bentley. You've got to get that fixed before you walk back out to the party." She walked to a mirror, pulled out her lipstick, and freshened up. In less than twenty seconds, she was back in the ballroom, celebrating the birth of the Savior with the elite of the Democratic Party—hoping that Bentley could truly succeed before she had to leave her future to the mere flip of a coin.

16

Not long before sunrise, Robert woke to find himself entangled with Cindy on the couch. They had dozed off with the kitchen light still on. The candle that Cindy had lit before their lovemaking flickered gently on the table, now half its original size but still burning brightly. He carefully adjusted her position on the couch, making her comfortable, and draped one of the thick blankets he had brought in earlier for the intended rollaway bed over her. Then, hoping that she would continue to sleep peacefully, he blew out the candle, turned out the light in the kitchen and went upstairs to take a shower.

Robert hesitated for a moment, the melodic strains of the unfamiliar yet calming music drawing him out of his thoughts. The blend of New Age and Celtic strings wasn't the usual kind of holiday music, but there was something magical about it—something that made him pause. The soft light from downstairs barely illuminated the hallway, casting shadows along the walls as he quietly stepped out of the bathroom.

The scent of rich coffee drifted up, mingling with the music, creating a warm and inviting atmosphere. Robert smiled to himself, appreciating the small, simple pleasures he hadn't really thought about in a long time. He made his way down the stairs, each step deliberate to avoid waking Cindy if she was still resting.

When he reached the bottom, he saw her—Cindy was already awake, sitting at the kitchen table with a mug in hand, her wheelchair positioned nearby. She had set the scene, the soft music filling the air, and the coffee pot gently steaming. She looked up as Robert entered the room, her face lighting up.

SCRABBLE

It was clear that Cindy was no longer asleep. The enticing aroma of bacon and sausage sizzling in the kitchen made him realize that she had likely wheeled herself over to start breakfast as soon as he had gone upstairs. His heart continued to stir as he considered the incredible reality of Cindy Wilstead.

By the time Robert finished and made his way down the stairs, he spotted Cindy in her wheelchair, busying herself in the kitchen. She glanced over her shoulder and cheerfully called out, "Merry Christmas and Happy Holidays!" over the soothing flow of beautiful music. "I love Christmas mornings, and maybe this is the best one of all." She spoke as she turned and wheeled herself back into the living room from the kitchen with a plate in her lap. She could see he was looking at the plate. "That's right; this is the best sausage you are ever going to have, right out of the best delicatessen in Old Town Alexandria."

Robert reached down, took a piece and delicately put it into his mouth. "This is it!" he declared. "This is great!" He continued to smile as he sat down to the best breakfast he had seen in years.

"Well, we've got plenty to eat, and I thought you could use a hearty Christmas morning breakfast to kick off the festivities, with my angel music playing in the background. I hope you enjoy it!"

"Festivities...what do you have in mind?"

Cindy pulled out a box, nicely wrapped, which Robert's experience told him was probably a shirt. "This is for you," she said, handing him the box.

"Can I open it now?" he asked.

"Well, of course you silly man...it is Christmas morning. Are we gonna wait for your birthday maybe? By the way, when is your birthday?" Cindy was playful and buoyant and alive in the morning, another attribute that made Robert want her even more. It all made Christmas seem that much more exciting for Robert, who had been alone on Christmas morning for as long as he could remember.

Robert started opening the box. It was not a shirt. "What is this?" he asked as he looked at a maroon cardboard box, which had the word "Scrabble" embossed in one lower corner. "A Scrabble game?" he asked as he smiled.

"Mister, if you mess with me, you play Scrabble!" Cindy playfully demanded. "You may think you're smart, but I want you to know that I am the finest Scrabble player on earth. If you can beat me at Scrabble, you can have anything you want...anything!"

"Well, I thought I already got that last night," Robert retorted.

"No, Bob," she said, "that was just the beginning...you have no idea what you could get if you beat me at Scrabble!"

As Robert looked through the game that had always seemed boring to him, it suddenly sounded fun. "Well, then you're on. When we finish breakfast and as soon as you're ready, I'll give you a Scrabble game you'll never forget!" he bragged.

"Okay, big guy, eat this breakfast and then let's see what you can do."

Twenty minutes later, the breakfast dishes were stacked in the sink as the two started their game of Scrabble which, over the next hour, became a battle. An hour later, the atmosphere had transformed into full-blown warfare. It was a Christmas morning unlike any other, culminating in an intense showdown as they tallied the points in the fifth and final game, where Cindy triumphed by a razor-thin margin.

After the game, Cindy took some time to resolve a delicate issue. It was time to change her colostomy device. She wheeled herself into the bathroom and took care of the situation as she had done so often for the last ten years of her life. For her it was routine. But, for Robert, there was a certain stench which began to emanate through the house that suddenly converted the joy of the moment back to the stark reality of a dark life. He could clearly see how it was all such a struggle, yet the woman seemed to move through it with such class, with such nobility. Maybe an infection, not well. How is it that she can be so positive, so uplifting and happy all the time? Robert pondered, how is it that this is one of the first times in years that I've made it through the night without thinking about death—not even once?

A COASTAL ROAD

The odor had been so powerful that he had walked out onto the porch to clear the smell of the fresh morning air blowing up from the beach. After working it through in his mind in several directions and running through the contrasts that in some ways had him so mixed up, he did not know what to think. He decided to reconcile it all by returning to the living room and sitting on the couch. He would ignore the smell, noting that it was dissipating. He did not want to talk to her about health issues; it wasn't the time for a downer. He reasoned that over time, he might learn to abide by all of this. At least he wanted to explore the possibility that it could be that way. This woman was so whole, so complete. He knew no one who had ever shown such a deep care for life. Her passion ignited a desire in him to learn more and reconnect with what he had ended for so many throughout his lifetime.

The skies were clear, and the temperature was in the mid-fifties, warm for the season, as Robert, clad in his running gear, unloaded the electric cart off the hoist in the back of the van. Cindy quickly switched from her wheelchair into the motorized cart with only slight assistance from Robert. He could see that she had done it many times before. Her considerable upper body strength allowed her to move with agility. Having never spent time with a wheelchair-bound person, he was continually amazed by everything she could do and how self-sufficient she seemed to be.

"So, how fast do you think you can go in that thing?" Robert asked.

"Well, Bob, let's put it this way: you don't want to race me into Cape May. You might get ahead of me for a while, but once we're two or three miles into town, I can push this thing up to about twelve miles an hour. I don't think you'll be able to keep up for as long as I can," Cindy challenged.

Robert was tempted to accept the offer, but he deferred in favor of a more friendly jog along the road leading back to Cape May proper. He wanted to talk. The Scrabble game had been tough enough and he didn't want to get beat again.

It was a more than perfect Christmas morning for both as they ran and motored along the coastal road into town. The temperature became even warmer as the sun periodically found a way to break through the clouds. All the shops were closed in the quaint downtown shopping district of Cape May. The restaurant in the old Grand Hotel was open and adorned with enough holiday revelry that it looked like an inviting place to eat. Robert and Cindy savored a non-Italian seafood lunch before heading back, with Robert walking and Cindy driving slowly. They exchanged little conversation, simply relishing each other's company as they made their way back to the cottage for an afternoon nap on the couch downstairs.

SECRETS OF SACRIFICE

By late afternoon, another outing to the lighthouse at Cape May was underway. The shadows from the setting sun across the bay on the Delaware shore stretched eastward. It was still a slow day, but now with larger numbers of tourists and visitors wandering about the shore and lighthouse. Christmas dinner had turned into a Christmas family outing as the relatively warm afternoon made it enjoyable for all. Cindy, in her wheelchair, wheeled alongside Robert as they talked and made their way up the ramp overlooking the beach to the south. From their vantage point, they could see the faint glimmer of light across the Delaware Bay at Lewes Ferry, where the ferry carrying cars and people had made its way six times daily to Cape May since the early 1930s.

Both were quiet and more pensive and even somewhat exhausted from the long night of lovemaking, short night of sleeping, and then the long day to follow. They spent much of the day reminiscing about their past experiences, discussing places they had traveled and things they had seen. The conversation was light and enjoyable, deliberately steering clear of sensitive topics. Robert shared stories of his trips to exotic locations, omitting any mention of the darker deeds that had occurred there. Cindy spoke of visits to major research centers and discussions with interesting doctors without reference to the painful surgeries and endless tests. The lack of seriousness had profited them both. As the sun set, questions arose.

"Bob, with everything we've talked about, I can tell there's something you really need." Cindy wheeled around to look up at Robert with her back to the sea.

"I hope you're not talking about another Scrabble game," Robert responded. He responded lightly but could see she was serious.

She smiled. "No, but I do think you need your children, your grandchildren...that whole relationship needs to come back into your life."

Robert was silent, looking beyond Cindy and out to sea. He focused momentarily on the gargantuan fire tower atop a cement battlement about nine hundred feet offshore. A relic of a once-proud 1943 coastal defense plan, the five-story steel structure with a flat observation deck was set up as a baseline to triangulate the position of suspicious ships or submarines.

They had seen better days—no longer standing proudly, they resembled a relic from a Star Wars trilogy more than a World War II tower. Leaning heavily to one side, they seemed destined to crumble and fall into the sea. He understood that feeling all too well.

Robert returned to the conversation, "I'm just not sure I could even think about that, let alone ever do it."

"I can't imagine being without my children, if I could ever have any," Cindy spoke. "When you've got them and you still have that whole part of your life, no matter how terrible things must have been, it just seems like that would have overcome the sadness more than anything else." They continued to move along in silence and then she asked, "Is the guilt really that powerful...or is it something else?"

Robert was not offended by the questions. He knew Cindy was the only person who could ask them. He had anticipated these inquiries over time but was still uncomfortable providing answers. "I've wondered that myself. I really don't know. I know I loved my wife, even though the marriage was so vacant."

"Yes, I have looked at that picture of her in the white dress. You keep it there on the mantle. It must be important to you."

"I don't know if it is or not," Robert responded. "So much of that life was just pictures... pictures of people frozen in time, smiling only for the camera, because there weren't many events that caused the smiles. I would often lay awake at night and think about when the last time we really made serious love or when we went for a walk along the beach, like you and I are doing right now—without her complaining about something... too hot, too cold, too tired. It was always something. I built her this place at Cape May, but she never came here.

When she did, she couldn't just enjoy the cottage on the ocean; instead, she was always in town buying up everything she could find in the stores. The credit card bill for a weekend at Cape May often exceeded the monthly mortgage payment on the beach house. In fact, I can't recall a moment like the one you and I shared last night. She was a busy woman—a wonderful mother—but she was always too occupied for romance, intimacy, or philosophical conversations, you know, the kinds of things you want to share with the person closest to you. When I'd come home from a trip... late at night, it was never special, no waiting up... no lights left on—just a dark house to come home to. Sleep was so much more important than us.

"We didn't talk much. I could never just sit down and talk to her about where space ends or some crazy subject like that without enduring a major chewing-out for being such a godless creature. Everything was just black and white. Yet, all the pictures were around, on the walls, the mantles, and shelves, and everybody was smiling. Maybe we were smiling because we had our health, and we were together. So often I was so bored, so depressed ... and I felt so guilty about being that way. I guess I never felt very special. Really, nothing seemed to move. It was always so dead, and to be honest, there were times that I just felt like a piece of furniture in the home. That doesn't mean I didn't love her. I did. I always sought a deeper spiritual connection because the physical aspect simply wasn't there—she didn't want that. When I finally got involved with someone else... to be honest, I can't even remember her name... I was defenseless. I suppose I was desperately searching for that deeper bond.

"So, did you ever get the deeper connection with whatever her name was?" Cindy asked.

"No, not at all. It was just a lot of wild nights trying to talk the talk and maybe walk the walk. In the end she was just a grown-up teenager, totally at ease with her generation, but completely out of touch with mine. It didn't go anywhere. When my wife died, I simply cut that girl out of my life too. There was nowhere to go but away."

"Sounds really difficult." Cindy was sympathetic.

After a considerable pause, Robert continued, "There was something about the whole concept of me planning to be with the other woman while my wife was in the air, maybe dying at the same time that just killed my soul. I couldn't deal with it. I don't know what it is—grief, guilt, or what. I knew at the time there was no way I could face my kids again, and until now, there was no way I could really spend any serious time looking at that picture of her."

"Then why not the kids now? Why don't you make it right? I mean, you're in your fifties, and life isn't over, but it can be sometime soon."

Cindy's statement hit home. Robert knew she was right. He knew there were reasons for the first time in his life to open himself up—completely. "Maybe once I tell you what I'm about to say, you'll prefer going home tonight instead of staying until tomorrow."

"I don't understand. What do you mean by that?" Cindy responded. She wanted to demand a more immediate explanation than she anticipated Robert would give her but decided to hold back.

Robert started walking back toward the lighthouse and the cottage beyond, while Cindy wheeled alongside him, eagerly anticipating his response to his previous comment. "I work as an investigator at a law firm, and I genuinely enjoy it. I truly am a private investigator, but only to a certain extent." What I did in the CIA and what I still do is something that I am neither proud of, nor would I ever want my children to know."

"Well, what is it...what can be so awful?"

"Put simply, I arrange assassinations."

With that comment there was a long pause. Cindy assumed that he would follow up as soon as he could pull his emotions together to talk further. "What do you mean? Assassinations of who?"

"When I go to work, people die. It's not the traditional assassin with a gun. But more like people dying suddenly of heart attacks, or over a long period of time, from disease. What's even worse," Robert's voice was breaking, "I've arranged several major accidents and even bombings. I cause pain, sadness, heartache, death. I'm not the sort of person you want your son to grow up and be like."

"You do this for whom?"

"For the government... your government and mine," Robert spoke coolly and directly, trying not to elaborate. As the walk ended and they sat in the living room of the cottage, the questions came slowly at first, then more rapidly. He found himself recounting his life story, starting from the FARC wars in South America to the assassination of the Colombian drug lord in Spain. It flowed slow, deliberate and continuous, like a complete confession to a priest. As he spoke, Cindy quietly cried, and by the time two hours had passed, she was hugging Robert tightly. Tears streamed down both of their faces. Finally, he returned to the discussion's starting point—the question of why he didn't reconnect with his children. This time, his response was even more chilling: "I have very little time left to live." The weight of his words hung in the air, creating a heavy silence between them.

Trying to break the silence, Cindy looked at him and spoke, "So, are you ill? I've got MD killing me. I have very little time left to live. I don't understand what you mean. Do you have very little time to live too? What's happening to you?"

"No, I'm not ill, but there are reasons why it is unlikely that I will live beyond the next week or so."

Cindy awaited the disclosure of something even more ominous than what she had just heard. Her heart felt heavy, battling against the sharp pangs of deep empathy. As he spoke, she inched even closer, and with each word, Robert could sense her growing love for him.

Robert stood up, leaving Cindy propped up against the cushions on the couch. He walked toward the window and ran his hands through his thinning hair as he gazed out toward the eastern void where nightfall had cast itself across the sea. "You know the things that I have told you...they all happened in foreign countries. "I've never caused anyone in America to die. That doesn't mean Americans haven't been killed or that many haven't been affected— but that's war; that's what we do." His tone suggested he was attempting to make a compelling case for a point that felt ultimately pointless. "I always knew that I was walking the line, but at least when these missions were carried out, it was outside the boundaries of the United States. I never pulled a trigger; I never did anything except make arrangements. Sometimes those arrangements required a fair amount of technical work, which I have been pretty good at over the years. But now...," he paused.

"What is it? What's going on now...you're frightening me!" Cindy spoke as she could see the tension building and blood vessels making his forehead wrinkle. "What is it?" she demanded again.

"It's simply this... I've been asked to terminate two people, both right here in Washington. Not outside the country, and it's got to be done right away."

"Why didn't you just say no?" Cindy asked.

Robert noted her naivety and shook his head, realizing this was as close as he would come to telling someone about his life who might care—at least a little, after he was gone. "Well, you know what's going on with the election. I think I've been pulled right into the middle of it. I've been assigned to take out a Justice of the U.S. Supreme Court and the most senior Congressman in the United States House of Representatives."

"You mean...?"

"That's right, kill them," Robert interrupted. There was silence again. He continued his vacant gaze out to the sea. "It's got to be done before New Year's Eve...so that means just a few days from now."

"Well, you're surely not going to do it, are you?" Cindy nervously asked, hinting at the answer.

"No, I'm not," Robert declared confidently. He sensed a sigh of relief from her, who sounded like she was suffering from severe shell shock.

"I'm so glad!" Cindy responded, relieved but uncertain whether to believe him.

"Therein lies the answer to your other question."

"What do you mean?"

"Why I am terminal," Robert said, turning to look at her. "I've never turned down any assignment before."

I have been trained not to turn them down. I have no doubt that when I do, they'll have no choice but to get rid of me. I'll be viewed as a national security risk and that will be the end of it: a bullet through the window, a knife on a side street...you know, some awful thing. I just hope it comes fast and it's not too painful."

Cindy sat stunned in silence on the couch, clearly affected by Robert's words. He recognized the distress he had caused her; she didn't need any more challenges in her life. "I'm sorry!" he exclaimed. "I doubt this is what you had in mind for a nice Christmas outing to the shore."

"Oh no, Oh no!" Cindy replied, "I knew that you would say no... I knew you didn't plan on hurting anybody...and that's all that matters now!"

Deep down Robert questioned the certainty of the decision not to go ahead with the assassinations. He could not ignore the influence to keep him from going back to what he had so effectively done before.

This new but incredibly impressive woman was in his life making a difference. At the same time, however, he was exacting a cost on her that he felt neither she nor anyone should have to pay. "There's probably still time for you to get down to Charlottesville before the end of the holidays," he offered. "If you want me to take you home, I will."

"No, of course not." Cindy replied. "What you do need to know is what are you going to do...where are you going to go, and what's going to happen. You can't just let someone kill you."

"Those are all good questions. I don't really have any answers." Robert was a matter of fact.

"What about those two people? If you don't, will someone else do?" Cindy asked, her voice still weak and crackling from the emotion of the moment.

"I'm afraid so. I think somebody else will. They are not just going to rely on one person if they in any way think it's shaky. They may not get it done as fast, but they'll get it done. I'm sure of that."

"But what do you mean...why do they have to do it right away? How does this affect the presidential election?"

"Oh, that's very simple," she replied. "The only thing I needed to ensure was that there was a Democratic governor in Mississippi, which there is. If Congressman Ormond dies of a heart attack in his sleep, Governor Meyers will appoint himself or another Democrat to the job." By the time the House meets on determining the presidency, there is a Democrat majority of 26 to 24 because previously Republican Mississippi now has a majority Democratic delegation. Not even a chance for a tie. The CIA gets its man...or better put, woman, in the White House. As far as the Supreme Court Justice goes, well you know, Ramona McCall. She went in as a Republican but is now always leaning towards the Democrats in just about everything. She's liberal and they love her, so she's got to go too."

Gathering her emotions, Cindy was confused. "I don't get it. If the CIA is trying to make things favorable in the House for the Democrats, then why would they want to have a liberal taken out of the Supreme Court?"

Robert walked back over, sat down on the couch, and began stroking Cindy's hair. "That's what makes this so crazy. The order to take out Justice McCall did not come from the CIA."

"What?"

"It came from the Department of Defense...U.S. Army Intelligence to be exact. So, what I think is going on here..." He paused. "With McCall out of the picture, there will be nothing preventing the courts from addressing the issues in Georgia and facilitating a second Electoral College vote in favor of Governor Houston. Once that vote reaches Congress, he wins." Remember, the Army and the Republicans don't know that Ormond will be gone by the time it gets to the House. So, I guess if I do both hits, Reid will be the next President."

Cindy interrupted, "You mean, they're taking sides!?" She shifted on the sofa, using her strong arm to lift one leg slightly off the other. "You nailed it. That's precisely the issue. Clearly, one person has no idea what the other is up to." They both want me to do their termination...I know it's hard to believe...too incredible to believe. That's what's going on and that's why my life is so totally screwed up. In fact, I will tell you this." Robert pulled Cindy into his arms and held her close, kissed her once, and then looked into her eyes. "I was going to kill myself...you know, finally finish it off just a few nights ago. You had come into my life, and you gave me...," his voice began to break, "hope."

Cindy climbed onto him again and hugged him tightly. "I'll give you all the hope I can!" she pleaded. I may not have a lot of time left either, but I'll get you through this...I really will!"

The two embraced for a long time in silence. Eventually, Cindy transferred into her wheelchair and wheeled herself to the table, which was softly illuminated by light spilling in from the adjacent kitchen. She struck a match and held it to the angel candle, watching the flame flicker to life. Robert watched as she cut the string on the tiny angel charm, which was around the candle, took her own necklace off and then looped the charm onto the gold chain which held a gold crucifix prominently in place on her upper chest. She then wheeled back over to Robert, climbed out of the wheelchair and back into his arms. "I'm your guardian angel. I'll help you. There's got to be a way."

After another long session of hugging quietly, Cindy returned to the kitchen and started fixing dinner. This time it would be spaghetti and wine—a lot of wine.

Within an hour, the lights were on, and they were talking, eating and even beginning to joke with each other again. To Robert, it seemed so bizarre, like shifting deck chairs around on the Titanic with the iceberg looming off the bow. He had no idea how she could really help. The fact that she even offered created an incredible sense of appreciation and he resolved to at least try to make the rest of the trip to the shore worthwhile.

After dinner, Robert started washing dishes. Cindy sat at the table watching him. The sink in the old cottage was not at a low enough level for her to help.

"So, what if you just called the CIA and the Army and told them you weren't going to go through with it? Just flat out say no and warn them to stay away or you'd go to the press?"

Robert chuckled nervously. "I can tell you don't quite grasp how this works. Then again, not many people do. First off, threatening to talk to the media is a breach of the National Security Act."

That's even if I'm right about everything. You must understand the way you prosecute breaches is you simply shut off the light, I mean get rid of the threat. Not even a secret FISA court for me."

"You mean, like they would just kill you?"

"Well yes, that's what I've been doing. I don't really know why the people were in trouble that I was dealing with but look at the Commerce Secretary back in the Balkans. I'm pretty sure he just was operating too freely with information, and it compromised the country's security at some level. Maybe he just got crosswise with the President. You promise not to do it, but when you breach that promise, if it's serious enough, you've got to go."

"Somehow this doesn't sound at all like America to me!"

"I don't mean to speak for the bad guys, but if you think about it, if you give someone a chance to go to court and blab all this to their lawyer and to judges and to everyone else, then whatever secret you're trying to keep, you can't keep. "You can't rely on judges and lawyers to shift everything into a secure 'hush-hush' legal environment. For one, that kind of environment doesn't really exist. And for another, even one more person knowing can sometimes be one too many. Just look at history. Whoever orchestrated the assassination of John F. Kennedy had to be silenced." That's why Lee Harvey Oswald was killed by Jack Ruby. That's why so many other people involved with that whole thing ended up disappearing and dying...I don't mean to defend this screwed up scheme, but that's just the way it works. As awful as it sounds, at least I understand it. I just never thought I'd end up with the short end of the stick here...In reality, I'm not any better than they are."

"So, you never thought they would ask you to do it inside the United States?" Cindy asked.

"Yeah, that's exactly it. Now I don't know what to do."

Cindy wheeled to a cupboard, looking for a dish towel. Finding none, she moved to a suitcase that Robert had brought which had several towels and threw one at him. The non-verbal aspect of the relationship was already taking over. Almost unconsciously, he accepted the towel and kept on working. "What about warning the judge and the congressman? I mean, you could call them directly and just let them know—anonymously or something?" he suggested, trying to grasp at any potential solution.

"I've thought about that. I'm just afraid they would go to the Secret Service. The Secret Service then goes to Homeland Security, or Defense Department and CIA, and the foxes are in charge of the henhouse—literally. They just find another way to do it."

"No, what I mean is send something to the press so that maybe by making it public, they'd back off," Cindy suggested.

"Yeah...," Robert responded slowly. "You know that means that I'm even deader than dead. If it comes out at all, they'll assume it was me. Then there'll be another guy just like me out trying to kill me. I know they've got a few of them. Since the War on Terror got going, they've gotten much better at it. It just so happens that I'm still probably the best."

"Good enough to keep someone else from getting to you?" Cindy asked.

"No, I don't mean that at all." Robert explained. "I've never had to protect myself. I've always been the hunter, not the hunted. I have no doubt that if they want to take me out, they can do it, and there's not anything in this world I can do to stop it, but maybe just prolong the agony."

THE BLUFF

With dinner cleared and an evening still to spend before the return trip to Washington, D.C. the next day, Robert focused on keeping the mood light. He tried to push aside the heavy thoughts lingering in his mind, determined not to ruin the whole trip. "So, if you could do anything in the world with the time we have left to kill, oops...I guess I shouldn't have quite put it that way, but I mean what would you like to do?" he asked, allowing a slight upbeat resonance to his voice. Robert chuckled lightly, appreciating Cindy's candidness. "Well, I certainly understand. It's not every day that someone gets to enjoy a moment like we did," he said, trying to match her lightheartedness. "But hey, I'm here for the company, no pressure."

Cindy smiled, her eyes twinkling with mischief.

"That's fine...and you are fine. Just remember that." Robert assured her.

"But we do have Scrabble," Cindy reminded him as she wheeled in the direction of the table. Within minutes the two were back at the Scrabble game, both trying to evade the perilous discussion of the past several hours. Cindy won the first game, and it was in the middle of the rematch that she spelled out the word "A-L-A-R-M" on a double word score. She paused. "There must be some way we could warn those people without the CIA knowing about you? There could be leaks from inside the Agency, or at least they could think that."

"They have forensics labs, handwriting experts, and every type of high-tech gadgetry you could ever imagine to figure out who sent what." As Robert looked down at the word she had just spelled, it caused him to pause. Cindy looked up at him as their eyes met. "I've got an idea," he said. "Maybe a really good idea."

"Well, let's hear it." Cindy urged him on.

"We've got all these old newspapers around here from so many decades back that it would be impossible to figure out where the lettering came from. We could just use some old generic paper, we could maybe..."

Cindy interrupted, "Make a warning message, right?"

"Yeah, that's it. As you put there in your words, sound the A-L-A-R-M!" Robert spoke, excited by the idea.

Over the next hour, they searched the house, looking at old newspapers—some from the Washington Post, others from the Philadelphia Inquirer, but all were dated. Robert explained to Cindy how the age of the fiber would make it harder to determine its origin. A forensic analysis would conclude the age, but records of fiber typing would be much more difficult with a current publication. In this case, the antique nature of the paper would be beneficial. As he started writing a message, Cindy quickly cut out vowels and consonants to give Robert a variety.

In time, he had spread out across the Scrabble board the small letters from small point newspaper headlines, letters approximately one-third the size of the Scrabble lettering, the phrase "TO CONGRESSMAN ORMOND AND JUSTICE MCCALL; YOUR LIVES ARE IN DANGER. ELEMENTS WITHIN THE UNITED STATES GOVERNMENT, INCLUDING THE CIA AND THE DEPARTMENT OF DEFENSE, INTEND TO KILL YOU IN ORDER TO FIX THE ELECTION. PLEASE INCREASE YOUR SECURITY AND BE WARY OF ANYONE IN YOUR TEAM WHOM YOU DO NOT ABSOLUTELY AND COMPLETELY TRUST. THE SECRET SERVICE HAS ALREADY BEEN COMPROMISED AND LIKELY CANNOT—OR WILL NOT—PROTECT YOU TAKE THIS TO THE US MARSHALL AND CAPITAL SECURITY. GET THEIR PROTECTION. GET IT NOW!"

"So, you don't think that they would figure that this might come from you?" The part about the Secret Service is quite specific." Cindy commented. "I'm not sure how else to put it. When this comes out, I don't want the President just offering Secret Service protection to them. "Remember what we saw on your TV the other night? The Secret Service was in the background, somehow superseded by both the CIA and DOD. We can only hope that the U.S. Marshal's Office and Capitol Security are not in the same predicament. If they are still legitimate, they should be able to protect a Supreme Court justice and a congressman, just like they had to do during Nixon and Watergate."

"I guess that makes sense. It still seems like you'll be the first person they suspect."

"Oh, I think they might. Many are involved in this."

This decision was not made in a vacuum. I've got another idea...as soon as this hits the media, I'm going to call my handler on both sides and demand more time to finish the job, sort of go on the offense."

"Brilliant!" Cindy exclaimed. "They will think you are still on the job, and you can buy more time and they won't suspect the warning came from you. Maybe the whole press thing will make them cancel it or something, what do you think?"

"Oh, I think it's a possibility. At this point, anything is worth trying." Robert then looked around. "We need some paper to mount this on, and we can't use as our backing something that could be traced to any store or anything made and distributed to a town this small. That could be easily traced."

"Let me see...," Cindy was thinking. "What about that paper, you know those two sheets from the office? Would that be good?"

"Yes, that might be," he was impressed that she was giving such reliable input, "You know plain white stock office paper in the D.C. area could be from anywhere. There's got to be millions of acres in this town. That's a good idea." The words were then carefully taped on the plain white 8-1/2 x 11 bond page.

That evening, there was no more Scrabble. Instead, the two spent their time talking and planning. Robert made it clear to Cindy that she would need to limit the time she spent with him until a resolution could be reached. He did not want her to be with him in the event the government decided to take him out. However, the idea of the bluff sounded very good. As he thought more about it through the night, he found himself falling asleep more easily. Then, somewhere between three and four in the morning, in the small quaint cottage on the south Jersey shore, Robert and Cindy made love again.

17

"Use words like outrageous! Bush League! Absolute fabrication! Bull Shit! "Anything like that is just ridiculous and barely worth a response, but I know you've got to say something!" Bentley Wilcox was screaming over the telephone at the press secretary for President Ronald Minton. Standing outside on the tarmac at the Bremerton, Washington Airport Executive Terminal, he found himself fighting the cold and a weak battery on his sophisticated iridium satellite phone. On the other end of the phone, President Minton's Press Chief was dealing with a crisis that was proving to be wholly inconsistent with the holiday season. The Washington Post was working full force to corroborate a secret message claiming that a plot had been formed within certain government agencies to assassinate a congressman and a Supreme Court justice. Since the allegations pointed to two specific agencies, the media was now pressuring the President for a response.

President Minton had busied himself throughout the holidays moving out of the White House and back to his home in rural Georgia. His White House staff, at least those that remained and who were largely staking their hopes on jobs in a Charlotte Reid administration, had stayed behind to handle the issues. With an unsettled election, they were busier than ever. Today, the tough questions were about the message in the envelope which showed up taped to the glass door at the Washington Post main office at 1150 Fifteenth Street NW.

"I can't believe that everyone gets so riled up over a rumor like this!" Bentley Wilcox continued to rail, "Here you've got Governor Houston with his press secretary hiring a thug to go out and knife a guy. I mean you've got that one about as obvious as day turning to night. It finally hits the news, and then, within days, some silly note shows up at The Washington Post. Suddenly there's a big plot that implicates us. Now, don't you think that's a bit too convenient? Hell, what I think is that it's simply an effort to create something bigger and wilder than the Governor's scheme to start at quarterback for his own football team. "That's what you're up against. Honestly, that's exactly what you should say—but in your own words, of course. If you were as blunt as I am, you wouldn't last a day in the Beltway!"

Wilcox concluded the conversation in time to join the Reid entourage as they climbed aboard Air Force Two for a flight back to D.C. The Vice President had two functions to attend on the 29th and the 30th. Both, of course, were fund-raisers, with the former fundraising for the DNC that she enjoyed regardless of the season. The latter event was a benefit for the Muscular Dystrophy Association. She had considered canceling it more than once. This time, she had set a firm deadline. With Houston's agreement to her offer, it would be the time and place for a nationwide announcement of the flip of the coin. With the action at the Washington Post it was more certain than ever to happen. As the others boarded the plane, Charlotte stopped Bentley at the base of the stairs, took him by the arm, and led him a few paces away for a private conversation. "So, what does this mean? I thought the Agency assured us they could get this done without a hitch."

"I don't know how they work," Wilcox was contrite. "I've already checked with them, and they say they've got their best person on it...and that's all they'll tell me."

"Well, how could such a thing be leaked? I mean," Charlotte's voice was frantic and nervous, "Is there a chance it's the CIA who's trying to take us out?" She was getting paranoid. "You know, they've got their people all around us saying that they are protecting you from somebody in the Defense Department. Then they put us in this situation and start leaking information that could ruin us in less than a day if anyone in their group decided to come clean. Whose side is anyone on here, Bentley? Bill's got his own security people. I could switch to them."

Bentley looked back at the airplane nervously, making sure that nobody could hear their conversation over the droning whine of the warming jet engines. "I'm looking into it, and it worries me a bit. But it's not time to panic. The Agency claims they'll do anything to get you into the White House, and I'm taking them at their word that they'll fix Congress. So far, nobody— and I mean nobody— I've spoken to has shown any inclination to back down.

"Well, you'd better be right, Bentley," Charlotte whispered, "But if you hear anything, then I want to make a pre-emptive move. I will go to the head of the Secret Service, have the CIA personnel moved out, and we'll take our chances with whatever this high-risk situation is that they keep warning us about. But I need you to analyze it and figure it out. I want to ensure these people are protecting us and not holding us captive.

Charlotte and Bentley could both see that everyone else had boarded the jet, except for the two CIA officers waiting outside and watching the movements of everyone on the tarmac and near the aircraft. Charlotte hoped they were not trained to lip read. Wilcox and Reid then boarded the plane, followed by the agents. Within eight minutes, Air Force Two was streaking over the Cascades, heading toward the eastern United States.

* * *

THE BRINK OF LOYALTY

The story, being far too hot to hold for the following day's paper, first hit the streets mid-day on the 27th, and earlier on The Washington Post's website. Two hours after that, the Post had a special edition on the street. By mid-afternoon, Robert, certain that the story was running on virtually all news services, made a call to Langley - office of the Deputy Director of the CIA. Following protocol, he called for another MOTS meeting, where he would feign confusion about the situation and once again pledge his loyalty to the cause. This would buy him time—hopefully the time needed to allow the publicity to encourage the CIA to call off the hit, that is, unless they did it at the MOTS. In that case, it would be all over. He had to take the risk. By evening, he received a return call confirming that the MOTS meeting would take place at 6:00 p.m., this time at the corner of M Street and Wisconsin, in front of Riggs Bank.

Not more than one-half hour after the Vice President's plane lifted off from the Municipal Airport in Bremerton, Washington, Robert was face to face on a cold street corner with Gerry Rothman for a one-way conversation. "Your team has some leaks! That's something I can't tolerate while trying to accomplish what I need to do. I need another week—seven days—to deal with Congressman Ormond. That's assuming this report to the Post will blow over in the next few days." Right now, everybody's got their radar up. In a day or so, it'll be old news. It can't hang around for long because it will get replaced by something else. I can get back to this. So, you just tell the Director that I've got to have another week. He's got to find out who the mole is that's got the loose lips. Sometimes I think you guys just aren't pros like you used to be." His words sounded tough like a mobster, but he could feel himself sweating as he talked—something he hoped Rothman was not sharp enough to detect.

Rothman was playing his role perfectly. He stood there like the great stone face, showing no emotion. He simply listened to what was said, kept his hands in his pockets, and, once Robert finished, turned and walked away.

It was not unusual for Robert to be left with a level of uncertainty as to how things would go. He knew he would be contacted at some point and informed as to whether he had an additional week or perhaps the mission had been called off. With any luck, and all the publicity, it would be the latter, but he also was preparing for the worst.

After turning in the Avis rental and returning Cindy to her home in Arlington on the evening of the 26th, Robert had started constructing a crisis plan of his own. He knew he couldn't make any moves that would certainly draw attention, such as withdrawing large amounts of cash from his Riggs Bank account, making substantial credit card charges, or planning any extensive travel. Anything odd would trigger an alarm which had the prospect of an immediate, deadly visit from both the CIA and the DOD. As he further evaluated the situation, however, his greatest concern was still with the CIA. The Agency knew him well. His former cohorts had a good sense for what he might do. The Army, for whom he had carried out only two prior missions, was less sophisticated in such things, and he figured it would also be less able to find him should he decide to run. Robert was confident that he still had some subtle moves to make that could be well beyond the detection of the CIA or the Army.

On the way back from dropping the van at the Avis lot at Dulles International, he stopped by his storage unit in a small industrial park in Reston, Virginia. It was here that he kept the equipment sometimes used in his missions for the government. It was a veritable assassin's museum, filled with relics from past missions. The once-sophisticated micro-tools used to calibrate the inertial guidance system of Korean Airlines Flight No. 007 were still packed in a small case in the corner. Wrapped inside some fixed steel boxes were several cases of gelatin known generally as plastic explosives, deadly but inert unless properly fused. A mere three ounces could incinerate everything inside a 5,000 square foot room in less than five seconds. It had been the weapon of choice for both covert operators and terrorists over the years.

Inside a chest of drawers situated against the far wall was a set of specialized inks and related materials he could use for forging counterfeit documents. This had been helpful in getting in and out of Chile and Spain. With a full-color printer, he could do a lot of things. Although he had never tried it, he always assumed he could probably counterfeit twenty-dollar bills if he wanted to.

The risk of keeping these items in a storage locker was considered minimal. It was certainly preferable to maintaining anything inside the row house in Georgetown. Robert did not doubt that, from time to time, a clandestine visit had occurred to his town home by people whose level of ability was such that he had been unable to detect the intrusion. The storage locker was just one of hundreds of thousands in the D.C. area. It was in a respectable part of town, and he considered the likelihood of a visit there to be extremely remote. As a precaution, he had installed a battery-powered transmitter, no larger than a quarter, on the inside of the storage locker door. If the storage locker door ever rolled up without the disc disarmed, then the next time that he came within a mile, he would receive no transmission. Thus, unless he had not replaced the battery, which he was careful to do once a year, no signal on his receiver would mean that someone had been in the storage locker and that he should avoid the area.

The bill for the storage locker for years had been paid through one of the children's trusts, a fact which had remained unknown to the children. The same blind trust also owned the Cape May cottage. The name of the trust and the address were generic and beyond reasonable detection, unless someone knew exactly where to look. He figured that the Agency likewise had long forgotten about the cottage. Most of the people who were at the Agency during the time of Veronica's death were long-since retired or on to other pursuits. For Robert, the storage locker was reasonably secure and the right place to store dangerous items.

Robert swept out the storage locker with a broom. He then took the blanket and the remaining non-perishable foods from the Cape May trip and stowed them away in the chest of drawers.

Robert then drove the forty minutes in still heavy night traffic into Georgetown. Rather than giving into fatigue, he loaded up another set of items consisting of those things in the row house which were special to him, such as the gifts from the children of the lawyers, a few remaining photographs of his wife and children, and a journal that he had kept from time to time. Putting them all in a box, he made the trip back out to Reston, where he stashed the items in the storage locker as well, finally to return to his place in Georgetown at approximately 12:45 a.m.

During the various trips to and from Reston, Robert had taken great care to make certain that he was not being followed. He assumed that the most likely chance of picking up a tail would be on his return to Georgetown in the evening. Someone could have followed him from there back out to Reston. So, he took a route which allowed him several chances to discover a tail. It was clear to him that there was none.

By the following evening, Robert found himself in a state of considerable anxiety over what might be happening. He had expected the CIA to get back to him by morning. He had been unable to contact Cedric Martin and the Army. His calls in that direction had gone unanswered, which did not surprise him. Therefore, he would try to sleep. Strangely, in the middle of the whole mess, sleeping had become something that he realized he could do. He would focus his thoughts on Cindy, and somehow, a pleasant dream about someone who cared seemed to dispel the ghosts of the past and the beasts of the night with such force that they would sometimes vanish for hours on end.

Robert had a plan. Maybe it would work, and maybe it wouldn't. But, just to make sure that no one pre-empted his efforts, he kept the safety on his 9mm off, and all the alarms in his Georgetown flat armed and ready to wake him in the event of the slightest possibility of an uninvited visitor. By 1:25 a.m., however, Robert was fast asleep. At 6:10 a.m., the phone rang, startling him awake. "Hello." He spoke softly into the receiver, his senses slowly sharpening enough to anticipate a call from Rothman, but it was not.

"Hi!" It was Cindy's voice. Robert loved her voice no matter how tired he might be. "I've got major league wheelchair problems today. I think we had too much fun on our trip and my electric motor has gone out."

"Well, I'm sorry to hear that," Robert replied. "So, how are you going to get around without it?"

"Well, I was hoping that maybe you could pick me up and take me to work." Cindy asked.

Robert paused for a moment, recalling that he hadn't seen or spoken to Cindy in almost two days. He didn't want to put her in harm's way at all and had expected to see her at work. Realizing this would give him a chance to see her even sooner, and without everyone around, he relented, "I guess I could do that if you could..."

"Breakfast? Is that what you were about to say?" Cindy's voice was buoyant and fun again. "But of course. We can't start our day without a good breakfast."

Robert loved her choice of the word "our." It seemed so right that he could hardly believe his good fortune.

* * *

BROKEN TIES

At 9:00 in the morning on the 28th, a dark blue sedan with Virginia plates drove past the Watergate heading north, exited the Whitehurst expressway and finally pulled over to the curb at the bottom of I Street and 30th Avenue. The day was gray. Winter had returned to the east coast following the holiday respite. From the passenger side of the car, a tall stoutly built man in a long dark overcoat and a nondescript black businessman's hat exited the vehicle and walked steadily up 30th into Georgetown proper toward M Street. He carefully avoided eye contact with the dozen or so people busily walking along the sidewalk. As he crossed the C&O Canal, he paused for a moment. He looked up and down the canal path, scanning from north to south, then turned to survey 30th Street, a one-way road that allowed traffic only from the west. After that, he reached into his upper inside coat pocket, made a slight mechanical adjustment by pushing a small lever, and continued walking eastward for about half a block.

The man then turned right off the sidewalk into the entryway of the courtyard and driveway of the Georgetown Suites Hotel. Before reaching the hotel, he made his way up the steps to the broad plate glass doors into the downstairs foyer of the office building which housed the Fischer, Cramer & Morrell law firm. He nodded to the sharply dressed African American guard standing behind the podium across the foyer, looked up the stairs, and asked, "Is that the law firm up there? The Fischer law firm?"

"Yes sir. Up the stairs, and through those doors." The guard pointed with his finger, his words conveying warmth and professional respect to the dark face he could see beneath the brim of the hat and above the overcoat, which opened to a red tie and heavily starched white shirt.

"Thank you," the man said politely and made his way up the stairs.

Once at the door, he confirmed the name of the law firm. The words "Fischer, Cramer & Morrell" were printed in gold leaf lettering across the door. He entered and first glanced at the receptionist's desk, noticing that no one was sitting there. He paused for only a moment. After looking around the lobby, he walked to the left, heading into the hallway, immediately arriving at the office with the name "Robert Cannon" in black lettering on a brass plate on the door. The door was open. He looked inside and stood there for a moment.

"May I help you?" A man's voice spoke from behind him, down the hall to the right.

"Uh, yes," was his slightly startled response as he walked further into Robert Cannon's office. At that point, Landon Cramer walked through the doorway with some curiosity as to who might be in Robert's office. As he walked through the door, the man reached into his upper coat pocket, pulled out a black .45 caliber handgun featuring clean lines with a customized silencer, quickly took aim and pumped two bullets into Cramer's heart. There was a slight gasp as Cramer wheeled backward toward the hall, first hitting the wall to the right of the doorway, never making it back to the hall before dying. The man then quickly grabbed the body and pulled it into the office behind the door, leaving a track of smeared blood on the carpet as he walked further down the hall. Over the next three minutes, the same event, deadly, awful and permanent, repeated itself. Stanley Fischer and Kevin Morrell were murdered where they sat behind the desks in their offices.

One staff person, having heard some commotion, had come out of the copy room in time to let out a scream. Her mouth was firmly covered by a gloved hand before another sound could be made. A bullet was fired through her head at point blank range. The other staff member never knew what happened. She had been in the break room on the phone, engaged in a personal conversation. The call ended abruptly when the phone line was yanked from the wall, and she was shot in the head. The man spent another two minutes wandering around the office, seeing if he could find anyone else to kill. Once satisfied that everyone was dead, he walked hastily to the door and made his way down the stairs.

The carnage was not over. Once in the foyer of the building, he stood for a moment, looked around and walked in the direction of the building guard. "Thanks for the instructions, I appreciated them," the man said.

"My pleasure, sir," the guard answered.

In the next second, standing just five feet from the guard, the man pulled out the handgun again and fired two subsonic rounds into the guard's chest. The massive man fell backward against the wall, slumping down in his chair. The shooter then scanned the foyer carefully. Fortunately, in the quasi-holiday mode, there was no one else in the downstairs area who might qualify for death by merely having seen him.

The stranger then turned, bound for the door and then walked slowly and unobtrusively away, through the archway gate, onto 30th Street. From there he walked to the C&O Canal, heading north along the canal two blocks to where a car was waiting. With him inside, it sped off to the north on I Street and disappeared in the busy morning traffic in northwest Washington, D.C.

18

It was approximately 9:40 a.m. as Robert, driving his Buick Lacrosse with the wheelchair in the trunk, made his way, along with Cindy, across the Lincoln Memorial Bridge and into D.C. As they approached the overpass to M Street, they noticed emergency vehicles and police crowding the entrances to Georgetown. Not seeing any fire equipment, they wondered if perhaps a movie was being filmed—a not uncommon occurrence in D.C., especially during the low-traffic holiday period. As he came closer, he saw two ambulances speeding south on M Street in the direction of the George Washington University Hospital.

Still uncertain as to the nature of the commotion, he drove south into the District and then north in a circular fashion headed east, then north to come back around into Georgetown, not far from his town home to the east of M Street. Arriving at around 36th and M, he looked south down the street and saw that the entire road was closed off, with traffic backed up so much that he couldn't turn left onto M Street. However, he could easily turn right and join the flow of traffic heading north from the blocked-off area.

As Robert made the turn, he looked down the street again and noticed that the activity was concentrated near the corner of 31st and 30th. With his office being at 30th, he became more concerned and suddenly pulled out in front of traffic, almost causing an accident as he negotiated a left hand turn across the backed-up traffic on 37th Street. He finally found a spot along the curb to park. "I need to see what's going on down there. That's just too close to our offices." I hope everything is okay!"

"What do you think it is?" Cindy asked.

"I'm just not sure, but I've got to go look. I'll be back. Just wait here in the car. I can get down there in two minutes." Robert responded.

Robert jumped out of the car and started running down the C&O Canal towpath in a southerly direction toward 30th Street. As he approached, the crowd grew denser. As he approached 30th, he could see a group of onlookers being held back where the archway gate to the Georgetown Suites drive was situated. Something was terribly wrong.

END OF DAYS

As Robert pushed deeper into the crowd, he noticed two additional ambulances parked with their lights extinguished. The scene was eerily calm, with people moving slowly. Unmarked cars began arriving, their sirens blaring, and plainclothes detectives from D.C. Homicide started to emerge, signaling the escalating investigation. Moving across the street to the north, he tried to gain a better vantage point and still avoid crossing the yellow police tape manned by at least a dozen uniformed officers. He could now see through the driveway gate, with activity concentrated around the thick lobby doors leading into the law firm. "What's going on? What's happening?" he asked a gentleman who looked to be a Georgetown University student, probably from India, in his early twenties. Several of the floors in the Georgetown Suites housed a number of these students in dormitory style.

"I think...I'm told at the lawyer's office—they've been killed— they've been shot and killed!"

Robert went cold for a moment and then a sudden sense of urgency caused him to want to bolt forward across the police line and into his office. In the next second, as he was about to lunge, assuming he could likely talk his way into the situation, his intuition told him that it would be much more difficult to talk his way out. He backed away, walking backwards and sideways with a frightened, almost hysterical look. He then began heading back in a westerly direction down 30th Street, looking over his shoulder and wondering if anyone had seen him.

A flurry of thought was sweeping through Robert's mind with as many confusing scenarios as in the collective minds of all the onlookers. No, it can't be, he told himself, I've got to wait...it can't be. He walked faster now to the pathway along the canal and turned north. He began to walk faster and faster as the impulses precedent to rage began to build within. Within another thirty seconds, he was running—sprinting faster than he had ever run before up the Canal pathway toward the car four blocks to the north. As he turned the corner where the 34th Street Bridge crosses the Canal, he spotted Cindy hunching over toward the dashboard on the passenger's side of the car. He bolted to the door and grabbed the handle to open it. The car was running, but the door wouldn't budge. Then he saw her look up, tears streaming down her face as she slowly reached for her door to press the electronic switch that unlocked it.

Once inside, he looked at her as she pointed to the radio, speechless and only pointing. In the next second, the electronic bumper music announcing a special report on WTOP News Radio played. *"THIS IS A SPECIAL REPORT FROM THE WTOP NEWS RADIO. VINCE GILLMAN REPORTING."* The melodic deep African American news reporter's voice boomed across the radio, *"FIVE MINUTES AGO, I REPORTED THAT THERE HAD BEEN A QUADRUPLE HOMICIDE AT AN OFFICE IN GEORGETOWN. WE NOW HAVE MORE BREAKING NEWS ON THIS TERRIBLE TURN OF EVENTS. I AM TOLD THAT POLICE ARE REPORTING THAT THERE HAS BEEN A SHOOTING AT THE LAW FIRM AND THAT IN FACT FIVE PEOPLE, THAT'S RIGHT FIVE PEOPLE,*

ARE CONFIRMED DEAD. FOR AN EYEWITNESS REPORT, LET'S SWITCH TO BARBARA WRAY AT THE SCENE. BARBARA?" His voice faded and a female voice cracking with emotion took over.

"VINCE, WHAT I HAVE LEARNED THUS FAR IS TERRIBLE. ABSOLUTELY TERRIBLE. THERE HAVE IN FACT BEEN FOUR PEOPLE BROUGHT OUT OF THE BUILDING SO FAR. TWO WERE RUSHED TO GEORGE WASHINGTON UNIVERSITY HOSPITAL AND I HAVE LEARNED THAT THEY ARE DEAD. THEY WERE DECLARED DEAD ON ARRIVAL. THERE ARE AT LEAST THREE MORE BODIES STILL IN THE OFFICE, ALREADY CONFIRMED DEAD. THE POLICE ARE LEAVING THEM WHERE THEY ARE AT THE MOMENT AS THEY FURTHER INVESTIGATE. SO, THAT IS THE FURTHER INFORMATION THAT I HAVE AT THIS POINT. THE TWO HAD BEEN RUSHED TO THE HOSPITAL, BUT THEY DID NOT SURVIVE. BACK TO YOU, VINCE!"

"OBVIOUSLY WE WILL BE BACK THROUGHOUT THE MORNING AS WE LEARN MORE ABOUT THIS SITUATION BUT, FOR NOW, THIS IS VINCE GILLMAN REPORTING FOR WTOP BREAKING NEWS."

HEART'S DESCENT

"I know it's *them*!" Cindy shrieked and then began to cry. "They loved me, you know! They let me into their lives...they gave me a chance...they were my family!" She continued to sob.

Robert could not produce any words. He simply stared at the steering wheel, sweating profusely as perspiration dripped from his face while his body recovered from the sprint up the pathway. For a moment, he feared that Cindy had been hit as well. Just as he began to shake off that thought, deeper realities started to set in. "Cindy, you've got to get a hold of yourself. We have to leave! They're gonna want to talk…to you…and to me and… If they get a hold of me, then I'm dead. I don't know. Maybe they want to kill you too!"

Cindy continued to cry. Robert's words seemed meaningless. He drove west across the bridge to the bottom of the street, turned right on I Street, proceeded one block farther and then turned right again, heading east across M Street back in the direction of his row house on Dumbarton Street. As he drove, he was also weighing all the odd possibilities to manage mind-numbing sentiments. With each thought, it only became more bizarre. Why would Cramer, Fischer, and Morrell be killed? What did they have to do with all of this? It was crucial to understand what the press knew. So, as he maneuvered his car into a curbside parallel parking spot two blocks north of his townhome, he asked Cindy to keep listening to the radio broadcast. No matter how painful it might be, he needed to know what was happening.

Robert again got out of the car on 33rd Street, walked south one block and then turned right going west on 32nd Street to the middle of the block. It was here that he moved quietly, but quickly, down an alley, leading him to Wisconsin Avenue, which intersected the north end of Dumbarton.

Robert knew he needed to retrieve essential items from his house, including $5,000 in emergency cash he had carefully stashed away for situations like this. He had always been prepared for the unexpected. Exiting the alley cautiously, he scanned his surroundings before deliberately choosing Dumbarton Street's one-way route heading south. The densely parked cars, all facing south, provided natural surveillance, allowing him to spot anyone suspicious.

As he walked northward, Robert's trained eyes swept the street, scrutinizing each vehicle for signs of occupancy or unusual activity. He noted the makes, models, and license plates, searching for anything out of place. His instincts honed from years of experience, he sensed potential danger lurking in every shadow. From Wisconsin, he looked carefully down the street southward, his mind breaking down each area of the road in front of each brownstone into a separate segment. He focused intently on the cars parked along the street, trying to determine if they looked familiar, while also scanning for any individuals standing nearby. Satisfied that the approach to his place seemed secure, he headed south along the east side of the street.

Reaching a point directly across the street and due east from the front door of his house, Robert looked again carefully and then walked across the street and halfway up the steps and stopped. He focused downward to the spot where he had applied the tape. Here's an expanded version of the text:

Robert's gaze locked onto the shattered lock, and his heart sank. A cold shiver coursed down his spine as the realization hit: someone had breached his sanctuary. The possibility that an intruder might still be lurking inside sent his senses on high alert. Instinctively, Robert scanned the street again, his movements deliberate and controlled to avoid drawing attention. His eyes darted from rooftop to rooftop, window to window, and car to car, searching for the slightest sign of danger. The tranquil street scene transformed into a potential kill zone, where bullets could rip through his body before he even heard the shot.

This was the perfect ambush spot — isolated yet surrounded by concealment options. The brownstone's proximity to the alley provided an easy escape route for a would-be assassin. Robert's training kicked in, weighing options and exit strategies. He knew he had to reassess and regroup. With all the fear closing in, he took a few steps backwards down the cement stairs leading to the front door and then turned and started walking on ever-numbing legs north along the west side of the street, wondering what commotion he might hear behind him.

There it was! An engine roared to life in a southwest-facing car parked on the east side of the street. Robert tried to glance without appearing overly aware. It was a dark blue Crown Victoria. Although he couldn't see the plates, it resembled an agency car. After all, the tape had been broken, and who else would be spending time at his townhouse but the CIA?

Robert picked up his pace and once reaching the top of the street, at Wisconsin, he looked back to see two men alight from the car and start walking rapidly up the street and northwardly in his direction. That was enough. He broke into a dead sprint, heading for the alley and dashing, as fast as he could, past the dumpsters, trash cans and cardboard boxes behind a restaurant.

Even at age 59, he was still confident that he could outrun most other officers over a long distance. It would only be another block to the car, and he feared that he might not be able to out - sprint younger agents over a short distance.

Making his way out of the alleyway, Robert swiftly covered the remaining thirty yards to his parked car, his senses still on high alert. He jumped in, out of breath, and jammed the car into gear. With a hasty reverse, he clipped the bumper of the car behind him, the jolt a brief distraction from his escape. Screeching into the street, Robert floored it, heading east out of Georgetown and into the gritty, run-down neighborhoods of northeast inner Washington.

As he drove, Robert could see that Cindy was still speechless. His heart was pumping so hard that his tongue was literally pounding up and down like an anvil inside his mouth with each heartbeat. In trying to recover, he was even ignoring her—at least for the moment. He continued to grapple with the increasingly complicated situation. The CIA at his home? Why? It only made sense if they were coming after him for not pursuing the assassination of the Congressman. But he still had until at least New Year's Eve to complete the job. So why would they want him now? Was merely asking for more time enough to ignite the Agency into committing such an atrocity? Could they do such a thing? Or, better, why would they? If they had just wanted to talk, they would not have chased him. Who really did that?

"AND NOW, THIS SPECIAL REPORT ON THE SHOOTINGS IN GEORGETOWN," Vince Gillman's voice was booming on WTOP again, *"WE HAVE BEEN FOLLOWING NEWS OF A MULTIPLE HOMICIDE EVENT IN GEORGETOWN THIS MORNING. ABOUT AN HOUR AGO, THE FIRST REPORT BROKE THAT A SHOOTING HAD TAKEN PLACE AND THAT AT LEAST TWO PEOPLE HAD BEEN RUSHED TO THE GEORGE WASHINGTON UNIVERSITY HOSPITAL. APPROXIMATELY TWENTY MINUTES AGO, WE LEARNED THAT TWO INDIVIDUALS HAD DIED, AND AT LEAST THREE OTHER BODIES WERE FOUND IN THE UPSTAIRS LAW OFFICES LOCATED AT 30TH AND M STREET IN GEORGETOWN. WE NOW HAVE ADDITIONAL INFORMATION THAT THE SHOOTING HAS TAKEN PLACE AT A LAW FIRM WITH THE NAME OF FISCHER, CRAMER & MORRELL."*

Cindy began to shriek. It was not crying, but rather it was terrible shrieking, as if no deep breath could be taken but every shallow breath was pouring out of her body faster than she could take air in.

"IT IS NOW CONFIRMED THAT SIX PEOPLE ARE DEAD. THE DEAD ARE IDENTIFIED AS THE THREE LAWYERS, STANLEY FISCHER, LANDON CRAMER AND KEVIN MORRELL. TWO FEMALE STAFF PERSONS HAVE LIKEWISE BEEN FOUND SHOT TO DEATH IN THE OFFICES. IN ADDITION, A SECURITY GUARD HAS BEEN REPORTED DEAD IN THE DOWNSTAIRS LOBBY OF THE BUILDING WHERE THE LAW FIRM IS LOCATED. THE MOTIVE IS OBVIOUSLY UNKNOWN AT THIS TIME. HOMICIDE INVESTIGATORS ARE MOVING QUICKLY TO FERRET OUT THE MOTIVE FOR THIS AWFUL HAPPENING. WE WILL KEEP YOU POSTED THROUGH THE DAY AS FURTHER DEVELOPMENTS WARRANT. THIS IS VINCE GILLMAN RETURNING YOU TO YOUR REGULAR WTOP NEWS PROGRAM"

"You're going to have to pull yourself together a little bit," Robert explained to Cindy. "We cannot stay in this car!" She glanced up but remained silent. After another minute, he parked along the curb in the roughest part of town—the northwest inner-city area known as "The Shooting Gallery" among those in the drug trade.

"Get out! We've got to move quickly!" Robert yelled as he popped the trunk, pulled the wheelchair out and began unfolding it by the passenger side.

"Why here?" Cindy spoke her first words since stricken so deeply by the grief of the moment.

"Because this car is not safe! They've seen this car. They know it! Maybe it's bugged? I don't have time to see if they can track it. But they probably can. Turn off your phone! We may need to toss it!. There's no way they are letting me get away from my house without knowing that they could track my vehicle."

EDGE OF REDEMPTION

Robert helped her into the chair, grabbing her purse and the precarious stack of items she'd been carrying to work. He placed them in her lap and began pushing her down the street with urgency. The rough, worn neighborhood seemed to close in around them - peeling graffiti-tagged buildings, litter-strewn sidewalks, and the pungent smell of trash from overflowing dumpsters.

Passersby cast suspicious glances, their faces a blur as Robert hastened past. The cracked sidewalk threatened to jolt her from the chair at every step. The air vibrated with the hum of idling engines and the distant wail of sirens. People parted to let them through, their whispers and pointed stares amplifying her unease. Within the next five minutes, they arrived at the Columbia Heights Metro Subway Station. Robert purchased tickets for both of them and then guided her toward the handicapped elevator, which took them several stories down to the

Green Line platform.

Here's the text with minor adjustments for clarity and flow:

As soon as they reached the platform, the southbound subway train arrived. They boarded swiftly, finding a secluded seat away from prying eyes. Once settled, they began to converse in hushed tones.

"If you were so worried, why risk going to your place?" Cindy asked, her brow furrowed.

Robert's voice barely rose above a whisper. "I needed the cash stashed there. A large withdrawal from Riggs Bank would raise red flags. They'd know I'm leaving the country, and they can't let that happen...not after today's events. They want me badly, Cindy."

Cindy's eyes widened. "They were trying to kill you at the office, weren't they?"

Robert's gaze darted around the train car before nodding almost imperceptibly.

"I don't know...I guess so. How would they ever know it was even me? The warning just showed up in the papers yesterday morning, and we just dropped it off the night before." Robert answered.

"Yeah, it doesn't make sense... not with so many other people involved in this," Cindy said. "It could have been any of them."

"Well, I've got my..." Suddenly, Robert was hit by a thought which could have dropped him to his knees had he not already been sitting. He whispered, "That paper. You know where I got that paper?"

"Well, yeah, it was from my desk...I assume you mean the paper that we put the words on...right?"

"That's right, but..." Robert now hunched over, feeling like he might vomit.

"What is it, Bob? Tell me...you are scaring me even more!" Cindy said in a low whisper, certain that no one else could hear and making sure that Robert could hear every word.

"That's the thing. Those papers were tucked under a check invoice—the carbon copy that had just been signed by Landon Cramer. That's it!" Robert stepped closer to Cindy, locking his gaze with hers as he spoke softly. I'm sure they found the impression of Landon Cramer's signature on the paper. It went from generic bond to paper that had a lawyer in our office's signature on it...you know what that means?" He spoke painstakingly.

"What?" Cindy shook her head, somewhat perplexed.

"It means that somehow, they got a hold of what got delivered to The Washington Post. They ran their tests and Landon Cramer's name showed up right on the paper. They can extract even the tiniest microscopic impression from regular paper. So, they knew who sent it. Who else would send this stuff but me? They know where I work. They probably assumed that Cramer and the other lawyers knew about it."

There was silence for little more than a minute. "You think they killed them intentionally?" Cindy asked incredulously.

""I don't know. Maybe they were just after me and accidentally ran into the lawyers. It's possible they wanted to eliminate anyone who might know something about this." They probably think I've told the lawyers all about it. I can't believe it...I can't!" Robert whispered, feeling his emotions get the best of him.

Within another minute, they were moving forward to the doorway to change trains at Gallery Place/China Town. This required them to make their way to the elevator, go up one level, and take the Red Line to Metro Center. "We need to get you home quickly. The D.C. police will be at your place asking questions, and there may be others looking for me." The door opened and they moved out onto the platform and up the elevator to the other train.

The wait at Metro Center was eerie. With access to the outside still as much as forty feet above them, and at the end of a long set of escalators, they could still hear only silence. He knew that at some point they would start searching their cameras. The eerie silence sent chills down Robert's spine, igniting a confusing mix of anticipation and dread within him. He had encountered death more than most people—a modern-day executioner, if you will. This was different. He was struggling with the emotion that was telling him something about this experience. Something that was investing a new kind of fear in him. It was something too genuine. Too hard for his surface senses to interpret. This time, he was protecting someone other than himself.

Finally, the westbound Orange Line train pulled into the station. They successfully made the switch and were soon racing away at top subway speeds, leaving behind the chaos and disappearing beneath the Potomac, heading into Northern Virginia. The number of subway riders was lessening, and they again had a chance to talk. "So, what was this plan you had?" Cindy asked.

"Well, it's all changed now," Robert responded nervously. "Trying to buy more time seemed like the way to go. I just wanted to have enough time to pull my money together and get out of town."

Cindy looked up at him, eyes tearful, as if any suggestion of leaving her was the end of her world. "What do you mean, get out of town...and go where?"

Robert realized he had caused her pain. "To New England, and then... to Canada." He looked directly into her eyes, leaned forward, and kissed her softly on the lips. "And yes, I wanted to take you with me. I just didn't know how you would feel about it. From Canada, we'd head on to Switzerland." I know of a clinic. In the village of Montreux on Lake Leman, a beautiful place. There's some of the finest medical care in the world. I needed time...time to transfer funds. "That's one of the reasons I needed to get into my place. The information I need to make these transfers is in that house." Otherwise, the only way to do it is I would have to go into Rigg's Bank in Georgetown and go through a whole exercise trying to get the numbers again to get all of this done. However, they've got to be watching me for that. I have no doubt!"

"I was hoping you'd say that," Cindy whispered, her eyes locking onto Robert's.

"You mean that I don't have any money?" Robert asked, managing a faint smile despite the gravity of their situation.

Cindy's face softened. "No, silly man. That you wouldn't consider leaving without me."

As the train emerged from the tunnel and reached the surface, Cindy gazed out the window, lost in thought. After a contemplative pause, she turned back to Robert.

"Is it safe to go to my house?" she asked, her voice laced with concern.

Robert's expression turned serious. "I'm not sure that it is." What choice do we have? If you're not there to answer questions, then the police are going to start putting out a bulletin to find you right away. I don't have any problem with you telling them the truth. "I picked you up because your motorized wheelchair was malfunctioning, and when we got close to the crime scene, I panicked. You're my alibi—you can tell them I wasn't there."

"Won't they want to know where you are?" Cindy asked.

"Yes, that'll be the big question. So, I can't stick around for long."

Cindy grabbed Robert's arm and pulled him closer. "You can't be away from me any longer." She spoke with unwavering devotion, and the surge of fear only seemed to amplify her love. "If they kill you, then they can kill me too!" she whispered urgently.

INFERNO OF SACRIFICE

Robert looked at her, wanting to throw his arms around her and carry her. He could feel the strength of her words that somehow projected a layer of warmth over the cold pain that filled the better part of his mid-section. Then, the train stopped at Ballston Metro Station. Robert wheeled Cindy off the train, down the ramp, and then as quickly as possible in the cold, brisk morning, another seven blocks down busy Glebe Road and then east to North Vermont Street.

As Robert approached the street, he made the same careful assessment of the scene as he had on his approach to Dumbarton Street. Nothing appeared out of place. He could not see any tell-tale signs of government cars on the street. Cindy looked carefully as well. He could see no obvious signs of police presence. It did not mean that they were not there, but risks would need to be taken to get Cindy home, which would be consistent with any statement to the police. He suspected the police would soon want to speak with her, as she was one of the few remaining employees of the law firm. He wheeled her up to the house and into the entryway. After a quick inspection that lasted about two minutes, he was relieved to find that no one had been in the house since she left.

Robert switched on the TV and keyed the remote to the local news channel. A report was half-way done, *"...IN THE BUSHES, JUST OFF THE C&O CANAL BIKE PATH. HE WAS PRONOUNCED DEAD AT THE SCENE. THERE IS SIMPLY NO MOTIVE AS FAR AS THE REPORTS GO AT THIS POINT."*

As the news report concluded, Robert began frantically switching between radio stations. He finally landed on one where a reporter was broadcasting live from his usual jogging route. *"I'M HERE AT C&O CANAL ABOUT ONE QUARTER OF A MILE SOUTH, DOWN POTOMAC RIVER FROM CHAIN BRIDGE. A TWENTY-TWO-YEAR-OLD MALE HAS BEEN FOUND IN THE BUSHES DEAD*

FROM WHAT APPEARS TO BE A SELF-INFLICTED GUNSHOT WOUND TO THE HEAD. THE WEAPON FOUND AT THE SCENE IS CLAIMED BY HOMICIDE DETECTIVES TO BE THE SAME WEAPON USED IN THE SHOOTINGS ABOUT TWO AND ONE-HALF HOURS AGO AT THE FISCHER, CRAMER & MORRELL LAW FIRM. IT IS STILL TOO EARLY TO COMPLETE THE FINGERPRINT ANALYSIS, BUT THE SIMILARITY IN WEAPONS IS ENOUGH FOR AUTHORITIES TO START TRYING TO PIECE TOGETHER THE RELATIONSHIP OF THE YOUNG MAN TO THE LAW FIRM." The reporter paused for a moment while listening to his earpiece. *"AND THIS ADDITIONAL INFORMATION, THE YOUNG MAN FOUND DEAD WAS IN FACT A BICYCLE COURIER WHO WORKED PRIMARILY FOR THE FISCHER, CRAMER & MORRELL LAW FIRM. WHAT WE'RE NOW BEING TOLD IS THAT IT APPEARS AS THOUGH THE LAW FIRM'S RUNNER (AS THEY CALL THEM), MAY HAVE GONE INTO THE LAW FIRM, SHOT EVERYONE IN THE FIRM, AND LATER THE SECURITY GUARD, AND THEN RIDDEN OUT HERE ALONG THE C&O CANAL BIKE TRAIL TO COMMIT SUICIDE. AGAIN, WE HAVE NO WITNESSES. NO ONE HEARD THE SHOTS AND THERE WERE SOME BIKERS IN THE AREA WHEN IT WAS SUPPOSED TO HAVE HAPPENED. SO, WE WILL KEEP YOU POSTED FURTHER AS WE LEARN MORE. BACK TO YOU."*

"I don't believe that for a minute! There's no way!" Robert exclaimed, his voice firm and resolute.

"Why not?" Cindy asked, her curiosity piqued.

"They want to shut down the case quickly, keep it from spreading to clean detectives at D.C. Homicide," Robert explained, his tone unwavering. "They aim to silence everyone, Cindy. That's their MO. They'll stop at nothing."

He paused, his eyes burning with conviction and anger.

"The CIA's involved, I'm certain of it. They've done this before — eliminate witnesses, destroy evidence. It's a classic cover-up tactic."

"I can't believe it! I can't believe that any of this is going on! I want to wake up from this nightmare!" Cindy's panic was coming back.

At that point the telephone rang. Cindy shrieked out of fright and nervousness. "What do I do?"

"You answer the phone," Robert responded. Cindy wheeled to the phone and looked at the Caller I.D. "It's the D.C. Metropolitan... "I don't see the rest of it, but I'm sure it means police," she said, her voice filled with fear. The phone rang repeatedly until she finally answered. "Hello." Robert listened intently to her side of the conversation, curious about how she would manage the situation. What she had to say would dictate his next move.

"Yes, that's where I work...very upset...I've seen it on the news. No, I didn't...No, I couldn't...because I'm disabled with muscular dystrophy and my motorized wheelchair was not running. You can come here and look at it if you...Oh, well of course...No, I was about to go, but then I heard it...on the radio and then on TV and I haven't gone anywhere."

Her explanation sounded convincing to Robert. He wondered how long that would hold them off.

She continued, "Yes...I know him. I've only been there for two weeks, so I don't know anyone very well." There was a long pause. "He lives in Georgetown somewhere... No, I'd be glad to help. Just tell me what you need me to say... anything at all." Her voice cracked. "Yes, they were very wonderful people..." Robert was impressed with her acting ability.

As Cindy spoke, the news broadcast shifted to the Fischer family. Photographs flashed on screen, accompanied by the reporter's voiceover.

Cindy wheeled closer, transfixed by images of the Fischer children.

Their bright smiles and innocent faces haunted.

An interview with neighbors began. Cindy turned to Robert, her voice barely above a whisper.

"Those children... they look just like the ones in your pictures.

Robert's expression turned grave. She sounded haunting, direct and painfully accurate. She began to cry.

Robert continued to lose his stoic grip. He looked at the pictures and then looked at the gifts under Cindy's tree all from the children of the Fischer, Cramer and Morrell families. It was all like the special corner in his townhouse, just not as much history. This was her first Christmas with them. He noted that it was also her last. The sentiment was taking over, along with his ability to control his inner emotions. These were children without fathers, lost to tragedy. He felt a deep, painful realization wash over him: this was the same suffering his own children had endured for much of their lives. Anger consumed him—he hated himself, he hated life, and he loathed anyone responsible for such devastation.

Robert had killed and destroyed families. Now it was not even a distant thought that he had taken fathers and mothers from children. For every act, he painfully thought to himself, there had been many lonesome, vacant lives relegated to painful disarray of the heart—lives that would never repair, faces that would never smile, and voices that would only speak in sorrow. How am I any better than the CIA. Hell, I'm one of 'em.

DISARRAY OF THE HEART

Robert looked at the woman sitting in the wheelchair weeping uncontrollably. The person who had brought to him what he was coming to understand as love. He sat there, watching her break down in tears, her body shaking violently in a fit of anguish, as if she were the very embodiment of all the grief in the world. He remembered how she had been so perfect and so strong and brought him so much joy. Even with the muscular dystrophy, it seemed to him at times as if she had ascended above it all. He had seen her move him beyond the dark world of reality, she had caused him to dream dreams. Now, her tears were bringing him back to a world where he did not want to be anymore.

Robert found himself wondering if it might have been better that he had never met Cindy. She had softened him—made him feel like he could talk to Landon Cramer. Maybe on that first day, he should have walked across the lobby to his office and ignored the receptionist, as he had done on so many occasions. If he had acted differently, perhaps a Congressman and a Supreme Court Justice would have been dead, but the fine men he had worked alongside for so many years at the firm would still be alive. Their families would remain untouched, and Cindy wouldn't have to endure yet another painful chapter in her already difficult life.

Robert's mind wandered to the web of deceit he'd spun among his lawyer friends. If he hadn't been entangled in the deadly trade, they'd never have been dragged into its shadows. Their unwavering trust blinded them to the truth. Landon Cramer and his partners, pillars of integrity, had never once doubted him. Their innocence and goodness made them oblivious to Robert's secrets.

It was not long before his mind carried him away to another time. He had been here before, that day years ago at the beach house in Cape May Veronica's death had frozen him. He wandered away, stunned and numb, overwhelmed by a profound sense of guilt. Now, he reasoned, here he was again, having lost the only other anchors in his life: first Veronica, and now Landon Cramer, Stanley Fischer, and Kevin Morrell. As distant as they were, it was still as close as it gets in my life.

Robert then looked at Cindy, her head forward, face cupped in her hands. Another perplexing similarity organized itself from the mass of painful recollections passing through his brain. Just as then, there was another woman involved. Strange, he thought, how Gina had been a mere object of escape. He had known that, even consciously thought the thought. It had been a real mid-life crisis that could just have run its course and ended—that is, if the commuter flight back to Dulles had not crashed. It would have been gone...over. I could be in Chicago with Veronica, enjoying life as a grandfather. Perhaps I could have been more like Landon Cramer instead of the current version of Robert Cannon.

In the next moment, however, he recognized that his reconstruction of the past was far too simplistic. The darkness, depression and loneliness had begun even before Veronica perished. It is so easy to edit out the complexities of life when looking back, as if the struggles are only in the present. There were challenges then, and there are challenges now. The intensity of the past is often forgotten—perhaps that's why a woman chooses to have more than one child, a soldier recovers from his wounds to return to the battlefield, and a person allows themselves to fall in love again.

However, some lessons are never learned, Robert continued to reason with himself. He closed his eyes hard, pressing them together, his body in a sort of painful grimace. He imagined how the bloody interlude at the law office must have played out. Two powerful forces were working within him—a sense of rage against whomever carried out the deed, and a deeply discernable sense of guilt—that in reality, he had been the cause.

"It's all my fault, Cindy!" He spoke, breathing the depressing silence of several minutes. "I'm so sorry for what I have caused you. It should not have happened this way."

Cindy sat quietly. She did not respond. She continued to hold her hands over her face. Robert could see the tears intermittently slipping through her fingers.

Robert continued, "There is so much I still want to tell you. I want...despite all this...to be close to you."

Within a few minutes, Cindy removed her hands. Robert could see her red emotion-ridden face. As he started to move toward her, she spoke only one word. "No!" She then climbed into her wheelchair and rolled to the window that looked out into the garden, which was now cold, leafless, and beset by winter.

Robert understood the signal; he could feel her pulling away. For a moment, he was unable to shake the self-pitying thought that everyone was destined to distance themselves from him—even a woman facing death with no one else by her side. Even she would reject him.

In the next series of thoughts, Robert reminded himself of her magnificence, the day they met, the weekend at Cape May, his seeming deliverance from depression that on all accounts, within his mind, was due to Cindy and no one else. He could not fathom even the momentary impact of her distance. She had been so forward, so accommodating, so driven to be with him at every moment. It was as if the last years of life might not be wretched; as if there was still time to live, even if that time was short. Maybe, he thought, that time had already come to an end. The murders at the law firm and the revelation of his past were more than anyone should have to bear. It all began to make painful sense. Robert felt the darkness closing in around him, bringing him back to where he had started—before he met Cindy. It was another hell to which he had relegated himself. Wonderful things in life, smiles, affection, heartfelt love, are all either fake or fleeting—easily superseded by time and events. These events have been very big, Robert thought to himself. He stood up and walked in the direction of the garage door. It was time to leave.

As he reached the door she spoke. "Where are you going?"

"I sense..." Robert's voice trembled. "Having me around will only make it worse. I need to go." The words were half real and half artificial, and not totally honest. He hoped she would ask him to stay.

She turned her wheelchair toward Robert but did not move across the room. "Maybe you are right." She was somber. Robert's stomach churned with her words. Deep inside he had hoped there would be some reprieve. He opened the door. Cindy spoke once more. "Bob. There were no chances left for me, that is, until Landon Cramer gave me that job. In the first week, I was visited twice by the children. "They loved me there. By the time you walked into my life, everything seemed perfect. I thought..." Her voice was measured, striving to remain steady. "I thought that my last year, or maybe even years—if I was lucky—would be fulfilling. I never pretended that Landon Cramer would keep me in that job for long." I'm going downhill, and I know it. By the time I could not work, I would have a family. They would visit me..." Then her words broke, "I hoped they would keep me from dying alone."

Cindy's words cut deep. Robert yearned to hold her, but his guilt held him back. He was the source of her pain.

"I'm so sorry," he whispered, the words escaping involuntarily. Yet, he meant everyone.

As he turned to leave, Cindy's soft voice halted him.

"I would stop them if I could, Bob. All this insanity... I wish I could!" Her words hung in the air, a heartfelt plea.

Robert's eyes lingered on hers, seeing the anguish and determination.

He could see her looking off into space, addressing the vacant room so much as speaking to him. She then sat up and spoke resolutely. "I would kill the CIA Director if I could."

Robert could not believe the words he was hearing. "What did you say?"

"If I could, I would kill him. He has ruined it for you and me and has taken away my hope. I am angry! I am hurt! So many others are broken today by him."

Robert felt a surge of hope as he witnessed her emergence from her previously shattered emotional state. It was a rare opportunity for conversation. "Why did you say that?" he asked, unable to resist the urge to know more, worried that his dark past might have offended her more than he had ever realized. He spoke further without allowing her to answer his question. "Cindy, it's not the CIA Director. He's like me. He carries out his assignments. The person who is behind this is Charlotte Reid. She's the killer here. It was her people who took out the law firm. I have no doubt. The problem is at the top. This kind of evil is a top-down problem. It's been that way for a long time. I never doubted that each bad thing I did had the President's approval. I don't know that, but I believe it."

"Then, maybe I will do something about her," Cindy spoke again with astounding resolution.

Robert thought he was hearing insanity. With the police intent on questioning Cindy, all she didn't need to do was send a threatening letter or worse to the Vice President of the United States. "Cindy, there is nothing you can do. Just let it go."

"I won't let it go." Cindy spoke quietly but certain. "Maybe it was just a dream," she mused, reflecting on the notion that in those final days, when she could no longer eat, speak, or even breathe on her own, there would be a steady, if small, stream of visitors by her bedside. Maybe a violin serenade occasionally from one of the children. Maybe one of the wives touching me like my mother used to. And maybe Landon Cramer coming in to give me work assignments that I could never do, but him talking to me like I'm on the mend and expected to be back at my desk the next day."

Cindy rolled her wheelchair to the kitchen counter near the

telephone. She picked up a piece of paper. "But you know, this tells me I have a chance."

"What do you mean?"

Cindy began to read. "You are invited as a special guest to the Greater Washington Area M.D. End-of-Year Holiday Fundraiser, at twelve o'clock noon on December 30th at the Kennedy Center. A special platform area shall be available to accommodate wheelchairs near the front of center stage. The event will be hosted by the Hon. Charlotte Reid, Vice President of the United States of America. Cindy stopped reading and began to speak in what Robert observed as almost a nervous babble. "I had no intention of just being another poster child for this event. "Now, I think I'll go. Maybe I can blow myself up, taking her with me! I could sneak a gun inside the engine of my wheelchair or hide it next to my colostomy bag. They'd never suspect that. Maybe, for once, this grotesquely awful part of my body can serve a purpose!" She reached for the side of her shirt but halted before revealing the device that had been both a burden and a benefit to her private life for as long as she could remember.

"Cindy, you're talking nonsense." He started to close the door in a move to remain in the house. She was too upset to leave alone.

"No. You leave!" Cindy yelled. "I don't know what I'll do, but I will do something. No one can get away with this! Not even the Vice President!" She could see his concern. "Oh, don't worry, I'll not drag you into it. I have not seen you since work, the day before Christmas!" she declared, holding head up and sitting as erect as her body would allow in a display of stoic pride. "If there is anyone that knows otherwise, they are now dead! Leave! I can make it on my own." She swiveled around on the wheelchair and returned to the window. Robert took one further look at the situation, was overcome by its futility, and walked out, closing the door behind him.

* * *

RECKONING

Making his way out onto Glebe Road, Robert did not know whether to travel into the city toward the District, or outward toward the Beltway. In either event, he had nowhere to go. He then drove west on North Fairfax Drive, staying on the main road for just a short while before pulling into a parking lot near the soccer fields at Fields Park.

Cindy's sudden change had surprised him. He could understand her grief, but the sense of rage was something he had thought her incapable of. Yet, as he pondered her words further, so much seemed to make sense. The people at the top decide who's good, who's bad, and who's got to go. They just get people like me to go out and do the job. The Vice President of the United States has gotten away with murder—this time—the murder of my friends.

Robert recalled driving north to New England, fully aware that all he had to do was make a call, yet terrified that he might never find the courage to do so. Facing his children, regardless of whether they ever knew the truth, would have created more shame than a person could endure in one lifetime. If he had just not accepted the Korean Airlines Flight 007 job.

Robert's thoughts turned to his children, a sudden longing to reconnect before it's too late. But the timing couldn't be more chaotic – CIA and DOD entanglements, the firm's murder, and his own mortality looming. As he sat in the Fields Park parking lot, uncertainty paralyzed him. The road ahead, literally and figuratively, stretched out in indecision. A one-way sign dictated a right turn, but Robert's emotions remained stuck. His mind raced: Which direction leads to safety? To family? To redemption? The questions swirled, leaving him immobilized, unable to move forward.

The weight of his circumstances bore down on him: No clear escape, no haven, no tomorrow guaranteed. Robert's world had shrunk to this solitary moment, this solitary decision – turn right or left? Yet, he couldn't move. The painful oppressive darkness of depression was making an otherwise partly cloudy afternoon dark and stormy. He wanted to shift the car into reverse, but he couldn't bring himself to do it. He longed to reach for the handle, open the door, and step out, yet he remained frozen in place. Overwhelmed by depression and gripped by an induced panic attack, he felt utterly helpless. Fatigue washed over him, and eventually, he succumbed to sleep.

The dream let him go to another place. It was in his past, maybe even before the children were born. Robert and Veronica had gone to a nearby high school track to run. It was a rare event where Veronica joined him at the track. He ran and she walked. This allowed him to pass her about every third lap.

Within minutes, it began to rain. There was no lightning, just a hard and unusually warm southern rainstorm having invaded the area from the south. Robert assumed it would be time to stop and head for cover. Veronica, true to her composed nature, typically wouldn't allow herself to be caught in the rain. Yet, to Robert's surprise, as he rounded the bend on the north end of the track and approached the grandstands, he spotted her at the far south end. She had chosen to forgo the shelter of the stadium and was walking resolutely through the downpour.

Robert was struck with a sense of joy and adventure that he had not felt before that time. He sprinted a fast hundred-meter dash along the straightaway to catch up with her. Once reaching her, he could see her curly dark reddish-brown hair pasted around her face by the rain. Never had he seen such beauty as he pulled her into his arms and kissed her in the downpour. She was kissing back, playfully frolicking in the rain like a clueless teenager thinking she was in love for the first time.

Robert took off, running the laps so fast that he was back to her in less than two. By this time, they were so drenched that they literally stuck together. Robert's intimate moment with Veronica suddenly twisted into a surreal nightmare. As he reached to remove her shirt, her body transformed into a lifeless, life-sized mannequin.

He froze, shocked and repulsed. The stormy backdrop and scoreboard lights seemed to mock him, a stark contrast to the eerie, artificial figure before him. Robert's mind reeled, struggling to comprehend the jarring shift from passion to plastic perfection. The mannequin's cold, stiff form felt like a cruel betrayal, a stark reminder of the darkness lurking beneath the surface.

His revulsion deepened, Robert recoiled from the synthetic substitute, his thoughts racing to escape the unsettling reality. The third was anger as he recognized the cruel trick that is possible only in the dream world.

Robert fought to wake up, struggling to pry his eyes open. Even when he managed to do so, he found himself caught in a haze, teetering between sleep and full awareness. As he blinked, he stared blankly around his car, trying to piece together his surroundings and figure out where he was. Closing his eyes, he attempted to recapture the dream of Veronica before it took such a bizarre turn.

How could I be so settled, so content in one moment, and so totally deceived in the next? How can so much be lost so quickly? Robert wondered as he continued to come fully awake, trying to regain connection with lucid thought, while still not fully conscious.

The wail of a police siren jolted Robert from his trance, causing him to jerk forward, nearly banging his forehead against the steering wheel. He quickly scanned his surroundings, trying to locate the source of the piercing sound, and concluded that it must be a highway patrol car on the nearby U.S. 66.

Momentarily the siren began to subside, but the feeling from the dream did not. He wanted to fall back to sleep, to know the Veronica he had never known. It took only a moment for Robert to realize how alone he was in his life, and how much he needed Cindy. A visceral longing worked its way through his mid-section. Robert's determination surged as he left Fields Park, driven by a newfound purpose. He arrived at Cindy's doorstep, urgency etched on his face.

"Cindy, listen! I've got a plan!" he exclaimed.

Cindy's eyes widened, curiosity mingling with caution.

"Teach me to drive your wheelchair," Robert asked, resolve in his voice. "I'll take on the Vice President. We can reclaim our lives, together."

A glimmer of hope flickered in Cindy's eyes.

"Maybe," she whispered, "just maybe..."

Robert's words hung in the air, a promise of redemption and shared purpose. The possibility of vengeance for Landon Cramer's loss and a future with Cindy ignited a beacon of hope.

"Let's do this," Cindy said, a resolute smile spreading across her face.

Together, they began to weave a fragile thread of hope, a chance to rewrite their shattered lives. Cindy looked up at him, first squinting as if she was looking into the sun, and then turning her head slightly as if she was struggling to hear. Robert paused at the door. Cindy then rolled back away from the door, suggesting to Robert that he could enter. As he stepped inside and shut the door behind him, she lunged at him, wrapping her arms around him with all the strength she could muster. "You would do that?" she asked, now out of her chair. He held her upper body tightly, her legs dangling lifelessly to the floor. The closeness between them was quickly becoming a source of comfort.

Robert responded, "You've given me some ideas!" Robert picked Cindy up, then cradled her in his arms and carried her to the sofa. For the next hour, despite all the anticipation of what was soon to happen, few words were exchanged. As the two simply held each other close, exchanging the warmth of one another's bodies in silence...

In time, Cindy looked at Robert, gazing directly into his eyes, and spoke. "I love you so much! You are the man I have always wanted...I can't believe after all I've gone through, I have you."

Robert felt an unyielding strength rising within. Never had he felt so deeply connected to a cause. In a world where reality seemed inescapable, he discovered a purpose he'd never known before. For Cindy, he would do anything. His resolve was also for the lawyers he loved, and the children whose lives had been torn apart. He thought of those he had killed, their families, and loved ones, and of himself, transformed into a monster he never thought he'd become. This crusade was also for his country, forcing him to confront whether he truly loved it. Cindy's love had taught him so much, and now it was time to act. Robert's transformation was underway, driven by the power of love and redemption.

Over the next hour, Robert laid out a plan for the upcoming end-of-year charity event, one he believed could work. He noticed that Cindy had returned to her former self, her renewed confidence fueling his own and making him feel invincible. With her support, anything seemed possible. While he couldn't allow her to take the risk, he resolved to take it on himself, determined to approach it with as much probability of success as he had with his many previous assignments.

19

"Bentley, we are running out of time! The press starts rolling tomorrow on the coin flip." Charlotte Reid was sitting at the end of a long table in the West Wing conference room. "When it hits the streets, I can't back out! Your solution is history!"

Bentley looked uncharacteristically sheepish for an acclaimed political wizard. "I can't guarantee anything at this point, Char... there's just too much happening, and that assassination rumor circulating doesn't help." "I'm not so sure," the Vice President replied. "It's definitely pushing the Chinese money story out of the headlines—page 37 in the New York Times."

"Well, I asked them to bury it. They were hesitant until I hinted about the coin flip... then they were suddenly ready to do anything for us."

For his part, Bentley was coming to grips with the fact that the American public was getting sick and tired of the relentless election gridlock. Even though Charlotte's plan had at first seemed so amateurish, so unlike hers, it was now gaining traction. He was getting word from the CIA that their officer was "in the cold," meaning out of contact and that the assassination of Congressman Ormond could no longer be guaranteed.

"So did you leak that dual assassination story, Bentley?" Charlotte asked, at the same time pulling out a make-up mirror and reworking her lipstick in a sort of irreverent slight to the room in which so many famous decisions had been made. "I think you did it... this story about the threat on Justice McCall—that's brilliant. It makes things look both ways, a very clever disguise!"

Bentley wanted to take credit, but he couldn't; he still had no clue who had slipped the strange, newspaper-lettered story to the Washington Post. It painted both sides in a bad light, which served his purposes well. "Char, it wasn't me, truly."

"Just seems like something you'd pull off!" Charlotte said, pulling a chair from the table and motioning for Bentley to sit beside her.

"Well, it just wasn't me." Bentley's response lacked any enthusiasm.

"Maybe I oughta fire you and bring on whoever it is that has figured out how to disguise your silly little plot and make it look like everybody's hands are in the till!"

"Maybe you shouldn't!" Bentley was facetious.

Charlotte continued the offensive. "Because whoever it is has taken the public's mind off this Chinese money thing. When the coin flip stuff hits tomorrow, the whole curious world will be somewhere else!"

Bentley interrupted. "It cuts both ways, so not so fast. You think anybody'll be focused on the football knifing deal from Houston's past? No...so he's getting some real suck out of this thing too!"

"I'm not so sure about that," Charlotte continued. "I'm still surprised Houston ever agreed. I think it gives us the upper hand in the media."

"How so?" Bentley asked.

"Because everyone hates this election. I've come up with the common man's solution. I get the credit—no matter what happens."

"Aren't you worried about the editorials?" Bentley wasn't convinced. "You know, headlines like 'Reid Hands Out Straws to Cabinet, Long End Wins!' or 'It's Eeny-Meeny-Miney-Mo Time at the White House!'"

A CLEAR PATH

"That's so cute, Bentley, where'd you come up with that? You had to spend some time to think those up!" Charlotte was becoming irritated; Bentley was not getting her message. "If you think it's so awful, then get your job done. I think the coin flip is a good idea, but if you change the circumstances, then even if the coin is in the air, I'll back out of it. I really will. No matter how bad it looks, because then I'll have a clear path. McCall will make sure it never gets to the House, and if it does, Mississippi will vote for me."

The Vice President paused, waiting for Bentley to respond, but he stayed silent. She pressed on, her tone firm and commanding. "If I win, I can fix all of this over the next four years—you know I can!" Her voice was resolute. "It'll give you more time here, right at the seat of power."

Bentley moved to sit at the table, but she abruptly kicked the chair across the room.

She stood up and grabbed Bentley in a rough, unaffectionate embrace, then stared straight into his eyes. "Go get that bastard killed! I'm afraid of my brilliant ideas! I can only live with 50/50 if you are a failure, and I don't want my man to fail!"

Bentley sensed he had shrunk in her mind and plans more than ever before. All he could manage was a brief, "Sure, I'll get it done," as he left the room, passing the saluting Marine guard on his way to his soon-to-be-vacant office at the Executive Office Building. He'd been counting on a move to the West Wing—to the Chief of Staff's office—but Charlotte now seemed to cast doubt on his role. As for the job itself, he assumed the CIA had ordered the hit on the lawyer's office in Georgetown to spur the out-in-the-cold agent into action. But this is not something he could tell the Vice President or anyone else—especially when he was still uncertain as to who really carried out the killings.

For now, it would be a two-track effort, both designed to save the republic; get the CIA off its duff or watch a coin flip at the fifty-yard line of an NFL game. To him, both had perilous prospects for failure—risks that he was not accustomed to taking.

Bentley sat down at his desk amid the moving boxes and picked up the phone. "That's right, the CIA director!" He barked into the phone, "I don't care if he's on vacation...I need to talk to him now...right now!"

* * *

By evening, Robert had made his way, again using the Metro and then a cab, to Reston, Virginia, where he opened a shop for earnest in his storage locker. By 3:00 a.m., after a trip to an all-night copy shop, he had powered up his equipment—computer, scanner, and various other tools—and produced new driver's licenses for himself and Cindy. Using a digital photo he'd taken before heading to Reston, he created aliases for them, each showing Montana state licenses.

It was another item which Robert worked very hard to develop that had even greater significance. After several more hours using Cindy's invitation, Robert had produced an invitation for himself to the United Way Fundraiser at Kennedy Center. In addition, he had duplicated the handicapped person's pass using the name Sydney Wilstead. But all other items, including social security number, address, description of disability and other relevant information were included. It looked authentic and he was rather proud of his work, even though fatigue was overtaking him.

By 6:00 a.m., he had curled up in the blankets he had brought to the storage locker a day earlier, certain it would serve as an adequate safe house amid the shifting plans. Initially, he had thought he was hiding due to his failure to eliminate Justice McCall and Congressman Ormond. Now, however, he found himself in hiding for an entirely different reason. There would be a termination, but one that neither the CIA nor the Department of Defense had planned on. This time, he planned on playing the role of the "Lever" to perfection.

TRUTHS LAID BARE

The sound of trucks and other vehicles pulling into the storage area awakened Robert. He had long since re-worked the locking mechanism so that he could control it from the inside. As he listened carefully to the noises outside the flimsy fiberglass door, he was relieved to hear what sounded like patrons of the storage lockers routinely getting their morning chores done. The sound of boxes being stacked, and furniture being hauled was easy to discern. It had a sort of domestic, unofficial sound. He finally lifted the door, looked around to make certain he was unnoticed, and headed out to the bus stop. Minutes later, he was on a Metro bus going west towards Dulles Airport.

Within half an hour, he was testing his Montana driver's license along with his newly created credit card. The driver's license was accepted immediately, without any comments. The credit card, however, was more complicated—it was a blank onto which he had printed the name of the Montana resident. He knew it wouldn't work with most card readers or ATMs.

As he waited nervously, the person at the Budget Car Rental counter manually punched in the number. This was the first real test of his plan in the outside world.

Robert felt a wave of relief as the standard magnetic strip on the card properly aligned with the information. There was a time when the pre-programmed strips would remain valid for at least a week before the banking system caught on and canceled them. But since the advent of the Patriot Act, they were only good for two or three transactions at best over a forty-eight-hour period, often using some unfortunate and unsuspecting person's account. The system had become much quicker at automatically shutting down suspicious credit accounts.

Any defect would have stifled the whole plan, slowing, if not stopping him, during the first step. Now, with a new card and a $9,999.00 credit limit at Maryland Bank, N.A., he was ready to move on to the next phase.

IRON RESOLVE

Robert rented a nondescript white Chevy Lumina and immediately headed back in the direction of the District. He avoided a stop at Cindy's home, by-passing it in favor of a quick trip back into downtown Georgetown. At 12:30 p.m., with just one-half hour left before the bank's Saturday closing time at 1:00 p.m., he entered the Riggs Farmers & Merchants Bank to make one last withdrawal. With the bank handling withdrawals, deposits, and no other bank business on Saturday, and with no electronic reporting to the Feds, he knew he could withdraw a substantial amount of money—an amount that would not be discovered until the bank balanced the Saturday activity on Monday morning. At the same time, he knew that he had to be careful to avoid a withdrawal that would trigger an immediate report to Homeland Security.

Upon hearing Robert's fabricated story about an urgent need for $25,000 in cash, the teller checked his five accounts on the computer and noted that they totaled over $1,500,000. She recognized him from his many prior visits to the bank and was more than willing to provide the Saturday limit of $25,000 in cash.

After leaving the bank, he drove around the block, up the street, and past his flat in Dumbarton. As he passed by, he slowed down and glanced over his shoulder down the street. He couldn't spot any signs of the CIA in the area but decided against stopping. There were essentials he needed, but he was acutely aware that the CIA likely anticipated those needs as well. This was not the time to take any chances.

Robert then worked his way down onto M Street, drove south to 30th and turned right down the one-way road. He drove past the office while looking momentarily through the archway into the Georgetown Suites Courtyard, and then focused on the large glass doors leading into the office building. There was still yellow tape across the door. It struck pain into his heart. It had to be ended, he thought to himself. Cindy is right. This sort of thing simply cannot be allowed to happen. Not in my world, not in her world, not anywhere in this country. He then drove back into Washington, across the Lincoln Memorial Bridge, and worked his way up into Arlington to Cindy's house.

The approach code he had devised with Cindy was straightforward: Robert would drive by her house on North Vermont Avenue twice, and she would then turn on the porch light in the middle of the day. On a bright Saturday morning, unless someone looked closely, it would be nearly impossible to notice. He parked his car on North Utah Street, a side street just a block east of Cindy's home, and began walking in her direction, feeling confident he would recognize danger when he saw it. As he approached, he carefully scanned the cars parked along the streets leading to her house. Nothing seemed suspicious, which led him to ponder when the CIA would make their move against him. The Agency could easily control the timing and location—especially in DC. He couldn't help but wonder if anyone had connected Cindy to him yet. Surely, they had already visited his home and ransacked the place by now.

Surely, with all the others at the law firm dead, they would be back to interrogate Cindy, again and again. Maybe the CIA was still waiting for him to follow through on Congressman Ormond? The thought lent him some confidence that that perhaps he had at least through New Year's Eve to stay alive. It was a bubble of hope which he knew could easily burst at any moment.

Robert walked across the front yard of Cindy's house, then quickly through a narrow side yard around to the back, entering through a door to the kitchen. He noticed Cindy sitting pensively at the kitchen table in her wheelchair. She seemed drawn and gaunt, far removed from the vibrant positive personality that he had recently known. He sat down at the table, reached out, took her hand, and began to speak. "Well, I'm ready to move the plan along, how about you?"

"It sounds like there's not much I really need to do." Cindy spoke in a down, almost disappointed manner.

"Teaching me how to operate that wheelchair and look the part is awfully important," Robert responded. "I can tell you this, I don't want you anywhere near where all of this is going to come down. I just want you to go to Cape May…to the cottage and wait." He then pulled out a piece of paper, laid it down on the table and pointed as he spoke. "I've got some money in Switzerland. Here are the bank account and control numbers. I've also arranged for a wire transfer to go out first thing on Monday morning. The order has been placed, and with any luck, the bank will handle it before they catch on to everything. When the wire goes through, I can't be sure if they'll be asleep at the switch or not, but I do know that within twenty-four hours, they'll be piecing things together and will be after me wherever I end up."

"I don't want your money, Robert…I want you. How does money help me in the direction my life is going?" Cindy asked, still tearful.

"In the first place, my plan is to get out of the country. In the second place, I want to take you to Montreux. It's a special place. And will be for us. Maybe we've got a year or two. Maybe the doctors there will be able to do something to allow you to live longer." Robert looked across the table, fatigued from a cold night spent in the storage locker, yet still determined to carry out the plan. "Here's your identity," he said, handing her a new driver's license. "And here's your new credit card. It's a MasterCard from Maryland Bank. It should work for about a week, but eventually, their computers will catch on."

She looked up at him. How did you do this? Where did you get these things?" Cindy was incredulous.

"Don't you think a guy should be able to make an honest living?" Robert tried to smile as well, but it was painful. He then changed the subject. "What do you say we go look at this contraption in the garage that you've been talking about?"

The two made their way out the back door with Cindy wheeling down the ramp leading to the garage. They both entered through a walk-in door to the rear of the garage and Cindy pointed to a motorized wheelchair sitting in the corner. "That's it…it's nothing pretty."

Robert walked over and began to examine the machine carefully. He unscrewed the engine cover and started to look carefully at the electronic housing and the chain drive-type transmission. "I'm going to need more room." he commented.

"I don't know what else we have." Cindy responded. "Maybe…"

Robert interrupted her, saying, "You're right," as he noticed her pointing to the motor housing on her current machine. "This one is larger. It provides more space over the engine, and possibly even underneath it, as long as things don't get too hot." He then carefully examined the two hollow metal bars that supported a tray for carrying personal items in front of the driver. The bars extended from the floor plate up to the small scooter-like machine, about two and a half feet high, angling back toward the driver.

A weaker crossbar assembly was attached at about two feet up the length of the pole, which angled forward to support the tray as well. This would allow a driver to carry a considerable number of items on the tray and yet at the same time, always have the tray largely in reach. "Yep, this is what I need. I'm going to have to make some modifications to this. It won't quite work the way it is."

"I don't really have any tools, so how are you going to do this?"

"Well, we've got my storage unit, and what I have there will have to suffice. I'm going to have to get right to it. I'm already operating on about two hours of sleep, and I've just got to get some rest before I move this along."

Throughout the mid-afternoon, Robert rested. Cleaning up after his long night's work in the storage unit, combined with very little sleep, had worn him out. At approximately 4:00 p.m., he loaded the older motorized wheelchair onto the carrying trailer, retrieved his rental car, and drove it to Cindy's home. Once there, he quickly attached the trailer to the car. Fearing that she might attract unwanted visitors, he hurried back to Reston for another night of work.

Once at the storage locker, Robert felt rejuvenated. His work became precise and methodical. Using a hacksaw, he cut the two-and-a-half-inch-thick, twelve-inch-long hollow poles that supported the tray and then reversed their positions on the motorized wheelchair so that the poles pointed forward. He repositioned the tray, allowing the poles to angle back toward the rider. With the front wheel turned entirely around, the support poles now leaned forward at an approximate forty-five-degree angle.

Robert began looking through metal boxes that he had stacked amid the cardboard boxes in the storage unit. Within a matter of minutes, he pulled out a green military ammo box, unclipped, and opened the lid. He reached in and pulled out several long, narrow cylindrical sticks that looked like small road flares. In addition to the warning labels on the side of the sticks were the words "Phosphorous Stun Rocket: 6 oz. Flare." He then slipped the eight-inch-long rocket into the three-quarter inch diameter hole on the pole frame supporting the tray. Noting it was not quite the fit he had in mind, he took out the hacksaw and took another three inches off the pole.

Once satisfied that both poles were properly positioned and re-anchored to the footrest of the motorized wheelchair, Robert pulled a small hand drill out of a locksmith kit. He then drilled an almost microscopic hole in each of the metal poles approximately one inch from their base. Then, after searching a few minutes for another metal box in the storage unit, he pulled out what appeared to be a spool of thread and walked to a makeshift tool bench, flipping on a light underneath a magnifying glass approximately eight inches in diameter.

Using surgical scissors from the locksmith kit, Robert began cutting thirty-three-inch lengths of fine fiber from the spool. He then reached into the kit and pulled out a simple one-inch needle, threading the fiber through it and tying off the end with a square knot. Next, he slid the phosphorous rocket down the three-quarter-inch shaft of the handlebar supporting the tray, pushing the needle through a microscopic hole in the handlebar where it met a soft material that penetrated deep into the body of the phosphorous flare.

After opening the battery compartment in the motor, Robert carefully examined the copper spring connectors. He returned to the magnifying glass, took out two more one-inch needles, and, using a small set of pliers from the locksmith kit, fashioned the needles into hooks. To complete the process, he taped the hooks to the inside of the plastic housing covering the battery compartment.

Over the course of the next hour, Robert followed a similar process by removing the handlebars, reversing them so they pointed forward, appearing like a modified racing bike handle. Again, it gave him a forward projecting end of the handlebar, though it was at a much lower angle than the support poles for the tray.

The next two hours were spent doing on a small scale what he had done on a very large scale in Spain a year and one-half earlier. The Spanish bomb had been a simple binary firebomb. He had packed five pounds of napalm gelatin into a glass cylinder which, together with some papier mâché modifications, had been painted to appear like a large hollow gourd for carrying water. In the upper ten percent of the glass cylinder was Semtex, a substance that even in the slightest mixing with the gelatin would make everything immediately unstable and initiate a chemical reaction, exploding into a huge fireball. In the Spanish operation, he had installed five such devices outside the hotel over several hours. Each device contained a thin glass membrane that separated the gelatin from the Semtex. This task was not for amateurs; even the slightest jarring could cause the membrane to break, resulting in a fiery explosion that could incinerate anyone nearby, including the bomb setter himself.

As a killing device, it boasted a very high success rate. When triggered by remote control, even a tiny crack in the membrane would unleash a massive fireball. Although not all devices ignited simultaneously, one would trigger another as the substances mixed, leading to secondary explosions that blew the wing of the Hotel De Leon into the street. This technique had been further perfected by Iraq's insurgents on the streets of Baghdad.

However, the current device was much smaller.

The glass cylinders were only slightly larger than golf balls. This would work well, given the plan to conceal them inside a colostomy device which Cindy would help him attach under his clothing. The colostomy bag would be the perfect place of concealment. It was an unlikely spot for a searcher to look, especially given the fact that if the seal was broken, an absolute putrid smell would engulf the area. Moreover, the smell would cut off any detection by bomb sniffing dogs.

Robert completed his work by filling the cylinders with gelatin but held off on injecting the Semtex into the small upper chamber. This he would do at the last possible moment.

WAR WAGON

After carefully loading stun rockets in the handlebars, Robert gently put the handlebar grips back in place. They would serve as able muzzle covers, removable on a second's notice. Then, just before leaving, he grabbed a handful of pressurized tear gas canisters. They were old, but after a brief test that cleared his nostrils more than he wanted them cleared, he knew they were still pressurized and would work in a crowd. These he would tape inside the plastic engine cover, next to the needle hooks already taped into place.

Arriving back at Cindy's home by mid-evening, it was time for a driving lesson. The weather was cold but clear, a fortunate reprieve for their plans. After loading Cindy into the car, Robert drove to the parking lot at nearby Quincy Park, where they could practice in relative seclusion.

To enhance their disguise, Robert tightly bound his legs together with one of Cindy's limb control straps, forcing himself to maneuver the vehicle without any use of his legs. As he adjusted to this awkward positioning, Cindy watched him closely, coaching him not just on how to drive, but also on how to present himself.

He leaned into the role, inferring pronounced muscular dystrophy by turning his entire upper body with a stiff neck, his eyes wide and panicked whenever he moved. The challenge was to control the wheelchair while maintaining that carefully crafted expression of slight terror. Initially, he found it difficult to juggle both tasks, but with Cindy's encouragement, he began to settle into the performance, slowly becoming more adept at masking his true intentions.

The natural tendency was to use his legs when driving. To succeed, he could not allow any voluntary motion in his lower body to show. All he would need to do is move one foot or a slight bend of a knee, and it would be a dead giveaway. Once bound together and turned to one side, his legs could not be moved unless he reached down with his hand and moved them over to the other side. In each event, the legs would need to fall limply hard to the left or hard to the right. For either to stop or be upright, or even to be in a semi-upright position, would risk exposing him as an imposter. Given the nature of the event, many attendees— especially those also in wheelchairs—would likely be able to spot a fake with ease. Robert knew he needed to perform well if he was going to succeed in their scheme. With every detail carefully considered, Robert tightened his grip on the steering wheel, steeling himself for the challenge ahead. The stakes were high, and any misstep could unravel everything they had worked for. He took a deep breath, focusing on maintaining the façade, ready to execute their plan with precision.

This, together with the M.D., would hopefully avoid any suspicion of such an extremely afflicted person.

The act would be all the more difficult for the reason that once Robert was in place in the Kennedy Center concert hall, he would need to feign a slight breakdown of his motorized wheelchair as a pretext for opening the battery compartment and attaching the wires to the battery to set up the detonator, as well as retrieve the tear gas canisters.

By about 10:00 p.m. the training session had ended and the two of them returned to Cindy's home, which had been visited only once by detectives from the D.C. Metropolitan Police Department. The purpose had been to conduct an interview with Cindy. They had asked about Robert Cannon. Where had she last seen him? Why he was absent from work? It was clear that someone was not buying the law firm courier story. It also occurred to Robert that the people who had any direct knowledge of even the slightest level of fraternization between Cindy and himself were dead. He was not worried about the D.C. police, but the CIA still had him spooked. Robert turned to face her, the dim light from the streetlamp filtering through the curtains casting shadows across her face. "Happy? Even with everything going on?"

Robert paused, surprised to hear her positivity after her earlier despair. He hesitated but felt compelled to speak. "What makes you happy at a time like this? We're about to change the course of world events tomorrow, and... I'm scared." Cindy laughed lightly. "Scared— that's relative. After what you've done, I doubt you understand that word."

Robert saw she still had no idea what lay ahead. "I've spent many nights awake, scared about everything. I've fought depression and wrestled with demons. I often thought I could drown it in whiskey or run so hard that surviving would be all I thought about."

Her expression shifted to concern. "I didn't know," she said softly. "I always thought you were strong, even invincible."

"Strength is often a facade," he replied. "Behind it is pain and fear. I've faced moments where I didn't know if I'd make it through the next hour. Tomorrow, everything could come crashing down, and I don't know what I'll do if it does."

Cindy shifted closer. "You don't have to face it alone. Whatever happens, we're in this together. That counts, doesn't it?" He nodded slowly. "You're right. But it's a heavy burden. I just hope I can keep you safe." Her eyes softened with determination. "You can, Robert. We'll watch each other's backs. We'll figure this out." He let out a breath he hadn't realized he was holding. "Okay," he said, a small smile forming. "Together, then." As they lay there, the world's uncertainties faded, replaced by shared purpose and the strength of their bond. They would face whatever awaited them side by side.

"Sounds awful," Cindy commented, seeming to understand.

Robert continued, "Well, I can remember thinking that if I just ran so hard that l had a heart attack, then I'd never have to put that gun to my head and finish it there. Sometimes I'd think about who care would even. Who might show up at the memorial...there surely would be no funeral. Probably just a few people at the grave site talking about me but knowing very little. I can remember thinking that if it was anybody, it would be those lawyers at the firm, and their children would be there acting like their grandfather had just died. "Why they loved me so much, I'll never know. I'll never understand. You felt it during your time there, and I could see what it did to you. I had it for years, but I just avoided it; I couldn't let my feelings get the best of me. Now, the only people who might show up at my funeral are gone!"

Robert continued to stare at the ceiling fan, noticing a slight squeak that triggered the technical side of his mind to want to oil it. But the practical side reminded him it was no longer necessary. The fan could squeak in this room for someone else. "I wish I could have told them how much I appreciated their kindness. I wonder if they ever opened the presents I gave the kids. Or was I too late? Kids with dead fathers won't think much about anything under the tree this year. I should have done it last year—or the year before. That just shows the kind of person I am—a guy with great intentions but never quite getting there, never really embracing life's important moments. And then…" he paused.

"And then what?" Cindy asked.

"And then you came along." Robert explained. "Suddenly I started to feel things; feeling things that released the hold that the darkness had on me. You know," his voice began to break slightly, "I've watched you function, taking on what must be such a horrendous challenge in trying to get through this part of your life. You do it with such dignity...and somehow...with so much grace. It's like you go around making everything better for a guy like me that has made it so bad for everybody else. When I'm around you, I feel like I'm in control of my life. I was able to turn down the assignment to kill those two people because you basically told me that I didn't have to do it." His comments slowed. He was, again, fighting back emotion.

Cindy turned sideways, extending her arm across his chest to hug his midsection as he sat slightly propped up in bed.

"That shows what a sad excuse for a person I am," Robert continued. "I needed you to tell me I didn't have to do these awful things. How I wish you had been in my life years ago. Maybe I would have been a different person. You know, if my wife had known what I was doing, perhaps with her support, I could have stopped..."

"There are a lot of maybes," Cindy replied. "There's a maybe that we need to think about, and when I said I was happy, this is what I meant. Maybe we can do something to avenge the killing of our good friends. Perhaps even more important, maybe it can be the beginning to the end of this kind of awful politics...this kind of treatment of people. That woman is a monster. It sounds like the people you've worked for at the CIA are just like her. Who do you think thought up this stuff, Charlotte Reid or the CIA?" she asked.

"I'm not sure it really matters. It's just an accepted way of doing business." Robert paused on his thought for a moment, surprised that Cindy had not lumped the Cedric Martin crowd in with the CIA. Maybe she's not catching everything I'm telling her. It's a lot to digest, he reasoned to himself.

"Maybe it won't be accepted if it becomes too high risk," Cindy continued. "You can't have the Charlotte Reids of the world around. With her in power, it's not a free country. She's effectively imprisoned the families of the Fischer, Cramer & Morrell firm for life. So, yeah...I am sort of happy—happy that something can be done about it. Because most of the time, especially when you're sitting here in this wheelchair, unable to do much, and suddenly you can actually do something—that means something, and that makes me happy."

Robert detected the pleasure and calmness of her voice. It seemed so strange on the night before what would be the greatest assassination since Kennedy. "You are really some political scientist! You make me feel like I can do it. I feel when we get to Montreux, you've got to know that I'm with you. I'm with you no matter how bad it gets. Believe me; I will spend every dollar of my Swiss accounts if I must, to make sure that you are as comfortable as you can be. As long as you are conscious of anyone around you, you need to know that it's going to be me. I'll be loving you; I'll be holding your hand, I'll be whispering."

"You make it sound terrible, like it's going to happen right away. You have to know this is a progressive illness. I plan on racing you in my wheelchair for quite a while. I hear these wheelchairs go faster in Europe than here," Cindy said, laughing to lighten the mood.

But the mood didn't change. Robert remained serious. "I love you.

There's no way to truly express how I feel."

"Well, you can start by succeeding tomorrow and coming back to me alive. You need to be at your best, so get some sleep."

Sleep did not come as quickly as Cindy had suggested. As fatigued as they both were from the long strenuous day of preparation, they still found time to make love and cling to each other as fears were tempered by hope—and hope, as they finally fell asleep, seemed to be the only thing that dreams are made of.

* * *

As morning arrived, Cindy was up early, finishing packing her bags, wheeling around the house and looking at various keepsakes that she knew she could not take with her. Robert had explained to her carefully about how they could change their identity on paper and live in anonymity in Switzerland for the next several years. Taking items that could be easily tracked back to family and friends could come back to haunt them. She would take some clothes and only a few other items and nothing more.

Robert showered, shaved, and prepared for the day as if he were just getting ready for another day of work. The adrenalin was building inside of him, along with a certain sickness in his gut which he interpreted as being, more than anything, a fear of failure. He knew he could not fail. He would have to make a difference, and this was the time to do it.

The Kennedy Center Fundraiser was scheduled to begin at 12:00 noon. At 9:00 a.m., however, they were both ready to leave. Cindy sat in her car looking into the eyes of the man leaning down through the open car window. "Now remember, you go to Cape May, and you stay in the house. Don't believe everything you hear on the radio. They can say a lot of things about what happened and to whom. There's going to be a lot of commotion. If I'm not there by 10:00 p.m., then you drive north. I wouldn't necessarily stay until morning. I would be out of there by midnight. You head for Woodstock, Vermont, and stay at the Kedron

Valley Inn. If I can't find you at Cape May, or if I don't get there in time, then that's where I'll go.

But we've got to be over the border and into Canada by Tuesday night because New Year's Day will be over, and people will be back to work. "The police and authorities will talk seriously, but they won't be serious until they finish partying. Any questions?" Robert looked at Cindy, trying to see into her soul. Cindy looked up at him and said, "No, just be there. Do what must be done and be there!" Robert leaned into the car, cradling her head in his hand, and kissed her delicately but lovingly. He backed away and stood in the driveway as she fiddled with the handicap controls for a moment, then put the car in reverse and began pulling out. He yelled, "Just look for me! Keep track of me if you can!"

She looked up and smiled and took control of the moment, and passionately proclaimed, like a lady to her knight in shining armor, "Fear Not! Fear Not!" He stood motionless, watching her as she drove away into the traffic on the cold Virginia morning.

20

The sun was breaking ever so slightly though the clouds to the east, painting a dirty yellow sky over the nation's capital as Robert crossed the Lincoln Memorial Bridge. Turning north on E Street, Robert entered the George Washington University Campus and pulled into the Columbia Plaza parking terrace at 2400 Virginia Avenue. It was early in the day, several hours before the noon event. He parked in a vacant overflow area designated for Kennedy Center events two blocks to the west.

Taking his time, Robert methodically followed the plan. He got out of his car, unloaded the motorized wheelchair from the rear platform, and ensured he was alone. Then, he loaded himself into the chair, binding his legs tightly together just above the knees with a leather strap. He put on dark glasses and began to practice, following Cindy's instructions.

Leaning and cocking his head in the way that Cindy had instructed him added to his appearance of being handicapped. It seemed to work, giving Robert plenty of cover to disguise his inexperience in driving the vehicle. Then, hoping that he could at least pass himself off as an MD victim for the next two hours, he started up the ramps, past the areas with parked cars, and out onto the sidewalk along Virginia Avenue. He then headed west, down the hill toward the Watergate Hotel, which was situated adjacent to the Kennedy Center.

The cold air gave Robert reason to have a blanket—one that he had chosen for a particular reason. A horsehair blanket would make it harder for dogs to detect the scent of his explosive materials. Even dogs have their limitations. He had handled them before.

Slowly working his way along Virginia Avenue, where it passes over the Whitehurst Freeway, Robert motored down to the front of the Watergate Hotel. There, he turned southward past the Watergate entrance and along the sidewalk in front of the Saudi Arabian Embassy, which was immediately across the street from the hotel. As he rolled past the Embassy, Robert realized this would likely be the first major terrorism event in years that no Middle Eastern-connected terror group could legitimately claim. He was early, so he stopped along one of the broad sidewalks leading to the Kennedy Center grounds.

The Kennedy Center events had become the principal news focus of an otherwise slow day. With Houston's acceptance of the Vice President's offer, the staff at both campaigns had worked overtime to put the best spin possible on the situation. Although an agreement had been reached days earlier, it was decided that the most effective and appropriate way to make the momentous flip of the coin announcement to the world would be at a fund raiser for a major charity. The Vice President's appearance at the greater Washington United Way End of the Year Benefit was fortuitous for both sides. To maintain secrecy, networks had been notified just twenty-four hours prior that both candidates would make a major statement regarding the Presidential election. Vice President Reid would be at the Kennedy Center, while Governor Houston would attend via live feed from the Convention Center in San Diego, where he and his family planned to spend New Year's. The media had been warned that this was not a telethon-style event, but a significant announcement aimed at resolving the national election crisis.

In the early morning darkness of the 30th, satellite trucks and mobile broadcast units began crowding the parking lot and road area on the north side, separating the Kennedy Center from the Saudi Arabian Embassy and the Watergate Hotel. By the time Robert wheeled by, it resembled a residential area for a large traveling circus.

It had also been a sudden turn of events for the umbrella of security forces in the D.C. area. The Secret Service, with its awkward arrangement with the CIA, was forced to quickly throw together a plan to protect the Vice President in the setting of a major media event. Although her regular support team could have easily made the adjustment to be in place, the notoriety of the event had elevated the whole process. The decision was quickly made and ratified through Homeland Security that the overlay protection needed to be at a much higher level of readiness and over a much broader area. The government scurried to be ready, wishing that it had had more time to plan. It was awkward; the security was already stretched to the limit with a current president and two would-be presidents to protect.

At 10:45 Robert made his move, crawling slowly up the ramp in the wheelchair and entering the broad outdoor marble walkways under the high columns that give the Kennedy Center its spectacular architectural signature. He proceeded along the east side of the building until he reached the northern most doors, which enter the Hall of Nations.

Robert took note that the security system had been set up to accommodate wheelchairs, given the nature of the event. He then waited until several people were lined up—some in chairs as well. He wanted to watch the process to avoid mistakes. The guards were courteous but thorough as they ran hand-held detection wands around the people and then allowed them to move to the next station, where the D.C. police were present with their bomb sniffing dog. Robert attempted to appear impatient but still accommodating as he waited his turn, realizing if he were to get caught, it would likely be at this second station.

The first stop was routine, but now, low in the wheelchair, Robert faced a no-nonsense German Shepherd. As the dog sniffed, he began to cough—a deep, phlegm-filled cough that launched slime into his hand, causing slight revulsion from the guards and the dog. Meanwhile, another guard scrutinized his driver's license, studying the name Sydney Wilstead. His counterfeiting work had been excellent.

The dog paused while sniffing the wheels of Robert's vehicle. He realized he hadn't cleaned the wheels after the machine had sat in his storage locker in Reston. Panic washed over him. *This is it!* he thought. Everything froze for a moment except his mind. Every operator had a backup plan, and Robert was no exception. If the situation started to break down, he had a three-second window to act. He reached down behind his left leg rest to connect the bare ends of two exposed copper wires he had installed.

There would be a slight shock, but the complete circuit igniting a very short electronic fuse to the tear gas and the phosphorus grenades all at the same time, right there at the entrance to the Hall of Nations. The almost simultaneous explosions, assuming they were large enough, might give him a fighting chance of escaping but little chance of avoiding being seriously burned. Three seconds was a long time. He waited, and dropped his hand, ready to make the move.

Fortunately, the dog backed off, the handler was further distracted by others lined up behind him, and even the dog avoided Robert's sudden grotesque fit of coughing and spitting. The counterfeit driver's license passed muster as well. He was signaled through and began making his way along the red carpet in the hall westward toward the huge windows opening onto a patio overlooking the Potomac River. There he turned left and worked his way up the red velvet carpeted ramps and ultimately down a side hall which led him into the beautifully ornate Concert Hall.

RAGE AGAINST THE MACHINE

Once inside, Robert maneuvered the motorized wheelchair along a ramp to a platform which had been positioned to cover the area between the fourth and the eighth rows, with a width of about twenty seats. It was the perfect accommodation for large numbers of people in wheelchairs, the best seat in the house for this special event. As he arrived, there were only three other chairs already in place on the platform, positioned toward the front. He estimated that there was room for about twenty more wheelchairs before the platform area would be fully occupied.

Robert was exhausted. His nerves of steel were showing some rust. His legs were cramping from the leather strap. He wanted to stretch but didn't dare. Instead, he appreciated having a few minutes to relax and prepare for the next part of the plan. As he looked around, he was impressed by the gold balconies, the ornate woodwork of the concert hall, and the high chandelier-laden ceiling. In addition to the seating in the middle for about 2000 people, he noted balconies at level for about six stories, presumably for the higher paying patrons.

People were beginning to file into the concert hall. Periodically Robert would notice Secret Service personnel walking onto the stage area, surveying the area and then leaving. With the center stage serving as, in effect, the point of attack, he had to carefully position himself on the center front of the platform near the fourth row. From there, he could aim carefully with little need for adjustment, so that he would have clear access to the stage which he estimated to be at about seventy feet. He was also within throwing range, and that was important. Once the smoke rockets were launched, there was little he could do to affect his target. For now, he would be discreet, sitting quietly and waiting as more wheelchairs crowded the platform.

By noon, the concert hall was full. The benefit had been billed as a final opportunity to write a deductible check before the end of the year. The director of the D.C. Muscular Dystrophy Association pulled out all the stops to ensure its success. Centering the event around the Vice President made it easier, but the holiday season posed challenges, as many people were out of town. He had to redouble his efforts to secure good attendance and major contributions.

As soon as the Reid/Houston election announcement became part of the program, major contribution pledges began popping up from all quarters—far beyond the Beltway, and far beyond the D.C. area. Even the commissioner of the NFL had called and asked to attend. The director was stunned. He looked forward to a very great and historic moment at the Kennedy Center.

Suddenly the stage doors to the left opened and a group of men walked onto the platform. Robert immediately recognized them as CIA. Again, it was CIA first, Secret Service second, an odd thing for America in Robert's mind, and perhaps in the minds of all Americans as well, to the extent any were aware of this strange circumstance. A flourish of music could be heard off stage, and then Charlotte Reid walked onto the stage arm- in-arm with the director of the D.C. Muscular Dystrophy Association and two other persons, the Commissioner of the National Football League and the National President of the United Way. She began to wave. Her electrifying smile and blonde flowing hair bracketed a stage presence that brought the audience to its feet, at least those who could stand. As usual, everyone on stage became minions in the wake of her powerful presence. During the minute of standing applause, others walked onto the stage and took their places behind the podium. Robert finally had Charlotte Reid right where he wanted her—an opportunity he would never have again. For a brief moment, he wished Cindy could be there.

The Director of the M.D. Association was first to take the podium and announce the agenda for the meeting. All stood again for the national anthem. The director then took the podium once more to introduce the Vice President of the United States. His introduction was gaudy and indulgent. Of course, he presented her as a friend to all persons in need, especially those suffering the scourge of Muscular Dystrophy. Everyone was all smiles, anticipating a huge contribution from Charlotte Reid and her husband, Bill. The applause erupted again, with a standing ovation from everyone in the room except Robert and the other wheelchair-bound individuals on the platform.

During the several minutes of the ovation, while the focus was entirely on the stage, Robert removed the caps from the ends of the handlebars, loosened the crossbars, and pointed them forward.

He then pulled out a small wrench and made final adjustments to lower the bars to point forward for what he continued to estimate was about as about two thirds that distance of an NBA court—almost point-blank for his small missiles. He did not have to be accurate. With the ordinance he was about to deploy, he just needed to hit the area near the stage. The phosphorous explosion, emitting a blinding flash and heat at 1,472 degrees Fahrenheit would stun everyone long enough for him to throw the heavy ordnance onto the stage. He then reached down and unobtrusively unlatched the cover over the motor compartment. As the ovation began to subside, Robert reached for the leather strap on his legs and loosened it enough so he would have complete freedom of movement at just the right moment.

Vice President Reid began to speak. "I'm here to tell you of great things which are happening in our country today. There are challenges we must overcome. In this room are people facing challenges that may never go away. Through cooperation, negotiation, and understanding, we can make some challenges disappear. Our nation is in crisis over this election. Governor Houston and I ended up in a virtual tie. We've turned to the courts and Congress, yet we still sense considerable consternation, misunderstanding, suspicion, and frustration with the system. As two individuals who seldom agree on much, we have found common ground on something we believe will be very good for this country. We have devised a solution for solving this momentous and historical impasse. It is a solution that is so simple and so basic that probably no one except for an NFL football referee will understand its utility."

Several people in the audience began to chuckle, not fully understanding the NFL referee's comment. Robert could hear the nearby camera men talking into their mouth pieces, moving all cameras close in on the Vice President, and preparing for a jump feed to San Diego.

"It is literally this simple," the Vice President continued.

It was time. Robert looked around the room once more, and then reached down and flipped the switch which allowed the battery to send a slight electrical impulse up the fibrous threads. In the next second, both handlebars became muzzles flaring with brilliance as rockets shot forward as fast as roman candles into the stage area. But the explosion was far beyond that of fireworks. The stage erupted with huge blinding phosphorus flashes. Within a second, another volley followed, met with frenzied gasps, and before any screams began, smoke billowed out in all directions from the flashes. Almost immediately, Robert started tossing the golf ball-sized incendiaries with their binary warheads into the smoke-filled area.

The podium and seating area were engulfed in flames, while fire began to race up the curtains, prompting everyone on stage who wasn't already burning to lunge for the wings, trying to escape the inferno that now resembled a massive pit of fire.

Robert then quickly pointed to the handlebars behind him, hitting the switch once more, igniting more phosphorus explosives to blind any security behind him, and making them unable to respond.

Having done the intended deed, Robert jumped off the platform to the right, crawling among the mass of people headed for the exit. As he did so, he began throwing the tear gas cylinders off into the smoke behind him, creating more havoc and further giving him the best opportunity to escape amid the confusion.

David Houston had been standing at the speaker's platform of the small performance theater in the San Diego Convention Center preparing to respond on cue to the Vice President's offer, when he heard a cameraman start to scream, "What in the hell..." Before he could fully grasp what he was seeing on the monitor, both Army and Secret Service agents grabbed him and literally lifted his 6'2", 200-pound frame off the ground, whisking him out of the room. As he glanced over his shoulder while being escorted out, he noticed bright flashes and chaos on the monitor, presumably from the Kennedy Center, just before the transmission went dead. No one was saying anything, just moving him quickly to a safer location.

Inside the satellite relay trucks next to the Kennedy Center, the technicians were screaming as others tore their headsets off, and simply jumped out of the trucks and started fleeing north past the front of the Watergate away from the area. It took less than thirty seconds following the first explosion for people to cram the Concert Hall exits. Soon, they were streaming out of the Kennedy Center in huge numbers, running onto Virginia Avenue. On the other side of the building, people were spilling out onto the balcony, some even jumping off, falling almost thirty feet onto the cobblestone median of Rock Creek Parkway below, like passengers leaping from a capsizing ship. Cars screeched and spun out of control to avoid those plummeting from above. Many were injured, and some lay dead from the falls.

"I've got a shot here!" the Secret Service marksman atop the Kennedy barked into his mouthpiece as he looked through the scope of his 8.59-millimeter L115A1 sniper rifle.

"Where?" Was the response from his team leader. "I see a muzzle pointing just across Virginia, fourth floor apartments third from the left!"

"I confirm!" Another agent, acting as a spotter, responded, seeing the very same person.

"This is team leader; you have a go!"

Immediately he pulled the trigger and a bullet at a muzzle velocity of 936 meters per second launched and entered the upper body of a CIA sniper who had been assigned to watch the streets around the Kennedy

Center. The hydrostatic shock of the soft grain anti-armor sniper round plowed right through the bullet-proof vest, stopped his heart instantly. He was dead before he hit the floor. "You've got one of ours! Don't shoot! This is the CIA you're shooting at us!" The nearby executive-protection supervisor screamed into his headset, hoping his radio was still on the Secret Services band—which was unusual for the CIA.

Robert crawled between and over seats, along the carpet, facing the floor among the pile of people surging toward the exit. The tear gas fumes were intense; his eyes burned, and he could hardly breathe. He looked into the anguished faces of those whose lives he had changed forever. It became a dark, frantic struggle, like a rugby scrum in a cloud of poison smoke. It was every person for themselves. Finally, through the chaos, he saw light and felt a surge of hope that he would not become a victim of his own actions.

Once outside, Robert ran with the hundreds of people spreading frantically in all directions. The first fire department vehicles were arriving and finding it hard to pull into place without running over dazed people lying on the streets and walkways, overcome by smoke inhalation, tear gas and burns.

This was one of those rare situations where the news organizations were largely neutralized and ineffective. "Ladies and gentlemen, this is a developing story unfolding in Washington, D.C. Reports indicate chaos at the Kennedy Center following a significant attack during a high-profile event. The implications are staggering, affecting not only those present but the entire nation. We urge everyone to stay indoors and avoid the area as authorities work to secure the scene. We'll provide updates as more information comes in. For now, we await word from law enforcement and emergency services. The camera shifted back to the anchor in New York, whose expression reflected the gravity of the moment. "We will continue to monitor this closely. Our thoughts are with everyone affected by this tragic event. Please stay tuned for ongoing coverage as we gather more details."

"AT THIS POINT WE DO NOT KNOW WHAT IS GOING ON AT THE JOHN F. KENNEDY CENTER IN WASHINGTON D.C. WE DO KNOW THAT THERE HAS BEEN SOME SORT OF MAJOR COMMOTION WHICH DOES IN FACT INVOLVE EXPLOSIONS AND FIRE, WHICH HAVE CAUSED PEOPLE AT A MUSCULAR DYSTROPHY BENEFIT ATTENDED BY THE VICE PRESIDENT TO FLEE THE BUILDING. WE HAVE NO CONFIRMATION IN ANY WAY REGARDING THE WHEREABOUTS, THE INVOLVEMENT OR CONDITION OF THE VICE PRESIDENT. WE HAVE HEARD NOTHING!"

The anchor hesitated, visibly grappling with the gravity of the situation while receiving updates through his earpiece. "LET'S GO TO CHRISTOPHER WORTHINGTON IN SAN DIEGO, WHERE GOVERNOR HOUSTON WAS SUPPOSED TO PARTICIPATE IN WHAT WAS BILLED TO BE A MOMENTOUS ANNOUNCEMENT REGARDING THE RESOLUTION OF THE ELECTION CRISIS." His voice strained to maintain composure, reflecting the sudden shift from anticipation to chaos as the nation watched in disbelief.

The reporter could be seen standing against the backdrop of the San Diego waterfront. He appeared disheveled, having moved quickly to a convention center patio area to report into a shoulder held camera. "THIS IS CHRISTOPHER WORTHINGTON IN SAN DIEGO WITH GOVERNOR HOUSTON...OR AT LEAST, WE WERE WITH GOVERNOR HOUSTON. WE HAD EXPECTED GOVERNOR HOUSTON TO PARTICIPATE VIA SATELLITE FROM THE CONVENTION CENTER WITH THE VICE PRESIDENT IN A SPEECH EXPLAINING SOME HERETOFORE SECRET PLAN THAT WE UNDERSTAND THEY HAVE COME UP WITH TO SOLVE THE ELECTION CRISIS. WE THINK WE KNOW WHAT IT WAS GOING TO BE. WE ARE NOT GOING TO SPECULATE AT THIS POINT GIVEN THE UNBELIEVABLE TURN OF EVENTS IN WASHINGTON,

D.C. WHAT WE DO KNOW IS THAT GOVERNOR HOUSTON HAS BEEN TAKEN AWAY TO AN UNDISCLOSED LOCATION BY THE SECRET SERVICE UNDER CONDITIONS THAT ARE STARTING TO RING IN OUR EARS LIKE 9-11 ALL OVER AGAIN. AT THIS POINT WE'RE REALLY UNWILLING TO SAY WHAT'S GOING ON BECAUSE WE DON'T KNOW." There was a slight pause and the reporter looked over his shoulder out towards the San Diego Bay.

"I NOW SEE HELICOPTERS, TWO OF THEM." He held his left hand up to his ear to get a clear message. "I'M TOLD THERE ARE TWO SEA KING HELICOPTERS COMING IN THIS DIRECTION FROM WHAT LOOKS LIKE POINT LOMA NAVAL BASE. I BELIEVE THAT'S A SUBMARINE BASE AT THE MOUTH OF THE HARBOR." The cameras began to search the sky for the helicopters and soon locked onto silver specks getting larger as they approached.

New York received a brief reprieve from the lack of visuals from D.C. as they aired footage of a Sea King landing. A team of twelve Marines in full battle gear deployed in the parking lot outside the convention center to await the arrival of a second helicopter. Moments later, the second chopper touched down. Governor Houston and his family were quickly hustled out into the parking lot and onto the aircraft. Within seconds, the Sea King lifted back into the air, peeling westward across the Bay toward Point Loma. The remaining Marines loaded into the other helicopter and swiftly followed.

Back in Washington, smoke was now billowing out of the Kennedy Center. Sirens could be heard coming from all points of the compass as the initial injuries were being hauled in the direction of the George Washington University Medical Center. With so many injured lying on the streets, the fire personnel were still having a difficult time getting heavy equipment into the building.

For his part, Robert was now walking easterly with a clump of people on Virginia Avenue where it crosses over the Whitehurst Freeway. He took note of the injury in a small park on the east side of the bridge where dozens of people were lying on the grass, still trying to figure out what had happened at the fundraiser.

Strangely, Robert felt compelled to stop and help. He paused, pulling out a handkerchief he had used to clean the batteries before inserting them into the motorized wheelchair's engine compartment. Using the cleaner part, he wiped the eyes of a lady in her late 70s sitting on a park bench, screaming that she couldn't see. Wetting the handkerchief in the park's water fountain, he wiped her eyes. After a minute, her vision began to clear. She started thanking him, and oddly, he sensed her appreciation, feeling good about himself—for just a moment. The feeling was not enough to keep him there. Although the park looked like the remnants of a battlefield where a Good Samaritan could have spent hours, he headed up Virginia Avenue to the parking terrace and down to the third level to get his car.

In New York, more reports from the scene were coming in. CNN had now joined FOX in rebounding sufficiently to enable crews to arrive and start reporting from the scene. "WE ARE NOW GETTING MORE INFORMATION," the anchor spoke nervously, still fishing for news, "THE DISTRICT OF COLUMBIA FIRE DEPARTMENT IS BATTLING A FIRE RAGING WITHIN THE BUILDING AT THIS MOMENT. WE CAN TELL YOU THAT THAT HUGE AMOUNTS OF SMOKE ARE COMING FROM THE BUILDING, AND WE ARE TOLD THERE IS A TERRIBLE INFERNO INSIDE." Suddenly, the screen behind the anchor shifted from the words "Attack on America" to a camera shot of the Kennedy Center from the south, near the Lincoln Memorial Bridge. Smoke billowed up from vents on the roof, but the fire had not yet broken through the building to the outside. "AS YOU CAN SEE THERE ARE FIRE PERSONNEL COMING AT THIS FROM ALL DIRECTIONS." Helicopters were hovering over the building. "AND WE CAN SEE TWO BLACK HELICOPTERS, WHICH HAVE NO INSIGNIA, HOVERING

OVER THE BUILDING AND WHIRLING AROUND IN VARIOUS DIRECTIONS. THEY DO NOT LOOK LIKE FIREFIGHTERS, BUT RATHER HAPPENED TO BE THERE FOR MILITARY PURPOSES. AND..."

The cameras turned from their view of the Kennedy Center to a view across the Lincoln Memorial Bridge as a long string of Humvees with soldiers in full combat gear began rolling across the bridge at high speed from west to east. "AND NOW WE CAN SEE THE ARMY COMING ACROSS THE RIVER FROM FORT MYER IN LARGE GROUPS. IT LOOKS LIKE SEVERAL HUNDRED SOLDIERS MOVING INTO THE DISTRICT. AGAIN, WE'RE NOT SURE WHAT THIS IS ALL ABOUT. ALL WE KNOW AT THIS POINT IS THAT THERE HAS BEEN A FIRE AND AN EXPLOSION AT THE KENNEDY CENTER. WE ASSUME THAT PRESIDENT MINTON, WHO IS AWAY AT HIS FARM IN GEORGIA, IS SAFE AND SOUND. BUT WE ARE NOT SURE ABOUT THE VICE PRESIDENT, WHO BY ALL REPORTS WAS IN THE BUILDING AT THE TIME OF THE BLAST."

The camera then made a distorted move as it looked upward into the sky and the reporter again anxiously continued, "WE SEE FOUR AIRCRAFT. LOOKS LIKE F-16S ORBITING, IF YOU WILL, OVER THE MIDDLE PART OF THE CITY. THE MILITARY HAS APPEARED TO RESPOND VERY QUICKLY, ALTHOUGH AS MANY WILL SAY WHEN WE GET THE WORD OF WHAT HAS ACTUALLY GONE ON HERE, IT WAS NOT FAST ENOUGH."

Ten minutes after lifting off from the San Diego Convention Center parking lot, Governor David Houston and his family were assisted down the hatch of the U.S.S. Salt Lake City nuclear attack submarine, moored at the Point Loma Naval Base, its home port. The plan was straightforward: get Governor Houston out to sea and away from the commotion unfolding around the country. As a candidate he needed to be kept safe. Holding no office yet, he did not need to be available to deal with this crisis. The military did not want to take any chances and had determined for him that the nuclear sub was the perfect place to be.

* * *

RIDE LIKE THE WIND

Robert had followed a traffic jam of impatiently – driven cars to escape the parking terrace at Columbia Plaza and then drove northeast on Virginia Avenue. The forced direction was south, across the Capitol Mall past the World War II Memorial, to the Jefferson Memorial, where he picked up Interstate I - 395 North. This allowed him to make good his escape through the southeast part of the District in the direction of Anacostia and the Maryland line. As he navigated through moderate traffic, he glanced to his left and saw the Capitol Building, the Senate Office Building, the Smithsonian, and other monuments on the east end of the Capitol Mall. Strangely, everything seemed quiet in this part of downtown. However, in his rearview mirror, the northwest sky was filled with smoke. The fire he had started was still raging. That was the plan, and it was a solid one.

As Robert crossed the Anacostia River Bridge, he could see in his that the traffic behind him was now being held up by D.C. police. He figured he had avoided the roadblock by not more than a minute. There would be more of them. He then turned on the radio, knowing that it would be best to listen to the developments in case the situation changed his plan to escape in the direction of Cape May.

"SPECIAL REPORT: WASHINGTON UNDER ATTACK!" The booming WTOP voice reported, "THE WASHINGTON D.C. FIRE DEPARTMENT HAS REACHED THE INSIDE OF THE CONCERT HALL AT THE JOHN F. KENNEDY CENTER FOR THE PERFORMING ARTS AND IS NOW REPORTING AT LEAST 10 PEOPLE DEAD. IT WAS FIRST REPORTED THAT THE VICE PRESIDENT MIGHT HAVE BEEN QUICKLY

REMOVED FROM THE BUILDING. THE FIRE IS NOW UNDER CONTROL AND SHE HAS NOT BEEN SEEN. HER MOTORCADE HAS NOT LEFT THE PARKING AREA UNDER THE BUILDING. IT IS SUSPECTED THAT SHE IS AMONG THE TEN PERSONS THUS FAR CONFIRMED DEAD. IT IS REPORTED THAT SEVEN PERSONS IN THE STAGE AREA ARE DEAD, AND AT LEAST ANOTHER THREE TRAMPLED IN THE RAMPAGE OF THE CROWD TO ESCAPE THE CONCERT HALL."

Robert was uncertain how to respond. His CIA instincts suggested that the number ten was an acceptable level of collateral damage. He had feared the death toll could be much higher, and that it might continue to rise as the fire cooled inside the Kennedy Center. Certainly, a toll of "one" would have been ideal, especially if that one was the Vice President herself. Shifting into his "casualties of war" mindset, he was unhappy about the additional deaths but rationalized that those in her entourage who perished likely deserved it; perhaps even the killers of the Fischer, Cramer & Morrell lawyers had been nearby and caught up in the chaos.

He continued east, and somewhere beyond the beltway the car radio was now featuring President Minton from his farm in Georgia who, in a somber Presidential voice explained, "AT ABOUT A QUARTER AFTER NOON TODAY, THE VICE PRESIDENT OF THE UNITED STATES WAS KILLED BY A PERSON OR PERSONS UNKNOWN AT THIS TIME, WHILE ATTENDING A CHARITY FUNDRAISER AT THE JOHN F. KENNEDY CENTER IN WASHINGTON, D.C. I MOURN, WE ALL MOURN, AND THE NATION MOURNS THE LOSS OF A GREAT LEADER. WE WILL NOT REST UNTIL WE FIND THE PERPETRATORS RESPONSIBLE FOR THIS. WE DO NOT KNOW AT THIS TIME IF THIS WAS AN ACT OF AGGRESSION BY TERRORISTS, A FOREIGN GOVERNMENT, OR THE WORK OF AN INDIVIDUAL OR GROUP WITHIN THE COUNTRY. ALL WE KNOW AT THIS POINT IS THAT SHE IS DECEASED, ALONG

WITH NINE OTHER AMERICANS, WHICH IS A SEVERE BLOW TO OUR COUNTRY."

You want a severe blow to our country? That happened when Fischer, Cramer and Morrell were lost, you son-of-a-bitch! Robert thought to himself and then flipped the radio off. He had heard enough and decided it was time to focus on something else—Cindy.

Two hours later, as he reached the Chesapeake Bay Bridge just beyond Annapolis, Robert expected a roadblock. The bridge was a perfect choke point for an eastern escape. He assumed that all bridges and major highways leading out of the nation's capital would be checked. As he reached the bridge, long shadows stretched across the ground from the low winter sun behind him. There was no roadblock in sight. Life felt simple and tranquil, the dirty air and harsh winter landscape giving way to a Currier & Ives scene. The Maryland eastern shore seemed like the perfect place to be, at least for one last time. It was his route to Switzerland, where he planned to spend Cindy's final years. For him, that was all that remained in life. There would never again be a catastrophe caused by his hands. Never.

Robert slipped down to Route 404 to cross the Delaware Peninsula, hoping to avoid the more obvious routes. As he made his way, now in the dark, toward Lewes Ferry he hoped the depression would be left somewhere behind him as well. He was seeing things that he had never noticed before, and they went far beyond Cindy. She was the catalyst and now he was the beneficiary. Quaint old farmhouses with white snow-covered roofs appeared warm and friendly. They could have been pictures on his wall when his children were young. The frozen waters of the Tuckahoe River would have been a place for ice skating and hockey with friends in another life. Old railroad trestles merging one steep embankment to the other, crossing over the road, reminded him of an electric train set his father made him for Christmas when he was six years old.

Now, an even more extreme thought was falling together. When it's over, when Cindy is gone, maybe somehow it will be time to see the children and the grandchildren. How is it, Robert thought to himself, that one woman could have such an impact and change my life so much? Indeed, his guardian angel had arrived. He was driven by the thought of being with her whenever, and however, that might be.

21

There were less than twenty cars rolling on to the ferry at Lewes, Delaware. The roar of the angry surf emanated from somewhere off in the dark, beyond the harbor breakwater. It was less than an. ideal night to go aboard any kind of ship, especially a relatively flat hulled ferry. The crossing of Delaware Bay would take seventy minutes. The shallow draft of the 250-foot-long boat, designed to carry 130 cars, would make for a rather wild ride. Once beyond the breakwater and into the bay, the choppy waters would transform the nighttime crossing into a perilous venture. Lewes, Delaware's oldest town, rests on the windblown eastern shore of the Delaware peninsula. It has endured hurricanes, Tories, Continentals, and Confederate raiders. There were even tales of German U-boats lurking at the broad mouth of the Delaware River, spotted and chased off by determined local fishermen during WWII.

VEIL OF CLOSURE

Although the town has changed a little with the years, the ferry operation has been constant since it began with a flat- bottomed steamer, augmented with sails, transporting wagons and carriages in 1874. It took the worst of hurricanes to interdict the scheduled trips. Seventy minutes across the bay to the New Jersey shore at Cape May, and seventy-five minutes coming back the other way, the ferry operated nearly every hour in the summertime, with a cut back in the winter.

Robert had just made it; he had caught the 8:00 p.m. transit, the last of the day. Once on board, the hard cold wind of the swelling sea kept passengers either in their cars or huddled inside the food court above the car and truck area at mid-deck. The rolling seas made eating an agonizing experience. Most of the thirty or so passengers sat quietly. Some would be green around the gills, likely throwing up over the sides before the trip ended. Far from the tourist season, for most passengers, this transit was a necessary alternative to the two-and-a-half-hour journey north to Wilmington, then across the Delaware just south of Philadelphia, where it was merely a river. But there was clearly a price to pay, and for some, it was far more than the relatively low crossing charge of $18.00 per car.

Robert avoided people wherever possible. In his winter coat, he sat still on an outside deck bench hunched over, eyes closed, hood over his head, and deep in thought. It was freezing, but the coldness strangely did not cause him to lose focus from his mission. He needed to get to Cape May—certainly for reasons, at least as he reasoned, of greater urgency than anyone else on the ferry. Seeing Cindy was foremost in his mind. The earlier events of the day blurred, and as momentous to the nation as they might be, they were seemingly insignificant to him. Would she be there?

The ship's insignificant presence on the waves felt profoundly symbolic. Much like his life, Robert had battled forces far stronger and more massive than himself. They controlled him, moved him. All he could do was float atop the water, like a rudderless vessel, hoping to reach a safe harbor somewhere.

Robert slipped into a daydream of his children, bouncing through his mind—still little, still babies. To him, they would never be grown up. He could remember holding them in his arms, rocking them to sleep and hoping for that moment when all the elements of joy from a good life would fill his heart. Suddenly, a chunk of ice crashed against the hull, and the children were gone. As he opened his eyes, only mildly startled, he found himself frantically trying to bury his evil life in the depths of the sea so his children would never be able to dig it up. All that he had left to show for the life bobbing on the surface were still pictures, snapshots of smiles posing for the moment, yet sad both before and after the moment that the shutter snapped. So many times, he had hoped that he might hold on to it for a second pose, a third pose, all together in series, a living motion picture. It might take the death out of life, or maybe give life to the still process of death. Then again, who really does control the sea—no one.

BALLOONS

Robert's thoughts momentarily distracted him as flickering lights danced among the clouds at the bay's northern end. Could it be an early New Year's celebration in Philadelphia? Lightning? Or perhaps an aircraft? He mused about who would be foolish enough to fly over the rough waters in such a winter gale. The day's extreme events were draining, sending Robert into a fuzzy haze. With his head buried in his hands against the cabin rail, he drifted into memories. Then, he was at a birthday party in Elgin, Illinois, on a warm summer afternoon. Two helium-filled balloons—one white, one purple—were tied to strings in his hands. While other children let theirs go, Robert clung to his as he rode his bike home. Halfway through his journey, uncertainty struck him, and he stopped to ponder for a moment before, in a single act of hesitation, he released the strings.

The balloons, attached by entangled strings, moved sideways with the wind, almost skirting the ground, and suddenly Robert wanted them back. He immediately sped after them on his bike. As he came close, they suddenly surged upward in a dramatic skyward motion. Robert was impressed by the freedom, the majesty, the power of the balloons flying skyward, out of his reach and away from the earth. He watched, and he watched, not wanting to take his eyes off the two objects reducing in size to small dots as they blew to the east.

On that muggy summer afternoon, Robert had pushed his little Huffy bicycle with the intensity of an adult storm chaser. It took him along the cornfield lanes, trying to maintain a route that kept him in range of the two party favors that he had released into the wind. The further way they carried, the more meaningful they became to him. The pursuit continued.

Eventually, after an hour's chase, the balloons were no longer so distant. They were getting larger, coming closer to the ground. They finally disappeared beyond a field of six-foot corn. As he neared the spot where he thought they might be, little Robert dismounted his bicycle and ran frantically from the lane into the field. He thrashed through the corn stalks, searching for the bobbing, fluttering balloons that had once floated so beautifully against the blue Illinois sky.

Suddenly, Robert came upon them. Two small, contorted shreds of rubber, bound down by string, and strewn across the sharp extremities of a few corn stalks. He reached up and pulled them from their distress as the flimsy rubber shredded and contracted into a meaningless nothing. Robert cried and cried and as there was a pop, and then thump! Robert was again almost knocked off the bench as he awoke to the powerful rhythm of the waves, rocking him to sleep in one minute and violently waking him up in the next.

COMING HOME

For a few long minutes, Robert tried hard to keep his mind silent. There was no chance to fall asleep again. The spray of the sea water in the wind caused his parka to glisten in the dim gray boat lighting, making him look like a statue covered by a thick sheet of ice. His thoughts needed help. He turned to Cindy. How could someone with such severe, almost insurmountable challenges move across the rough seas with such ease and grace? How is it that she can always be smiling, or on the verge of a smile, while my face hardly remembers what that feels like? Once again, he thought, she doesn't kill people for a living—I do!

Robert watched the beacon from the Cape May lighthouse periodically cut through the fog from a point off to the east. He then noticed the sound of the ice regularly banging against the hull, which had been only intermittent out on the channel in the middle of the bay, but now increasing rapidly. Likewise, the tossing of the boat was now becoming even more intense. Excitement began to build within him. This meant the shore was near. Somewhere, within view of that lighthouse, was the woman who made all the difference. She was the remedy to his cynical life without purpose. He would see her through to the end. If he could make a difference, prolong her life, and give her comfort during her most extreme moments of crisis, he would do everything possible to be the guardian angel she was becoming for him. The pulsating light of the Cape May beacon provided Robert with the same direction it offered the ship. He needed to be close to her, to dock with her in the safety of her harbor, where no storm could sink him and where he could end his meaningless drifting across the surface.

Within minutes, Robert was driving down the ramp, off the boat. He quickly made his way into West Cape May and then out to Sunset Road, a long stretch covered by beachfront vegetation as thick as the winter would allow. There were only a few intermittent streetlights, and the wind was relentless, causing his rental car to shudder against the cold. He then turned south towards the shore, past the entrance to the state park which led to the lighthouse he had seen from the ferry. He turned west on Lincoln Avenue, passing by the renowned two-story Victorian homes of the type that were Cape May's signature. The road narrowed and became very dark. The streetlights of the town had never stretched this far. The last turn made his heartbeat even faster. He knew that at the end of the road she would be there in the cottage by the sea, in the place that had for so long been so empty, so full of still photographs, but now full of love.

Robert finally slowed to a stop, signaling left to pull through the gate on the ocean side of the road, intending to drive down the tree-lined lane leading to the gravel circular drive and front door of the cottage. Just before clearing the gate, he noticed the absence of lights. The house, particularly the front porch area, was dark. It struck him as odd that she, of all people, would forget—especially after he had shared how, during his marriage, coming home late to an unlit house had bothered him greatly.

Robert paused at the gate area, not pulling forward, not backing up. He stopped and started, sensing an awful pain gripping the middle of his being. He did not retreat from his certainty that he knew she was there because the gate was open. But the lights were not on. Why?

It took longer than normal for his professional faculties to start kicking in! Robert realized that his desire for Cindy might dull his sense of caution. That was a thought that he had lived with already for several weeks. His instincts were not anywhere close to dead. In the next second, looking further off to his left back through the thick but still porous coastal evergreens, Robert thought he saw something unusual. He abruptly backed up, swinging his car around, flashing his bright into the woods. It was there! A black executive sedan, likely a government vehicle, accompanied by an equally official-looking black Suburban-style SUV, caught his eye. Government cars! he thought. In the next instant, wet gravel and snow flew in all directions as he slammed the car into reverse, pulling hard onto Lincoln Avenue before screeching into drive and laying down heavy rubber as he sped east toward Sunset Road.

Watching in his rear-view mirror, the lights that Robert had expected and yet had not hoped for, were now turning on to the road behind him. He counted one set, and then two sets, as they bounced onto the road, clearly showing two vehicles in a rush ignoring potholes and icy spots to catch him. His CIA officer's mind, the mind of the 'Lever" now shifted into its high gear—as it had so many times before in the heat of battle. His heart was burning with fear that they had Cindy. He was quickly surmising that they had followed her to Cape May, and now all that he had hoped and dreamed of, just a few months, a year with the woman he loved—it all now was in serious peril.

As Robert raced along the road, he estimated in his rear-view mirror that it would only be a matter of time before the law enforcement vehicles closed in on his underpowered rental. Spotting an opportunity at a curve, he suddenly turned left onto the road that would connect him with the long straightaway of Sunset Road. Instinctively, he veered hard right after only a few seconds and pulled into the parking lot of the Cape May Lighthouse State Park, shutting off his lights and pulling behind an eight-passenger van. It was the sole other vehicle in the dark parking lot on the lee side of the coastal sand dunes.

Robert reached for his glove box and pulled out his 9-millimeter automatic pistol, checking to make sure a round was chambered, and waited. All was quiet for a moment, long enough to hear his heart beating harder, not just in his ear, but in his neck and chest - even harder than it had at the Kennedy Center attack. Then the stillness broke, but only for seconds, as an echoing roar filled the air when both pursuing vehicles raced by, continuing past the parking lot, slowing only slightly before speeding toward Sunset Road. The sound of the engines dissipated into the night. All was silent again, except for the pounding of his heart.

STAND OF THE UNBROKEN

It was time to plan. But the options seemed easily whittled down to only one issue—find Cindy and find her quickly! There was no question in Robert's mind that as soon as his pursuers could not spot him farther down the straightaway of the Sunset Road, they would go no farther east. Maybe they would roll into downtown Cape May before turning around. But very soon, they would come back. That was a certainty. If they were in the business at all, they would carefully search the parking lot and State Park area, and any other side roads that they had overlooked in the heat of the chase. As he considered where to go, he dismissed the idea of charging back up the road to the cottage. He estimated they would likely return around the same time, creating a situation he might not be able to control. It was too risky; they would be back in the area soon.

Robert focused on the only remaining move he could where he might still have some tactical opportunity. He started the engine and lurched forward, plunging the car into a dense thicket on the east side of the parking lot. He got out of the car, struggling against the branches of the bushes that were jammed against the car door. He ran across the parking lot and toward the beach, taking the boardwalk path between the fenced off sand dunes at high speed. Within seconds, he was at the water's edge. Initially he turned east on the sand, intentionally leaving tracks headed in that direction. But he then turned west, running as fast as he could, splashing through the edge of the dark pounding winter surf, hoping that if his car was found, his pursuers would go east along the beach and again in the direction of Cape May. Also hoping that someone would not appear atop a sand dune and put a bullet through his head before he finished this first part of his plan, Robert broke out into a sprint in the direction of the nearby breakwater.

Before long, Robert was forced to climb onto the rocks and over the massive breakwater below the lighthouse as he made his way west along the beach. Soon, he was back on sandy ground, feeling the cold water erode the sand beneath his feet with each retreating wave. There, he could move in concealment, using the coastal sand dunes to shield himself from the few beachside cottages just inland. He estimated that it was about a mile run along the beach to the cottage. He would need to run a mile faster than he had ever run before.

Suddenly, Robert slipped on a rock and fell onto the ice-covered sand. He had lost his grip on the gun, allowing it to fall. He started searching frantically, realizing that unless he picked it up before the arrival of the next wave, the gun would be washed away in the darkness. He could see the fractal lead wave coming. In the next second he saw the gun, lying flat in the sand like a large half buried seashell. He grabbed it just as a wave rolled in, then ran up off the beach away from the water, hoping that he had covered his tracks well before he climbed over the breakwater.

THE THUD

Thud! At first Robert heard it. His ears started to ring. In only a speck of time, he felt it. At first, he thought he had been shot. He instinctively started searching for the wound. But the thud came again, and again. Not in his head where a trained government agent would shoot with the assumption that the target was wearing a bullet proof vest, but in his chest. It started in the upper back and then rolled through his torso from forward to his chest. At that moment, Robert realized he was running out of breath and losing strength. This doesn't happen to me! he thought. Then it occurred to him: I might be having a heart attack. A thud followed by an intense inner emptiness surged through him, followed by dizziness, another thud, and more dizziness. It stopped him in his tracks; he looked behind him to the east, then reluctantly sat on the cold sand.

Robert sat as still as he could, giving credence to the thought that maybe his years of running would help get him through this one—at least long enough to find Cindy. He sat still with his legs crossed, hugging his 9-millimeter. He tried rocking back and forth, hoping to regain his strength, while at the same time trying to assess whether he had any meaningful circulation through his body. He sat for seconds. Soon seconds became minutes. He was wasting time. The rocking helped. His gasping for breath shifted to labored but more normal breathing. As he attempted to stand, he realized he still lacked strength. Leaning forward, he began to crawl westward along the beach, pushing himself through the sand like an aging alligator, moving with glacial slowness.

After several minutes of crawling, Robert worked his way slowly to his feet and staggered further inland towards the dune. His mind closed in on the thought that all the forces of life seemed to be trapping him at this moment, including, of all things, a heart attack which he planned to survive at least long enough to see if Cindy was in the cottage. Finally, he found himself on his feet, walking slowly. Robert began to adjust to the thought that if he could just see her once more, even for a moment, it would bring some completeness or closure to what felt like a wretched, wasted life. That might be the best his world had to offer. The best.

Over the next few hundred yards, walking became a bit easier. Robert stopped briefly, leaned forward with his hands on his knees, regained some strength and started plodding forward again. He hoped he had covered over half of the mile. He would now need to keep low and conceal himself as he made his way along the coastal sand dune between himself and the cottages. The harsh wind continued to blast, and the surf thundered loudly to his left. On top of everything else, he sensed the first stages of hypothermia setting in. He could no longer distinguish the shaking from his chest pains and the shivering caused by the cold.

In time, Robert came to a place where the line of shore-front cottages ended, replaced by a long strand of ice coated coastal evergreens standing tall behind the sand dune. This signaled to him that he had almost arrived. Only a hundred yards or less to the remote Cannon family cottage.

Robert stopped again. He laid down against the dune and checked his 9-millimeter to make sure it was dry. He tried to blow into it, to clear away the sand, but lacked the strength to force any serious air out of his lungs. He continued, half-crawling, half-walking, in a frantic effort to reach the cottage and save Cindy. After covering about sixty yards, he spotted a faint yet definite rose-colored glow over the dune, near where the cottage stood by the open beach. It was one of the few cottages along the shore without a dune obstructing the view of the ocean from its ground-level patio. He recognized the color well—the warm reflection off the redwood burgundy walls of the living room. He also assumed that the CIA had made it back from the chase into Cape May and might be on the lookout for someone as crazy as him closing in on the home.

Another thought started to take over. After failing to catch him, maybe they would return and be even more compelled to harm Cindy. The thought ignited a surge of determination within him. With renewed energy, he stood up, climbed over the rickety three-foot wooden fence that barely held its purpose, and charged into the woods. He knew these trees and brush offered the concealment he needed, allowing him to approach the house without being seen. The familiar path wound through the undergrowth, and he moved quickly, dodging branches and low-hanging limbs, driven by the urgency to reach Cindy before it was too late.

FLAMES OF VALOR

The pounding of the surf was deafening, drowning out any sound of Robert's movements. And then just as he stopped to crouch momentarily in a dark spot in the thicket, he saw a figure move out through the break in the dune and then run down directly toward the beach away from the house. It was a fast-moving figure dressed in dark clothing. Robert knew it presented an opportunity, which despite the physical struggle, he would need to take. As he nestled against the wooden dune fence, Robert felt the coarse wood digging into his back, grounding him in the moment despite the pain. He focused on his breathing, each gasp a reminder of his deteriorating condition. The man was still visible in the distance, cautiously advancing along the beach, his silhouette framed against the crashing waves.

Robert's heart raced—not just from exertion but from a primal instinct to survive. He calculated the man's trajectory, assessing how long it would take for him to reach the spot where Robert's footprints vanished into the sand. With the pounding surf echoing in his ears, he forced himself to remain still, every muscle tense with anticipation.

As the man drew nearer, Robert strained to hear any sound beyond the roar of the ocean. He could feel the adrenaline coursing through him, sharpening his senses. The pain in his chest felt secondary to the mission at hand. He had to wait for the right moment—wait until the man was close enough to intercept, but not so close that he would spot Robert's hiding place.

Just a few more moments, he thought, as the man continued his deliberate advance, oblivious to the hunter lying in wait.

Robert took careful aim at about 30 paces, coolly cranking off one round and then a second. The figure sprawled wildly backwards into the water and was immediately enveloped by a massive wave as if the sea had to make certain that one of the combatants from the field of battle would be permanently removed.

Robert had eliminated one person, which meant one less gunman to deal with at the cottage. In a normal operation, he would have gone over the fence, found the body in the surf, and inspected it to see who he was dealing with. At this point he lacked energy, and he knew he was running out of time. He worked his way back up over the dune and into the woods and again, began his half crawl, half walk effort toward the more important objective, the beach house and Cindy.

Robert was certain that the incessant rumble of the waves on the beach had disguised his two shots. He would take no chances, moving quietly forward, using his last effort to get to a white grape-stake fence that ran north to south through the woods and ended at the top of the dune. The fence which he had painted in the calm of the summer would be too high to climb over. Perhaps it would even be too weak to hold him, creating a deadly giveaway were he to break it down. So, he crawled back toward the sea, up the crest of the dune, and around the point where the fence buried itself into the sand. He then rolled down again, this time into the yard of the cottage, realizing he was at a spot where he had once put up a swing set for his children. He began crawling forward toward the house which was now not more than twenty feet away.

Robert could see the soft light from the kitchen spilling onto the rough, brown, partially snow-covered grass in the yard. He had once dreamed of a summer with Cindy—working on fences, doing yard work, adding caulking to the windows while she cooked inside. Long evenings on the seaside patio, sipping coffee and wine, seemed like a perfect future. Now, all that mattered was getting to her and ensuring she was alive.

He decided the best course of action was to quickly cross the twenty feet of yard, ascend the six wooden steps to the deck, and enter through the sliding glass door where his victim on the beach had likely come from.

As Robert ran forward, hunched down, not to avoid detection but to protect himself from a wave of salty spray that had just blasted around the edge of the terminus of the sand dune, he remembered how his house had had little protection from the sea. The breaking surf coming at him from the left was now being carried sidewise through the air as an icy salty sleet.

After ten paces toward the house, Robert slowed. The thud in his chest began again. He sensed a certain dizziness and stopped to gather his bearings. He felt a strong desire to stop, to curl up in a ball on the ground and just deal with his own envelope of pain. Each step was so labored and now he struggled just for a few quality breaths of air, one after another. Yet, having come this far, he hoped he could put his physical issues off—just for a few minutes more. Robert stood erect, more erect than he had since the climb over the breakwater near the lighthouse, gathered his thoughts, and moved forward again to the southeast corner of the house. It had been his intention to first look in a window, but he saw a shadow being cast onto the deck. which he interpreted as someone about to come out of the sliding glass door.

In the next second, Robert saw a man wearing a parka and a hood walk out onto the deck, holding a bulky set of night vision binoculars to his eyes and looking out across the beach to the east, obviously trying to track the person who had left only a few minutes earlier. Amid the strange thuds, Robert took courage in the assumption that he still had the element of surprise. Robert knew that even with night vision binoculars, it would be hard to spot the body floating in the surf. He feared it might have washed up onto the beach, 60 to 70 yards away, where it would be more visible.

Gathering his remaining strength, hoping the thudding in his chest would subside, he moved around the corner, raising his 9-millimeter and shouting, "Make one move, and I'll blow your head off!" He approached the base of the steps. As the man turned, the wind blew his hood off, revealing a startled Cedric Martin. "No, it can't be!"

"Cannon, is that you?" Cedric's booming voice cut through the storm. Robert took in Cedric's broad, bald head and dark face.

"You move, and you're dead, you son of a bitch!" Robert yelled, struggling to project his voice over the crashing surf. Anger surged within him as he tried to figure out why Martin was there instead of the CIA. He wanted to squeeze the trigger.

BLOODY HANDS

Robert began walking up the stairs as Martin backed away, hands in the air, across the patio and away from him. Robert sensed danger but at the same moment a frantic need to get into the house to find Cindy.

"Where is Cindy?!"

Martin smiled, dropping his hands slightly, and nervously chuckled, "Robert...she doesn't exist!"

"What have you done to her?" Robert again yelled loudly moving up onto the patio, while at the same time cautiously protecting himself from any threat from within the house. He tried hard to stand erect, to disguise the awful pain that told him should be clutching his chest and lying on the ground. Then suddenly he had made it to the sliding glass door. He could see inside. There she was, Cindy, sitting in her wheelchair staring at him with what he recognized as a perplexed look, something he could not readily interpret. "Cindy! Are you okay?" He yelled into the room.

The reaction of his heart to seeing Cindy was starting to compete with the coronary in progress. He heard no answer but then looked at Martin to assess what might be going on. Martin began to talk, "Robert you've got to listen to me...it's over." Martin started to drop his hands even further and began to walk forward. For a moment, Robert was frozen by his confusion, but then he raised the gun, taking aim. He knew he could blow the soldier away if necessary. He began to squeeze the trigger, comforted by the thought that soon Cindy would be in his arms.

Then, in an instant, he felt a massive explosion near the back of his neck, lifting him off the ground and sending him flying off the patio onto the mud, heading toward the sea. Stunned, he tried to raise his head to look back at Cindy, but his body wouldn't cooperate. Even turning his head felt impossible. He was numb, the cold creeping in from his extremities toward his heart.

Strangely, the chest pain was gone—replaced with a sort of stolid vacuous sensation that, despite all his painful agonizing moments, he had never experienced before.

As Robert clawed at what he had first thought was sand, now he could see that it was blood, the blood-soaked, bloody hands of his worst nightmare. It had all come back just to this, he thought. Again, he tried to raise his head—to see Cindy just once more - wanting it more than anything. But as the blood oozed out of the back of his head, the bloody hands were all he could see. It became darker for him as the thunder of the surf and howling wind of the storm started to subside, darkness canceling any other sound as well. If Cindy is calling, I cannot hear her, he thought. All was darkness, almost.

Realizing that he could not look behind him, in one last effort he lifted his head, looking out to sea. He saw something, something very different. It was so easy to recognize. The oval portrait of Veronica in her flowing white dress, no longer on the wall in the cottage but now full size and stationery amidst the bounding surf on the beach before him. Strangely, her long dark curly hair began to move, to blow across her face. The hair brushed against her beautifully sculpted lips, which he had longed to kiss since the first day they met. Now, he watched her emerge from the surf, walking toward him with arms outstretched, glowing amidst the storm's darkness. In that moment, the stillness gave way to motion, and where there had been only shadows, there was now light, and light was good.

He gazed in astonishment for a moment, trying hard, in the small portion of his mind that remained, to clarify what he was really seeing. Thought of Cindy was gone. He wanted to raise his blood covered hands out of the cold mud to reach for Veronica, but he could not. He dropped his head gently against the sand and was finished.

* * *

The words would have been muffled, even if he could hear them, as Cedric Martin checked the body before returning to the house through the sliding glass door, closing it behind him. "Thanks, sweetheart, for getting my work done for me," he said. That was a close call. After all, he was The Lever. Let's go home." She nodded consent without speaking a word, then returned her .38 special to a leather pouch on the side of her wheelchair.

EPILOGUE

The TV set in the corner of the living room in Charlottesville, Virginia, moved to the lead story on the evening news. "AT A JOINT PRESS CONFERENCE FOLLOWING A RARE CLOSED SESSION OF THE UNITED STATES CONGRESS, DEMOCRATIC PARTY LEADERS FROM BOTH THE HOUSE AND THE SENATE, JOINED BY MEMBERS OF THE DEMOCRATIC NATIONAL PARTY COMMITTEE, ANNOUNCED THAT THEY ARE WITHDRAWING ALL OBJECTION AND PROTEST TO THE ELECTION OF GOVERNOR DAVID HOUSTON FOR PRESIDENT OF THE UNITED STATES. ALTHOUGH DETAILS OF THE CONTENTIOUS DISCUSSION ON THE FLOOR OF THE UNTIED STATES HOUSE OF REPRESENTATIVES HAVE NOT BEEN DISCLOSED, PARTY LEADERS EXPLAINED THAT UNDER THE CIRCUMSTANCES OF THE ELECTION BEING SIMPLY TOO CLOSE TO CALL, AND THE TRAGIC ASSASSINATION OF THE VICE PRESIDENT AND PRESIDENTIAL CANDIDATE CHARLOTTE REID, IT IS IN THE BEST INTEREST OF THE NATION TO MOVE ON AND NOT STAND IN THE WAY OF GOVERNOR HOUSTON'S INAUGURATION ON JANUARY 20TH. FOR NATIONAL SECURITY REASONS THE MINUTES OF THE SESSION WILL NOT BE RELEASED FOR NINETY-NINE YEARS.

WE DO UNDERSTAND, HOWEVER, THAT COMING OUT OF THE SESSION IS THE FACT HOUSTON'S RUNNING MATE, SENATOR TALMADGE SMITH, HAS RESIGNED FROM THE VICE PRESIDENCY, EVEN BEFORE THE INAUGURATION. NO FURTHER FACTS ARE KNOWN ON THIS. THE SENATE WILL CONVENE TOMORROW TO SELECT A NEW VICE PRESIDENT."

The broadcaster then switched his pose to a second camera. "WE

NOW GO TO OKLAHOMA CITY TO HEAR FROM GOVERNOR HOUSTON."

A somber David Houston sat behind a desk at his Nichols Hills estate in Oklahoma City, looking straight into the camera, and spoke without a teleprompter. "WE'RE ALL SADDENED BY THE TRAGIC PASSING OF VICE PRESIDENT CHARLOTTE REID. AS IN A GOOD CONTEST, WE WERE ADVERSARIES ON THE FIELD, BUT NEVERTHELESS CITIZENS OF THIS COUNTRY OFF THE FIELD JUST LIKE EACH OF YOU. AMERICANS KNOW THAT AMERICA SHOULD COME FIRST, AND AT THE END OF THE DAY, BOTH SHE AND I WERE PREPARED TO PUT YOU AND THIS COUNTRY AHEAD OF OUR DISPUTES. THAT'S WHO WE ARE, NOTHING MORE AND NOTHING LESS. THEREFORE, I ACCEPT THE DECISION OF THE HOUSE WITH A HEAVY HEART AND WITH SOMBER RESPONSIBILITY, KNOWING THAT MY JOB IS ONE TO HELP UNITE OUR COUNTRY AND AVOID DOING ANYTHING THAT MIGHT TEAR IT APART."

The news broadcast returned to the anchor in New York, showing a split screen with a white hearse followed by a procession of modest cars turning into the entrance of a nondescript small-town cemetery. "ON A DIRECTLY RELATED STORY ROBERT CANNON WAS LAID TO REST IN A PRIVATE GRAVESIDE MEMORIAL THIS MORNING, ATTENDED ONLY BY A SMALL GROUP OF FAMILY MEMBERS. CANNON WAS KILLED IN A GUN BATTLE WITH A SPECIAL DEPARTMENT OF DEFENSE TEAM WORKING IN COORDINATION WITH THE DEPARTMENT OF HOMELAND SECURITY LAST WEEK IN CAPE MAY, NEW JERSEY, FOLLOWING THE ASSASSINATION OF VICE PRESIDENT REID. IN PIECING THE MYSTERIOUS CASE TOGETHER, GOVERNMENT AGENCIES ARE STILL UNSURE AS TO HIS MOTIVE, BUT SUSPECT THAT IT WAS CONNECTED TO SEVERE DEPRESSION AND

DESPONDENCY OVER RETIREMENT RELATED PROBLEMS CONNECTED TO HIS PREVIOUS JOB AT THE CIA. THE KILLINGS HAD RAISED THE IMMEDIATE FEAR THAT THE ASSASSINATION HAD BEEN AN ACT OF FOREIGN TERRORISTS. THE JUSTICE DEPARTMENT, HOWEVER, HAS ANNOUNCED THAT IN THE COURSE OF ITS INVESTIGATION IT HAS CONCLUDED THAT CANNON ACTED ALONE, AND THAT THERE WAS NO CONSPIRACY OR INVOLVEMENT WHATSOEVER WITH FOREIGN ELEMENTS OR TERRORISTS OF ANY KIND."

U.S. Army Major JoAnn Martin reached for the remote to turn off the television. Wheelchair-bound since a clandestine anti-ISIS operation in Somalia two years earlier, she had come out of retirement for temporary duty to serve her country. This required her to work alongside her husband, Major General Cedric Martin, a dark forces operator known publicly as "Col. Cedric Martin." The job had initially been to merely screen activities of Robert Cannon in carrying out an assignment from Cedric. As Major Martin had more effectively worked her undercover assignment, however, and with all the information reported by her immediately following Christmas at Cape May, all plans changed. The Department of Defense was no longer content with the assassination of Justice McCall, especially after discovering the CIA's intention to kill Congressman Ormond. Instead, they planned to eliminate Robert's few friends and then give Major Martin the green light to transform the "Lever" into a vice presidential assassin.

Major Martin sat up erect in her wheelchair, took a deep breath, and for a moment had a tear in her eye, and only one, as she pondered all that had happened during the weeks in December when she had been known in a Georgetown law firm as a woman named "Cindy."

END